The Love Haters

The Love

Haters

KATHERINE CENTER

ST. MARTIN'S PRESS
NEW YORK

First published in the United States by St. Martin's Press, an imprint of St. Martin's Publishing Group

THE LOVE HATERS. Copyright © 2025 by Katherine Center. All rights reserved. Printed in the United States of America. For information, address St. Martin's Publishing Group, 120 Broadway, New York, NY 10271.

Designed by Devan Norman
Endpaper illustration © Aleksandra Novakovic /Shutterstock

ISBN 978-1-250-28382-5

For Gordon Center, the reigning world champion
Greatest Husband on the Planet.

Thank you for always making everything better.

The Love Haters

One

IT WAS QUITTING time on a Friday, but Cole Hutcheson didn't care.

Nobody cared too much right then, in fact. Because we were all about to get laid off.

Or, too many of us were, anyway.

That's when Cole showed up at my cubby, perched on the edge of my desk, and asked if I wanted to spend a few weeks in Key West filming a video about a US Coast Guard rescue swimmer.

My answer, of course, was, "Sure."

Did I know what a rescue swimmer was? Could I locate Key West on a map? Could I tell you anything about the US Coast Guard—other than it had something to do with *guarding the coast*? Did I even like the ocean?

All no.

But it didn't matter.

That's how it was in this business: the cutthroat world of mid-level video production.

That's also how it was when the company director—a tall lady with tall shoes who we all just called "Sullivan"—was planning to lay off a third of the department over the next month. Most likely the newest employees. Which included me.

She sent an email about it, of all things. An email so full of jargon about *rightsizing* and *rebalancing* and *adjusting to levels of demand* that I had no real idea what it said.

I skimmed it, honestly. And went back to work. For a few minutes.

Until the stampede of office-wide panic.

I would have said yes to the Coast Guard project, anyway. But I guess Sullivan's email made me say yes *faster*.

As soon as I agreed, Cole—my work superior—gave me all the details. Rapid-fire, in our now mostly vacated office. It was fine. He was doing me a favor. This was the kind of assignment that could demonstrate my value.

As of today, I needed to get on that.

I grabbed a notebook to jot down the important stuff.

"It's a Coast Guard air station in Key West," Cole said.

"Shouldn't it be a *water* station?" I said, half joking.

Cole ignored me. "It's to shoot a recruiting video. They want to film a rescue swimmer on a helicopter—"

"A swimmer *on a helicopter*?" I interrupted.

Now Cole squinted at me like he couldn't decide if I was serious.

Then, he made a decision. "Right," he said, and started to stand up. "Maybe this isn't for you."

"Wait!" I said, holding out my hands like *Stay* until he eased back down.

But Cole was studying me. "Do you know *anything* about the Coast Guard? At all?"

The stakes of the situation were not low. If I could've pulled off a lie, I'd have lied. "Not really," I said.

"You're not gonna be right for this," Cole said, with a headshake.

"I am gonna be *perfect* for this," I countered. Bluffing, of course. "It's the fact that I don't know anything about the military that makes me the best choice."

Cole waited, crossing his arms over his chest to brace against whatever bullshit I was about to offer up.

"It's a promo, right?" I went on, thinking fast. "Which means our target audience will be people—*like me*—who know nothing. I can teach them as I'm learning! I'll have a fresh perspective. I'll see things others won't."

I wasn't even sure what the job was yet, honestly.

But whatever it was, I needed it.

More accurately: I needed to *not get fired*.

Cole sighed and then seemed to make the real-time decision to continue this conversation on a provisional basis. In a tone you'd use with a toddler, Cole said, "The Coast Guard flies helicopters out over the big ocean so their swimmers can rescue people out of the dangerous water."

A new visual came to my mind. I had definitely seen images of rescue guys jumping out of helicopters into the ocean. "That's the Coast Guard?" I asked. "The guys in the flippers?"

Cole blinked so slowly it read as sarcastic. "Yes. But don't call them flippers."

I tried to think of another word for flippers.

"They're *fins*," Cole said. Then another headshake. "This should go to someone else."

"No, no!" I said. "I've got this."

"If I hear the word *flippers* again, you're out." Then he added, "I almost gave this to Jaden."

Cole gave most things to Jaden, who had been here two months longer than me. "Why didn't you?"

Cole shrugged. "He can't swim."

Okay, don't tell anybody: *I also couldn't swim.*

"Not swimming is a deal breaker?" I asked.

"I mean, yeah," Cole said. "Half this job will happen in the water."

"In the water?"

"In it, over it, near it."

"Not *under* it, though, right? It's not, like, a scuba-diving deal?"

Cole thought for a second. "No. These guys are swimmers, not divers."

"So *on* the water—not *in* the water."

"Unless things go horribly wrong."

I shouldn't have asked. But I did. *"Horribly wrong?"*

Cole shrugged. "The helicopter could go down in the ocean."

"Does that happen?"

"It *can* happen. It has happened."

Oh, god. I took a breath.

"And if it does happen," Cole went on, "you need to know how to swim. Because helicopters flip upside down as soon as they hit the surface."

Maybe he *should* give this to someone else.

But I nodded, all cool, like *Sure.* Then, I asked, in a *Remind me again* tone: "Why do they flip upside down?"

Cole blinked. Clearly, he thought everyone already knew this. "You know those big spinny blades up top?"

I gave him a look. "Yes."

"Just below them is the engine."

I nodded, like, *Huh.*

"So helicopters are top-heavy," he continued.

"So they just—roll belly-up?" I asked.

"Only if they crash."

"But they don't crash, right?"

Cole shrugged. "Sometimes they do. When it happens, it happens. The crew has to train for it. They have to get strapped into a simulator . . . and then practice getting out. And whoever we send for this project has to do that training, too."

Wait—what?

"I'm sorry," I said. "Whoever's doing this video has to get *flipped upside down inside a helicopter underwater?*"

"In a simulator," Cole said. "Insurance requires it."

I shifted to a poker face. "Cool."

I decided not to ask any more questions.

"Anyway," Cole went on, refocusing. "Just making sure you're fine with water."

"Yes." I nodded definitively. That wasn't a lie, right? I mean, who isn't *fine with water*?

"Great," Cole said. "Because I'm trying to help you out here."

He was? "You are?"

"Yes," he said, impatient. "Jaden's out, but I could've gone with Dylan. Or Arjun. Or Mila." Other recent hires who were now also on the chopping block.

"Why me, then?" I asked, surprised I was on his radar.

"Because Sullivan's about to lay off fifty percent of the company."

"Fifty?" I said. "I heard it was thirty-three."

"It's fifty. It's going to be a bloodbath. She's restructuring everything. She's hired consultants. You heard about her divorce, right?"

I nodded.

"Did you hear he cheated on her with his Pilates instructor?"

Oof. That was rough. I shook my head.

"And he did some kind of sneaky shit with the lawyers where he walked away with most of their money."

Now I frowned protectively for Sullivan. Who I had never talked to.

"That's what I'm saying. She's got some rage to burn. And she's channeling every ounce of it into turning this company into a profit machine. And that means getting rid of people like you."

"People like me?"

"But I want you to stay. Because if she fires all the talented people, that makes my life harder. And I don't need my life to be any harder."

"You think I'm one of the talented people?"

"I do." Cole shrugged.

This was news to me. "Since when?"

"Since the other night. When you told me about your dreams."

Oh, god. Had I done that?

I thought back. We'd had a company dinner. I might have had a little too much to drink. Cole and I were the last two people in the rideshare heading home, and okay, to be honest . . . I might have gotten a little weepy about my long list of recent disappointments. And—ugh, yes—possibly overshared a few things.

Dammit, Katie! I scolded. *Don't tell people about your dreams!*

"Sorry about that," I said, wincing.

"It was strangely endearing," Cole said. "I normally don't notice junior employees too much. How long have you been here? Six months?"

I wasn't *that* junior. "Twelve."

He nodded. "The tears got my attention. You also told me about getting jilted—and I've been jilted myself."

Was he sharing? Did he want me to commiserate? Were we about to bond?

But then he went on. "You just seemed so . . . what's a nicer word for *pathetic*?"

"Pitiable?" I offered.

"Exactly. Pitiable. Do you remember when you blew your nose straight into your blouse like a Kleenex?"

I did now.

"You also told me about the videos you've done for your 'Day in the Life' project," Cole went on. "And I went home and watched one. And it was surprisingly good."

This conversation was like a Ping-Pong game. "It was?"

"Your cinematography is strong. Your camera angles are unexpected. And you get fantastic emotion out of your interviewees."

That *was* a specialty of mine, for better or worse: making people cry.

I didn't realize how good that encouragement would feel until it was happening. Cole might be overly confident, and a smidge narcissistic, and not exactly my favorite person in the office. But he was good at his job.

And when a person who's good at something says that you are also good at that same thing . . . it's nice. No matter how much trouble Cole Hutcheson was about to cause me, I have to admit that him flat-out acknowledging my professional strengths like that was inspiring.

Because I really had been jilted.

And I really did love my work.

And I really did not want to get fired.

"That's why you're helping me?" I asked.

Cole counted off on his fingers. "I'm helping you because: One, now I've seen your stuff, and it's good. Two, if you get fired, that makes my life harder. And three: this job fits your topic."

My topic.

Oh, god. Had I told him about that, too?

I worked at this corporate video company on the weekdays. You know what corporate videos are, right? They're like if a TV commercial and a documentary had a baby—but the TV commercial had all the dominant genes. Hallmarks of corporate videos include branding, marketing, and client pleasing. Plus, lots of upbeat, royalty-free music.

Nothing wrong with that.

It was a fun job in a nice building with pleasant colleagues. I had health insurance and a paycheck—at least for now. No complaints.

But. The thing about doing creative work for hire is that you're not exactly following your own vision. You're following your vision of what you think somebody else's vision is.

Which isn't the same thing.

So, on the weekends, I did my own thing.

A passion project.

I made charming little six-minute mini-documentaries for my fledgling YouTube channel.

And the mini-documentaries were about . . . heroes.

That was my topic.

I profiled people who had pulled children out of burning cars, or intercepted robberies, or plunged headfirst into riptides. I filmed them at their homes morning, noon, and night and got them to tell me the story of the heroic thing they'd done—and why, and how, and if it had changed them, and what it meant.

A "Day in the Life." That's all. A little portrait of an ordinary person who had once decided to do an extraordinary thing.

The idea had come to me at a time when I was feeling, shall we say, just *so disappointed in humanity.* A time when I really needed to hear stories like that: of kindness and heroism and sacrifice. Of people doing *good.*

It worked this way: I spent exactly twenty-four hours with each subject, filming every aspect of that one day—from drinking coffee in the morning, to putting on socks, to feeding the cat, to driving to work. All that was B-roll, which is videographer-speak for filler images, except I didn't use it as filler. I used it as the whole framework. While I was there, I interviewed the subjects to get the story of the heroic thing they'd done, from start to finish, in great detail. That's an art: Asking the right questions. Getting the real story about what it was like—really like—to be a hero.

I filmed the interviews, but then I just used the voices. Heroic people telling their own stories for six minutes—with lots and lots of B-roll flashing by on the screen to keep it interesting.

I'll just say it. The videos were cool.

Unnoticed, but cool.

Here's a twist. So far, I'd only featured women. Not for feminist reasons, exactly—but because I truly spent a full-circle day with these folks, even sleeping at their houses. They had to agree to that up front in the contract. One full day of me filming *everything.* You could get impossibly amazing shots that way: people blow-drying their hair in slo-mo, or doing morning sit-ups at sunrise, or the steam rising off that first cup of coffee. Not to mention pasta noodles twining on forks, phone calls with sick parents, cuddles with pets. Sighs, frowns, laughs. Tears.

Personal things. True things.

The fact was, I just wasn't going to ask some random man out of nowhere if I could sleep over at his place alone.

Not even a hero.

Maybe I'd add some men to the series when I was rich and success-ful and could bring a crew with me. Or a bodyguard. But until then, it was ladies only.

But next, Cole said, "That's why I'm giving you this. The guy we're profiling for this promo is a bona fide hero. So you should go to Florida and make the official video—but, while you're there, do a 'Day in the Life' with him on the side."

Ah. What was it I just said about saying yes and figuring it out later?

Okay, fine. This guy *being a guy* was problematic. But I'd seen enough opportunities come and go to keep that to myself.

"What kind of hero is he?" I asked.

"You definitely saw it on the news. It was everywhere a few years back. He saved a golden retriever that fell off a cliff."

I sat up. "Jennifer Aniston's dog?"

"Yeah."

"I know that video," I said. "That video was everywhere!"

"Right? I know. It would have been everywhere anyway because the footage was so dramatic—"

I was nodding now. "He got lowered down to the beach on that wire, and then he climbed all the way back up to that tiny ledge—"

"A hundred feet—"

"And the dog was in so much pain, it was snapping—"

"And he hummed the song 'Heart and Soul' over and over until it felt safe."

I nodded. As heroes went, this one was pretty top-notch. "Remember that little paw he splinted?" I said.

Cole nodded. "And then he put the dog in a rescue basket, and climbed in with him, and did the hoist."

Guess Cole had seen it a few times, too.

"What was his name again?" I asked, like it was on the tip of my memory.

"The media nicknamed him Puppy Love."

"Tom something," I said, thinking.

But now Cole tilted his head at me. "Wait. Did you watch it all those times and *never realize that was the Coast Guard*?"

I tried to think of a more respectable answer than *yes*. "I knew he was some type of rescuer person?"

Cole shook his head. "This is why they need promo videos."

I waved my hands. "Look, I wasn't focused on the *military details*. I was focused on the heartwarming . . . -ness."

To my surprise, Cole accepted that. "It was very heartwarming," he said, in a tone like maybe it was a little too heartwarming.

"That video would've been huge no matter what," I said. "But then add Jennifer Aniston into the mix? That moment when he delivers the dog into her arms—and *she's crying*?"

Wasn't that what we were all looking for? Something real?

"That's great television," Cole agreed.

A pleasant moment of harmony.

Then I said, "And the swimmer they want us to profile just happens to be him?"

"It's not a coincidence. It's *because* it's him. It's a recruiting video, after all."

"But . . ." I thought back. "Didn't that guy refuse to do interviews?"

"Correct."

"What changed his mind?"

Cole cocked his head, like *Hello?* "His *superior officer* changed his mind."

"I seem to remember him saying, 'I'm not a hero. I was just doing my job.'"

"That's absolutely something he would say," Cole said. Then he added, "Though he doesn't usually say much," like he knew him or something.

I waited for more.

But Cole just went on, "So getting him in your YouTube series would be a great catch. Like, a career-saving catch. If this guy did a 'Day in the Life' with you, it would take over the internet. You'd be on easy street."

I mean, probably not. Documentary filmmakers were pretty much never on easy street. Unless they happened to be Ken Burns. It was kind of the lowest-ranked filmmaking passion you could pursue. None of the glamour of Hollywood. None of the money or fame. Just quietly trying to tell the stories that you felt should be told—and then trying to convince the world to listen.

Plus: covering obscure topics that nobody cared about until *after they'd seen the film*? Never easy.

But Cole had a point. Everybody already loved this guy. We were all desperately curious about him, or had been at the time—and our curiosity was still unsatisfied.

The fact that he didn't want to be famous had made him more famous.

A six-minute documentary about him would definitely get some traction.

And by *traction*, I mean *millions of views*.

Would it save my career?

It couldn't hurt.

"Why are you helping me, again?" I asked Cole.

"You'd be helping *me*," he said. "Because I'm actually the one who's supposed to do this project."

"*You're* supposed to do the promo?"

Cole nodded. "The hero himself requested me. And put in with his superiors to get our random Dallas company hired for the job."

"So why aren't you doing it?"

"I don't want to."

Why did his voice sound so bitter?

"Why would that guy request you?" I asked. "And why wouldn't you want this huge opportunity? And, while we're at it, why would Jennifer Aniston's Puppy Love let me, of all people, do a 'Day in the Life' with him—when he fully refused everything with everyone else?"

Now Cole was nodding. "Good questions," he said. Then he tapped my notebook, like I should write the next thing down, and said, "And the answer to each of them is the same."

I got my pen ready.

But then Cole made me wait a good, solid eternity before finally saying:

"Because that guy . . . is my brother."

Two

DID COLE HUTCHESON, mid-level production editor at a mid-level commercial video company, seem like he would be the brother of a certifiable hero and internet sensation?

Umm, *no.*

Cole didn't possess anything you might call *star power.*

In fact, he was one of those people you really didn't notice much. Unless he was actively irritating you—interrupting you in a meeting, for example, or asking you to do something that was technically his job as if you were his secretary (which you most definitely were not)—he was just kind of . . . there.

The idea that Cole was the brother of Puppy Love?

Mind-boggling.

And yet, who was I to complain?

If my slightly superior work colleague wanted to help me not get fired, I was hardly in a position to say no. Was it my fault if he had some kind of beef with his brother?

But guess what the beef was?

His brother was too awesome.

This guy had the coolest nickname in the world, for one: Hutch.

And things went downhill from there.

"He's a total badass," Cole explained, making me write it all down. "He's morally upstanding and physically unstoppable. He does two hundred push-ups a day. He can hold his breath underwater for three minutes. He has never had a cavity. He's more of a machine than a human. He just goes around all day doing good deeds."

"So he's . . . too likable?"

"He's the opposite of likable! He's perfect."

"Not sure those are opposites."

"He's totally serious all the time. And he's not a talker. He never talks. He never has fun. His main hobby is frowning."

"His *hobby* is frowning?"

"He has no inner life," Cole went on. "He's all exterior, no interior."

"Everybody has an inner life," I argued.

"Not Hutch," Cole said, like *Trust me.* "He just works out, drinks water, eats healthy, and rescues people all day long. He never drinks. He won't even have one beer. And he hasn't dated anyone in a year."

"So?" I said. That could happen.

"Wait till you see him."

"What?"

Cole shrugged. "He's good-looking, okay? A guy that good-looking doesn't stay single unless he hates love."

"You think he *hates* love?"

"I'm just saying," Cole said. "His life choices speak louder than words."

Huh. "I haven't dated anyone in a year. Do *I* hate love?"

"I don't know," Cole said. "Do you?"

It was a good question.

Maybe.

A year. I hadn't noticed until I said it: I'd been single for a year.

But I hadn't thought I *hated love.* I'd thought I was just recovering from it.

You couldn't hate love, could you? Was that even allowed?

But, actually . . . what had love ever done for me? Other than frustrate, exhaust, mislead, and disappoint me? Hadn't it just been a waste of time and energy? Maybe I'd been too gullible. Watched too many Disney movies. Imprinted on too many nineties rom-coms.

Maybe I should have been a little more discerning.

"I don't think I hate love," I finally said to Cole. "But that's actually not a bad idea."

I PERSONALLY HAD been jilted one year ago by my fiancé, the now-very-famous Lucas Banks. Who had been a perfectly nice unsuccessful musician for years—until one of his TikTok videos blew up on the very same night he asked me to marry him.

Truly: the ring had been on my finger about three seconds before his phone started buzzing with notifications that a song he'd posted that morning had hit 100,000 views. People were sharing it. And duetting it—adding instruments and harmonies. At first just ordinary people—but then, suddenly, Noah Kahan jumped in, and before dinner was done, it had over a million. *Views.* In one day.

I was as excited as anyone, at first. Lucas and I sat in that fancy restaurant until closing time, hunched over his phone, our brand-new engagement fully forgotten as we watched the numbers climb and witnessed him *making it big* in real time—meeting eyes over and over in astonishment, like *Can this be happening?*

Next, Lucas had talent coaches reaching out and sponsorship offers with agencies—and his whole life just changed.

In *weeks.*

Some folks who make it big on TikTok only have one song—or, honestly, just seventeen seconds of a song. Some of them don't even know how to sing at all—have never even been in a recording studio. I read an article with one manager describing a guy with millions of fans—who couldn't even keep time. She flew all the way to New Jersey to sign him . . . and then she left empty-handed.

But Lucas was the real deal. He'd been writing songs since middle school, and he played piano *and* guitar *and* harmonica, and he had a whole backlog of songs he could release, one right after the other. When his big chance came—he grabbed it with both hands.

I was happy for him. I *was*.

But it wasn't exactly a journey I could go on *with him*. I was working full time at the University of North Texas back then, in their advancement department, making fundraising videos. I couldn't suddenly just abandon my standard forty-hour workweek, pack up, and take off like a roadie. I was an adult.

Lucas hit the road alone, playing clubs and filming more videos, and then he got invited to open for the Jonas Brothers on tour, and then he was just . . . gone all the time. I saw more of him on my phone than in real life.

Maybe it was inevitable that he would cheat on me.

Did everybody else see that coming?

It's probably a good thing that we never got around to going through with the wedding. Once the frenzy started, he just couldn't make time to sit down with the calendar. We never set a date, and I didn't pressure him. I kept telling myself we had a whole lifetime to make it happen.

But then came the internet scandal where Lucas was photographed canoodling with Lili Ventura—herself newly married—and the photos started showing up on gossip sites.

By *showing up*, I mean *avalanching*.

Sites I would never have noticed, by the way. But then people started texting me marked-up screenshots of Lucas's hand on Lili Ventura's ass, circled with commentary like, IS LUCAS HAVING AN AFFAIR??? and HOW DARE HE OMG!!!

Lili Ventura got the brunt of the internet judgery, to be honest. Lucas somehow got a pass.

But not from me.

I obsessed over the pictures, *A Beautiful Mind* style.

How could I not?

Did Lucas have his arm draped silkily over Lili Ventura's shoulder in the red carpet line at the Grammys? Were they holding hands in that crowd shot by the entrance? And did he grind up behind her in that pic at the Grammys after-party?

I was no FBI analyst, but . . . yes to all.

The night it all blew up, I texted him in LA with no preamble: Hey. Are you cheating on me with Lili Ventura?

To no one's surprise but mine, he didn't reply.

The next day he called, sounding hoarse, and said, "Let's talk when I get home."

But we didn't really need to talk.

I could tell from his voice. And the five hundred photos on the internet.

"It's better to know now," my cousin Beanie had insisted, and she was probably right.

Apparently, that was a full year ago—and now I was well into my current project of *thriving anyway*. I'd kicked Lucas out, and bought all new bedding, and taken up crochet. In a late-night compulsive urge for instant self-improvement, I'd cut my own bangs with a pair of kitchen scissors. I'd purchased an air fryer, developed an audiobook addiction, and changed day jobs, from making promo videos for a university to . . . another job making promo videos. For anyone who hired us.

I was fine.

It was a relief, to be honest. I was never cut out to be fame-adjacent. And there were upsides. Breaking up meant I'd never have to sit quietly and pretend to be enraptured while Lucas played his guitar at me again. Or listen to him parse a conversation with his agent for three hours over dinner. Or—best of all—ever have to go to another awards show.

Awards shows were the worst.

For me, in particular. Because I was basically the opposite of everything that's valuable at an awards show. I wasn't famous, or rich, or stunningly gorgeous, or even particularly talented.

All I had, ultimately, was my connection to Lucas. Which wasn't nearly enough to protect me.

I learned this the hard way at my very first Billboard Music Awards the first year Lucas was famous. I was so proud of him, and I felt sweetly giddy at the prospect of doing something so glamorous. I went shopping and found a vintage-y, floral-print dress that I, personally, thought was gorgeous. I had my hair done and my nails painted. I *moisturized my calves*.

I fully expected to feel like Cinderella at the ball.

And guess what? I did. At first.

Until I started getting texts that the internet hated my dress.

Photos of me next to Lucas started popping up all over *even before the show was over* with questions like, Why did Lucas Banks bring his mother to the Billboard Awards? and Who is the frumpy lady with Lucas Banks? and Is Lucas Banks dating Mrs. Doubtfire?

Sorry—did you miss the one where someone thought I was Lucas's *mother*?

I was *twenty-six*. And he was four years older than me!

And, for the record, none of those comments was actually true. I did not—and *do not*—look like Mrs. Doubtfire.

Now you're wondering what I *do* look like.

For a long time, that was a hard question for me to answer.

I don't know. I just looked . . . pleasant.

Unremarkable, but friendly—like your nonthreatening best friend. Five-five. Collar-length brown hair. Arms, legs, boobs—the usual. The single most remarkable thing about me was that I had nondescript hazel-ish eyes with a blurry little pie-piece section in one iris that was light brown. And it wasn't even that noticeable. *I* never even noticed anymore. And as far as I knew, Lucas had never noticed at all.

Which was probably lucky, in the end. The last thing I needed was some song about me called "Pie Eyes" or something.

The point is, the most unusual thing about me was something you could see only if you were really, really looking.

And none of us were. Myself included.

I guess I was kind of like those before-and-after pictures of women who've had cosmetic surgery where you're like, "Why did she do that to herself? She was fine before."

I was the "fine before."

Or, at least, I'd thought I was.

Until the entire internet disagreed.

Did I cry myself to sleep that night? And declare I'd never leave the house again? And then wake up the next day and immediately decide to remedy my frumpiness by starting what you might generously describe as a "starvation diet"?

Like you wouldn't believe.

Have you ever heard of those starvation experiments they did back in the 1940s with conscientious objectors to the war? The ones where the men ate so few calories that they lost their minds a little—and one of them accidentally-on-purpose chopped off some of his own fingers?

That was the regime I decided on.

In fact, I watched a whole documentary on it. They gave the men in those studies just over 1,500 calories per day.

So I set my own limit at a thousand.

If those guys had gone crazy, I was going to go *crazier.*

Which felt, in the moment, like a power move.

My goals were twofold: (1) to be a size zero—or less, and (2) to never let the tops of my thighs touch each other again.

It was such an odd idea, when you think about it: that I could hurt the world back by hurting myself.

But it was the best I could come up with at the time.

I'll fast-forward and tell you that I *did* make it to a size zero—almost—and I *did* stop my thighs from touching—and all it required was obsessive dedication and singular focus to the exclusion of all else.

I never wore a printed fabric again, either. From that awards show on, I wore black jeans and a black T-shirt every damn day without fail.

Black socks and underwear, too.

And that was that. I lived that way for a full year: cranky, hungry, obsessed with all the food I wasn't eating, and hiding in plain sight.

I used to daydream—frequently—multiple times a day—about shoving my face into a rotisserie chicken and eating my way back out.

The journals I'd kept my whole life had always been full of poems and drawings and thoughts on the books I was reading and leisurely reminiscences of the people and places who had meant things to me. But during that year? They were nothing but lists of calories. A typical entry:

2	black coffee
10	celery stalk
80	apple
284	boneless skinless chicken breast
70	½ cup nonfat Greek yogurt
86	veggie egg-white omelet in nonstick pan
0	72 oz. water
34	½ cup kale, steamed
182	salmon filet (wild caught)
94	cup of steamed broccoli
160	½ avocado—slices
1,002	TOTAL (*Do better!*)

This was literally everything I had to say about my day. This list was a full 3-D rendering of my inner life. And, for the record: this would have been a heartbreaking list. Any total over a thousand was *catastrophic*.

Shouldn't have had that black coffee.

Anyway—I amassed hundreds of these. That's what my journals became. Just like the starvation study confirmed back in the forties: when you're starving, that's all you think about.

I must have become very boring. Honestly.

Sometimes, very late at night, I'd wonder if that was partly why Lucas cheated—before shaking myself by the emotional shoulders and reminding myself, again, of something that I mostly, usually, was determined to believe: It was never the *cheatee's* fault. It was always the cheater's.

Maybe I *had* become boring. But nothing about that forced Lucas to *bang Lili Ventura*.

They were broken up now, by the way.

More important, guess what I did after I kicked Lucas out of our apartment?

I ate a gallon of chocolate chip cookie–dough ice cream.

Not a pint. A *gallon.*

It was a melted soup by the time I finished, but I got there.

And then I ate nothing but ice cream for a week. And then . . . I bought a bunch of books on body positivity and read them all, unfollowed Lucas and everyone associated with him, gave my thighs permission to lovingly caress each other again . . . and declared an unstable truce with my body.

Quite the healing journey. I'd come a long, long way in a year. I was proud of myself—and my thighs.

But I was still a beginner, if I'm honest.

It was one thing to be body-positive in theory—and quite another to do it in reality.

I was still wearing black jeans and T-shirts every day. I was still keeping to the sides of the world, hiding behind other people in group photos, avoiding mirrors.

I'd changed my thinking, and changed my behavior, and given myself permission to just eat anything I wanted. I'd even—and this might've been a stroke of genius—found some beat-up old art books on the $1 cart of a used bookstore, bought them all, and used them to make a self-acceptance journal. This became a nightly project— cutting out pictures of plump, cellulite-laden Baroque ladies who had been painted naked (admiringly, it seemed) by old masters like Rubens and Titian and Botticelli and pasting them admiringly into a drawing sketchbook.

The idea was to pay attention to images of women who hadn't been photoshopped. To unlock myself from our current era's beauty standards. To draft a peace accord with my thighs. To redefine "beautiful" broadly enough to fit my current, non-starving, thigh-touching self into that category. To be at home in my body as it was—whatever that meant.

A tall-ass order.

But I really was kinder to myself now.

I just hadn't put that progress to the test.

As harsh as it had been to starve myself that way, there was a certain comfort in my vastly oversimplified thinking. It reduced all the chaos of the world into one simple metric that—in theory, at least—I could control. As long as I stayed under a thousand calories a day, I was safe. Nothing bad could happen to me.

To which Lucas, and Lili Ventura, and the entire internet, had said, *Challenge accepted.*

What do they call those moments when your fiancé cheats on you with a pop star in front of the entire world? *Opportunities for personal growth?*

I'd grown, dammit. Literally and metaphorically. In all the good, bad, and terrifying ways possible.

Which is why that night, in our after-hours office, after I'd just fully committed to a not entirely specified number of weeks in Key West, on a job I wasn't qualified for, with a man whose own brother thought he was *too perfect* . . . when Cole Hutcheson raised his hand for a high-five and said, "And don't forget to pack your bikini!"

I burst into tears.

Three

"YOU DIDN'T," MY cousin Beanie said on FaceTime when I told her about it.

I winced. "I did."

Beanie—a personal shopper—had moved from Texas to New York the week before the Lili Ventura scandal broke a year ago.

And, ever since, we'd FaceTimed every day.

The kind of video calls where you chat driving to work with your phone in the cupholder, and then home again with your phone on the passenger seat. Then, at home, you set it in the basket while you do laundry, and balance it on a bunch of bananas in the fruit bowl while you make dinner, and prop it on the sink ledge while you take a shower. The kind of video calls you do with genuine loved ones, where no one's even trying to look good—and you're mostly seeing the ceiling fan, or the inside of a pocket, or part of a nostril.

Right now, I was packing for Key West, and Beanie—just back from a super-busy work trip to Paris—was getting all the updates. I had her wedged into the pocket of my suitcase while I packed, and she had me resting on her dresser while she unpacked.

"Did he think you were crazy?" she wanted to know, re: my weeping at the word *bikini*.

"I told him it was allergies," I said.

"Did he buy that?"

"I don't think he cared much, either way."

"Maybe it really was allergies."

"And what would I be allergic to?"

"Um, to *bathing suits*. Obviously!"

True enough. I hadn't owned a bathing suit since middle school.

I felt a familiar squeeze of dread. "Also, I can't swim."

"That's not news."

Of course it wasn't. Beanie knew more about me than I knew about myself. We'd grown up together on the same block. Our dads were brothers, and after my mom left us and moved away—when I was eleven—I pretty much spent the rest of my childhood trying to live with Beanie and convince her mom to be my mom, too.

Beanie was basically my cousin, sister, and lifetime bestie all rolled into one.

We had "gone swimming" my whole life, of course. It's too hot in Texas in the summers not to be constantly hitting the neighborhood pool, and the beach, and the lawn sprinklers whenever possible. But "getting wet and splashing around" is not the same thing as swimming.

The summer after my mom left, when all the cousins were supposed to take proper swim lessons, I'd refused to go—in part because the boy cousins kept teasing me about how often I burst into tears.

By the *next* summer, my dad had started dating a lady named Angela, who—I want to emphasize—*had some nice qualities*, but who also wanted to guide me through puberty by telling me over and over to suck in my stomach.

Beanie knew all about that, too. And she was *not* Team Angela.

I do think Angela meant well, in her way.

I'm not excusing her. But intentions don't *not* matter. She wasn't trying to hurt me. She was trying to help. It's just that her version of helping, as Beanie always put it, was "supremely fucked up."

She thought the most important thing a woman could possibly be was *tiny*.

Within six months of marrying my dad, Angela had put me on a diet. I was twelve. Looking back at photos from those years, I'm always shocked at how much I looked exactly like all the other ordinary kids.

But I guess Angela wanted me to be extraordinary.

She was trying to teach me the rules of being a successful woman as she understood them. And it never occurred to her that women might be able to write those rules for themselves.

Don't worry—I did my best to resist. I snuck Cheetos into a secret stash under my bed. I met Beanie at the Stop-N-Go on our bikes for Fudgsicles. I processed it all with stacks of self-help journals.

But the fact remains: I abandoned swimsuits forever after that lady showed up in my life.

So I couldn't lay *all* of my insecurities at Lucas Banks's feet. Some of them were courtesy of Angela. Some of them came from just being a girl in a world that is appallingly mean to girls. Do any of us escape unscathed?

I really was fine now. Most of the time. As long as I could keep my clothes on.

Beanie had made it her personal mission to get me back into the water. "You never used to care about that stuff!" she'd say. "We splashed at the beach all the time!"

"That was before I knew about sucking in."

Beanie thought the swimming component of my new assignment was, and I quote: "A glorious opportunity to work through your stepmother-based trauma."

"*Glorious* feels a bit strong," I said.

"You can confront your body-image demons and learn a new skill at the same time," Beanie said, way too chipper about the idea. "You didn't tell your boss you couldn't swim, right?"

"He's not my boss. He's just my work superior."

"But did you tell him?"

"I didn't. I lied to get the job."

"You *omitted the truth*, which is not the same thing."

"Either way, I'm about to spend many upcoming weeks 'on or near' the water."

"Which part of this is bothering you?"

"All of it. They're going to make me do safety training. In the water!"

"That sounds reasonable," Beanie said.

"But don't you think they'll make me wear a swimsuit?"

"Of course not," Beanie said. But then, like we both needed more convincing, she added, "They'll probably put you in a flight suit. Or something."

"And then there's the drowning problem."

Beanie shook her head at me. "You'll be with *rescue swimmers*," she said. "You couldn't drown if you tried."

"Watch me."

Beanie leaned in to the phone to give me a look.

"I'll be flying in a helicopter with them," I said then, the truth of how very unqualified I was blooming in my mind. "Out over the ocean. For *weeks*." Then, realizing there was no way around it, I sighed. "I should call Cole back and confess."

Beanie was aghast. "Absolutely not. You just said these rescue swimmers work out ninety minutes a day *for their job*. If anyone on this earth needs a full month of cavorting with military men who are—and just based on the math, I think we can all agree—*scientifically* sexy, it's you."

I shook my head, like *Nope*. "Not *cavorting*," I said. "Just working."

"If you say so," Beanie said.

I added: "Besides. The swimmer I'm profiling hates love."

Beanie paused. "*Hates* love?"

I nodded. "He's a love hater."

"What does that mean?"

"He's all rules and no heart! He's all action and no reaction! He's all body and no soul."

Beanie peered at me through the phone. "Who cares?"

"He's not even human! He hasn't dated anyone in a year."

"*You* haven't dated anyone in a year."

"I'm in recovery!"

"Sounds like he needs some *company*," Beanie said, as if *company* meant ten different things at once.

"Not from me, he doesn't!"

But now she was nodding like she'd had an idea. "You should sleep with the love hater."

"Oh, my god!"

But Beanie doubled down. "Yes. This is the cure for everything."

"He *hates love!*"

"You could stand to hate love a little yourself."

"What are you saying?"

"I'm saying maybe an all-body, no-soul fling with a hero robot might help you toughen up a little."

"I don't need to toughen up."

"Yes, you do."

"I'm not *sleeping* with my subject, Beanie. This is my *job*."

"The point is, you need an adventure. Don't self-sabotage!"

"The point is," I countered, "this is not an adventure. This is an attempt to not get downsized."

"Why can't it be both?"

But now I was shaking my head. "What was I thinking? Why did I lie about the swimming?"

"You'd rather just hand this job over to that brown-noser Mila?"

"At least she can swim."

"Swimming's not that hard," Beanie said. "Just take some lessons."

"Lessons?" I said, like I'd never heard of them before.

"You've got the weekend in Key West to settle in before work starts," Beanie said. "Do a full-immersion class." Then she tilted her head like she hadn't meant to make that joke—but she'd allow it.

"Very funny."

"You don't have to win a gold medal at the Olympics," Beanie said. "You just need to master the dog paddle."

It was, actually, kind of a good point.

Beanie, in fact, had lots of points that were good.

It was the most annoying—and secretly helpful—thing about her. She was the queen of self-help books. Pick any bookstore, I swear, and go to the self-help section—and Beanie had read them all. Read them, highlighted them, copied quotes onto little three-by-five cards. She had memorized Brené Brown's entire body of work. She could recite Maya Angelou's words of wisdom like they were Shakespeare's. And after Lucas got famous, she'd forced me to read her favorite book by love gurus John and Julie Gottman—whose work overflowed with relationship advice gold.

None of which I could remember right now.

Except for this: strong relationships had to create a *culture of appreciation*.

A whole book, and that was all I'd retained: People in good relationships had to appreciate each other—say thank you, give compliments, notice what their partner was getting right—in ways that created a cushion of warmth and kindness that eased everything else.

Brilliant! Right? Super helpful! Or, at least, it would have been if Lucas had read the book. Or even *not been checking his TikTok DMs* while I was telling him about it.

I guess, even then, we were past the point where self-help could be helpful.

But the truth was, as much as I made fun of Beanie . . . she got more than a few things right.

"I haven't even told you the worst part," I said then, not sure I wanted to say it out loud.

Beanie picked up the phone to make eye contact. "What's the worst part?"

"When Cole was running down the equipment list," I said, "he said he was shipping the lightest camera to Key West for me."

Beanie frowned. "The *lightest* camera?"

I nodded. "Because every single thing that goes onto a helicopter has to be weighed."

Beanie tilted her head. "Why?"

"Because if helicopters try to carry too much weight, they will sink out of the sky."

"So they have to—what? Tally up the weight of everything on board?"

"Exactly," I said. "Equipment. Fuel. Rescue victims."

But Beanie wasn't getting it. "Why is this the worst part?"

"Because," I said slowly, knowing it would be real after I said it out loud, "*I* am one of the things that will be on board."

Beanie's eyes got wide as the statement hit. "You have to weigh yourself?"

I nodded and closed my eyes. "And then I have to announce the number to the pilot. In front of the whole crew. So he can add it to the total."

"That can't be right!" Beanie protested on my behalf. "We're not living in a nightmare!"

"I am, apparently," I said.

"There has to be a way around it."

"I'm telling you," I said, "I googled it. This is how it's done. They have a preflight check before every mission, and any unspecified weight has to be . . . specified."

Beanie winced. Then she said, "Okay." Then, apparently unable to come up with anything else, she said the thing she always said when a problem was unsolvable. "What doesn't kill you makes you stronger."

I closed my eyes. "I think it might actually kill me."

Beanie sighed in solidarity. "That might actually be for the best."

BEANIE HAD BEEN the person to convince me to stop weighing myself in the first place.

After the breakup, she'd taken some personal days to come back for a visit, back when I still couldn't get out of bed. I had lain on the sofa, wrapped in the trompe l'oeil tortilla blanket she'd given me for my birthday, and I'd watched her clean my entire apartment—takeout container by takeout container.

"This is very soothing," I said, as she walked past me with another full Hefty bag.

"It's not just soothing," Beanie said. "It's *cleansing*. It's a rebirth. By the time I head back to New York, you're going to be a whole new person."

That weekend, she took my digital scale—aka my closest friend—and wrapped it up in one of Lucas's forgotten T-shirts, doused it all with lighter fluid, and set the whole thing on fire out by the street.

"This thing is ruining your life," Beanie said, as we watched the flames. "Free yourself."

She'd also scrubbed my apartment top to bottom—bathroom to kitchen and back. She vacuumed and dusted and decluttered so hard, she took six grocery sacks to Goodwill. Then she turned her attention on me—made me take a shower, get a haircut, go for a pedicure, and floss.

But even after the glow-ups, Beanie wasn't satisfied. She stood in my living room and looked around.

"It's awfully beige in here," she said.

"It's not beige, it's 'Oyster.'"

"It's just so *blah*."

"It's not *blah*. It's sophisticated."

"You need some pops of color."

But I shook my head. "I *hate* pops of color."

"Too bad."

Beanie dragged me out shopping, and before I knew it, I had four new orange throw pillows. After she was gone, I thought about donating them to Goodwill, too. But, out of guilt, I just stacked them in a closet instead.

Beanie had promised me, in the wake of my failed engagement, that I was due for a renaissance. "You're going to come back to life in ways you never could've imagined," she swore.

I wasn't sure orange throw pillows were the key to that renaissance.

But I wasn't sure they *weren't*, either.

Sometimes Beanie was right.

The promised revival had proved elusive in the months since she'd burned my scale. But Beanie never lost sight of it. And so now, on the phone, she was evaluating this Key West job with a different set of goals than mine. I was asking questions like, *Can I take this job and still physically survive?*

Beanie, in contrast, was asking if this journey would help me *thrive*.

And that's how our conversation seesawed, like they always did, between Beanie both pushing me to go and telling me not to. This was how we processed things—thoroughly. By switching sides until we'd covered all the angles.

"What I still don't understand is"—Beanie was now saying on our FaceTime, switching from *You deserve this!* to *Is this really a good idea?*—"why this coworker of yours isn't going himself."

"He and his brother don't get along."

"He won't even be there, but he arranged for your lodging?"

"The company did. It's his aunt's place. She's a real estate tycoon."

"You don't say."

Now *I* was the one who was pro me going. "I'm telling you," I said, "I stalked the place on Vrbo. It's a block of old-timey motor court cottages she fixed up. So charming! It's all on the website. They could be in a magazine. And, according to Cole, she's going to let me stay there for a deep discount. The only catch is that I can't tell her why I'm there. At first."

"You have to lie about why you're there?"

"I have to be strategic with my timing."

"And who cares about the discount? Isn't the company paying for it?"

"Yes, but this stretches the budget. If it costs less for me to go, I can be there longer. Which means I can—hopefully—do a 'Day in the Life' with the love hater."

Beanie nodded. "But you said he didn't do interviews."

"Cole says he can talk him into it."

"How, exactly?"

"I don't know, but it doesn't matter."

"Um, it kind of does. And it's weird that he doesn't want you to tell his aunt why you're there."

"At *first*," I said, like that was normal. "Just until the job starts."

"I'm just not sure about this coworker."

"He doesn't want me to *lie*," I said. "He just wants me to . . ."

"Omit the truth?" Beanie offered.

I gave Beanie a look. "To refrain from sharing the full story. For a day or two."

"It's sketchy."

"It's temporary." Then I added, "Three minutes ago, you were sending me to bed with the love hater!"

"Fine," Beanie said. "I support you." Then Beanie accidentally dropped her phone into her pile of laundry. After she fished it back out, she said, "You're doing better than Lucas, anyway."

I brought my own phone close to peer in at her. She normally refused to say his name. "What?" I asked. "Am I?"

"He got interviewed on *The Tonight Show*—didn't you see?"

"I don't follow him anymore."

"Of course not. Good for you. And don't watch the interview. It's depressing as hell."

"Does he talk about Lili Ventura?"

"No. About you. About how stupid he was to leave you."

Ah. "Well," I said, taking a breath, "he *was* stupid."

"Preaching to the choir, lady."

"Should I feel sorry for him now?"

"No! And don't google him, either! Here's what you need to know: He misses you, he never should've cheated, you were the only real thing in his life, and he hates himself."

"He hated himself before. That's, like, his whole thing."

"He should have read that Gottman book," Beanie said, like we'd tried to hand him all of life's answers on a silver platter. "He should have applied the culture of appreciation to himself!" Beanie was just making chitchat—just casually judging a person who'd hurt me in a pleasant, gossipy way.

But when she said it, I gasped.

"What?" Beanie asked.

"Beanie!" I said. "That's genius!"

She frowned. "Which part?"

"The culture-of-appreciation thing," I said. "Turning the Gottmans on yourself."

Beanie paused to think about it.

"They're talking about relationships," I said, "but you don't just have relationships with other people. You have one with yourself, too."

Beanie waited.

"I definitely have a relationship with myself. It's judgmental and toxic, but it's there."

Beanie squinted to indicate she did not condone the toxicity.

"I mean, an abusive relationship with yourself is still a relationship, right?"

Beanie frowned. "I guess? Technically?"

"If I created a culture of appreciation *with myself*, maybe I could make the relationship better. And maybe it could create that cushion of warmth and kindness they talk about. And then maybe things like having to *announce my weight to a room full of military superjocks who work out ninety minutes a day* would be a tiny bit easier."

Beanie tried to arrange her face in a hopeful shape. "Sure! It's worth a shot, right?"

This was just the tiny crumb of hope I needed. "I don't have much time, though," I said. "I should've thought of this a year ago."

Beanie pointed through the phone. "No negative self-talk! You can't rush life-changing insights!"

Next, she walked to her bookshelf and pulled down a dog-eared Gottman book. She paged through to the right spot and started rereading: "The main strategy is just to notice what your partner is getting right." She peered at me, thinking. "Maybe you can just work on noticing what *your body* is getting right. Things you like about it. You *do* have some of those, right?"

Things I liked about my body? What an odd thought.

"I have a few, I guess," I said.

Beanie looked doubtful. "What are they?"

I took a breath. "I like my earlobes," I declared.

Beanie flared her nostrils. "Earlobes don't count."

But I took offense. "Yes, they do!" I brought the phone close to my ear and pulled an earlobe forward to show her. "Look at this little beauty! Look how soft and tender and velvety she is! And she's the perfect shape: plump and pillow-like." I pulled the camera back. "My earlobes," I declared, "are what all other earlobes wish they could be."

Beanie looked impressed. "Okay, then. That's a start. I love this fangirl energy." Then, like she was starting a list: "Earlobes, check. What else?"

But coming up with a second thing was harder. I frowned.

"That's your entire list? *Earlobes*?"

"What's *your* list?" I challenged.

"It's private," Beanie said, standing up a little taller. "But it's a hell of a lot better than *earlobes*."

"Tell me your list!" I demanded.

"No."

"This is mean! Tell me!"

But Beanie had decided to use curiosity as a motivator. "Make your beauty list first," she challenged. "Get ten things on it, and then I'll tell you mine."

"You don't even have a list," I said, like *Bullshit*.

But Beanie didn't take the bait. "Get to ten," she said, "and find out."

Four

DID MY COMPANY splurge for a nonstop flight from Dallas to Miami?

They did not. Though they did ship my *equipment* direct.

Instead, I flew all day—with a random stop in Newark and a plane change. And was there turbulence on both flights? And was I in the middle seat both times with no access to *any* armrest? And did the aisle guy on the second leg spend the entire time coughing—hacking up one lung after the other every sixty seconds?

Don't make me say it.

And then as soon as I landed in Miami at last, a lady racing for her gate with a full, Venti-sized Starbucks cup in her hand crashed into me and doused me so thoroughly that cinnamon latté soaked into everything but my socks.

And then! After walking all the way to baggage claim—reeking of coffee and holding my wet, and now very cold, T-shirt fabric away from my chest with pinched fingers—I waited for my bags.

And waited.

And waited.

And then, finally, when the last unclaimed bag on the carousel (hot pink with flowers) was definitely not mine (black with a black luggage tag), I went to the service desk and got the astute commentary: "It's probably lost."

And let's not get started on the thousand-hour wait at the rental car counter.

Let's just sum up: the *getting there* was terrible.

But the *arriving*? That was something else entirely.

First of all, it was a 58-degree October morning in Dallas, Texas, when I left, and it was an 86-degree October afternoon in Key West when I arrived.

So that's a start.

I've done a ton of traveling for my job. They put you up in one anonymous box hotel after another. And the places you go are all exactly, almost spookily, the same. Same strip malls, same chain restaurants, same hotel art.

I'm not complaining. There's a comfort in all that sameness.

But I just need to note that everything about going to Key West was . . . different.

Even the drive to get there was different. The Overseas Highway really is a *highway over the seas*. I googled it: forty-two astonishing bridges connecting all of the Florida Keys over the water for 113 miles—and one of them is seven miles long.

I mean, *come on!*

I'd never seen—or done—anything like it, work trip or not. Zooming over the water that way, surrounded by blue ocean and clouds, windows down, ocean breezes just slam-dancing around in the rental car. Just when I'd start to miss land, the bridges would set me down on another key, and I'd zip along past palm trees, and docks, and sun umbrellas, and beachy restaurants with turquoise signs about key lime pie and conch fritters.

Nothing about this felt anything like any job I'd had before.

And that was before I'd even arrived at the final key—Key West— and seen the Victorian buildings with Easter egg colors and metal seam roofs. The second-story verandas, and picket fences, and brick-paved streets. The mangrove trees and coconut palms. Everything was scaled for walking. The stores and restaurants had music playing. Pedestrians strolled along everywhere. Not to mention the wild roosters strutting around like they owned the place, with their red combs and black plumed tails.

The whole town just felt like one endless festival.

So, yeah. Not your average corporate video shoot.

Cole Hutcheson's aunt, Rue—who I'd never even heard of a week ago—was *waiting for me* when I pulled into the crushed-shell parking lot at the Starlite Cottages. She came right out to the car and *gave me a hug*.

That's exactly the condition I was in when I met her for the first time, by the way: rumpled, sleep deprived, still damp, and stinking of someone else's cinnamon latté.

Rue, for her part, was the opposite of all those things.

She wore a caftan with hot-pink and white hibiscus flowers printed all over it, and clacky raffia sandals, and a long drapey necklace. Her bright silver hair was short in a pixie cut, and she was sporting the most enormous, thick-rimmed, stop sign–red glasses I'd ever seen—with red tassel earrings that matched.

"Oh, *sweetheart*," she said, taking in the sight of me. "You've had an ordeal."

Just from the sympathy in her voice, it felt like she already knew the whole story.

"Where are your bags?" she asked, looking around.

"Lost," I told her.

She eyed my shirt. "Is that . . . ?"

I nodded. "A lady in the airport's full Venti latté."

She frowned, like she was formulating a plan. "Well, first things first. I'm Rue." She stepped back to hold out her hand for a post-hug shake.

I took it. "I'm Katie."

"I've got your cottage all ready," she said then. "But I think first you need some clothes. And some food. Though I'm not sure in what order."

I wasn't sure, either.

"Clothes first, I think," she decided then. "My treat. Then a late lunch. Also my treat."

I loved her instantly. How could I not? Plus, she said she was going to let me turn in my rental car and "rent" her Mini Cooper—for a very nominal fee. All because Cole had asked her to.

"But don't you need something to drive?" I asked.

"No, no," Rue said, shaking her head. "I have a Dutch town bike. It's all I ever use—unless I'm road-tripping."

She gestured behind her at a sleek black bike—complete with a basket festooned with flowers.

What can I say? I believed her. If she preferred her bike, she preferred her bike. The less money I spent, the longer I could stay, and the longer I could stay, the more footage I could get, and the more footage I could get, the better *both* videos would be, and the better the videos . . . the lower the chances I'd get fired.

When Rue led me to a nearby boutique, I followed.

The shop was called Vitamin Sea, and it was like stepping into a kaleidoscope.

It was mostly clothes: dresses and tunics and skirts and sarongs—all in the brightest of bright oranges and pinks and reds and yellows. Blues and purples, too. So much color my eyes had to adjust, like when you flip on the lights in a dark room.

Bob Marley played on the speaker system, and as I followed Rue around the store, my steps fell into the rhythm of the music, and I found myself thinking how very different this was from, say, arriving in Omaha to start a project for Unity Home Mortgage.

Did I say it was like a kaleidoscope? Maybe more like a coral reef.

While we browsed, Rue told me all about buying the Starlite Cottages as an investment property when she'd retired—but then loving the vibe there so much that she moved into one of the cottages herself. Then her best friend from childhood, Ginger, lost her husband, and Rue convinced her to move in next door. She'd fixed the cabins up as vacation rentals, styling them lavishly in a "vintage tropics" look—with banana-leaf-print wallpaper and rattan furniture, and replacing the dated kitchenettes with new ones from IKEA.

Four of the ten cottages now had permanent residents.

"Not an old folks' home *technically*," Rue said, "but we're not exactly teenagers."

Rue had also bought the last remaining building on the same city block—which fronted onto Duval Street—and so she owned the building we were standing in, too. Other tenants included the Italian restaurant next door, an art gallery, a bar with a whole back wall of pinball machines, and, upstairs, a dentist, a travel agency, and a concierge doctor.

"It's a lot of math," Rue said, "but it keeps me out of trouble."

The boutique was bright, and sunny, and it had—how to put it— a soothing flow?

It had been such a long journey, and I didn't fully have my bearings, and so it took me longer than it should have to put the pieces together. I was, in fact, subtly mouthing along with the words to "One Love" and totally unprepared when Rue turned around with a pink-and-orange floor-length caftan, held it up in front of her, and said, "This one."

I stopped walking. "I'm sorry?"

"This is the one. I feel it," Rue said, now stepping closer to hold this max-brightness, *full-bolt-of-fabric* garment up to me.

I was shaking my head before it touched me. "No, no, no," I said.

"I'm thinking yes, yes, yes," Rue said. "These colors are perfect."

"I'm not a—" I started, head still shaking. "I don't really . . ." I looked around. "Isn't there anything plain?"

"Plain?" Rue asked, unable to imagine what I meant.

I rotated 360 degrees, scanning the tropical prints. Of course, obviously, I knew there was zero chance I would stumble upon a black T-shirt and jeans section in a tropics-wear boutique. But there had to be at least a piece or two that hadn't been designed by someone on active psychedelics.

I stretched up my neck for a better view, straining for a glance of maybe a navy blue. "I'm not really a bright-colors person," I said.

But Rue looked me up and down. "Sweetheart, life is short. Let's fix that."

Panic was setting in. Where was my damned suitcase? In vain, I looked out the front window, as if someone from the airport might screech up right now and toss it out onto the sidewalk.

"Okay, okay," Rue said, reading my face and relenting. "You don't like colors."

"I *like* them," I said. "I just don't *wear* them. On myself. And, plus," I added, now panic-babbling, "this is a *lot* of colors. Right? It's like Lilly Pulitzer threw up in here. After eating some bad key limes. And taking acid. On a tropical vacation."

Rue was having none of it. "Just think of it as a robe. You've worn *robes* before. You've got one at home, right?"

I nodded, but solemnly.

"Don't tell me," Rue said, reading my face. "Your robe at home is black."

"Charcoal gray." I nodded, with a wave of longing.

Were my *eyes* filling up with *tears*?

"Okay," Rue said, accepting that she wouldn't be getting me pumped up about this Astrobrights situation anytime soon. She held up the caftan again. "Just for a little while. Only temporary. It's better than being naked, right?"

At last, some agreement. "It is better than being naked," I conceded.

Rue kept us focused, steering me toward the dressing rooms. "Just keep it on while we wash and dry your"—a little pause here—"outfit. And then you'll be back to your old self in no time."

She patted me on the shoulder as I disappeared through the dressing room curtain.

Temporary, I thought, *okay.* Then: *Better than naked.*

The dressing room felt strangely smaller than usual, until I figured out why. "There's no mirror in here?" I called to Rue through the curtain as I unbuttoned my jeans, noting that my coffee-stained (black) underwear was still wet.

Should I take that off, too? I wondered, thinking maybe I shouldn't get coffee on the merchandise. Ultimately, I wrapped my bra and panties up neatly in my T-shirt and set the pile on a little bench, sneakers on top, and then, feeling more naked than I'd ever felt in my entire life, lifted the caftan up over my devoid-of-undergarments body, dropped it over my head, and let it undulate down like a silk parachute.

"The shop owner doesn't believe in mirrors," Rue called back. Then, unrelated: "I grabbed you some flip-flops."

"The owner doesn't *believe* in *mirrors*?" I asked, adjusting to the watery cool of the silk.

"She thinks fashion should be more about how you *feel* than how you look."

What an appalling idea.

In a tone like *We can outsmart this lunatic*, I asked, "Do you have a pocket mirror?"

"I happen to agree with her," Rue said.

And then, in that instant, I just knew.

Rue . . . was the shop owner.

I peeked my head through the curtain. "Rue," I said, squinting against her inevitable answer. "Are *you* the owner?"

"Of course I am, sweetheart," she said. "Now get out here."

Reluctantly, I stepped out, draped shoulders to ankles in a long, bell-sleeved, silky, orange-and-white, *patterned-so-aggressively-it-was-almost-violent* caftan.

Feeling like I'd been body-snatched.

"Stunning," Rue proclaimed, taking in the sight. "How do you feel?"

The only word that came to mind was "Surreal?"

"Don't think," Rue said, implying I was doing it wrong. "Just *experience*."

I gave it a second. Then I said, "My experience feels surreal."

"Try spinning," Rue said, like that might help.

"In a circle?"

"Yes," she said, turning me by the shoulders to wind me up.

I did it, but clompily.

"Faster," Rue said.

Obediently, I turned faster. She was my new landlord, after all.

And then a fun thing happened: the fabric started to glide on the air and float out around my calves, like a pinwheel. For a moment, until I got dizzy and stopped, I felt several things other than weird: the smooth wood floor under my bare feet, the wind swirling around my legs, the very bizarre—but not totally unpleasant, if I'm honest—sensation of *having no underpants on* . . . and, as I looked down at the bright fabric fluttering below, a micro-flash of the delight you can only get from glimpsing something beautiful.

Genuine delight—just for a half second.

There, and then gone. Like a firefly.

As I came to a stop and watched all the fabric settle around me, Rue held up a hair clip with a hot-pink hibiscus flower hot-glued to it.

"I want to put your hair up," she said, and it didn't even occur to me to protest.

"Rue," I said then, as she twisted my hair. "I'm very sorry about the Lilly Pulitzer commentary. From before."

But Rue patted my shoulder as if it hadn't bothered her at all.

"Don't even think about it," she said. "It's a lot for a chromophobe."

"For a—*what*?"

But Rue just nodded.

"A *what* kind of phobe?" I asked again.

"Chromophobia," Rue explained then, gently, like she was breaking the news of my diagnosis, "is a fear of color."

"I don't have chromophobia!" I said.

But Rue gave me a minute to consider it.

I thought about all the neutral colors in my apartment. My Harbor Gray living room and my Abalone curtains and my Pearl River cabinets. Not to mention my black underwear. And then I thought about Beanie's safety-cone-orange throw pillows that were still—eternally—stacked in my closet.

"I'm not *afraid* of color," I said. "I just don't wear it. Or enjoy it. Or have it in my house. Disliking something is not the same thing as being afraid of it."

Rue nodded like she was more of a lover than a fighter. "Maybe we should get you a bite to eat," she said. Then she snipped the tags off the caftan and dropped some rhinestone flip-flops at my feet.

"I've got my sneakers—" I started to protest, but Rue was already gathering them, along with everything else, into her arms.

"I'm just going to pop it *all* in the wash," she said, disappearing toward a back room and leaving me alone in the store.

Alone, with Bob Marley still slow-jamming on the speakers.

Not to mention braless and underwearless, with a silk hibiscus in my hair.

We were not in Dallas anymore, so to speak.

As I waited for Rue to come back, I let myself float around the merchandise, idly touching the fabrics as my silky caftan tickled the skin of my calves, with nothing else to do but experience my body in a whole new way. Beanie would hear a lot about this later—if I survived to tell the tale.

At least, thank god, there was no one else in the store.

And then, as if I'd given a cue: the shop door opened with a jangle of its handle bells.

And in walked a man.

A man that I could tell—before I'd even fully seen him—was very . . . tall.

Six-two, I decided on the spot. I'd put money on it.

Six-two, with big buzz-cut energy, and . . . manly.

Had I ever used the word *manly* to describe anyone before? Did people even still use that word? And yet there it was. I felt it the way you feel heat from a fire.

How tall—and *manly*—exactly did this guy have to be for me to sense all that *without even looking directly at him*?

Disaster! Right? I mean, could there be a worse person to have walked in at this moment? I would've happily traded him for any other kind of interloper. A blind grandmother would have worked great! A distracted mom on her cell phone! A myopic child with very thick glasses!

Anything but this guy!

Oh, god! And I didn't have any underwear on!

I held very still. Maybe the bright colors could function as camouflage?

Or maybe, if I got really lucky, he'd think I was a mannequin.

And—hey—that wasn't the worst idea in the world. I kept my eyes on the floor and stiffened my joints. I was standing right next to the register, by the jewelry counter. A perfect spot for a mannequin. People don't pay attention in stores, anyway, I told myself. This manly man surely had his own urgent island-wear shopping to do.

I tried not to breathe. *Be the mannequin.*

What was this guy doing here?

Didn't matter—didn't matter! *Just stay still.*

And then, just as I was daring to hope for the best, he took a step closer to me, peered over, and said, "Hey there."

His voice had just the slightest roughness to it. Kind of sandpapery.

As if listening to enough of it might smooth you down.

In a really good way.

That settled it. I'd have to start moving my limbs. But I drew the line at eye contact. "Hello," I said to the floor.

"I'm looking for Rue?" he said then. "Is she around?"

"She's in the back," I managed to rasp out. Was my throat closing up? Could *not having underwear on* in a moment like this cause you to suffocate?

"Thanks," he said, slapping his palm on the jewelry counter a couple of times before heading off in that direction. I think I was actually holding my breath when he turned—still walking, backward—and said, "Great hibiscus, by the way."

Hibiscus? I looked up.

And there he was.

My gaze snapped to his like a magnet. And then all questions of tallness or manliness or anything else disappeared. All I could see at first was his face—dominated by big, serious, dark eyes. Eyes are not an uncommon feature, of course—but I had never seen a pair so buttery brown—or such a combination of friendly, and intrigued, and . . . somehow melancholy.

Maybe it was the shape of them? Or the slight frown at his brows?

Can you smile and frown at the same time?

Apparently yes.

Other features appeared after that. Tan skin, with a plum-red mouth, and a defined jaw that pulled my gaze down to a truly mesmerizing Adam's apple.

Had I ever been mesmerized by an Adam's apple before?

Or even *noticed* one?

I'm sure this face-to-face contact lasted only a second. But it felt like *Matrix*-style bullet time. As though I was taking in the angle of his eyebrows, and the slope of his nose, and the deep intensity of those eyes, frame by frame, in ultra slo-mo.

It wasn't love at first sight. You can't fall in love with a person you don't even know.

But it was . . . something.

Longing at first sight, maybe? *Yearning?*

Salivating?

That face of his was *beautiful*.

I felt positively overtaken by the sight of it.

I wanted to buy it, and own it, and take it home.

And then, with what could only be described as the most charming, earnest, barely there smile in all of history, the guy touched the back of his own head—and yes, it was a longish burr cut—to indicate the hibiscus hair clip. *Great hibiscus.*

Ah. "Thanks," I said—and then, like a hopeless overachiever, I eked out a few more syllables: "Rue picked it out."

"Of course she did," the guy said, as if Rue beflowered every person she met.

Why was everything happening in slow motion?

Why were those melancholy eyes of his the most dreamy things I had ever seen?

And when he gave me a little goodbye wave and left to go find her, why did I feel a momentary flash—despite everything—of wishing he would stay?

Questions to ponder.

Especially once I realized something else about that face.

I'd seen it before.

That beautiful face, those serious eyes, that hypnotizing aura . . . belonged to Tom Hutcheson. Also known as Puppy Love. Also known as Hutch.

Hutch: Brother of Cole. Nephew of Rue. Rescuer of Jennifer Aniston's dog.

Hutch. The frowner. The *love hater.*

The guy I was here to profile.

I put my head down on the glass top of the jewelry case then, and I tried to keep breathing, wondering if my new subject was the most scientifically good-looking human I'd ever spotted in the wild . . . and I waited for Rue to show up. Which she did, a thousand hours later, and found me *still there,* slumped over the counter, only to say: "Oh, sweetheart. You must be *starving.*"

Five

THE CAFTAN WAS a slippery slope.

I sensed it from the start, if I'm honest. *This will not end well.*

Smash cut to me, the next morning, with bed-head hair, standing in my adorable three-hundred-square-foot vintage motel cabin in a baggy LIFE'S A BEACH T-shirt—also from Vitamin Sea—that I'd slept in, engaged in what can only be described as a spaghetti-Western-style stand-off with . . .

A brand-new bathing suit.

Draped very aggressively on a hanger on a peg near the mirror.

I'd caught Beanie before work on FaceTime for an emergency consultation.

"So," Beanie was saying, mining essential details from the five-minute verbal dump I'd just woken her up with. "You asked this lady about swim lessons, and now she's forcing you to take a swimming class? *This morning?*"

"Kind of."

A more accurate description might be that she "warmly invited me to join her." But "forcing" captured some of the vibe, too.

"And she bought you a swimsuit?"

"*Comped* me a swimsuit," I corrected. "As a gift. From her tropics-wear boutique."

"That was nice of her."

"Too nice," I agreed.

Beanie dropped her voice. "Oh, I see. You hate it."

"I don't hate it," I said. "I just hate the way it's looking at me."

"How is it"—here she made air quotes—"'looking at' you?"

"Like it's the predator, and I'm the prey."

"This feels melodramatic," Beanie said.

"The point is, now I have to *put it on.*"

"Okay, then," she said, bracing for impact. "Show me the suit."

All business, I rotated my phone until the menacing garment was in frame.

Was I expecting validation? Here's what I got: "What are you talking about?" Beanie demanded. "It's adorable."

It had a vintage pinup-girl look: a red-polka-dot one-piece with a halter top and a sweetheart neckline with a short little pleated skirt at the bottom.

If something that barely covers your lady bits can really be called a *skirt.*

"It's adorable *in theory,*" I said.

"Put it on," Beanie commanded.

"I don't want to. That's the truth. I just really don't want to. And the class is about to start."

"Just do it," Beanie urged.

"The thing is," I said, "I've been staring at it for fifteen minutes, and I can't seem to make it happen."

"Why not?" Beanie asked.

"A funny feeling in my chest seems to be holding me frozen."

"What's the feeling?"

"I think it's fear."

"You're *afraid of a bathing suit?*"

I turned the phone back my way so I could make eye contact and said, "I mean, I don't think it's going to come to life and strangle me or anything. I just . . . don't want to wear it."

Beanie gave me a look.

But I stood up for myself. "Don't act like this is ridiculous."

Softly, hoping not to hurt my feelings, Beanie said, "It *is* ridiculous."

"Hey," I said, "I don't need your judgment."

"I guess I just don't understand the problem. It's red. It's fun. It's got that cute little sweetheart neckline."

None of this solved anything.

Beanie went on, "People wear swimsuits all the time. It's fine."

"Not for me."

"But why not?"

"Because . . ." I had never tried to articulate this before. "Because it feels like being naked."

"But you're *not* naked in a bathing suit," Beanie protested. "You're in a bathing suit. All the important stuff is covered."

"Not for me."

"What else do you want to cover?"

"You know," I said, waving my hand. "Just—everything."

Beanie thought about this. "So there's some stepmother-based shame there," she said.

"Definitely."

"And some self-criticism."

"For sure."

"Don't you think you're being a little hard on yourself right now?"

"I'm not the only woman in the world with body-image issues," I said.

"But you might be the only one in a standoff with a bathing suit."

"You're not helping."

"Don't be one of those women who insists on thinking she's ugly," she said.

"I don't think I'm ugly," I stated. Then, much quieter and possibly hoping not even to be heard, I followed that with: "But other people might?"

Beanie was incredulous. "What?!"

I wasn't passing her feminist muster.

"I'm sorry!" I said, seeing her point. "I'd so much rather just march confidently around town, not giving a shit what anybody thinks—and I *do*! Mostly! When I'm in jeans! But a *bathing suit* . . . It's like being a knight with no armor. It's like being a quarterback with no helmet. It's like being a hermit crab with no shell!" Then I spotted a way to change the subject. "You saw that article, right? How hermit crabs are starting to *prefer* trash to real shells? They're using bottle caps and PVC debris. And apparently all that plastic isn't healthy for them!"

"Don't change the subject. That adorable swimsuit isn't trash. And you're not a hermit crab, by the way."

"It's just so *vulnerable*," I said.

But was *vulnerable* even a vulnerable enough word?

"I didn't realize you were so hard on yourself," Beanie said, like she was revising her whole opinion of me.

"I'm not! Usually. Ninety-nine percent of the time I'm completely fine and comfortable and even happy being me. *As long as I can keep my clothes on.*"

That was reasonable, right?

But Beanie was sizing me up now. "Doesn't the level of what you're feeling right now feel kind of . . . *intense*?"

I wasn't sure. *Did it?*

"Maybe it's more than just *issues*." Beanie was nodding now.

Oh, god, she had her diagnosing face on.

Next, she looked almost excited as she said, "Maybe it's a phobia."

"Look," I said, "normally I'm fine. I don't go anywhere near swimsuits, and I'm fine."

"A life spent avoiding bathing suits? This really does sound like a phobia, right?"

That sounded a little strong. "It's not a *phobia*," I said. "It's a normal female reaction to having an ordinary, imperfect body in a world overrun by Photoshop and AI."

"Normal for *you*, maybe."

But I defended myself. "The point is," I said, "I'm here for work. I'm here to film a kick-ass promo and save my job. I'm not here for a swimsuit competition! Or to sign up for some kind of *Sports Illustrated* parade! Or to release my thighs out into the wild!"

But now Beanie was googling. "Question," she said. "Do you *know* that it's crazy to be afraid of a swimsuit?"

"Of course I do!"

"Well," Beanie said, "at least it's not psychosis."

"Beanie!" I pleaded, glancing at the time. "This is serious."

"I am serious. What you're describing really sounds like a phobia." She got quiet for a second. "And I'm just double-checking, but I'm pretty sure the cure for phobias is . . . yeah. The cure for a phobia is to do the thing you're afraid of."

"To *do* it?"

"Yeah. The fact that you're afraid to put on the swimsuit means you have to put on the swimsuit."

I dropped my shoulders. Classic Beanie.

"It's called exposure therapy," Beanie went on. "You have to do the scary thing over and over until it's not scary anymore."

"But . . ." I said, trying to make my voice sound reasonable, "I don't want to."

I stared at the swimsuit, and it stared back.

"Look," Beanie went on. "Before, you were just scared. But now you have a diagnosis from the internet. And a higher purpose. Now," she said, like this changed everything, "it's a hero's journey. You are conquering your own long-held fears."

Beanie waited as long as she could for me to get on board with this new concept.

Finally, she said, "Didn't you just say this swim class was full of eighty-year-old ladies?"

I had definitely mentioned that somewhere in my opening monologue. "Uh-huh."

"Problem solved," Beanie said then. "You'll have the best-looking thighs there."

TWO MINUTES LATER, I was stepping one long, naked, imperfect leg and then the other into that godforsaken swimsuit . . . while I pep-talked myself.

I could do this! This wasn't so impossible! I might not be good at *bathing suits*. But I was *very good* at doing what needed to be done! I was good at achieving goals. Maybe a higher purpose was just what I'd needed all along.

I pulled the suit up, snapped the straps over my shoulders.

Then I wrapped a complimentary beach towel around my waist like a sarong.

And then, with a deep breath of self-encouragement, I took the hibiscus clip Rue had given me, and I clipped it to my hair just above my ear.

Then I put one sparkly flip-flop in front of the other out my cabin door, across the little porch, down the steps, along the walkway, and past the palmetto plants—cheering myself on the whole time—until I arrived at a wood deck near the pool where the ladies were gathering before class as they waited for their lifeguard-slash-swim instructor.

It felt a little bit like an out-of-body experience, but I did it.

Exposure therapy. This was good for me.

And just for the record—and I am not exaggerating here—it was the cutest crew of old ladies I had ever seen in my life. A group I would come to know as The Gals.

I had been so scared to walk out there. I had expected a lion's den—and instead found myself surrounded by lambs: kind-eyed women with grandma vibes who cooed welcoming greetings as Rue gave me a hug.

They were all smiles and color—decked head to toe in vibrant tropics-wear like a flock of hummingbirds. Hummingbirds who believed color was the answer to everything—and who possibly had a friends-and-family discount at Vitamin Sea. All of them had lost husbands, and—with the exception of Ginger, who was Rue's friend from childhood—they had all met when Rue taught a journaling class called the Joys of Grief.

That was seven years ago. In the time that followed, the four of them became a tight group—traveling, shopping, going to matinees—and one by one they'd all wound up moving to Rue's cottages. Theirs were lined up side by side, and they cooked group dinners, often grilling outside when the weather was fine, and always chatting with other Starlite guests by the pool.

"Half retirement home, half resort" was how Rue had described it yesterday. A little living-your-best-life miracle.

Rue led the introductions with basic details to get us started: Childhood friend Ginger, her red hair faded to blonde in a sensible bob, was a retired prosecutor. Benita, who immigrated to the keys from Argentina with her husband, had run a restaurant for thirty years before passing it on to her kids. Nadine, originally from Jamaica, was a librarian who read a hundred novels a year and chose all the books for the Starlite book club. Not to mention Rue herself, in a hot-pink one-piece that matched today's glasses, draped in a sheer floral cover-up that fluttered in the wind.

A heck of a lineup.

Here they were: ready to swim.

It was such a relief. I'd thought I couldn't do it—but here I was, doing it. And it wasn't so bad. Maybe I'd shock the hell out of myself by turning out to love it, I thought.

Until I saw Rue reach up to wave at someone.

I followed her smile, and then I saw, unlatching the picket-fence gate . . .

Hutch.

The same Hutch from yesterday.

The love hater himself. And also the guy with the saddest eyes I'd ever seen.

Looking very much like he might be . . . our swim instructor.

I looked around in panic. Because Hutch the rescue swimmer was *the one person* in Key West who I couldn't take swim lessons from.

Beyond how embarrassing it is to be near *a person that beautiful* when you are feeling the exact opposite, and beyond the weirdness of being not-that-far-from-naked in front of a person you're about to work with in a professional capacity . . .

Hutch couldn't know that I didn't know how to swim.

Because I'd *omitted* that to get the job he didn't even know I had.

It was bad on so many levels. But especially: once Hutch knew I was making the video promo, he could probably get me fired. For the lying, if nothing else.

Given all the secrecy around my taking Cole's place, it wasn't hard to intuit that Hutch might not be too thrilled to find out I was his new videographer.

Was there a way to escape?

Because the less he knew about me, the better.

"Morning, ladies," Hutch called.

Today, I got a good wide-shot gander at him. Yes: he was the perfect amount of tall. And wearing board shorts, and flip-flops . . . and nothing else. Also, and I'm not exaggerating: *a specimen of human perfection.*

But in a normal way—if that's possible?

Like a person who just happens to really put his body to very good use.

His muscles were solid. His calf muscles were—I don't know— like something out of an anatomy textbook? I would swear he'd been sculpted out of marble by some very attentive ancient Greek if his skin tone wasn't so . . . buttery? As if he'd been baked to perfection in some mouthwatering oven?

I shook my head to reset. This guy was my job. *Get it together!*

But I hadn't even adjusted to the visual of Hutch himself before I got another shock.

Hutch was followed through the gate by the most enormous horse-sized dog I'd ever seen.

"Hutch!" the ladies all started calling. "Come meet your new student!"

What were the options again? Fight, flight, or freeze?

Flight would have been a great option. Fight could also have worked in a pinch.

But I must have been a herd animal in a former life, because—once again—I froze.

I froze hard.

No method acting required today. I *was* a mannequin.

What was happening? I felt like I'd been tricked. I never would have signed up for any class within a hundred miles of here if I'd known *Puppy Love* was the instructor!

And yet, here we were.

Mentally, I braced for impact.

At some point, this sea of old ladies was going to part, and he was going to behold the sight of me—and I'll just pause here to cry a little bit—*in a bathing suit.*

I blew a mental kiss to my beach towel for being the last thing standing between me and utter despair.

I don't actually know how to put into words what I was afraid of in that moment. I didn't really think that this man was going to do anything weird when he saw me. He wasn't going to slap his hands over his eyes like he'd just seen a cyclops, or bend over and start retching, or turn and run screaming from the pool.

He was a rescue swimmer! For a living! And also, apparently, a swim instructor for eighty-year-olds. He'd seen the human form in plenty—*plenty*—of variations.

What was I really afraid of?

If I'm really honest . . . if I truly think about it . . . I think it was just the idea that he—or, honestly, anybody—might see me the way my stepmother had. That he might encounter me out in the open, so exposed, with so little left to the imagination . . . and find me . . . unappealing.

Or any of a whole tasting plate of other words starting with *un*:
Unattractive. Uninviting. Unsalvageable. Unpleasant. Unacceptable.
Unlovable.

This was it. This was the phobia.

Being exposed, in plain daylight, with nowhere to hide—and then
being . . . rejected. By anyone. Even a stranger.

A beautiful stranger in this case, but still.

I wasn't afraid of *bathing suits*. I was afraid of *being seen*.

I'd spent my whole life avoiding moments like this. And here it was,
happening.

I thought I might die. And then I was disappointed when I didn't.

Because here's the twist. Things didn't quite play out as expected.

The sea of old ladies *did* part, and I *was* left standing alone, totally
defenseless, with next to nothing on, my collarbones and shoulders and
upper arms exposed to the world, but before Hutch could even look up
to take in the sight of me . . .

His Clydesdale-sized dog beheld me first. And then it broke into a
gallop.

Right for me. Toward me. *At* me.

I'm fond of dogs. I'm a dog person.

But if I thought just standing around in a bathing suit was scary—
I needed a few reminders about fear. This beast *launched itself*—lips
flapping, ears undulating, teeth unveiled, giant paws galumphing—
across the wooden deck and straight at its target.

Me.

There wasn't time to move or even duck. It happened so fast, we all
just stared. This thing hurtled itself toward me—and the next thing I
knew, we were both skidding across the wooden deck and sliding to a
stop in a heap.

Leaving my beloved beach towel limp and lifeless, many feet
behind me.

Not to mention my hibiscus hair clip.

The dog—unfazed—was up on its feet in no time, licking my face
while I tried to adjust to the stinging scrape on the back of my leg. Or

maybe it was my hip. Or maybe my butt. Most likely all three. Is there a term for that place on the outer back of your thigh-hip-butt?

The only word that came to mind was *haunch*.

Did humans even *have* haunches?

One thing was for sure. It was a real body part—and it was now riddled with splinters.

Hutch was there in seconds, helping me back up and hoisting me to my feet. "I'm so sorry," he said in astonishment. Looking down into my face with those dark, melancholy eyes and an undeniable concerned frown.

Dazed, I thought of Cole saying that frowning was Hutch's favorite hobby.

So on-brand.

But Hutch was still apologizing. "He never runs to anyone but me."

"Did he think I was going to *catch* him?" I asked, now frowning myself.

"He's a Great Dane," Hutch said, "but he thinks he's a chihuahua."

From all the women clucking scoldingly at the dog, I gathered his name was either "George" or "Bailey." Or both.

"Where does it hurt?" Hutch asked.

"It's fine," I insisted, my whole back quadrant stinging like fire. "It's fine."

But to no avail. Hutch was now walking me and my swimsuit over to a seating area so he could—and I'm just as horrified to say this as you must be to hear it—*examine my wound.*

"Oh, no. There's no need for this," I said as Hutch bent me forward, ass out, over a table.

"We're going to need some tweezers," I heard him say to someone.

"I'm really okay," I protested again, just as Ginger showed up with a pool chair cushion for me to lean over.

"Let him help you, sweetie," Benita said. "He knows what he's doing."

Now Hutch was pulling up a footstool to sit on so he could lean in close and take a good gander at what—fine, let's call a haunch a haunch—could only be classified as *a large section of my butt*.

Next, Rue showed up with tweezers and a first-aid kit for Hutch— and a glass of champagne for me.

"For the pain," she said, conspiratorially, as she patted me on the shoulder.

I kicked it back like an old-timey soldier downing whiskey before a post-battle amputation.

The crowd sighed and made wincing sounds as they got in close to look.

"How bad is it?" I finally asked.

"You look like a cactus," Benita said.

"Should someone take a picture and text it to you?" Ginger asked.

"Oh, god, please—*no one* ever do that," I begged.

"It's just a few splinters," Hutch said.

"How many?" I demanded.

"Forty?" he guessed. "Fifty?"

That was not the definition of *a few*, but okay.

Then I heard his voice shift as he called to the class.

"Ladies, why don't you get started without me? We're gonna be here awhile."

"You don't have to do this!" I protested from my position over the cushion. "I can do it myself."

"Unless you're a contortionist," Hutch said, "I really don't think you can."

"Rue can do it!" I insisted then. "Right, Rue?"

But Rue was already in the pool. "I'd love to, sweetheart," she said, "but I'm squeamish."

Defeated, I collapsed over the cushion.

"Don't worry!" Nadine called. "He's not a big talker, but he's great at first aid!"

Down below, under the table, the beast who had done this to me was settling into a lion's pose like nothing had happened.

For just a millisecond there, I'd thought that dog had saved me. If he had stopped just a bit shorter, I could have hidden fully behind his gargantuan torso until it was time to slip into the pool. He could have been my salvation.

But now, of course, as my precious beach towel lay forgotten on the deck like a dead jellyfish, and as Hutch leaned in so close to peer at my backside *that I could feel his breath brushing my skin*, it was clear this dog was the opposite. He'd shoved me out of the frying pan and into the hellfires of deepest humiliation.

All the dread I'd felt for how this morning would play out?

I should've doubled it.

Wait. *Tripled.*

The ladies set about splashing in the pool, and Hutch got to work on the splinters, leaning against my lower back for support.

A line from one of my favorite movies went through my head: *"I'm tempted to marry him so I can tell people how we met."*

I felt little pinches from the tweezers and the near constant brushing of his fingers as he felt for the edges. Hutch's face, I swear to god, was six inches from my butt the whole time.

If that.

"You were in the shop yesterday," Hutch said then, striking up a conversation in that let's-pretend-this-isn't-weird way the gynecologist does when she busts out the salad tongs.

"Yes," I said, playing along.

"You were wearing one of Rue's . . . garments."

Well, that was thoughtful. An opportunity for me to say, "My regular clothes were in the wash."

"You looked like an Orange Crush."

Was he teasing me? "Is that a compliment?"

"I guess that depends."

"On?"

"On if you like Orange Crush."

So this was Hutch. Now that we were meeting—if you can call a man pulling splinters out of your nether regions *a meeting*—I found myself reviewing Cole's prep info on his brother. According to Cole,

Hutch was serious, and never joked around, and hardly ever talked. He was a former Eagle Scout, a former high school class president, the epitome of a responsible adult, and a total alpha.

Cole had warned me that nothing about Hutch was in any way *fun*.

Yet here he was: teasing me a little.

Maybe he sensed my panic. Or maybe he had some of his own.

"I'm truly sorry about all this," he said next. "I've honestly never seen my dog do anything like that. And I've had him over a year."

I looked down at the dog, now resting his head on his paws, under the table.

"Is his name George?" I asked, studying him. "Or Bailey?"

"Both," Hutch said. "It's George Bailey."

"Like in the movie? *It's a Wonderful Life*?"

"Exactly," Hutch said, like not everybody knew that reference. "He's a rescue," he added then.

"You rescued him and named him after Jimmy Stewart?"

Hutch shifted position to get a better angle. "He was part of a puppy mill, so he didn't even have a name at first. The puppy mill was raided, and they pulled out sixty-seven dogs. He was two years old, and he'd never been outside. He'd spent his whole life in a cage."

"Oh, god," I said, my heart squeezing.

"Nobody wanted him," Hutch went on, "because he was so big, and he had this skin condition that kind of looked like leprosy. Also, he'd never been socialized—and he was afraid of people. With a dog this big, that's never a good thing."

"But he looks great now," I said. "He could be a show dog!"

"They wanted to put him down. They thought he was hopeless."

"But you didn't?"

"I just had this feeling about him," Hutch said. "And I'm pretty good with dogs."

"You know," I said, "even when he was running right at me, even as huge as he is—he never looked scary. The *moment* was scary—but the dog . . . seemed happy."

"I think he is happy now," Hutch said. "His paws are all healed up from the wire floor of the cage—though there's still some scarring. His coat's all grown back. The heartworms weren't too bad—and they're treated now. And honestly, it wasn't that hard to socialize him. I really think, all that time, he was just waiting for someone to love."

Again—I'll note that Hutch was surprisingly chatty for a person who was "not a big talker."

Did I have the right guy? Did *Cole*?

I felt this conversation shifting my perspective on my own current suffering in real time. The gorgeous, velvet-eared dog resting under the table had spent *two years* alone in a cage. Without ever going outside. Or getting petted. Or having a treat. Or getting to play.

Compared to that, my personal morning's humiliation didn't seem so bad.

"When I first brought him out of the rescue shelter," Hutch said, "he had never seen grass before. He was scared of it. He'd touch it with a paw and then back up to the sidewalk."

"Is he still scared?"

"No. Now he rolls and rolls in it. It just took some time. And some exposure therapy."

Exposure therapy. Quite the theme today.

I watched George Bailey scratch his ear with one of his paws.

"So he's living the good life now," I said.

"Yeah. That's the idea. He plays in the park, and basks in the sun, and eats like a king. And somehow I've wound up letting him sleep in my bed, too. Or maybe it's more accurate to say he lets me sleep in his."

"This is the happiest happy ending I've ever heard of."

"The only thing I haven't been able to solve is his fear of thunder."

George Bailey shifted to lie on his side. "He's afraid of thunder?" I asked.

"It's called brontophobia," Hutch said. "It's common in dogs."

Newly diagnosed with a few phobias myself, I got it.

"Poor guy," I said.

"Yeah," Hutch said. "He's fine with *rain*. It's just thunder—something about the rumble. He starts shaking and panting, and then he has to come climb on top of me."

"Does that help?"

"Not really."

"Is there—a medication for it?"

"Yeah, there's doggie Xanax. But he can't take it."

"Can't? Or won't?"

"Both, actually. The first time he took it, he threw up all over the place. Every time I've tried again since—in case that was a fluke—he refuses."

"He refuses?"

"If I try to hide a pill in a treat, he spits out the pill. And if I bury it in a pile of dog food, I'll find the whole plate licked clean with an un-touched, pristine pill sitting right in the middle. They have pill shooters for dogs—but he won't let me near him with it."

"Wow."

"Yeah. It's pretty hard to make a Great Dane do anything he doesn't want to do."

"So he just panics until the thunder stops? You can't do anything for him?"

"I do lots of things for him. They don't help, but I do them anyway. I hum. I pet him. I've got a snug vest to put him in that's supposed to be comforting. Mostly, I just spend hours trying to explain that the thunder can't hurt us. But he never believes me."

"He's lucky to have you," I said.

"I'm lucky to have *him*," Hutch said.

"Maybe you both can call it even."

FIVE MILLION HOURS later, as Hutch finished pulling out the last of the splinters—and was dabbing antiseptic all over the scrapes—The Gals finished their swim and came over to tease him, gathering in a semicircle around my upturned butt like they were contemplating a piece of art.

"This is quite a first date," Nadine said.

"It's not a date," Benita corrected. "It's a medical emergency."

"Aren't they so adorable together?" Ginger asked The Gals.

Coos and murmurs all around.

"That's more talking than I've seen Hutch do in all the time I've known him," Benita said then.

"What were you two chatting about?" Nadine wanted to know.

I turned back to look at Hutch, and I realized he was done. He'd turned his attention to putting away the supplies.

I felt like I needed to stand up for him. "He was apologizing for George Bailey," I said, just as Rue showed up nearby—now in a post-swim cover-up with a wide straw hat.

"Will she live?" Rue asked.

Undecided.

"Probably," Hutch answered.

"Good," Rue said. "Because she still needs her swim lesson."

Shit. Busted.

"Was she . . . here for the swim lesson?" Hutch asked.

I wanted to say *No*, but of course the answer was yes. And Rue knew that.

This is the trouble with lying, I guess.

"She doesn't know how to swim," Rue told Hutch then. "Can you imagine? On vacation in the keys and hasn't owned a bathing suit since middle school."

Oh, god. I'd overshared.

That's when Benita picked up my towel, and the little hibiscus hair clip, and came over to me. She set the clip on the table and wrapped the towel around my shoulders. It was bigger than I remembered, and I sank into it so gratefully—just as Rue said to Hutch, blithely spilling all my secrets, "She needs to learn to swim before Monday. Could you give her some private lessons?"

How did she make *private lessons* sound so provocative?

"I'm pretty busy," Hutch answered, glancing in my direction.

As he said it, George Bailey appeared by my side and then leaned against me like he was mooring to a dock. I stroked his head.

Maybe this whole splinters-in-the-haunch situation was a blessing of sorts. Maybe it would help with my swimsuit phobia. I mean, how hard could it be to work with this guy now? He'd seen more of me, at this point, than I'd seen of myself.

"You need to learn to swim *before Monday*?" Hutch asked.

It was Friday.

"I just need a refresher course," I said, fully lying. "I'm a little rusty."

Hutch frowned in earnest.

"I don't need to win any gold medals," I went on, quoting Beanie. "I just need to beef up my dog paddle."

"I'm not sure that's enough time," Hutch said, "even for a dog paddle."

"I'll take anything," I said. Anything was better than nothing, right? "Whatever I can learn before Monday, I'll take it."

But he was shaking his head. "I'm busy this weekend."

But, as I thought about it, it didn't even have to be that soon. I started at the air station on Monday, but the first few days were always just getting the lay of the land. "Actually even a couple days after Monday could work."

Hutch kept his serious expression. "I guess we can manage something."

"Thank you," I said. "And thank you," I added then, "for pulling all those splinters out of my ass."

Hutch stifled a smile and said, "Anytime."

Six

BEANIE COULD NOT *believe* that in all that time I never introduced myself to Hutch as his future videographer. She was aghast. "That man had his hands all over your backside for all that time, and you never found a moment to mention it?"

"I prefer the term *haunch*," I said.

"You should have told him," Beanie said, undeterred.

"Um. I was a little swamped by all the soul-crushing humiliation at the time," I said. "And getting busted for lying."

"He doesn't know you lied about being able to swim."

"Not yet. But he will."

Beanie nodded. "It's going to be *indescribably* weird when you see him at the air station."

"I couldn't have told him, anyway," I went on, still defending myself. "Cole told me not to say anything about anything until after the job started."

"To the *old lady*," Beanie pointed out. "This guy is not an old lady."

No. He certainly wasn't.

"She was nearby," I said. "She would've heard me."

"I'm just saying Monday morning is going to be weird as hell."

No argument there.

I knew Cole was supposed to be doing this project. But Cole wasn't coming. Was that my fault? That was between Cole and the Coast Guard.

Yes. My showing up at the air station would be weird for Hutch.

But not even a tiny fraction of how weird it would be for me.

Without a doubt, this was the first time in my career I'd start a project knowing that the subject had already—slowly, over a long period of time—had his hands all over a part of my body that had been, shall we say, *devoid of gentleman callers* for far too long.

I mean, if there was anybody to pity in this situation . . . it was me.

I SPENT THE weekend staunching the flow of my dread with over-preparation.

My shipped equipment arrived on Saturday—as did my lost luggage.

Apparently, all I needed to restore my equilibrium was my Sony FX6 camera, my beat-up shoulder rig, and my sturdiest tripod from the equipment room back at the office.

Plus, my trusty black underwear.

I unpacked it all like I was reuniting with lost pieces of myself.

A higher-budget production would have a separate director of photography and production editor, but I'd be doing most things myself. To be honest, I enjoyed doing both. It was part of the storytelling process for me: capturing the moments, and then, later, hunting back to find the best clips to tell the story.

This promo project was different from others I'd worked on, though.

Most of the projects I got were the usual: a CEO at his desk, in a suit, looking calm and important and in charge, talking about some product or service his company had paid ours to highlight. Still shots on tripods, a simple script, and a spokesperson struggling to make it sound natural—later scored with vaguely uplifting, very on-the-nose, royalty-free background songs with titles like "Happy and Trustworthy."

But the US Coast Guard was different.

They wanted the *un*usual. They wanted a video that would stand out, and get attention, and captivate. "This is a *recruiting* video," Cole had explained, "for a grueling, exhausting, death-defying job."

"That's a tough sell."

"Exactly," Cole said. "That's where you come in. Explain the unexplainable. Describe the indescribable. Show them what they can't see."

Was this a pep talk?

I wrote down, *Make it look exciting.*

But Cole had leaned over the notepad and then jabbed at the paper with his finger. "No. You don't need to 'make it look exciting.' It *is* exciting. Your job is to capture that excitement."

"Got it," I said.

"It's a kick-ass job," Cole concluded. "And it needs a kick-ass video."

So . . . my job for this assignment was to film *everything* and find the moments that would capture the story. That's why I would stay so long. A full-immersion deep dive into the job of a rescue swimmer—in hopes that I could surface with genuine treasure.

MONDAY MORNING, AS I got dressed for my first day at the air station in my black-on-black everything, I felt many feelings—including (1) excitement to get started; (2) a full-body tension I've now dubbed *moderate fear of helicopters*; and (3) dread.

I dreaded the moment when Hutch would realize everything. But it wasn't just Hutch I was dreading.

I was also intimidated by . . . the military. I'd been trying to study all the names and ranks, but I couldn't keep anything straight. It seemed likely I would say, or do, one wrong thing after another. I couldn't even remember the written rules I knew of—not even counting the unwritten ones I didn't. Would I forget to salute? Sit when I should be standing? Make eye contact with the wrong rank of eyes?

Is anticipatory humiliation a real thing?

Scratch that question.

Yes, it is. My bathing suit could vouch.

I took Rue's red-and-white Mini Cooper for the twenty-minute drive to the air station on Stock Island—but because I didn't have clearance to enter the premises, I had to park in the visitor lot outside the gatehouse and wait for my liaison, one Lieutenant Junior Grade Carlos Alonso, to meet me, vouch for me, and get me past the guards.

"So sorry about the wait," the lieutenant said, after a big friendly handshake, once we were past the gates and walking toward the air station itself. "We sent a clearance form to fill out, but we never received it back."

Great. *Thanks, Cole.*

"What should I call you?" I asked then. First things first. "Lieutenant Alonso?"

"Carlos is fine."

I frowned, like that didn't seem right. "Should I salute you or something?"

Carlos, as bright and youthful as a puppy dog, gave me a smile like *I* was the puppy. "We're pretty informal here."

"So should I just—act normal?"

"Sure," Carlos said. "You're a civilian. Nobody expects you to know the rules."

Carlos was friendly, but that was only the beginning. As we entered the no-frills industrial air station building, Carlos introduced me to one smiling Coastie after another—all sticking out welcoming hands to shake. It was a parade of friendliness. Friendliness in flight suits. So much friendliness, in fact, that by the time we'd made it down the long corridor to the conference room, I had relaxed a little—despite myself.

Bad move.

Because the only person I really should have been dreading was the one I was there to see.

Though he didn't recognize me.

Not at first.

We walked in, and Hutch—looking official in a drab-green zip-up flight suit with patches—stood to greet us. And all he seemed to see . . . was that I wasn't Cole.

"What's this?" He blinked over at Carlos. "I thought today was the video?"

"It is," Carlos said. Then, beginning his introduction: "Aviation Survival Technician First Class Tom Hutcheson, please meet—"

But Hutch's melancholy frown turned to a suspicious one. "Where's the video guy?"

Carlos gestured at me. "This is the video guy."

"Where's *Cole*, the video guy?"

"Who?"

"The guy who's filming the video. Cole."

"Um," Carlos said, now frowning at me. "I guess they sent this lady instead?"

"Cole is unavailable," I said, reciting what Cole had told me to say. Then, as if we might move on: "I'm Katie. We met—"

But I didn't even get to finish with "at Rue's" before Hutch put his head down, muscled past us, and charged out of the room.

Seven

"GUESS HE HAD something else—urgent—to do?" Carlos said, as we stared at the vacant doorway.

But then, through the A/C vent, we heard Hutch's voice next door, leaving an angry message in a straight-to-voicemail situation.

His words were as loud and clear as if he had never left the room.

"I just walked in to start filming," Hutch began, his voice tense, "and found out you sent someone else. Do you have any idea how many hoops I had to jump through to make this happen? The paperwork? The letters of petition? The logistics? I just about killed myself—and then I worked out the timing just right so you could be here on October fourth so we could all be together for the first time in over a year, for Rue's sake, if nothing else—and all you had to do was *show up* . . . And that's too much for you? Even that? It did occur to me that this might happen. That you might actually keep holding this grudge forever. If that's really who you want to be, then I guess I can't stop you. But what about Rue? What about everything she gave up for you? There's only one thing she's ever asked of us, and it was to be together on *one* specific day. You're going to miss it—again?"

Carlos and I glanced at each other, then kept watching the vent.

Hutch went on with his message. "I recovered a body yesterday. A twenty-year-old guy who got caught in a rip current. His whole family waited on the beach while we searched." Another sigh. "Do you have any idea how short life is? Even *long* lives are too short. Why are you wasting time? I keep trying—but nothing from you. I want so badly right now to say that I give up. But I can't do that, Cole! Because as much as you hate it, and as much as I hate it right now, too—you're the only brother I'll ever have."

The vent went quiet.

Wow. For a guy who was not a talker . . . I guess he had some things to say.

Then Hutch appeared in the hallway, his frown tight, practicing what looked like controlled breathing. He took several deliberate steps until he had joined us again.

Carlos proceeded as if nothing was weird. "AST One Tom Hutcheson, may I present documentary filmmaker Katie Vaughn."

I was really more of a mid-level employee with potential. But documentary filmmaker worked, too.

"Hello," I said, holding out my hand.

Hutch took it, looked up—and recognized me at last.

Delayed reaction.

Me: no longer butt-up leaning over a patio table in a polka-dot one-piece, but in normal clothes with all my gear—my personal dignity a little shaky, but present and accounted for.

"You're—" he started.

My haunch stung at the recognition. "Katie," I said. "I'm staying with Rue. In one of her cottages. Cole set it up."

"I see," Hutch said, nodding. "Cole set it up when he decided to send you instead of himself."

I mean, *yeah.* I shrugged.

"Does Rue know? That you're here to take his place?"

I shook my head. "He swore me to secrecy."

Hutch pushed out a sigh. "Until when?"

"Until it was too late for her to make him change the plan?"

"So you knew?" he asked, like we'd been in cahoots.

Knew? Knew what? That this was an offer I couldn't refuse? I'd have to be fully unconscious *not* to know that. "I knew," I began, standing straighter, "that Cole was not available for this project and needed a replacement. And that his aunt Rue might not be happy about it."

Hutch gave a nod, like *Noted*.

I waited out the pause that followed.

Next, Hutch stretched around to get a gander at my haunch. "How's your—"

"It's fine," I cut him off, in a tone like *We're done with that topic forever.*

Hutch brought his eyes back up to my all-business face. Then, in a one-final-question tone, he asked, "And you didn't introduce yourself the other day at the pool because—?"

I thought about trying to come up with some convoluted explanation for him. But the only thing that came to me was the truth. So I didn't fight it.

Instead, I just said: "I was too busy drowning in humiliation."

IT'S FAIR TO say that I really didn't know this guy Hutch very well—so my ability to read his emotional state might not have been perfect. But, as he led me off for the scheduled air station tour, there wasn't too much doubt about his vibe.

I think the technical term is *pissed off.*

The kind of pissed off that's *so* pissed off it seems weirdly calm.

Eye-of-the-storm pissed off.

Even though Hutch was clearly endeavoring to be professional, and even though he was polite the whole time, I could just tell. It was clear from the poker face, the one-word responses, the nostril flares, and the way he walked—no, *strode*—two feet in front of me at all times.

This, honestly, was the nonverbal Hutch I'd been led to expect.

But I had a job to do, so I just did it: asked questions, and took notes, and snapped photos. But this guy definitely didn't want me there.

It's a weird feeling: being *unwelcome.* I tried to compensate with enthusiasm, panic-talking with ridiculous commentary, like "Those helicopters are so orange!"

I guess the US Coast Guard didn't suffer from chromophobia.

Needless to say, my goofy cheeriness didn't help.

Hutch kept up a robotic pace, showing me the remaining offices, the presentation room, the break room, the preflight meeting room, and the hangar—the site of my infamous "so orange" comment, yes, but also several other idiotic statements, like, "Look how shiny they are!" and "The floor is so clean!" and "Those rotors are *enormous!*"

Yeah. Pretty bad.

But can I say something about all those dumb things I said? They were *true.*

The helicopters really were shiny—and so much bigger than when you see them motoring across the sky in the distance. The hangar really was spotlessly clean. And the rotors really were enormous—almost prehistoric in scale. I felt an actual, honest-to-god feeling of awe as I beheld them in that hangar.

It was unexpectedly moving.

It felt like a shrine to all the best parts of humanity.

Which was something I would've said to Hutch, if he'd been receptive at all. I might even have thanked him.

Instead, I was trapped. Anxiety-babbling about décor.

Finally, for the grand finale, he took me outside, pausing to don a pair of aviators, where a helicopter was about to take flight for a training mission. The crew was already on board, and the blades were spinning up top—and there is no possible way to explain how loud it was. For the first time, I understood the term *choppers.* Those blades really do chop the air—and you can feel the vibrations from one side of your body to the other.

"This chopper is really loud!" I called to Hutch once I'd caught up, continuing my streak of inane commentary.

Hutch turned back. "They're only called *choppers* in the movies."

"You guys don't call them *choppers*?"

"We call them *birds*."

Birds. Huh. "Why hasn't that bird taken off yet?" I called next, trying it out.

He looked at me long enough for me to decide that he was at least 10 percent cooler and more intimidating with those aviators on.

Then he answered, "Procedures and checks."

I watched it, thinking I'd see it lift up into the sky any minute. But I guess those procedures and checks were pretty thorough. Time lumbered along, and many minutes later, still standing there, side by side, surrounded by the vibrating air, I squinted toward Hutch in the sunlight and heard myself call, "Did you know that the word *helicopter* comes from Greek?"

Hutch looked over.

"People assume it breaks down into *heli* and *copter*," I went on, "but that's not right. It's actually *helico* and *pter*."

No response.

Come on! This was the most interesting thing I'd learned all weekend!

"*Helico*," I pushed on, still at top volume, "means 'to spin,' and *pter* means 'to fly.' You know: *pter* as in 'pterodactyl.' And of course *dactyl* means 'fingers.' So *pterodactyl* means 'flies with fingers.' Which is true, if you look at their wings. They're just fingers with skin stretched between."

Had I gone off the rails at *flies with fingers*? Possibly.

But this information *was* objectively fascinating.

I waited for Hutch to become fascinated.

But he refused.

So I went ahead and asked, "Are you angry right now or something?"

He tilted his head, like that was the most ridiculous question ever. "No."

"You look kind of cranky."

"No."

I put a hand on my hip. "You seemed a lot nicer the other day."

"You hadn't taken my brother's job the other day."

There it was. At least now we could talk about it. "I didn't take it! He *gave* it to me!"

"This"—Hutch gestured around at everything we were doing—"was supposed to be happening with him."

"That's not my fault."

"You could have said no."

"Why would I do that?"

"Because you can't even swim!"

"Shh!" I said, looking around as if the helicopter noise wasn't swallowing every sound we made. "You could get me fired."

"Maybe I *should* get you fired. You lied to get this job."

"I didn't *lie*," I said. "I just *didn't volunteer the truth.*"

"Also known as lying."

"Look," I called over the noise, "this is how my industry works. You say yes, and then you figure it out."

"Unless you drown first."

That went dark fast. "I'm not going to drown."

"No?"

"No! Because you're going to teach me how to swim."

"Maybe I should just report you."

"Reporting me won't get you Cole. He'll send every underling there is before he comes here. And the next one you won't be able to blackmail."

Hutch looked away.

"Look," I said, "I know you didn't want to do this. I googled you. You refused every Puppy Love interview request! You refused *60 Minutes*! And NPR! And Jimmy Fallon! You're not looking for cheap fame. You just want to do your job in peace."

Hutch let out a slow breath.

"And I'm gonna be honest," I went on. "I overheard everything you said in that voicemail message for Cole. It came right through the A/C vent like a loudspeaker. So I know this is only happening right now because the higher-ups wanted it to. And I know you're trying to make the best of things—and that's how our little rinky-dink, Dallas–Fort Worth metro area video company got this gig. And I know you're trying to heal some deep rift with your brother. And you're mad that I'm here and he isn't. But, honestly . . ." I paused for dramatic effect. "I think you should get over it."

Hutch dropped his shoulders. "You do, huh?"

"I do. Because I may not be what you wanted—but I'm definitely the next best thing. I'm good at my job. And I'm a nice person. And I genuinely respect who you are and what you do. And guess what? We can help each other."

Hutch flared his nostrils, like *How?*

"If you"—I pointed at him—"don't get me fired, then I"—I touched my collarbone—"will help you reconnect with your brother."

"How exactly would you do that?"

I made it up on the fly: "Well, he's my producer, so we're in pretty frequent contact. I take it from earlier that he's not too keen on taking your calls."

Hutch looked away.

"Who knows if he'll even listen to that voicemail?" I went on. "He might just delete it. Or never even notice it. I *talk* to him. I can put in a good word for you." But that didn't sound strong enough. "I can put in *lots* of good words for you! Help him come around. Convey your talking points."

I was just brainstorming at this point.

But Hutch was considering it.

I kept going. "I can advocate for you. However you need me to. We can get creative."

When Hutch looked up, his body language had shifted. The sun had shifted, too, and started to cast its famous late-afternoon golden rays. It was lighting up the ends of his burr haircut like dandelion fluff, and backlighting his flight suit, too.

Which I suddenly realized was a strangely sexy garment. Maybe it was the suggestiveness of what that drab green was camouflaging. Or maybe it was the badassery of the arm patches. Or the dependability of those black utility boots. Or the official gold lettering on his name tag that read TOM HUTCHESON—AST USCG.

Or maybe it was the fact that the obscenely noisy helicopter we'd been standing next to this whole time had taken off while we were shout-talking, and I hadn't even noticed. Now it was just a distant buzz on the horizon. Now I could hear the wind *shhh*ing around us—and see long, tufted grass waving at the edges of the runway, making this moment seem bright, and alive, and tinged with possibility.

"You'd do that?" Hutch asked.

But now I'd lost my train of thought. *Thanks a lot, military-wear.* "Do what?" I asked.

Hutch shifted his weight. "Advocate for me. With Cole."

"Of course. We can form an allegiance."

"Alliance," Hutch corrected.

I shrugged, like *That's what I said.* "You help me. I'll help you. Everybody wins. That doesn't sound too bad, does it? Everybody winning?"

"No," Hutch agreed. "That doesn't sound too bad."

"So we're allies?" I asked, to confirm.

Hutch eyed me. "I suppose so. On a trial basis."

"Great," I said. Then I added, "Because Cole never cleared Rue's car to drive on the base. So do you mind if we carpool to work?"

AND SO, WITH that . . . we went inside to do our first official interview.

Disastrous timing. If there's not an old saying "Never interview a subject on the very first day," there should be.

By the time we got back to the hangar, the lighting and sound guy from Miami was there. He'd been escorted in by Carlos and had already finished setting up. He had a rat ponytail and wore a T-shirt that featured a clip-art video camera and the words I SHOOT PEOPLE . . . FOR A LIVING.

He'd arranged a chair in front of one of those big, orange, shiny birds I'd been admiring earlier, using his own camera on his own tripod, and when I checked the framing, it was perfect—a wide angle with a depth of field set just right to blur and soften the background a little while still keeping it bright and imposing and impressive.

I studied it for a minute, and then I said, "We should lose the chair."

"You don't want him sitting?"

Most interviewees sat: more conversational.

But I shook my head. "I want him standing."

Standing like an alpha. With his feet shoulder-distance apart and his helmet under one arm. Shot from an underside angle to make him look even taller and emphasize the heroism.

But the lighting guy didn't need all those details.

He took the chair away.

I positioned Hutch in an at-ease stance on a mark taped to the floor at a two-thirds split in the frame. Then I checked everything in the monitor.

Perfect. Except something was missing. Hutch had taken off his aviators when we came inside.

I walked back over to Hutch. "Give me your sunglasses," I said.

"What? Why?"

"I want to try something."

Hutch took the case out of a zipper pocket and handed it to me.

I took the glasses out, opened them up, and then stepped close to position them on his face. Wow, did all military men radiate this kind of buzzing electricity? Or was it just Hutch?

It distracted me a little. For a second, I kept my hands up on either side of his face, trying to focus and decide if the glasses were a *go* or a *no-go*.

"What are you doing?" Hutch said.

I stepped back. "Seeing if you look cooler with your aviators on."

"I don't," Hutch said.

I wrinkled my nose. "I think every woman in America might disagree with you."

"We are *inside*," Hutch said then. "There is no sun here."

"Details," I said, waving it off.

"You don't wear sunglasses inside a hangar."

"Nobody knows that."

"*I* know that."

"They make you look cool," I said, like *Why are you fighting me?*

"I don't need to *look* cool," Hutch said—implying, but not actually saying, *I am cool.*

"Real life and video are not the same thing," I said.

"But," Hutch argued, "if you put on sunglasses when there *is no sun*, then you're just wearing them for show. Which amounts to trying to look cool. And I don't know if you know this—but if you have to try to look cool, you're not. By definition."

Fortunately for the shot, he looked cool either way.

I flared my nostrils, stepped close again—feeling that same electrical force field of his body—and reached up to take them back off.

But just as my fingers touched his temples, Hutch said, "Did you know you have a little pie piece of brown in one of your eyes?"

I held still. "Yes."

"Not really a pie piece, even, because the edges are blurry, like it was airbrushed."

I hadn't thought of it like that before.

"Does it have a name?" Hutch asked then.

"Does what have a name?"

"When part of your iris is a different color like that?"

"I don't know," I said. "Probably?"

Hutch kept staring straight at my eyes. My finger pads were still touching the sides of his glasses. "Well," Hutch said, like he was summing everything up. "It's cool."

"Cool?" I asked.

"Your pie piece," he said. "It's cool."

"And I didn't even have to try," I said.

I was supposed to be taking off his aviators. So I did.

"Exactly," Hutch said. "You're a fast learner." Then, before I turned away, Hutch had another question. He lifted the sunglasses and said, "Why didn't you just ask me to put these on myself?"

Huh. I thought for a second. Why *hadn't* I done that? "I guess I'm just used to handling the props."

"These aren't props. These are my actual glasses."

Bit of an overly fine point. "Now that you're in a video," I said, "they're kind of both."

TIME TO GET started. I checked the frame again and sent a silent prayer of thanks to the heavens that Hutch looked even better on camera than he did in real life. There are people in this world you just can't help but want to stare at, and Hutch was definitely one of them. Frown and all.

Good for him.

But also good for my career.

Plus, he turned out to be appealing. As a person. Pilots and flight mechanics kept walking by, catcalling him and teasing him with "Work it, baby!"—and he'd duck his head in the most irresistible aw-shucks way and smile at that spotless concrete floor. He clearly disliked being the center of attention—but he was also a really good sport about it.

Not to mention the moment when—and I swear this has never, ever happened before—I caught my foot in one of the lighting cables and knocked over one of the big lights—and myself. The lighting guy caught the light just in time, and Hutch, out of nowhere, caught *me*.

"Got ya," Hutch said. Before I even registered that I was *in his arms*, he had me back on my feet and was picking up his helmet and returning to his mark.

As if rescuing people was as no-big-deal as breathing.

Which I guess maybe it was—for him.

"Thank you!" I called, brushing myself off. Then adding, "That never happens, by the way." Right? I knew my way around a set. I didn't just go around from job to job, tripping on lighting cables like a loony bird.

I blamed the weirdness of this weird day. And Hutch. And his aviators.

I got back to work and checked the monitor one more time—noting that drab green and Coast Guard orange were complementary colors.

Sometimes you just know when you've got a project in the bag. Hutch looked so good on-screen, I'd have watched that interview with the sound off. This video was going to rock, I thought. I had no option but to crush it. This guy was *born* to be interviewed.

Until the interview actually started.

Let's just say that Hutch turned out to be . . . not exactly a natural.

The not-a-big-talker version of Hutch showed up just when I needed him to be the opposite.

The camera—even after I'd messed around for twenty more minutes—did not disappear from his mind. He stayed aware of it constantly, the way you might stay aware of a hungry wolf just outside the light of your campfire.

To seem natural when there's a camera lens trained on you takes a certain amount of pretending for anyone: pretending it's not there, or that you don't care, or that it doesn't bother you. But Hutch, it turned out, was not great at pretending.

By *not great*, I mean *abysmal*.

Probably a good thing in real life. But on video? *Disaster.*

I tried everything I could think of to help him to relax. Jokes, flirting, making crazy noises, laughing too loud at everything he said. I was like a dog photographer with a squeaky toy, I swear.

But Hutch remained painfully monosyllabic.

I won't suck out your soul with the details of the first hour-plus. It was basically me just asking questions like, "Can you introduce yourself?"

And Hutch robotically saying, "I'm Tom Hutcheson. I'm an aviation survival technician—an AST—for the United States Coast Guard, commonly referred to as a rescue swimmer. I have eight years of service."

Tone of voice? Body language? Vibes?

All totally unusable.

We'd have to record intros again later.

"Tell me about being in the Coast Guard," I said.

"There's not much to tell."

Okay, that was clearly false. "Something," I prompted. "Anything."

So Hutch answered, "There are twenty-six Coast Guard air stations in the United States—including Alaska, Hawaii, and Puerto Rico— scattered about three hundred miles apart along the coast."

Oh, god. We were doomed.

He was beautiful but useless.

Honestly. Where was the guy who had mocked me for using the word *chopper*? Where was the guy who had just explained to me *how coolness worked*?

I wanted to interview *that* guy.

"Tell us about that chopper behind you," I teased, hoping to provoke him.

But Hutch just replied: "Some air stations run the MH-65 Dolphin and others run the MH-60 Jayhawk. We also deploy fixed-wing air-craft."

"What's the most interesting thing you do in your job?" I asked, hoping he might tell a story of a death-defying rescue, or wax rhapsodic about how fun it is to fly in helicopters, or even explain what I'd just learned from the internet: that all swimmers were experts at sewing and they repaired their own gear.

But Hutch just shrugged and said, "Saving lives."

Most interviews last between two and five hours. After *an hour and a half*, and a snack break, he finally loosened up—a little. I hadn't wanted to waste any of my good questions on him early, when he was still so stiff, because I knew none of it would be usable later. He could announce a UFO with that body language—or cure cancer, or declare he'd seen a mermaid—and it wouldn't matter, because the *way he was saying it* was dull as hell.

It wasn't until I ran out of starter questions that things shifted.

Maybe he wasn't *not-a-talker*. Maybe he just wasn't a small-talker.

Maybe he wasn't a starter-questions kind of guy.

Or maybe the novelty wore off, or maybe he got used to the camera, or maybe I was just finally asking him something real . . . but after a hundred minutes, at last, I finally started catching glimpses of the real Hutch.

"I watched a movie about the Coast Guard—" I started.

Hutch crooked an eyebrow. "I know that movie."

The eyebrow felt encouraging. I went on, "And in this movie, a rescue swimmer yells at a man for panicking in the water. Is that a common thing in the real Coast Guard? Do you yell at the people you rescue?"

Hutch gave me a look.

Was that the worst question ever? Maybe.

But it sure got him talking.

"No," Hutch said. "That's not common—and no, we don't yell at the people we rescue. People panic in the water all the time. Desperation makes people do crazy things. They'll fight you—or try to climb on top of you—even when you're the only hope they've got. Not to mention that hypothermia can make people lose their minds. They can get so cold they take their clothes off."

"They can get so cold they *take their clothes off*?"

Hutch nodded. "It's called paradoxical undressing. The muscles keeping the blood close to your core become exhausted, and then it all rushes to the extremities—which makes people feel like they're burning up."

Hypothermia suddenly seemed scary in a new way.

"But you probably don't see a lot of hypothermia in warmer climates, though, right?"

"You can get hypothermic in any water that's lower than your body temperature," Hutch said. "It just takes longer."

Now we were getting somewhere. "What are the biggest hazards rescue swimmers have to face in the water?"

"Wildlife and boaters," Hutch said, not even pausing to think.

"Wildlife, like—?"

"Jellyfish, crocodiles, and sharks."

"There are sharks here?"

"There are sharks *everywhere*."

"Everywhere?"

"One time in Puerto Rico, I got hoisted at the last second, just as a dorsal fin was coming right at me."

Now I felt aghast. "So you go to work every day knowing you could get eaten by a shark?"

"I try not to think about it."

I shook my head at Hutch, like *What the hell?*

But Hutch just said, "Sharks don't really think of humans as prey. Your odds of getting killed by a shark are one in 3.75 million."

"Says the man who almost got eaten."

Hutch shrugged. "You can't be scared of everything."

"Sure you can."

"You're more likely to be killed by stray fireworks than a shark."

I let that stand. Then I said, "Tell me about AST school."

Hutch met my eyes. "What do you want to know?"

"I read that only fifteen percent of people who start AST school actually make it through. One year, out of a thousand who started the process . . . only three graduated."

"That sounds right. There are some graduating class photos with *only instructors*. No students at all."

"So what's that about?"

I braced for a list of techniques.

But instead, Hutch lifted his handsome, symmetrical, film-worthy face, and I could see in his eyes that now, at last, he'd finally forgotten the camera.

At last, he was just talking to me.

Then he said, in a voice that suddenly felt as real and human as I'd heard all day, "It's about being there for people on the worst day of their lives."

I felt the truth of that like a twinge in my chest.

"AST school is tough," Hutch went on. "It's competitive. It's dangerous. It's grueling. It pushes you beyond your limits and then some. They make it that way on purpose. They force you to find out for your-

self just exactly how much you can take . . . and then go beyond it. Because when you go out on a search-and-rescue mission, and when you
deploy into the ocean—*not going* is not an option. And then it's just you
all alone out there. You, and your stamina, and your determination—in
an environment that wants to kill you. It's you against *everything*, and
you have to win. Because you are the last thing standing between your
victim and the sea."

Hutch looked down for a second, like those words were not just
words to him, and then he looked back up. "So that's all there is. Swimmer
school taught us about one thing, and one thing only. Survival."

Eight

BEANIE CALLED THE next morning and woke me five minutes before my alarm.

"It's time to do another one," she said, like she would accept no protests.

"*Another one* what?"

"I gave you a grace period because you've been adjusting, but now I'm cracking down. We really are doing this."

"What are we doing, again?"

"Making your beauty list."

"Oh, god," I said, turning over. "You sound like you've trademarked it."

"It was your idea."

"Was it?"

"Yes. As usual, you're your own worst enemy."

"Can I get an extension?"

"No. Just pick something."

"I'm still asleep!"

"That's clearly false."

"Maybe I'm dreaming."

"Quit stalling."

"Fine," I said, rolling up into a sitting position and scanning my body to just pick something at random.

"And don't just pick something at random," Beanie warned.

"I wasn't!"

"You have to *mean it.*"

I rubbed my eyes. "What's the assignment again?"

"You're making a list of things you genuinely love about your body. Things you think are beautiful. Not things that you think *other people* would see as beautiful. *You.*"

"Right," I said, still scanning.

"Don't overthink it," Beanie commanded.

"Fine," I said. "I could've saved this for the grand finale, but apparently you have me cornered, so I'm picking 'ankles.'"

"Ankles!" Beanie protested. Then she made a buzzer sound, like *Wrong!* "You cannot pick *ankles.*"

"Ankles," I said, doubling down.

"Do you even have ankles?" Beanie demanded.

"What the hell kind of question is that?"

"I don't remember anything about your ankles. They're completely unremarkable. I'm calling bullshit."

"My ankles," I declared, awake enough now to feel protective, "are exceptional."

"Prove it."

"I will," I said. And before anyone could stop me, I'd leaned back onto the bed like a pinup girl and taken glamour shot after glamour shot of my feet in the air from every angle I could muster. And then I texted them all to Beanie in a burst.

"Did you just send me"—she paused to count—"seventeen photos? Of your ankles?"

"Read 'em and weep."

But Beanie did not weep. Instead, she Jedi-mind-tricked me into standing up for them even harder. "I don't know," she said. "They look like ordinary ankles to me."

"Ordinary?" I asked. "Are *ordinary ankles* that mesmerizing? That sleek? That *sophisticated*?"

Before she could answer, I cut her off.

"These ankles," I went on, "could live in Paris! And wear berets! And drink champagne for breakfast every morning!"

"Okay—what are you even saying right now?"

"*Look* at that taper near the arch! And the curve above the Achilles tendon! Not to mention the . . ." I hadn't brushed up on my ankle anatomy, so I had to google for a second. "Hang on. Not to mention the . . ."

"Please tell me you're not googling parts of the ankle," Beanie said.

"The *lateral malleolus*," I supplied then, triumphantly, "and how symmetrical it is with the *medial malleolus*. You don't see *that* every day!"

"I guess you don't."

"I'm telling you, these ankles are lethal. They could work for the CIA. You could gouge somebody's eye out with these babies. You could *cut glass*!"

"Wow," Beanie said.

But I was fully awake now. She'd started this—and now I was going to finish it. "Can *you* cut glass with *your* ankles?"

"I don't think so," Beanie said, like she was happy to be defeated.

"There you have it, then. Case closed. You may add 'ankles of death' to my résumé."

"Ankles," Beanie said slowly then, like she was writing it down. "Adding that to *earlobes* makes a grand total of two things that you love about your body."

"Two down, infinity to go," I agreed.

"We'll get there," Beanie said then, her voice warm. "You're definitely getting the hang of it."

BUT WAS I?

After we hung up, I blissfully admired my ankles for about three more seconds before remembering with horror that today was a swim-lesson day. Hutch—I checked the time—would be arriving here in under an hour, and I hadn't prepared emotionally in any way. Much less brushed my teeth, or had breakfast, or showered.

Wait—*did* you shower right before getting into a pool?

A quick search turned up a *not* definitive *yes and no*. Depending on how you felt about showering. And pools.

You might think that the prospect of hanging out in a swimsuit with Hutch might seem less appalling to me now that I knew him better. Or now that we'd formed a fragile alliance at the air station and agreed to carpool. Or possibly now that I'd met my humiliation deductible with that splinter-removal situation.

You might think that, but you'd be wrong.

It wasn't *less* mortifying to see Hutch now. It was *more*.

Plus, we were meeting back at the same place—the Starlite pool. We were revisiting the scene of the crime. We wouldn't be *moving away* from the memory of what he'd been forced to do to me, we'd be *reviving* it.

Add to that: now he was my subject. Officially. I'd spent a whole day with him—following him around, arguing with him, psychoanalyzing him, studying him, filming him, and noting his surprisingly charming habit of humming "Heart and Soul" to himself all the time.

Now I was a hundred times more aware of his shoulders, and the length of his stride when he kept a few paces ahead of me, and the exact spot on his nose where his aviators rested. Now I had noticed the dimple in his chin—more of a groove than a dot—and couldn't un-notice it. Now I knew how much everyone seemed to admire him, how he chewed on his lower lip when he was thinking, and how, even when he was smiling, he never fully erased that serious darkness in his eyes.

Now I liked him more, I guess.

Which made me want to prance around in front of him in a bathing suit *so much less*.

Though, at this point, what I did or didn't want had kind of ceased to matter.

Because Lieutenant JG Carlos Alonso had just emailed me yesterday with the date of the scheduled SWET training required by my company's insurance.

So, of course, I googled SWET training—and realized it was the upside-down-helicopter, escape-hell training that Cole had mentioned back at the start. Training I'd been hoping he'd made up to scare me. But nope. It was real. SWET stood for Shallow Water Egress Training— aka seat-belting people into a fake helicopter seat welded inside a metal frame and then *turning it upside down underwater.*

Oh—no. No, no, no.

They couldn't really be making me do that.

I rifled through my file folder on Hutch and found his number, making a new contact for him so that I could send the text: SWET training??????????????

To which he replied: You'll be fine

To which I replied: Or DIE IN A WATERY GRAVE

And that's when my phone rang. And it was Hutch.

And I didn't even say hello. I just answered with, "Don't make me do this."

"*I'm* not making you do anything. Your company is."

I shook my head. "I'm dead. This is the end."

"We'll figure it out," Hutch said.

"How, exactly?" I demanded. "I can't even *dog-paddle*! You want to turn me upside down like Houdini?"

"We'll work on some tricks."

"Okay, look, I didn't mean to," I confessed then, my voice starting to tremble, "but after I googled SWET training, I accidentally wound up watching a few videos of exactly how it works . . . and I don't think . . ." I took a deep breath. "I'm really not sure that I can actually do it. I suspect I'm going to have a genuine panic attack. And then I'll cry and confess everything, and then I'll get fired for being a totally unqualified liar—and rightly so, *because I am*—and then that's it for the rest of my life: I'll be a bitter, unemployable outcast who never reached her potential because she couldn't swim."

"I guess that's one possible outcome," Hutch said.

"I'm sort of joking—but also really, really not. You know?"

When Hutch spoke again, his voice was softer. "You're not that un-qualified. It's not like you're making a scuba video."

Okay, that was oddly helpful.

Hutch went on. "You can do it. I'll help you. Tomorrow's my day off."

But his kindness just surfaced the tears I'd been suppressing. "What was I *thinking* taking this job?" I asked, pawing at my eyes. "I'm one hundred percent going to drown."

"You're not going to drown," Hutch said then.

"You can't know that."

"Yes, I can," Hutch said, and then unwittingly quoted Beanie: "It's a pool full of rescue swimmers. You couldn't drown if you tried."

ALL TO SAY: now I really had to learn to swim.

There'd be no weaseling out of this swim lesson—or anything that would follow.

As I showered and got ready—*blow-drying my hair*, of all things—I formulated a plan. I'd wear my Day-Glo orchid-print caftan in hopes of temporarily blinding Hutch, and then, when it was time to slip out of my new, voluminous, maxi cover-up to get into the pool, I'd create a distraction—maybe accidentally-on-purpose knock over a pool chaise?—and then slip unseen into the water while Hutch was dealing with it.

That could work, right?

But, as it turned out, no furniture had to be harmed.

The real scene played out very differently than I'd imagined.

I'd pictured Hutch and me arriving at the pool alone—facing off like gunslingers. But we weren't alone. Rue and The Gals were already there, drinking coffee, wearing their raffia sandals, and all seated on one side of a table like a panel of judges—saying they thought it would be "fun to watch."

We were also *not alone* because Hutch brought George Bailey along.

George Bailey, who once again launched into a full-tilt gallop as soon as he saw me in hopes of catapulting himself into my arms—and ended up shoving me backward into the pool, and then landing on top of me in the water.

Remember ten minutes before, when I was *blow-drying my hair*?

Yeah.

Fortunately, it was the shallow end. I only had to splash around in panic for a handful of seconds before feeling the rough pool floor under my now-bare feet—and then noticing that George Bailey was standing next to me, smiling and panting, head and shoulders comfortably above the waterline while my flip-flops bobbed upside down beside us.

I stood up, water pouring off me in a deluge, and pawed my flattened bangs away from my eyes.

"Oh, sweetheart," Rue said.

Then Hutch, looking down at me from the edge, asked, as if I'd know the answer, "Why does he keep doing that?"

I took so long to attempt a reply that Hutch gave up waiting and took off his T-shirt, peeling it up over his head.

I'm sure in real life it happened in an instant. But in my memory, it unfolded in slo-mo: Hutch reaching down to grab the shirt hem, and then stretching out all his shoulder muscles like a cobra before tossing the shirt over a nearby chair, and standing resplendently shirtless before me and all of Rue's lady friends.

I should clarify: I wasn't an ogler, normally.

I'd interviewed many, many men for many, many videos—and not had a problem with accidentally ogling any of them. I had been nothing but professional with the quality-assurance manager at Altman Foods, and the VP of the Dallas Chamber of Commerce, and the regional environmental manager for Hanson Homes. I was a total pro.

But this was different.

This was some kind of perfect storm of job requirements, physical proximity, removal of clothing, and . . . Hutch.

Who was, as Beanie had foretold . . . just scientifically . . . just *mathematically* . . .

Very good-looking.

Though I should point out that he wasn't some bodybuilding, man-chesty, wall-of-muscle he-man. He was just a standard, incredibly fit swimmer dude who was now suddenly half-naked—and wearing swim trunks that I think we'd all approvingly describe as *rather snug*.

I mean, The Gals and I hardly had a choice. Who *wouldn't* be rubbernecking in that situation?

If anything, we were all hapless victims.

Rue noticed us all watching him, and then she said, "Do a trick for The Gals, Hutch."

Hutch looked like he'd heard a few requests like this before.

He shrugged over at the ladies. "Handstand?"

They all cheered, and Ginger wolf-whistled.

"Okay," Hutch agreed. "One handstand, and then I've got to teach this one"—he hooked his thumb in my direction—"how to swim."

"I'm just brushing up on my—" I started to correct him.

But then I fully lost my train of thought as Hutch walked that unclothed torso of his over to the deep end, clasped his hands over the lip of the pool edge, lifted and stretched his entire body up into a straight handstand, and then launched himself into a totally feet-first backward dive into the water.

We all stared as an awestruck group.

The ladies all cheered as he disappeared under the surface, skimmed low and deep along the bottom, like a marine mammal, and then surfaced right in front of me. What on earth must it be like to just live in your body so comfortably and enjoy it like that?

"Hi," he said, shaking out his buzz cut.

"Hello," I said, still dripping.

"Do you want to get rid of that?" he asked, gesturing at my sopping-wet cover-up.

I looked down, puzzled—as if I'd forgotten my body was even there.

Then I started trying to unwrap myself from the wet fabric. But all the yards of fluttery cotton that had seemed so floaty and freeing in the air were something different in the water. The cover-up was twisted and tangled around me like wet gauze.

I wasn't immobilized, exactly, but I was struggling enough that Hutch decided to help out. The ladies watched, and so did I, to be honest, as Hutch moved his hands all around my body, tugging, peeling, and unwrapping. At one point, he held a stretch of fabric up at an angle and unwound me like a top. Then, for a grand finale, he stripped the limp wet cotton up over my head, positively disrobing me in broad daylight.

I mean, he left the swimsuit in place. But still.

When he finally tossed the wadded-up pile of fabric to the side of the pool, the ladies clapped. George Bailey, for his part, climbed up the steps, shook the water out of his fur—and decided to sun himself on the patio.

"I really am sorry," Hutch said, watching me watch the dog. "I'm baffled over why he keeps doing that. Do you have this effect on other dogs?"

"Never," I said, now trying to neaten my hair by tucking it behind my ears.

Hutch started walking toward the deeper water and gesturing with his head for me to follow.

When the pool surface was just above the waist, we stopped.

"Are you nervous?" Hutch asked.

There was no way to fake it at this point. My hands were cold. My breathing was tight. He knew I was in deep. There really was no turning back.

I met his eyes and nodded.

"Have you done any swimming at all before?" he asked.

Now we were in diagnostic mode. I gave him all the information I could think of, like I was visiting the doctor. "My mom used to take me to the pool all the time when I was a kid—but there was no real swimming involved. Just splashing and getting wet and cooling off. I mostly stayed on the steps in the shallow end. We went to the beach, too—but again, it was mostly splashing and making dribble castles. I was supposed to take proper lessons the summer after fifth grade, but my parents got divorced and that whole plan fell apart."

Hutch nodded, like he was adding all that up. "Do you have any happy memories of being in the water?"

What a funny question. I thought back. "I remember my mom carrying me on her hip in the water. She liked getting in to cool off, and she'd chat with the other moms, and I'd ride along. I remember cuddling against her like a baby koala bear."

Hutch held back his reaction a second, like that was not the answer he'd expected.

"So," he asked next, "no formal instruction at all?"

I shook my head. "But I'm sure I'd have forgotten it all, anyway."

Now Hutch shook his head. "We don't forget muscle memory. It's implicit. Anything you could do back then, you can still do. We just need to jog your body's memory."

"Not sure how much there is to remember."

Hutch nodded, like, *Noted.* "Don't worry. Even if it's for the first time, everything we're about to do, you already know how to do. It's just that now, you'll be doing it in the water."

First, he just wanted me to walk around in the pool. To just get used to the feeling of being submerged, of the resistance and drag, of how the water swirled and eddied.

All easy.

Then he walked us both to the edge of the pool where the ladies were watching. They lifted their coffee cups and croissants in a toast, calling out things like, "You got this!"

He held on to the edge of the pool with both hands and squatted down to submerge his head, blowing bubbles as he went.

When he came up and waited for me to copy him, I said, "I'm so sorry."

Hutch frowned. "What for?"

"This is utterly beneath you."

But Hutch shook his head like I was nuts. "Everybody has to start somewhere."

"You *jump out of helicopters* for a living," I countered. "And now here we are, blowing bubbles."

"I love blowing bubbles," Hutch said, and there was that frowny smile again.

By the end of the lesson, I'd mastered the arts of bobbing, relaxing, and floating. All of which are harder than they sound. We'd also spent a shocking amount of time doing exercises that forced Hutch to put his hands all over my body.

Floating, in particular, required him to give graduate-level lessons on buoyancy, hydraulics, water temperature, and muscle mass—all while propping up the stiff frame of a student who he just could not convince to relax.

"Relaxing is *hard*," I kept saying. "I don't know what to do."

"That's the point," Hutch kept explaining. "Relaxing means *not doing anything*."

"Not doing anything isn't my style."

"Be a jellyfish," Hutch suggested.

"That's easier said than done."

Hutch's point was that once I could float—and once I *knew* that I could float—it would change everything. "The lungs are basically air balloons," he said. "And what do air balloons do in water?"

"Float?" I ventured, wondering if it was a trick question.

"Exactly. Your body isn't going to sink like a stone because it's not a stone. It's a living, porous, air-filled thing. It *wants* to float." Then he told me to take a deep breath, hold it, and lean back to rest on the water. Which I did. And it worked: my head and shoulders stayed up at the surface. "Now gently kick your feet," he said, and, as I did, my legs rose toward the surface, too.

And then there I was, floating.

Which felt amazing for a second—before I exhaled the question "What if I need to breathe?" and then started to sink.

But Hutch's hands were there to catch me in a flash—one under my shoulders, and one under the backs of my thighs, keeping me steady.

"Exhale fast and then inhale again quick," Hutch said. "You'll have time. Water is forgiving."

I inhaled, and then I kicked my feet back up toward the surface, and then Hutch took his hands away. "See how easy it is? Plus it helps that you're a woman."

Good god. I guess he'd noticed. "Why?" I asked, trying not to let out too much air.

"Women have more body fat than men do."

"Where are we heading with this?"

"And fat is more buoyant than muscle. Arnold Schwarzenegger would sink like an anchor in the ocean."

"Really?" I asked.

"It's true. Women actually are statistically less likely to drown."

"Because of the fat?"

Hutch nodded and patted his belly. "That's why I keep a few extra biscuits in the tin."

Was he serious? "I don't think you know what biscuits are."

"Feel it," Hutch said, patting himself again like an invitation.

That broke my float. "No, thank you," I said, going vertical and touching my feet to the bottom.

"Do it!" Ginger called from the dugout.

"Life is short!" Benita agreed.

"Feel how nice and soft it is," Hutch urged again, demonstrating.

"*I'll* feel it!" Nadine offered.

But I just kept shaking my head, like *No way*.

Hutch nodded, like *You got this*. "For educational purposes."

I glanced at the ladies. They gave a thumbs-up in unison. Then I moved my palm toward him, and as it got close, Hutch pulled it to him and pressed it against the flesh at his belly button. I swear, as soon as he touched my hand, everything shifted into slow motion. I saw his big hand covering mine as he pulled it toward him—and then I anticipated the feeling of his skin slicking under my palm for several suspended seconds before it actually happened.

"Feel that sponginess?" Hutch said, pressing both our hands against his torso like we were bouncing on a mattress. "That little layer of blubber is my best friend in the ocean."

Layer of blubber? Were we just making up the meanings of words now?

"That's hardly a *layer of blubber*," I protested, my eyes locked on my hand and what it was doing.

"It helps me float, it protects me from hypothermia . . ." He let my hand go. "And it makes me a really good snuggler."

Wait! Hold on.

Was I detecting a note of flirting? Was the love hater *flirting* with me?

He was supposed to be all muscle, no heart.

Except, I guess—the heart *is* a muscle.

Still. It couldn't be flirting. I'd have to research it later. It had been so long, I wasn't sure I'd recognize it in the wild. Though what would that search question even be? "What's the difference between flirting and not flirting?" "What does it mean when men talk about snuggling?" "Should you touch a man's extra biscuits?"

Next, without my permission, my hand brought itself over to my own tummy, pressing against my own buoyant, insulating, life-saving sponginess with a new appreciation.

And then the funniest thing happened.

As our lesson ended, and Rue and the ladies dispersed from their courtside seats, and as Hutch started freestyling toward the edge of the pool, his shoulders churning the water, I felt something shift in my psyche.

All day long, I'd been dreading asking this guy to do a "Day in the Life" video with me—an idea I was 90 percent sure he'd hate. I'd been trying to force myself to do it the way you make yourself do homework: I knew I *needed* to. But I hadn't *wanted* to.

Now, suddenly, I wanted to.

Suddenly, I was truly, deeply curious about a day in his life.

Hutch hoisted himself up in one virile motion and flipped around to sit on the pool's edge. Then called over to me to ask, "Any questions so far?"

"Yes," I answered, sloshing my way closer to him.

Hutch waited. Then, when I got close, I stood there, half-submerged, and said, "Would you by any chance be willing to do a small, extra mini-documentary with me for YouTube—on top of the one we're already doing?"

At the question, Hutch dropped his head in that aw-shucks way of his and then lifted it again to frown in my direction.

"Why would I want to do that?" he asked.

Was that a no already? But I wasn't finished. "It's just a series I do—on the side—about . . . heroes?"

"You didn't answer my question."

Oh. Right. "Because it could be powerful and inspiring?"

Hutch didn't react. So I added, "And profound. And beautiful. And it could capture . . . deep truths about your life."

"What if I don't want to capture deep truths about my life?"

How to answer that? "Then you don't have to watch it?"

"But other people will."

"Yeah. That's called being famous."

"I don't want to be famous."

"Too late."

Hutch thought about that. Then he nodded. "Maybe. But I don't have to make it worse."

We didn't have to keep going. There were no signs of hope in this conversation.

"So that's a no, then?" I asked.

Then, as friendly as pie, Hutch said: "That's not just a no. That's a *no way in hell.*"

Nine

NO WAY IN hell.

Not a lot of wiggle room there.

To be honest, I hadn't been completely truthful with Hutch during our alliance negotiations when I told him that I was in contact with Cole *often*.

I was actually in contact with Cole *from time to time*.

But tonight, just hours after Hutch's very hard pass on my mini-documentary, was one of those times.

I didn't even recognize Cole's number when the call came in, if that says anything. Mostly we just sent nuts-and-bolts texts.

This phone call didn't stand on pleasantries, either. No chitchat, no small talk . . . Just Cole launching right into his only question: "Did Hutch say yes to your 'Day in the Life' thing?"

"Um," I said, as if I might have to think back. "No. He did not."

"He said no?"

"Technically, he said *no way in hell*, but, yeah. Same idea."

"That's not good," Cole said.

"I agree."

"No, I mean, that's really not good."

"Why? What?"

"Sullivan," he answered.

"What about her?"

"She fired the first two people today."

Oh, god. "Who?"

"You know that new girl Janine with the tongue ring and the purple bangs?"

"I love her!"

"Yeah, well, too bad. She's toast."

"Who else?"

"Jaden."

"Jaden? Your protégé, Jaden?"

"Yeah. He's gonna have to move back in with his mom."

"Wow," I said.

"And Sullivan called me in today to ask about *you*."

I frowned. "Ask what?"

"If you were any good. If you were worth keeping. That kind of thing."

"What did you say?"

"I said you *were* good and you *were* worth keeping—and that I thought you were really going places. Which is true, by the way."

"Thank you."

"But she didn't seem convinced. So I had to get creative."

"You had to *get creative*?"

"I told her that you were already filming a 'Day in the Life' video with Hutch."

"What?!"

"And, okay, that it was almost done. And that I'd seen some clips, and it was awesome. And that you were going to be the next big thing. But I also emphasized the many, many shirtless shots of Hutch. And then I mentioned—in an unrelated way—that Hutch is single."

"Implying—what, exactly?"

"Implying that if she doesn't fire you, you might be able to set her up with him."

"Cole! What the hell!"

"I may also have showed her some old beach photos of shirtless Hutch looking handsome."

I put my head in my hands. "Whyyyy would you do that?"

"Look, we have to use everything in our arsenal. Word is, Sullivan's in she-wolf mode."

"What does that even mean?"

"She's got a man-starved vibe about her."

"I thought you said she was all work all the time!"

"Well," Cole said, "she's had a rough year. And a six-minute mini-documentary on Hutch might really appeal to her. On a deep level. Do you see what I mean? He could turn this whole thing around. Especially if you can get him to jump-rope shirtless."

"What are you saying?"

"I'm saying when you've just had a mouthwatering meal, you don't turn around and fire the chef."

"But don't you see how you just made things worse?"

"You should be thanking me. Your head was on the chopping block. And guess what else? She was into it! She wants to see that 'Day in the Life.' She got so excited she even talked about all the vacation time she's never used and how she might just come to Key West."

"Do *not* let her come to Key West!"

"If you hurry up and get this video made, she won't have to."

"That makes no sense. There *is* no 'Day in the Life' video with Hutch. It's *not* almost done—and, as of yesterday, it's never going to even start!"

"You're going to have to fix that."

"How, exactly?"

"Ask him again. Nicer."

"He already said no."

"Tell him the truth. Tell him your job is on the line. He's got a savior complex. Use it against him."

Why did that sound so sinister?

"I have a nuclear option," Cole said next. "But I'd rather not use it."

"Why are you helping me?" I asked him then.

I don't know what I was expecting from his answer, but Cole just said, "If you get canned, then I'll have to take over the Coast Guard project. And then I'll have to make a video about what a hero my big brother is. And I don't really want to do that."

I let that land.

"So we're in this together," Cole went on. "You're doing something for me that I really don't want to do, and I'm saving you from getting axed and crying in the elevator like Jaden."

Did I want to cry in the elevator like Jaden?

I very much did not.

I sighed, and said, "Fine. Okay. I'll ask again. Nicer."

I WAS ABOUT to call Beanie to process all this . . . when the phone in my hand started ringing—and it was Beanie.

"I was literally just about to call you," I said, by way of a greeting.

"How are you feeling?" she asked. "Are you holding up okay?"

For a second, I thought she was talking about the layoffs. But she couldn't know about those. "How am I feeling about what?" I asked.

"About Lucas!"

Lucas? "Why would I be feeling anything about Lucas?"

"Oh," Beanie said. "You haven't heard it yet."

"Heard what?"

"Lucas just dropped a new song. And it's about you."

I held very still. Then I said, "How do you know?"

"Because it's all about him dumping you."

"I'm not the only person he's ever dumped," I said. Right? By that criteria, there were at least three other candidates—that I knew of.

"Yeah," Beanie said. "But the title of the song is 'Katie.'"

Ah. Well, then.

Beanie went on, "It's all over TikTok. And YouTube. And everywhere else. The video is him just wandering around in a field of grass, and looking forlorn, and wearing that little knitted hat you made for him after he found out he was allergic to wool."

"*That*," I asked, "is taking over the internet? Lucas in a knitted cap?"

"It's all about how stupid he was to let you go."

"No argument there."

"And then it ends with a lyric that's so epic, this girl I follow already got a tattoo of it."

"What's the lyric?"

"Love is what happens to you while you're busy making other plans."

"That's John Lennon! He plagiarized John Lennon!"

"Nope. I saw a thread about this. John Lennon's version says 'life,' not 'love.' '*Life* is what happens to you while you're busy making other plans.' Also some people are saying it was Henry David Thoreau. Or Beyoncé."

"It's still plagiarism."

"Not according to a bunch of random strangers on the internet."

"He can't change *one* word and pretend he didn't steal it!"

"Who cares?"

But now I was worked up. "It's not even a good point! Love *doesn't* happen to you while you're busy making other plans! That's not how love works at all. When you're in love, you don't want to make *other plans*—you just want to make plans with the person you're in love with. That's the whole thing!"

"Why do you care?"

"Because he doesn't know what love is."

"That's not your problem anymore."

"But now it's everybody's problem! Somebody who is terrible at love decided to define it for the rest of us—and now it's becoming *tattoos*."

"Yeah, well. Everybody loves that lyric."

"Except for John Lennon's ghost."

"The point is, it's a hit. You should listen to it."

"I will never listen to it."

"Never is a long time."

"Fine. I'll listen to it on my ninetieth birthday. I'll drink a whole bottle of champagne, listen to this song, and then throw myself off a cliff."

"Don't throw yourself off a cliff. Throw *Lucas* off that cliff."

"Great suggestion."

"Anyway, it's topping the charts. I feel you should get a royalty or something."

"*John Lennon* should get a royalty."

Lucas and his timing. I had finally—finally!—found something I was more interested in than feeling terrible about him . . . and now here he was again, demanding my attention.

"What will you do if he calls you?" Beanie asked.

"I won't answer."

"Good. Perfect. Stay strong."

"I don't need strength. I have indifference."

"That's because you haven't heard the song yet."

DID I LISTEN to the song?

Of course. The second I hung up with Beanie.

And was it good?

Fine. Affirmative. It was good.

Annoyingly good.

The kind of song you put on repeat and it sends you into a poetically bittersweet groove that makes you reflect on life and love and what it all means in a way that hurts just right.

I never said he wasn't a good songwriter. Plagiarism aside.

But did the song make me waver? Did it make me wish I could turn back time and be with Lucas again?

Honestly? Not really.

If anything, it made it pretty clear that I had moved on. Thanks to some very intense journaling, some bossy life advice from Beanie, and the stability that comes from standing on your own two feet for a while.

I'll also add: it really kinda takes the shine off a man once he's cheated on you.

Plus, to be honest, the sunny memory of Hutch's handstand dive into the swimming pool kept lighting up the corners of my consciousness.

Not that I needed that visual of Hutch to be okay. I was just fine on my own, thanks.

But if it was free for the taking . . . I'd go ahead and take it.

Ten

I SPENT THE next week trying to make the "Day in the Life" happen.

Hutch had said *no way in hell*? We'd just have to see about that.

I decided that if I couldn't get him to say yes, I would come clean and tell him that my job was on the line.

But I didn't want to have to do that. I didn't want to abuse his sense of pity.

I wanted to talk him into it, fair and square.

I cornered him with lists of reasons why telling his story would inspire the world—but none of them worked. I tried arguing that Rue would be proud of him—but he said she was proud enough already. I made an impassioned argument that the world was on a slippery slope of self-centered thoughtlessness that we all needed to push back against.

But his *no* held firm.

I tried catching him at different times of the day, too: while swimming laps, or running sprints, or doing pull-ups. I tried asking as we carpooled to and from the air station. I practiced arguments in the mirror to myself—from detailing how stepping outside our comfort zones could help us grow emotionally to explaining patriotism to *a person in the military.*

But, yeah: nothing.

The only argument that had any promise was also the one that seemed morally wrong: to tell him that I needed to be rescued.

I drew the line at that—at first. But as time wore on and his rejections piled up, I started to wonder.

I did need to be rescued, after all.

I wasn't going to blackmail him. Or force him. I would just give him the full picture. He was free to make whatever choice he wanted. You could even argue, I decided, that the true morally suspect behavior was withholding information from him that he might have been interested in.

The truth is, it's hard to make yourself ask for something that you know the person you're asking doesn't want to give.

Toughen up! I pep-talked myself. *This is your career.*

But what was I going to do, interrupt him in a preflight meeting? Demand his help over the sound of the sewing machine while he was mending his gear? Stop a safety training as he walked the crews through the items stashed in the pockets of their flight vests? Was saving my job really more important than Hutch teaching these folks about the knives, rations, oxygen tanks, signal mirrors, and life rafts that might one day save their lives?

This was the kind of thing Hutch did all day.

Can you even imagine?

Picture it: Hutch describing, say, the technique for placing a tourniquet on a victim, including serious details like "If you can't get the bleeding to stop, add a second tourniquet," and adding, half joking: "Just twist it until they scream and then give it one more twist." And then me, on the heels of that, jumping in to say, "I'm so sorry to interrupt. Quick question: I'm in danger of getting fired. Can I sleep over at your house and film you jumping rope shirtless?"

No. Just no.

My problems, my worries, my *whole life* seemed positively silly in comparison.

For example—safety tip from Hutch in that same meeting that I sat in on: "If you're ever in a boating accident, and you smell fuel in the water, do not launch your flares."

I mean, the man was on another level.

He didn't need some person he barely knew putting more demands on him.

I might have dropped the subject entirely—if not for the drumbeat of Cole's texts.

Did you ask again?

Better hurry up.

That dude from California just got the axe.

Plus, I was busy. This job was a steep learning curve for a person who knew nothing about the military. Coast Guard terms I learned in the first week alone included: *rollers* for waves; *sortie* for a trip out in the helicopter; *ensembles* for the different swim gear ASTs wore for different weather conditions; *night sun* for the external spotlight over the waves in the dark. Plus, SAR for "search and rescue," PIW for "person in the water," and NVGs for "night-vision goggles."

Oh, and this one seemed important: *bingo*. As in, "to hit *bingo*." In the helicopter. Which meant to reach the point where, if you didn't turn around and RTB ("return to base") *immediately*, you would not have enough fuel to make it back to shore.

A lot of new terminology. None of it trivial.

I kept a notebook and wrote it down, went back and highlighted, and had to ask Hutch endless questions like, "I'm sorry: What's a VFR chart?"

Plus, can I just add? Even when I wasn't hauling ass to get up to speed on military terms, talking to Hutch was also just . . . fun. He was an interesting guy. Watching him go through his day at the air station prompted endless questions in my head.

And don't forget: I was making a video about him.

All day, I followed him around with a camera, and then, after I got back to the Starlite, I went through the footage. Hutch basically took up 90 percent of my waking hours. When I wasn't talking to him, I was filming him, and when I wasn't filming him, I was combing through the footage, looking for the best moments.

And do you want to know what I saw?

Hutch holding the door for people. Hutch sweeping the air station hangar while humming "Heart and Soul." Hutch stopping to gather up litter in the parking lot. Hutch genuinely laughing at other people's jokes. Hutch picking up breakfast tacos for the crew. Hutch offering other people his umbrella in the rain and insisting that he didn't mind getting wet. And one I saw over and over on the footage that I didn't quite understand: Hutch picking up pennies whenever he saw them on the ground, checking them out, and then tossing them back down so someone else could have the good luck.

"What's the deal with the pennies?" I asked one time, on our commute home.

"The pennies?"

"You always look at pennies."

"Do I?"

"You check them when you get change. And you go through the coin jar in the lounge. And you always pick them up if you see them on the ground."

"Everybody does that. It's good luck."

"Only if you keep them. But you don't."

"I have enough luck as it is."

"It's like you're looking for something," I said then. "What are you looking for?"

Hutch looked over. Then he said, "After my mom died, when I was a kid, I got this idea that if I could find a penny from the year she was born, I would know she was okay. So I started looking. And now I collect them."

"You collect coins?"

"No. I collect pennies from 1965. Only pennies. Only 1965. The year my mom was born."

"Are they valuable?"

"They are to me."

"How many do you have?"

Hutch shrugged. "A jarful or so. I haven't counted in a while. I just like finding them, you know? It's like my mom's saying hi."

"Huh," I said. "I thought you just really loved pennies."

"Naw," Hutch said. "I just really loved my mom."

ONE THING WAS for sure: Cole Hutcheson could not have been more wrong about his older brother. He wasn't a love hater. Or an empty machine. Or a strong silent type. He wasn't empty of thoughts, or devoid of feelings.

And he wasn't hard to talk to at all.

He was almost too easy.

He was so easy that I had to make a rule for myself never to ask him about rescue-swimmer things in the off-hours, or military things, or *job* things—lest I waste material that should go in the video.

So we talked on our commutes about favorite music, and favorite movies, and favorite foods. We talked about old friends and places we'd lived. We talked about bucket lists, and mistakes we'd made, and things we still hoped to get right.

It turned out, Hutch was a mad fan of nature shows—though he called them *wildlife podcasts* to make them sound more exciting. He was a fountain of trivia about the natural world, happily explaining how most insects taste with their feet, and how dogs have two compartments in their noses—one for breathing and one for holding smells—and how ducks have wraparound vision and can see the entirety of the sky without having to turn their heads.

If we ever had a quiet moment on our commute, I could just say, "Tell me about bats," and off he'd go.

But it wasn't just Hutch talking on those drives.

Good listeners make it easy to overshare, and Hutch was a shock-ingly good listener. Before I knew it, I was saying all kinds of things that mattered. Sentence after sentence would just burble up and *happen*. I told him about my mom leaving us when I was a kid and running off with her dentist. "Her *dentist*," I said. I told him about Beanie's self-help obsession. I told him about Lucas getting famous, and how things fell apart. I even told him about the way I'd proposed to Lucas—almost a month before he had proposed to me.

"You proposed to him first? And then he proposed to you again later?"

I nodded. "We had these four bridges that went over this stretch of freeway near our house, and they had cyclone fences on them. You know those ones with the twisted wires?"

"Yeah."

"People used to stick Styrofoam cups in the holes between the wires to spell out team names and stuff. Or like, 'Go to the prom with me, Stella!'"

"Got it."

"And one day I started thinking I might do a Burma-Shave proposal on those bridges."

"What's Burma-Shave?"

"It's an old-timey shaving cream. And back when highways were first becoming a thing, they used to put rhyming signs by the side of the road to advertise. So, have you ever heard the rhyme, 'Don't stick your arm out too far. It might go home in another car'?"

"Yeah. We said that as kids."

"That's Burma-Shave! Each phrase was on a different sign, so you'd pass them in real time as you drove."

"Huh."

"There were tons of them—brilliant ones. Like: 'Special seats—reserved in Hades—for whiskered guys—who scratch their ladies.' Or 'If your peach—keeps out of reach—you better practice—what we preach.' Or—this is my favorite: 'Soap may do—for lads with fuzz—but sir, you ain't—the kid you wuz.'"

"These are brilliant."

"I was freelancing for a documentary about the company, so I had those rhymes in my head all the time. And then one day I just heard one in my head, proposing to him, and I decided to write it in cups on those four bridges—and then drive underneath them with Lucas."

"What was the rhyme?"

"'Make you happy?—Yes I can!—Lucas won't you—be my man?'"

Hutch nodded, impressed. "Genius."

"Right? But it didn't work."

Hutch frowned and glanced over.

"I had to drive him under the bridges three times before he noticed. And then, when he finally saw it, he refused to give me an answer."

"He—what?"

"He said that guys should propose to girls, and not the other way around."

A new type of frown from Hutch. A *That's crazy* frown.

"So he never answered. But then he took me to a fancy restaurant a month later and did it 'right.' Like with flowers and candles."

"Your way was better."

"Right?! Thank you."

"If somebody proposed to me that way, I'd have said yes before the last bridge."

"Exactly! That makes me feel better."

"Were you feeling bad?"

"No. It's just . . . He's a singer, and he just released a new song, and it's about me. So that's been a little weird."

"Wait," Hutch said. "Your ex-fiancé Lucas isn't—?"

"Lucas Banks. Yeah."

"And so his new song 'Katie' is—?"

"About me. Yes."

Hutch kept driving, trying to take it in. "Are you messing with me?"

"Nope."

"You used to be engaged to Lucas Banks?"

"He wasn't famous when we met. He was just a dude playing guitar in coffee shops—for free."

After a moment, Hutch said, "But are you sure that song is really about you?"

"Yes?" I said. "The name kinda gives it away."

"Yes, but it's about a girl with hazel eyes."

"So?"

"Your eyes aren't hazel."

"They aren't?"

Hutch shook his head. "Hazel's like a brownish green, and yours are a bluish gray."

I pulled down the visor mirror to check. "Are they?"

"You don't know what color your own eyes are?"

"I always just called them hazel."

"Maybe the pie piece was throwing you off."

"Maybe."

"And you'd think he'd mention the pie piece, too, by the way."

"He never noticed it, though. So he couldn't have put it in the song."

"How could he not have noticed it? I saw it the first day."

"The first day?" I asked. "When you were"—I hesitated—"doing splinter removal?"

But Hutch shook his head. "The first day in Rue's shop. When you had that hibiscus in your hair."

I nodded and took that in.

"I looked it up, by the way—your pie piece. It's called *sectoral heterochromia*."

I looked over. "Well, that's a mouthful."

"Heterochromia is having different colors in your eyes—like, some people have one blue eye and one brown eye. But sectoral heterochromia is just a section of the eye that's different."

I nodded like I was fascinated by the scientific terminology. But I was really more fascinated by how Lucas, a man I'd dated so long, could have noticed so little about me. And, for that matter, how I could've noticed so little about myself.

After a while, Hutch said, "Well, it's a great song."

I sighed. "I guess it is."

"He must have loved you, to write a song like that."

"Yeah, probably," I said, looking out the window. "He just didn't love me . . . *good enough.*"

ALL TO SAY, Hutch and I wound up spending a lot of time together. I followed him around all day at work. We shared a commute to and fro. We had an urgent swim-lesson regimen to stick to.

My self-imposed deadline for getting that "yes" for a "Day in the Life" before SWET training day had seemed so reasonable at first—but then the training got postponed a few times. Which allowed me to put off asking, and gave us time to pack in extra swim lessons.

Add in the fact that Rue and The Gals grilled dinner out by the pool almost every night, drinking sangria in fluttery caftans and watching the sunset—and that Hutch dropped me off, went home to pick up George Bailey, and came back to swim and stay for dinner almost every night, too.

With someone else, it could easily have been *too much.*

But somehow, with Hutch, it just wasn't. The more we spent time together, the easier it was to spend time together. It was like there was this extra layer of energy whenever we were around each other that just kind of amplified whatever was happening. Something that would be serious with somebody else felt earthshaking with him. And anything mildly funny became hilarious. He laughed a shocking amount for someone whose *main hobby was frowning.*

We just got along.

Even swimming was fun, as impossible as that sounds.

I guess exposure therapy really works. The more you do a thing, the less weird it starts to feel. Plus, Hutch was so comfortable in the water. He made a good lead. Add to that, this wasn't some spring break situation—all about preening and looking good. This was work.

Work that involved blowing a lot of bubbles and doing cannonballs.

You know how going on vacation can sometimes make you into a different person? This was kind of like that. Nothing around me was the same, and so I didn't have to be the same, either.

This wasn't the usual, ordinary old me. This was *me in Key West*.

I'd splash around with Hutch in the pool and then slip that fluttery cover-up back on and spend the rest of the evening noshing on dinner at the patio tables with him and The Gals, George Bailey lying in the grass nearby.

Maybe it was the island breezes. Or the sangria. Or the warmth of the sun. Or the lovely feeling of being surrounded by the easy chatter of friends. But there was something special going on that I couldn't ignore. It felt like a different way of living that had something good—and something long overdue—to teach me.

Eleven

EXCITING NEWS.

I found a definitive cure for swimsuit phobia: sheer terror of something else.

On the morning that SWET training was finally happening, I found that I did not have my usual hitch of fear at the idea of putting on a swimsuit. I was too busy fearing *death*.

So much so that when Beanie FaceTimed and demanded something for my beauty list, I tried to give her *fingernails*.

"Unacceptable," Beanie declared. "Do something real."

I was too tired to fight her. I let out a long sigh while I thought about it.

And then my second try accidentally delighted her.

"Okay, then," I said. "How about my sectoral heterochromia?"

"Your—what?"

"It's that little pie piece of brown in my eye."

"Do you have a pie piece of brown in your eye?"

"How has no one ever noticed this?"

No one except Hutch.

I held the phone up close to my eye. "See that brown patch? It's very rare." Then, proudly: "It's a *genetic anomaly*. You can't just buy gray-blue eyes with a pie piece of brown like this off the rack."

Beanie squinted. "I thought your eyes were hazel."

"Why would you think that?"

"Because you always say they're hazel. And that's what the song says."

"Well, the song is wrong. And so was I."

"Doesn't it say *hazel* on your driver's license?"

"Fine," I said. "We've all been wrong forever about the color of my eyes. Even me. But now we stand corrected."

"Who corrected us?"

"What?"

"Who inspired us to suddenly notice your eye color in a new way?"

Why did this feel like a trap? I straightened a little bit. "Hutch looked it up."

"I knew it!"

"Knew what?" I asked, with that feeling of suppressed hope you get when somebody else might think the thing *you also keep wanting to think*.

"The Love Hater likes you!" Beanie shouted.

I gasped. "He doesn't!" I said, my voice all scoldy. But I had to turn the phone camera away while I squinted an unbidden smile off my face.

"He noticed your pie piece, and he *redefined the color of your eyes*," Beanie said. "I don't think it's up for debate."

"I don't have time to debate, anyway," I said. "I'm late to go drown in a helicopter-crash simulation."

"That's today?" Beanie said.

"That's today."

"You should definitely *almost* drown," Beanie said. "But not all the way. Just enough so he has to give you CPR."

"Hanging up now," I said.

"Make him put his mouth on you!" Beanie ordered, as I tapped the red *X*.

To be truthful, I didn't logically think that I would drown during SWET training. I grasped the almost mathematical impossibility of drowning in a pool while surrounded by highly trained, peak-condition, professional rescue swimmers.

It wouldn't really happen.

It just felt like it would.

In fact, my feelings didn't seem to understand math at all—because if you'd asked them, they'd have told you I was certain to drown. One thousand percent.

One thing about this morning was for sure: I had frittered away a full week goofing around with Hutch—and still hadn't gotten that *yes* for my "Day in the Life."

Tonight. After SWET training. I'd ask him again tonight—and tell the truth about why.

If I survived.

I'D BEEN HOLDING on to hope that they might let me wear clothes for SWET training, but then Hutch told me to bring a swimsuit.

I'd accumulated five suits since taking up residence at Rue's place—100 percent of them because Rue kept buying them for me. She'd show up at my door with a gift bag from Vitamin Sea, and my shoulders would drop. "Put it on," she'd command, and I never knew how to say no.

"Rue," I'd asked recently, "why do you keep buying these for me?"

Rue just squeezed my hand and said, "Because I'm fond of you."

I could feel that she meant it, and I let the warm comfort of that settle over me for a second before pressing on: "But do you buy tropics-wear for everyone you're fond of?"

Rue was staying all business—waving me off with her hands to go try on the suit while she took her usual seat in the rattan chair with palm-leaf upholstery. "Only the ones who remind me a little of myself."

At that, I paused. "Do I?"

Rue nodded. "Myself forty years ago."

"Were you"—I dropped my voice to a stage whisper—"a chromo-phobe?"

Rue nodded, like *Can you believe it?* "Picture all this," she said, gesturing grandly at herself, "in beige."

Beige? I wasn't sure that I could, honestly. There she sat in a red-and-orange caftan with teal accents that matched her oversized Iris Apfel glasses, looking like she was *born that way.* A fearless seventy-year-old from the jump.

And I said as much.

"No one's born fearless," Rue said. "You have to earn it." Then she added, gesturing at the swimsuit dangling from my hand, "Every time you have to be brave, you get to be a little braver next time. That's what life is for."

"I don't think I want to be brave," I said.

"I know." Her face was all sympathy. "That's why you keep hiding."

What can I say? She had me.

"But I'll tell you a secret," she said. "It doesn't matter what anybody thinks if you're having fun. And all the fun is in color."

I tried that idea on for size.

"My wish for you," Rue went on, "is a vibrant, bright, glorious life. That's why I keep bringing you these vibrant, bright, glorious swimsuits."

"So am I your pet project or something?" I asked.

"Is that so terrible?"

"No," I said. "It's nice, actually."

"Good," Rue said. "Now go get changed."

Next thing I knew, we were contemplating my reflection in the mirror as I adjusted to the exposure, and the temperature shift, and the feel of the bare floorboards under my feet.

Every time you have to be brave, you get to be a little braver next time.

The suits, without question, were fabulous. Any past chromophobia of Rue's was fully conquered. She brought me one-pieces with vibrant stripes and plunging necklines, and two-pieces bursting with tropical flowers, and one hot-pink bikini with petal-shaped ruffles.

I got it. I could appreciate them.

But not one of those suits was in any way appropriate for SWET training.

Hence, the morning-of panic.

I finally just gave up and left the cottage wearing my usual black jeans.

When I showed up at the car, Hutch called through the window, "You've got a suit with you, right?"

"A bathing suit?" I asked, like I'd missed his message.

Hutch frowned. "Yes. A bathing suit."

Of course I did. "But isn't it to simulate a crash?"

"Yes," Hutch replied cautiously.

"Well," I said, looking down at my clothes. "This is what I'd be wearing in a crash."

"We're not simulating it that much."

I felt like I was making a pretty good argument. I looked down at my outfit again.

Hutch didn't wait for another protest. "You need a suit. Go change."

I shot him a look like a cranky teenager but then turned back toward my cottage.

"And not one of those flowery ones!" Hutch called after me. "This isn't the yacht club! Be professional!"

"Flowery ones are all I have!" I called back.

But that wasn't entirely true. Rue had recently gifted me an all-black one-piece that she'd special-ordered.

"Fabulous," she'd declared, after I put it on. Then she nodded approvingly. "It's endlessly flattering. Even if it looks like a bathing suit for a funeral."

"Do they make bathing suits for funerals?"

I'd squinted into the mirror as we both took in the visuals, but I found myself quietly agreeing with her. Whatever mathematics or geometry or optical illusions were going on . . . I approved.

It was a massive life milestone. To see myself in a bathing suit in a mirror and not all-out wince was unprecedented. But there was no getting around it. This suit was flattering.

Flattering, but racy.

It was a gathered halter top that connected to the body of the suit like two curtains falling from my shoulders. And let's just say that everything I had going on in the chest area was nestled into those curtains, and something about the way the fabric arranged itself was somehow both perfectly modest and wildly lascivious at the same time. You know those ads in *Vogue*, where the models' clothes are totally legit and classy—and yet somehow mind-bendingly salacious all at once?

Like that.

This plain black one-piece swimsuit given to me by Hutch's *elderly aunt* was somehow, deep down, like some kind of oil slick of naughtiness. It was *worse* than the flowery ones. At least the flowers on those could serve as camouflage.

When I arrived back at Hutch's car, I was wearing my black jeans and T-shirt over the black one-piece. "I think I should go change into one of the floral ones," I told Hutch, climbing in.

"No flowers," he said, like *We talked about this*.

"I'm not sure this one is appropriate."

"Bikini or one-piece?" Hutch demanded.

"One-piece."

"What color?"

"Black."

"That's it. That's the one."

"But—"

"We're already late. Let's go."

That's how I wound up reporting for military training in a swimsuit so provocative it might get you kicked off of a nude beach.

To be fair, it was Hutch's fault for being overly bossy without all the visual information.

But don't worry. He was about to get it.

Because we'd been doing swim lessons so faithfully, I had definitely come a long way, skills-wise. I could hold my breath underwater, and blow bubbles, and make my hands into little fins, and scissor my legs for propulsion. I could push off and swim freestyle from one side to the other. I could dive down and retrieve a toy off the pool floor.

But that didn't mean I was *good*.

I was fine for a total beginner, but I was still a total beginner.

And now I had to survive a helicopter crash.

My head felt woozy. I kept forgetting to breathe.

I once read that the mind can only truly focus on one thing at a time. And there's no doubt that given the choice between (1) being looked at and judged unfavorably and (2) drowning upside down in a community pool, my mind had the good sense to know that dying was slightly worse.

Which felt like progress.

But as I took off my jeans and then my T-shirt for the test, Hutch rushed over and said, "Hey—hey! What are you wearing?"

I was flustered by both the question itself and the fact that Hutch was putting his arms around me as he asked it, like he was trying to hide me. I mean, how terrible do you have to look for a man to sprint across a pool area to cover you up? That was my first thought.

"I'm wearing *what you told me to wear*," I said, feeling a sting of humiliation.

But now he was wrapping me in a beach towel. "*That's* your black one-piece?"

I nodded, looking down at it. "Rue bought it for me."

"Of course she did."

"What's that supposed to mean?"

"It's totally . . ."

And I don't know what I was expecting him to say or what I assumed his objection was, but I guarantee it never occurred to me that his complaint—or anyone's—might be that I looked *too good*.

Looking too good was not generally a problem for me.

But that's when Hutch finished with, "Sexy."

"What?" I asked.

"That swimsuit," Hutch said, like *Stay focused*. "It's way too sexy."

Never in my life had I been scolded for being too sexy.

I looked up—in awe—to check his face. Was this really his complaint?

Sure enough—there were those frown-wrinkles above his nose. And those dark, worried eyes. And a dead-serious expression.

If he was teasing me, he was the worst teaser in the world.

"You *told* me to wear this!" I said. "You made me go change!"

"You said it was a one-piece."

"It *is* a one-piece."

"A one-piece that got caught in a lawn mower, maybe."

"Look—"

"Put on a different one."

"I don't have a different one."

"This is all you brought?"

"I wanted to wear *jeans*, remember?"

But Hutch was in action mode now. He apparently decided to solve all our problems at once by yanking my towel away with a magician-like flourish, and then sweeping me up into his arms, charging toward the pool, and tossing me into the water.

Okay. Did not see that coming.

Hutch jumped in after me, and then he and Carlos each grabbed one end of the simulator's aluminum frame to lower it, seat and all, into the water. Then Hutch called me over.

I looked at the frame and hesitated long enough that Hutch sloshed over to me, took my hand, and pulled me toward the contraption. And I let him. If I wanted to keep my job, I had to make this video. And if I wanted to make this video, I had to go up in a helicopter. And if I wanted to go up in a helicopter, I had to pass this SWET test.

So there really were no decisions left to make.

Which was helpful, in a way.

Hutch's sudden irritability was also strangely helpful. It gave me something else to think about.

Hutch let go of my hand and I touched the aluminum of the frame, almost like I was checking to make sure it was real. Then Hutch motioned for me to swim under and come up in the middle. I did, and then climbed into the seat, which was half-submerged in the water. Then I buckled myself in. Hutch was holding the front of the frame, so I was face-to-face with him, and Carlos was holding the back.

"Here's how it works," Hutch said. "You have to do this successfully three times to pass."

I nodded.

"You can push against the frame to get yourself out," Hutch went on, "so it's less about actually swimming than it is about getting your bearings once you're upside down. You've been upside down before?"

I gave him a slightly insulted look.

Hutch gave a shrug as he said, "Use that look you're giving me as a starting place. Tell yourself you've been upside down before. Next step: unbuckle—but this isn't a car seat belt. This is a five-point harness."

I nodded. Five points seemed like a lot of points.

Somehow, in the seconds that elapsed next, my heart had started thudding in my chest.

"It's simple," Hutch said, reading my face. "You just turn the release, and all five of them fall away. Easy."

We practiced a couple of times. It was—technically—easy.

But my throat felt cold. Was that even a thing? *The cold throat of fear?* Was I inventing new ways to be terrified?

"Okay," Hutch said then, when he'd taught me everything there was to teach me. "You ready?"

I was not.

"Here we go," Hutch said. "Take a breath."

Together, Hutch and Carlos manually turned the frame over. And then I was upside down underwater and just as disoriented as Hutch had promised. And then, obediently, like a Hutch Hutcheson tribute band, I heard my mind say, "I've been upside down before."

And he was right. The thought *was* comforting. It *was* a good starting place.

From there, I did the next step and released the harness.

And, damn him. It was easy.

Unbuckled, I could feel my body drift from the seat, which took me to the next step: time to move. I grabbed the metal frame at the side and propelled myself out, but I guess maybe I pushed a little too hard, because the side of my butt scraped the frame as I went by, not badly, not enough to hurt, but enough that something—a bolt, maybe—caught on the elastic of the leg hole of this cursed bathing suit, and for a second, I was caught.

Just a short second, honestly, but long enough for me to panic and thrash around in the water like a fish on a line until I freed myself.

Then I surfaced, breathing hard, but triumphant.

I met that worried face of Hutch's again, and he just said, "What took you so long?"

"My bathing suit got caught on a bolt or something," I said, still breathless and still proud. "But I tore myself free."

"Caught on a bolt?" Hutch asked, like that had never happened before.

"Yep," I said. "Just for a minute. But I'm good now."

But was I?

I felt a little whispery tickle at my backside. I reached back to investigate, and that's when I felt some loose fabric, floating free.

My smile dropped. "Hutch," I said.

"What?" he asked, looking down.

"Don't look!" I said, pressing my hand against my butt—and, to my surprise, feeling not just loose fabric, but also a fair bit of . . . *skin*. I knew it was true, even as I said it: "I think I ripped my bathing suit."

Hutch's frown deepened. "Where?"

"The back."

"The back? Like your shoulders?"

I shook my head. "Lower."

"Your waist?"

Another shake.

Hutch's eyes got wider. "The *backside*?"

I widened my own eyes to confirm.

Then, "How much of it ripped?"

I felt around, and then winced at my assessment. "Most of it, by the feel of things?"

Hutch lowered his voice. "Are you saying your ass is hanging out of that nonexistent swimsuit right now?"

I met his eyes and nodded.

Hutch threw his head back to the heavens for a second, like this was too much. Then he looked me in the eyes and said, "Let's shut this down for today."

But I grabbed his arm. "No! I'm just getting the hang of it."

"You can't just swim around in this pool with your butt hanging out."

I clutched his shoulder. "If we leave right now, I will never come back. I can't. I won't. And then I'll have to forfeit this job and my whole career and everything I've ever wanted."

"Wow," Hutch said.

"I'm not kidding," I said.

Hutch searched my expression then, and at last, he nodded. "Okay," he said. "I have an idea."

"Thank you," I said, and I watched as Hutch reached down, grabbed the hem of his own black rash guard, and peeled it up over his head.

Then he handed the wet fabric to me in a wad and said, "Here."

"*Here* what?"

"Here, put it on."

But I shook my head. That wouldn't solve my problem. "It's just going to float up."

"Not like a shirt. Put it on like a diaper."

I frowned. "Like a *diaper*?"

"Put your legs through the armholes and then we'll tie a knot around your waist."

"Okay, there are a lot of other words you could've used besides *diaper*."

"Come on," he said. "People are waiting."

I looked around. People *were* waiting.

"Okay." I nodded, but then I just stared at the pile of wadded-up nylon until Hutch took it from me.

He found an armhole and stretched it wide, and then he lowered it under the surface near one of my feet and said, "Step through."

What else could I do? I stepped through.

Then I did the same on the other side.

Then I stood there, still as a department store mannequin, as Hutch worked his upside-down rash guard up my legs, pulled the hem of it tight around my waist, and twisted it into a knot. Then he pushed and pulled at the fabric (and by extension me) for a minute before declaring, "That'll hold."

"This is lunacy," I said.

"Is your naked butt still hanging out of your swimsuit?" Hutch asked.

"No," I answered.

"Then let's get this SWET test finished."

Twelve

IN THE END, I passed the test.

I was afraid I might get caught again, so Hutch went underwater both times to watch me—but I did fine. When it was time to get out of the pool, he hoisted me out by the armpits and wrapped the towel around me before anyone—I hope—could see my makeshift bottom half.

Hutch thought it was all hilariously funny.

Endlessly, hilariously, bent-at-the-waist funny.

I couldn't even go home and hide after that. I had to go back to the station with everybody else and walk around pretending my human dignity hadn't just been steamrollered into oblivion.

I would have loved to try to forget about it. But I couldn't.

Because Hutch could not stop laughing.

By the time we were driving home, I was pretty mad about it.

"Would you please stop laughing?" I said, rolling down the window.

"I'm not laughing at you," Hutch said. "I'm laughing because of you."

"You laughed at me all day."

"I saved you first, though."

There was an upside, though: no swim lessons tonight.

After Hutch dropped me off, I took a long shower and had just put on a fresh uniform of my usual black T-shirt and jeans when Rue showed up at the door with yet another gift bag.

"Rue," I said. "You can't keep buying me clothes."

"Sure I can."

"I've seen the price tags in your boutique."

"Who else am I going to spend my fortune on?"

"This is all because I remind you of your former self?"

"This is all because I've decided I can help you. And I need a project."

I pulled an embroidered black-and-white cotton blouse out of the bag.

"Put it on," she urged. "It's perfect for you."

Yes, she kept dressing me up like a paper doll. But her heart was in such a good place. It was only a shirt, after all. I could meet her halfway. As long as I could keep my butt safely tucked away in my jeans.

I kind of hoped Hutch might not come back to the Starlite for dinner that night—in part because I knew he'd tell the whole bathing suit story to The Gals, and in part because it really was time to level with him, for real, about why I needed him to do the "Day in the Life." We were at the deadline.

But Hutch did come back. And he sat down right next to me and The Gals as we drank our predinner sangrias, and then, as predicted, he regaled the whole group with the tale of my makeshift-diaper moment, relishing every detail.

When Rue sent us for some more ice, on the walk back across the lawn, it was finally time to make the ask. Maybe he'd feel guilty about all the laughing he'd done at my expense and capitulate. I had to take the shot, either way.

I was about to say it. I really was. I had just opened my mouth to say, *I need to ask you to save my job* . . . But that's when Ginger met us with my phone in her hand. "Here you go," she said. "It's been buzzing off the table."

I took it and, as Ginger and Hutch went off to take the ice to Rue, I fell behind to check the screen. There were twenty texts—with new ones still dinging like crazy—all pure outrage: OMG and !!!!! and the scream emoji.

All question-asking of Hutch was forgotten. I scrolled through to find my best source for clarity: Beanie. Her text just said, Call me before you click that link.

But another text came in on top of it from a former colleague I hadn't seen in a year, and it had the link in it. Right there. So clickable. And the impulse to find out what the hell was going on was so strong that against Beanie's very clear advice, I clicked it.

The second I saw the headline, I clapped the phone to my chest, instinctually making sure no one else could see it.

I looked again. Had I really seen what I just saw?

A millisecond confirmed it.

Yes.

It was an article on a gossip site. In a bold font, the headline read:

REAL-LIFE "KATIE" FROM THE SONG EXPOSED!
EX-FIANCÉE OF LUCAS BANKS HAS REALLY LET HERSELF GO

Under it was a photo of me. For proof.

Proof that I looked . . . terrible.

But it wasn't some sneaky paparazzi photo. Not some grainy, stolen image of me. Not even a recent one.

The photo with this article was from *five years ago*. Before Lucas got famous, and before we were engaged, and before I'd ever been mocked online. I had posted this photo *myself*. It was just a screenshot from my social media—back when I used to do that kind of thing. It was the kind of sweet, naïve picture you'd post if you thought it was only for your friends. I was smiling, and wearing a different, but similar, floral dress to the one the internet had hated so much at the Billboard Awards.

It was a photo, in fact, that I'd always liked.

A photo I'd always thought was kind of . . . pretty.

I scanned the article—all about the "true story" behind the song. And then it described a version of my life, somehow managing to get the basic gist of it all pretty right and 75 percent of the details totally wrong, the reporter concluding soundly that after Lucas cheated, I became suicidal and gained fifty pounds. Or a hundred. Depending on the source.

The confidence of the tone was astonishingly destabilizing. The author of this article—a person who went by the simple moniker "Lissi G"— was so certain about everything, it made me pause for a second.

Had I become suicidal?

There *were* some pretty dark days in there.

Had I gained fifty pounds?

Given that Beanie had burned my scale, we might never know.

But one thing was certain. *This* girl in *this* photo hadn't done either of those things. Because her future heartbreaks hadn't happened to her yet.

I peeked back at the phone in my hand, and as my brain realized what my body was about to do, a ticker-tape warning started zipping across my mind: *Don't check the comments. Do* not *check the comments!*

. . . Even as—*yeah*—I checked the comments.

What was I hoping for?

I have no idea. I knew it was a bad choice. I knew the internet wasn't going to rise up in inspiring unison to defend me. I was not—and *I knew this*—going to see comments like, "Hey! Leave this girl alone! She's lovely, and she's fine, she seems like a nice person—and it's this *exact toxicity* that's going to bring down human civilization."

All checking could possibly do was make things *so much* worse.

But my hand moved of its own will, anyway, and my fingers stroked the screen, and my eyes followed the text down.

And then, there they were.

Hideous.

Hopeless.

Nightmare.

This just ruined the song for me.

I can never unsee this.

She should kill herself.

I knew that "She should kill herself" was kind of the "Have a nice day" of the internet . . . but it was still beyond jarring to see it.

At last—too late—I squeezed my eyes closed and summoned the will to click the phone off. I felt an ache in my core like I'd been stomach-punched. Then I raised my arm, drew it back, and pelted the phone with all my might across the yard, watching it bounce a couple of times in the grass before landing out of sight.

When I turned, Hutch was heading my way to check on me.

He saw my face, and then he looked from me to the patch of grass where my phone was and back again.

"Don't go after it," I said, feeling like my voice was far away. "Don't even touch it." Then, to make sure he really understood: "If you go anywhere near that phone, I swear to God, I will light myself on fire."

Hutch gave an alarmed nod that said, *Message received.*

And then I just started walking.

There was nothing to do in this moment. I wasn't going to show him the article. I wasn't going to talk about it. I sure as hell wasn't going to just *resume my pleasant evening.*

No plan, no thoughts—just instinct.

Time to move.

"Hutch, where's she going?" Rue called as I went by. "Dinner's ready."

Dinner, I thought. *How ridiculous.*

I left the cottages behind—no purse, no phone, not even any shoes— and just strode out into the city streets. I wasn't headed anywhere. I didn't have a plan. I was just a person *on fire with humiliation*—doomed to try to outrun the flames.

I have no idea what route I took, or what streets I walked, or how much time went by.

Eventually, I wound up crossing the cobblestone streets of Old Town and slowing down, finally, at Mallory Square, where Rue had told me folks gathered every night to celebrate the sunset.

It was sunset now, and the park was full. The mood there in no way matched my scorched-earth vibe. The wind careened by. Party boats churned past. People perched on the empty cruise ship docks, leaning on each other's shoulders as they watched the water and the sky. Others milled around, watching a guy playing acoustic guitar, and a Hula-Hooper doing some mighty impressive tricks, and a guy busking on a unicycle and playing an accordion. Even the food vendors were adorable: Conch Fritter Fred, Pineapple Rita, a lady selling two-bite key lime pies.

Why did everybody else *being okay* just make me feel worse?

I found a metal railing by the water and leaned against it, gripping the cool, smooth bar with my palms.

I didn't know what to do with myself. I felt panicked. Trapped. Caged inside my body. And all I wanted, all I could even think about wanting, was out.

But there was no way out.

That's the thing about having a body. You only get one, and you're trapped in it from beginning to end.

What would Beanie say right now? I didn't have to think too hard on that one.

First she would make me name some new body part that I loved— a knuckle, or a nostril, or a cowlick. And then she would tell me to stand up for myself.

And my voice would tremble as I told her, "I don't know how."

And then she would insist, very gently, that I *wasn't* stuck inside of my body. It wasn't some prison my soul was caged in. The two things were—and only ever had been—one thing. I was it, and it was me. We were the same.

It was a simple truth: I couldn't abandon myself.

And as much as that was a curse, it was also a blessing.

I got it. I knew what she meant. I had a choice, and, as complicated as it was, it was also so simple. I could agree with all those ghouls on the internet . . . or I could make a choice to disagree. As that realization took hold, I saw it in my head like it was happening. As if a jeering crowd surrounded me on this very dock: the *me* from that photo in her floral dress, down on her knees. I could walk over to join the crowd and jeer along with them . . . or I could kneel down next to myself, and put my arm around that girl, and help her to her feet. I could squeeze her in a tight hug, and say into her ear—closer and louder than everyone else: "I see you. They're wrong. You're beautiful."

What would happen if I did that?

They might jeer at both of us, I guess.

Though . . . if *she was me* and *I was her*, they were already doing that, anyway.

I remembered an article about bullying that said onlookers often didn't stand up for bullied kids for fear that they would become targets themselves. But research showed that was almost never how it went. Even one other kid standing up for the victim could change the outcome.

I could choose to be that one other kid. For myself.

I could stay with her, and help her up, and we could turn to watch the sunset, side by side. I could keep one arm around her, and we could watch the sky darken until the moonlight sparkled on the waves, and listen to the water lapping the dock, and be okay together.

What if I showed up like that every time?

That exact crowd had lurked in my imagination for years—some amalgamation of every person who had ever made me feel bad. Every stepmom who had ever told me to "suck in," every photoshopped lady in every magazine, every mean-ass person on the internet.

If you don't reject the harsh things people say to you, then I guess, at some point, that means you accept them.

That crowd was my imagination, after all.

The comments had been real—maybe, I guess. If anything on the internet is real.

But everybody who followed me after I threw my phone in the grass?

Those people were all me. My fears. My worries. My unchallenged beliefs.

Maybe standing up to them wouldn't be that hard after all. I didn't have to fight them. I didn't have to outsmart them, or argue, or win. All I had to do was turn toward myself.

Was that a strategy? Would that work?

I had the strangest feeling like it might.

And what, at this point, did I have to lose?

THAT'S WHEN I felt, more than saw, someone show up next to me at the railing.

I turned. It was Hutch, and he had Rue's bike with him. He'd followed me.

He smiled, squinting in the warm orange light.

"You followed me?" I asked.

"Rue told me to," he said.

We all knew better than to disobey Rue.

"But I would have done it, anyway."

I nodded, and I looked at the bike.

"Thought you might need a ride home," Hutch said.

A sailboat was gliding by on the water.

"Do you know you don't have any shoes on?" Hutch asked then.

I looked down. Sure enough, I didn't.

Hutch kicked off his own sneakers and left them next to my feet.

I didn't put them on—just turned my attention back to the water. "That's a kind offer," I said.

"What's going on?" Hutch asked then.

Half an hour ago, I would have said, *Nothing.*

But if I was going to try to stand up for myself, it might be easier if I had some company. It was a risk, though. It was possible that Hutch might decide to stand with the crowd. I looked over at Hutch's fit, fearless profile. There was no way on earth he'd ever experienced anything like what I was feeling right now.

But that didn't mean he couldn't be on my side.

I took a breath and decided to take a chance on him.

"When I used to be engaged to Lucas Banks," I said, "that first year he got famous . . . I went with him to an awards show. And I wore a vintage, funky dress with flowers on it, and the internet decided I looked terrible—and then *went insane* writing hateful comments about me."

I glanced at Hutch.

"Thousands," I said. "I won't repeat them."

He nodded, like *Okay.*

"In the wake of it," I said, "I was very mean to myself. And I kind of stopped eating. For a year or so. And I tried very hard to be"—*How to put it?*—"skinny enough to be invisible." But maybe that wasn't right. I shook my head. "Skinny enough to be safe from criticism."

Hutch squinted, like *Huh.*

"And I might have lived that way forever, except that then Lucas cheated on me, and then left me, and then I fell apart, and then my cousin Beanie staged an intervention and set my scale on fire."

Hutch nodded, like *None of this is weird.*

"And, after that, slowly, I got better. I've been working on it very hard—finding a way to be okay. Burning that scale really helped. Also, getting away from Lucas. And keeping a journal. And . . . coming here." I waved my hands. "Stuff. You know. Personal growth. Exposure therapy. Rue makes it hard to be invisible."

Hutch stepped closer.

I took a breath. "But then today . . ." My voice disintegrated. I wished the epiphany I'd just had would take all the sting out of it— but it didn't. I looked up at the sky and tried again. "Today, an article

popped up on a gossip site with a photo of me, saying—" I felt a hitch
of worry that I shouldn't mention specifics. *What if Hutch agreed with
them?* But I pushed on: "Saying . . . that I was ugly."

Wow, that word tasted bad in my mouth.

But I will never be able to repay Hutch for the total, unmitigated
shock that overtook his face as I said it. "What?!" he said.

I nodded. "Saying I was so ugly that I should kill myself."

And then, Hutch did a funny thing: He laughed.

A quick little laugh. And then a headshake.

That got my attention. I frowned. "Are you laughing?"

Hutch shrugged. "I mean, it's funny."

"Is it?"

"It's mean as shit, but it's funny, too."

What did that mean, exactly—for him to think it was funny? *Nothing* about this was funny. Was he so obtuse that he couldn't see that?
Was he so callous that he enjoyed laughing at other people's pain? Did
he have such a terrible sense of humor that he didn't know the difference between *funny* and *life-destroyingly cruel*? Was he so unrelent-
ingly handsome that he had no capacity for empathy about what being
called ugly might even feel like?

I swallowed, then steeled myself, then met his eyes. "What about
this, exactly, is funny?"

Hutch frowned, like *What else?* "How jealous they are."

"What?"

"The people leaving those comments. They're so jealous."

"Of—what?"

And then, in the most straight-shooting, unselfconscious way, in a
tone like *What else could we possibly be talking about?*, Hutch said,
"Of you."

Then, when I didn't respond in any way, Hutch prompted: "Of how
pretty you are."

Important addendum: I was not one of those pretty girls who didn't
know she was pretty.

Equally important extra addendum: apparently, Hutch thought I was.

I just stared.

"Right?" Hutch went on, reading my face and intuiting that I might have come to a different interpretation—but unable to fathom what it could be. "Those people are on the internet, looking at a photo of the ex-fiancée of a famous singer. The ex! And you're so pretty, they have to go after you."

"You haven't seen the picture, have you?"

"I don't have to see the picture." He pointed at me. "You're right here."

Bizarre. I'd worried that telling him might change how he saw me. But it never occurred to me that it might change how I saw myself.

Hutch tilted his head and frowned. "Wait," he said. "You didn't—*believe them*, did you?"

I wasn't sure how to answer that.

"Katie, tell me that's not why you've been crying."

But I couldn't. Because I could feel myself starting to cry again.

"Oh, my god," Hutch said, breaking away and pacing off—by all indications, *angrily*—before U-turning back.

Wait. Was he *mad at me* right now? What was going on?

But then, from a bit of a distance, Hutch shouted, "Those assholes!"

Not *me*, then.

"I can't believe you believed them!"

Or maybe a little.

Hutch went on: "A famous singer wrote a chart-topping love song about you, so they have to bring you down. You have something they don't—*many* things they don't. You have that guy pining for you. You have a ballad that sings your praises all over the airways. Your name is on everyone's lips. And look at you!" Hutch gestured at my whole vibe, and then he took a few steps closer. "You've got that—mouth, and those . . . lips. And you've got this—I don't know—brightness that radiates out, and this effect on people." Hutch was closer now. "I can't figure out what it is, but it's something about the way you laugh, or maybe the curve of your neck, or . . ." He paused, just inches away now, and took in the sight of me. "It's just a fact. It's just reality. You're just . . . You're like a human hot-fudge sundae or something."

In the past, I'd coped with the meanness by just shutting down—like a little pill bug curling up into a ball. But this time was different. Hutch wasn't letting me shut down—or maybe he was just giving me a better option. Because if I did that, I'd be missing this exquisite monologue about how great I was.

No way was I missing that.

"You think I'm . . . a *human hot-fudge sundae?*" I asked, wondering if that might be the nicest thing I'd ever hear.

By the time I asked that question, Hutch was close enough to reach on either side of me and hold on to the railing behind, pinning me there. And then he raised his face to mine, just inches away.

And then—deliberately and slowly, so I could make no mistake about it—he nodded.

Um. Was giving myself an imaginary hug the best idea I could think of ten minutes ago?

Because this was *also very effective.*

"But—" I protested. "But you've been laughing at me all day."

There was that famous frown again. "That's not the same kind of laughing."

"It isn't?"

"No," Hutch said, with conviction.

"But you . . ." I wasn't sure how to say it. "Today, when you covered me up with a towel . . . it was like you couldn't stand it."

"That's right," Hutch said. "I couldn't stand it."

I took a ragged breath.

But then Hutch said, "In a *good* way."

What did that mean?

"Did you think I did that," Hutch asked, "because I didn't like the sight of you?"

I held very still.

"Katie, it was the opposite."

"What does that mean? The *opposite?*"

"It means I liked the sight of you *too much.*"

I kept frowning.

"The kind of laughing I was doing today," Hutch said, "was not the kind of laughing you do to hurt someone. God, I hope you knew that."

"I wasn't sure what kind of laughing it was, actually."

"It was the kind of laughing you do when you're supposed to be testing a woman for crash readiness during a workday for your job and she strips down to a swimsuit right in front of your eyes and the sight of her somehow makes your brain stop working."

"Your brain stopped working?"

Hutch nodded. "It did."

"Why?"

"Because every time I'm around you—and today was the worst of all—I want . . ." He shook his head. "I just want . . . *everything*."

I looked down. I'm not sure why my eyes filled up with tears again, but they did.

But Hutch ducked down again to catch my gaze and bring me back. Then he stared into my eyes. "Do you understand what I'm saying?"

I wasn't sure. "What are you saying?"

"I'm saying that when I'm not with you, I'm thinking about you. And waiting to see you again. And we've spent all day, every day together for weeks now—and it already feels like it'll never be enough."

He was gazing at me so openly, I got caught spellbound.

And then I thought, *He's going to kiss me.*

He was so dark and serious. So intense. So unwilling to look away. It was the intensity that happens from closeness—that tug that magnets have when they get close enough. It was the way he seemed to want so desperately to say things that he couldn't fit into words.

You know that feeling when someone's about to kiss you? That tension? That palpable anticipation? How everything slows down and seems to *matter* in a whole new way?

That was the feeling I had. And it pushed out all the others.

There was no internet in that moment. No Lucas. No struggle against the howling winds of self-hatred. There was only Hutch, and his frowny eyes, and me. Everything else blurred away.

Was this how this ridiculous day was going to end?

Not with me weeping at the edge of the ocean—but with a kiss?

I could feel my breaths rolling in and out of my lungs like waves.

I could hear the ocean all around us. I could feel the sea breeze whispering past. I felt lost in something bigger than myself—time, or space, or maybe just Hutch's gaze. I have never in all my life looked into another person's eyes for so long. But I couldn't look away.

And I didn't want to.

And then Hutch leaned in closer. "You can't believe them," he said then, his voice sounding mesmerized, dropping his gaze to my mouth. "How could you believe them?"

And with that, he bent his head. And the truth—that he was definitely, absolutely, one million percent going to kiss me—seemed utterly impossible and completely inevitable at the same time. I wondered if this would be the kind of kiss that would eclipse all other kisses.

It felt *that* life-changing.

Then that same hand of mine that had checked all those comments without permission decided to go in another direction. To reach for something good this time.

I brought it up behind Hutch's buzz cut and palmed its velvety texture.

And then I gave a slight, *kiss me* tug.

And that was all the permission Hutch needed.

He dove in and pressed his mouth to mine.

Thirteen

WAS IT THE best kiss in the history of humanity?

Um . . . yes.

I think all the history books will agree.

Hutch tightened his arms around me in a way that felt like a rescue. And then he kissed me so well, and so intensely, and so relentlessly, and so meltingly that I forgot everything else. The virtual haters disappeared, and so did the real-life partyers all around us, and so did the sunset, and the ocean—until there was nothing left but his mouth on mine, and the tightness of his arms, and all the tenderness in the world.

The longing, too. Like embers that had been fed a little kindling at last and were flaring up into flames of joy.

I won't say that one kiss fixed every broken thing in my life. But I will say this: having someone stand up for you and then kiss you sense-less by the water at sunset is a hell of a thing. Something quiet and forgotten and neglected in my soul got an undeniable dose of healing.

I'm also not declaring that kisses are magic.

Though maybe the right ones at the right time with the right people are—who knows?

But joy is a kind of magic, for sure. And if kissing Hutch at the water's edge in Mallory Square doesn't qualify as joy, then there's nothing on this earth that does.

I could have stayed there all night. I might have, in fact.

Except that not long after we got started, we had to stop.

Because that's when Rue called Hutch's cell phone.

Actually, it was all The Gals. On speaker.

"Did you find her?" Rue asked, sounding worried. "She left without her shoes."

"I found her," Hutch said, resting his forehead against mine, his voice sounding a little rough.

"Well, bring her home," Rue said, like *Hurry up*. "She hasn't even eaten."

AND SO, BECAUSE we all knew better than to disobey Rue, Hutch lifted me up onto Rue's bike and positioned me sidesaddle on the steel rack over the back wheel.

"Can this rack hold me?"

"On a Dutch bike, it can," Hutch said.

The chain had a solid guard I could rest my bare feet on, and once I'd wrapped my arms around Hutch's waist, we were off.

But slowly. Gently. No rush.

I relaxed into it. The wind ruffled my hair, and I leaned against his back and wrapped my arms around his waist. For stability. Mostly.

For a little while, we didn't talk. Just got used to the motion, and the feeling of balancing together. A lot had been said. And done.

But then Hutch said, "I'm torn between wanting to take you back to Rue and wanting to steal her bike and keep you to myself."

I thought about Rue—what a force of nature she was. "She's lucky to have you," I said. "I've never seen a nephew so devoted."

Hutch nodded. "She raised us, so I owe her a lot. Plus, I like her."

"I like her, too," I said.

"She retired to Key West when she bought the Starlite. I was sta-tioned in Kodiak then. I put in for here on my next tour, thinking I probably wouldn't get it, but then"—we went over a little bump on the street—"I did."

"That's lucky," I said.

"It really is," Hutch said. "I've been here a year, but tours are usu-ally four, so I've got some time before I move on. I'm trying to make the most of it."

Hutch was good at cycling. Despite everything—having no helmet, and no shoes, and not even really having a seat—I felt at ease. The side streets were quiet. I could hear the tires ribboning along the road. It was easy to talk.

Next, I asked, "Rue raised you after your mom died?"

"Parents," Hutch corrected. "After our parents died."

"Oh," I said. "Wow. I'm sorry."

"It was an accident," Hutch said. "I was twelve and Cole was eight, and there really was no one to take us after that."

"No one except your aunt Rue," I said.

"*Honorary* aunt," Hutch explained. "We were headed for foster care when Rue stepped in. She'd never wanted kids. But she couldn't *not* help."

I felt my admiration for Rue rising. "Was she a friend of your mom's?" I asked.

"No . . ." Hutch said.

"A work colleague or something?"

"I never talk about this," Hutch said then. "It's so strange to talk about it."

I frowned. Was I asking sensitive questions? "We don't have to talk about anything," I said.

"It's okay," Hutch said. "You've shared a few things tonight."

"More than a few," I agreed.

Hutch paused for a second, and then he said, "The accident my parents died in . . . My dad caused it."

At that, I shifted position—from leaning against him dreamily, my head resting on his shoulder, to sitting up alert, watching his body language from behind.

"He'd just gotten a promotion," Hutch went on, "and he'd taken us out to dinner, and I definitely remember him having at least one drink from the bar because I asked if I could get my Sprite in the same kind of glass. But I don't really know how many drinks he had, or if he might have been a little"—Hutch hesitated a half second before deciding on—"impaired."

I waited, watching over his shoulder.

"On the drive home," Hutch said, "he blew through a stop sign at the bottom of a hill and T-ed into another car." Hutch hesitated, and then he added: "Rue's car."

"Oh," I said, as Hutch kept pedaling.

Hutch shook his head, and I watched his neck muscles flex with the motion. "He didn't seem drunk. He wasn't a big drinker. But Rue's husband, Robert, was killed instantly."

Hutch had slowed, and I wondered if he would stop, and get off, and find a bench to talk face-to-face.

But he didn't.

Maybe it was easier to say it this way.

Hutch went on. "Rue says there was an overgrown tree blocking the sight of the stop sign. That's her explanation—plain and simple. That my dad didn't know to stop, or even slow down. I've never mentioned that drink from the bar to her. But of course she would know one way or the other from the autopsy."

"So whatever they told her, she didn't tell you?"

Hutch shook his head again. "No, and I didn't ask." Then he kept going. "After the impact, Rue was able to climb out of her side, but when she came around to try to open Robert's door, he was caged in. He must have already been dead. But Rue didn't know that yet. Somebody—a man, a bystander—pulled her back and away. The collision must have ruptured a gas tank. The fumes were so strong, everybody could smell them. The whole front of our car had crumpled like an accordion—and both my parents were still inside. I was able to get out, and I got Cole and led him away. Seconds later, the whole scene exploded—both cars, and everything in them. I can still remember the heat on my face."

Hutch fell silent.

So did I.

"It's funny," Hutch said next. "There aren't too many things I can recall about that night. The fire, I remember. How tightly Cole gripped my hand. But I can still see so clearly—almost like on a movie screen—the sight of Rue fighting the man who'd dragged her to safety."

I saw Hutch lift the back of his hand to wipe his face.

Now I tightened my arms around him, and leaned against him in a legitimate hug.

"Wow," he said. "I've never told that story before. To anyone."

"You've all been through a lot," I said.

"I guess I'll keep going," Hutch said then, "and add that our whole town knew about what happened, and whose fault it was. Some dipshits in my middle school took to calling my dad a killer—which I couldn't even argue with, technically. Cole was still in grammar school, and somehow he got lucky and escaped the worst of it. I always think the one who had it toughest was Rue. She did a good thing, taking us in, and she loves us now, but it wasn't easy. She and Robert were high school sweethearts. They were happy. It's not like two squirrely boys were any replacement for the life she lost. And then, suddenly, she was driving car pools, and signing permission slips, and tied down in ways she'd never wanted. But she rescued us. She saved us. I'll never forget it, and I'm grateful every day."

"That's why you're so attentive to her," I said.

"It's not just duty. Rue is a lot of fun."

"She really is."

"That's why I don't want to be famous, though. Every time something about me shows up in the news, it brings it all up again. And then Rue does what she's been doing since I was a kid: tells me she's fine, puts on a brave face, and then goes outside to cry."

"That's why you didn't want to do any interviews? It wasn't just"—
I tried to come up with a better term, couldn't, and then finally went
with—"false modesty?"

"It wasn't any kind of modesty," Hutch said, not taking offense. "It
was just knowing, from firsthand experience, that when people are talking about you, most of what they're saying is wrong."

"I'm so sorry that happened to you. All of you."

"Me, too," Hutch said.

"Now I'm wondering if we should be doing this Coast Guard video,"
I said.

"I wouldn't have volunteered for it," Hutch said. "But there's an
upside if it helps recruitment."

"Unlike just being Puppy Love–famous for no reason."

"Exactly," Hutch said. Then added, "So you better do a good job."

"I always do a good job."

"Anyway, it's not up to me." He shrugged. "Or you, either, for that
matter." Then he added, "But I thought if it could bring Cole here, at
least, that could make Aunt Rue happy."

"Sorry," I said, wondering if I'd made things worse.

"Not your fault."

"I had no idea," I said.

"We're okay, now. Mostly. Kind of. It's been a long time."

"Your story makes my internet bullies look almost cute."

Hutch shook his head. "There's nothing cute about those assholes."

I tightened my arms around him. Somehow, all this seemed to raise
more questions than it answered about Hutch. Was this why he didn't
drink? Was this why he'd signed up for a life of rescuing people? Was
this the reason for whatever beef Cole had with him?

I wanted to ask, but I didn't.

We'd both shared plenty for one day.

One thing was pretty clear, though. I would not—absolutely *not*—be
asking Hutch if I could borrow his star power to make a "Day in the
Life" video to save my job. Now that I knew the reason he didn't want

to, I didn't want to, either. Making a video to recruit rescue swimmers was one thing. Protecting me from Sullivan was another.

First order of business, when I got back to the Starlite, was to find my phone in the grass. Then to text an answer to Cole's waiting question: Will he do it?

No, I texted back. Absolutely not. Case closed.

Fourteen

I DID NOT spend the rest of that night reading more comments.

That kiss from Hutch turned out to be the exact encouragement I needed to stay in the real world. The funny thing about the internet is that it's basically a collective hallucination. If you don't join in, it doesn't exist. I mean, it *does* . . . but in another very real way, it doesn't.

Now that I had passed my SWET test, I had real-world things to do.

Like flying in a Coast Guard rescue helicopter.

Take *that*, internet.

The morning of the flight, I chose "pinkie" for my beauty list, much to Beanie's head-shaking disapproval.

"It's like you're not even trying," Beanie said.

But I doubled down and texted her a photo.

I'll tell you something: my admiration for that pinkie was sincere. The proportions were great. The nail shape was elegant. The knuckles were . . . cute? Everything about that little digit, once I started paying attention, met with my approval. And, now that I was defending my choice to Beanie, I couldn't help but notice that I *also* admired my ring finger and my pointer.

"That's a three-fer," I declared. "Stop complaining."

"What about your middle finger?" Beanie challenged then, like it was being snubbed. Then: "What about your *thumb*?"

I wasn't sure why my middle finger hadn't made the cut, but the thumb was easy. "My thumb is a little stubby."

"That's your homework right there," Beanie said then.

"Homework?" I said, like *What is this, school?*

"Find something to admire about that thumb," Beanie said, "and add it to the list."

So that's what I did while I waited in the Starlite parking lot for Hutch to pick me up. I felt strangely nervous to see him again after all the sharing and night bicycling and . . . smooching . . . and so I hyper-fixated on that thumb.

This homework was hard. What is there to admire about a thumb?

It *was* a little stubby. That was just a fact. What was I supposed to do, lie to myself?

And yet, I also agreed with Beanie. I couldn't let that negativity stand.

The Gottmans said the magic ratio was five to one: for every one negative interaction between partners, it took five positive ones to cancel it out.

So I forced myself to list five things I admired about my thumb.

Obviously, the nail was the headliner. A well-proportioned blend of rounded and square. I appreciated the little crescent moon of the nail bed, now that I thought about it. I enjoyed the way it tapered in between the knuckle and the base of my hand. How many was that? Two more to go. What else? The stripes of my knuckle wrinkles? Nicely arched? Okay, now I was reaching. But it counted. I turned my thumb around to look at the pad of it. Smooth and soft.

Done.

I texted Beanie my list of five things with a GIF of a cartoon thumb. Then, with great seriousness, I kissed the knuckle and said *to my thumb,* "I should never have called you *stubby.* You *are* stubby, but you're also many other beautiful things," just as Hutch was pulling up in his truck.

We'd deal with the middle finger later.

Did Hutch see me kiss my thumb?

We'll never know.

Because even before I'd opened the door, I could see his usual frown was different today.

It wasn't the earnest, concerned, lovable frown I was used to.

This frown was . . . sharper? Darker? Harder?

I didn't know how to read it. Was he irritated? Vexed? Enraged about something?

After that life-changing kiss from the night before, I'd assumed things would be a little different . . . but *in a good way.* I'm not sure I was expecting another *kiss,* but a warm smile, if nothing else.

But instead . . . as I climbed in, I got nothing except that frown.

No warmth. No camaraderie. No unspoken intimacy.

No eye contact, that was for sure.

There he was, in his Coast Guard–issued navy-blue T-shirt and shorts, with his hands on the wheel, his eyes straight ahead, and a cartoon scribble of angst above his head.

So, no: I did not regale him with a funny little anecdote about kissing my own thumb.

Instead, I laid low.

"Hey there," I said, buckling up. "Good morning."

Hutch gave a no-eye-contact nod and got us going.

"First flight today," I said, testing out the conversational waters.

Another nod.

"Thanks again so much for all your . . . kindness yesterday," I said then.

"Of course," Hutch said, more whisper than voice, sounding oddly formal.

"I'm not sure what I would've done without you."

Yet another nod. Then some breathing.

Thumb forgotten, we drove for a few minutes in silence. More minutes—*many* more—of silence than we'd ever let happen before. I suddenly remembered Cole saying that Hutch was not a talker.

Finally, I said, "Is everything—okay?"

"Everything's fine," Hutch said.

Everything didn't *seem* fine. But who was I to say?

Something was going on. Did he regret the kiss? Did he regret telling me about his parents? Or had he—god forbid—gone on the internet after he got home, read all those posts, decided that all those mean assholes were right about me after all—and shifted sides?

It wasn't impossible.

The internet did seem to have a knack for persuasion.

Whatever was happening, it wasn't good.

I spent the rest of the drive trying to get him talking—about *anything*—but never getting past the two-word answers. Or getting any eye contact. And when we arrived at the air station, he made himself scarce pretty fast. So I went around getting B-roll shots of the hangar. I didn't see him again until the meeting for the preflight check, where he walked in, avoided my eyes, and took a seat across the room.

Like, at the mathematically farthest point from where I was.

Maybe this was just how he was during missions? I'd never flown with him before. Maybe I was just seeing the all-business Hutch?

In one of our interviews, Hutch had explained to me the concept of a *flight bubble*—a mindset that crew members got into before any sortie, where the flight itself had their full attention.

Maybe that's where Hutch had gone, mentally? Inside his flight bubble?

I'd have to work on mine.

Because this flight did not exactly have my full attention.

The meeting started with a discussion of whether the morning fog was impacting visibility too much to fly—concluding that no, it was within a safe range. Next, there were check-in questions with each member of the crew about their readiness. I'd read that everything in aviation starts and ends with a checklist—and that was definitely true now.

As the meeting progressed, my worries about Hutch gave way to other worries. Specifically to one particular, much more primal worry.

Because this meeting had no choice but to end in the moment I'd been dreading from the start. The moment when I'd have to stand up and *announce my weight* to the room.

No getting out of it now.

Had you forgotten that I'd have to do that before this flight?

Because I sure hadn't.

The silent drive with Hutch had distracted me for a minute, but once we were in the conference room, there was no way out.

As the meeting wore on, the dread grew. By the end, I had a significant tied-to-the-train-tracks feeling.

But here's something you might not know about the US Coast Guard. It's not the same crew flying every sortie. The crews change depending on days and schedules. Procedures are standardized so that everybody can work with everybody, and this makes it easy to come together in emergencies and work with different people.

Today, we had a pilot named Mira, a copilot named Noah, a flight mechanic named Vanessa, and Hutch.

Plus me. And my camera.

During the meeting, I'd decided to announce my weight together with the camera's, thinking I could imply with my voice that the camera was exceptionally heavy. I liked the obfuscation of this plan. The plausible deniability. Anything was possible in this scenario! I could be a *waif* for all they knew. A waif carrying a Mack Truck of a camera.

It would have to do.

Maybe I wasn't scared of the helicopter at all. Maybe I was just scared of *the meeting about the helicopter.*

But I guess I got lucky.

It turned out, we did *not* all have to announce our weights out loud in that meeting. All those numbers would happen later, in the equipment room. So this nightmare scenario I'd been fearing for weeks of having to stand up in a room full of cool people and announce some number that would randomly *define my value as a person* . . . just didn't happen.

Isn't that how it always is?

The thing you're afraid of is never the thing you should be afraid of.

Instead, in the equipment room, as we got our flight helmets—which were blue and sparkly, like bowling balls—the pilot, Mira, took me quietly aside to a scale in the corner. Just an ordinary scale. And just the two of us, alone.

"I just need to get your number," she said, lifting up a clipboard.

"Oh," I said. Then, "That's it?"

Mira nodded. "That's it."

Relief bloomed in my chest. "I'm not going to look, if that's okay."

"That's totally fine," Mira said, woman-to-woman.

I stepped on, and then she looked down, and then she wrote a random number on her clipboard, and . . . that was that. All that buildup for a beautiful kind of nothing.

Next, she said, "And the camera is—?"

"Twenty-two pounds," I said. Honest, this time.

She wrote that down, too.

"You don't need to weigh the camera?"

"Not really."

"Is that because people only lie about their body weight?"

Mira nodded. "Yep. When people self-report in their distress calls, we always add another ten percent."

"I would've been truthful," I said. Or as truthful as a person *fully guessing* could be.

"I sense that about you," Mira said.

"Thank you," I said. Then I added, "You are now the only person on earth who knows that number. Including me."

"Am I?" Mira asked. "Wow. I've already forgotten it."

And because she was a pilot in the US military, and because I didn't know if it was allowed . . . I didn't hug her right then.

But I wanted to.

HELICOPTERS ARE SO loud that pilots have to communicate through headphones and mics. If you ever see a movie with people in a helicopter just *talking to each other normally*, go ahead and call it: false.

You *can* talk in a helicopter, but you have to shout.

Helicopters are so loud, in fact, that in addition to wearing flight helmets with noise-canceling headphones in them, crews put foam earplugs in, too. It's *that* noisy.

That's one big problem for pilots: hearing loss. Also back pain from all the sitting and vibrations. And neck problems from the heavy helmets and the night-vision goggles.

It all takes a toll.

But my personal toll on this flight turned out to be smaller than I'd feared.

They let me wear my civilian clothes, for one, which was a relief. I just wore my trusty black jeans and T-shirt and sneakers with an orange safety flight vest.

Not the worst look in the world.

The helicopter was already waiting outside the hangar by the time I emerged with my gear, and I looked over to see Hutch coming out of the men's locker room in his swim ensemble—which was, in essence, a black wet suit with black swim shoes.

Which made him look distinctly superhero-esque.

He also carried a pack with other gear, a bright yellow swim helmet with an attached snorkel and goggles, and a set of long black fins and green safety gloves.

I stopped walking at the sight of him.

I just froze for a second—totally starstruck. He really was a rescue swimmer. This was what he wore *to jump out of helicopters. Into the open ocean. To save people's lives.*

This man, right here, who had kissed me by the ocean at sunset *yesterday.*

The memory overtook me for a second—before reality elbowed its way back in.

I was standing right between Hutch and the helicopter he was striding toward, so it wasn't crazy to think that he might join up with me to walk together. Or wave hello. Or acknowledge my existence.

But he did not.

I watched him walk right past me, like I wasn't even there.

Seriously. What the hell?

But I guess that was a question for after work.

Now, as the rest of the crew walked out toward the waiting helicopter, Mira, the pilot, fell into step next to me and said, "If you feel nauseated in the air, let us know."

Her flight bubble didn't preclude acknowledging my existence.

"Nauseated?" I asked.

"You'll probably be fine. But it's a different feeling from what you're used to on planes. So keep your eyes on the horizon. And if you start to feel sick, say something. There are things we can do to help with that. But if you throw up, the flight crew will have a lot of cleaning to do."

Don't throw up. "Got it."

"You ate some breakfast today, yes?" Mira asked then.

"Yes," I lied.

"You'll be fine."

As we arrived at the helicopter, still as majestic and orange as ever, Mira and the rest of the crew started visual checks of the equipment and Hutch appeared beside me.

"Did you eat breakfast today?" he asked, looking straight ahead, like we were spies trading secrets.

I shook my head. "I was too nervous to eat."

Hutch nodded, like *Thought so*, and then he pulled an energy bar out of a zipper pouch on his flight vest. "Take this."

"Thank you," I said.

"More snacks where that came from," he said, patting his vest and still sounding as all business as a person talking about snacks can.

Huh.

IT WAS JUST supposed to be a training mission. Crews fly training missions on every overnight shift to keep their hours up and stay in practice. But not long after we'd lifted off, just as I was trying to decide if I was nauseated or not, a call came from Sector for a fishing boat in distress with one soul on board.

I wondered if there was any other branch of the military that referred to people as "souls." I'd have to google that later.

The training mission turned into a rescue pretty fast.

The two pilots were up front, and the flight mechanic was in a seat behind them on a track that slid side to side so she could work from either door of the aircraft, and I was in the back—buckled into Hutch's usual seat. Hutch, for his part, sat on the gray-painted metal floor, beside the rescue basket that was folded and stowed in the back.

I *guess* we had room for one more person. But it would be snug.

It's not the *flying* of the helicopter that's disorienting—it's the *hovering*. You really do have to find the horizon line to keep your bearings. Hutch kept glancing at me—worried I might barf, no doubt. But there would be no vomiting. Not today. As a point of pride.

I'd *implode* before I let that happen.

Instead, as soon as I had my sea legs, so to speak, I focused on filming. I got interior shots of the cabin, the water below, the crew, and the equipment.

Because the pilots were up front, piloting, and because Hutch apparently didn't want to talk to me, the job of explaining what was going on fell to the flight mechanic, Vanessa. "When we reach the scene," she said, talking through the helmet mic and headphones, "we'll descend to fifteen feet above the highest crest, and then Hutch will deploy into the water. Once he's out, and we've lowered whatever equipment he needs—the basket or the sling—we can strap you into the gunner's belt so you can lean out and get some good shots."

"Lean out"—I clarified—"of the helicopter?"

"Sure," Vanessa said. "You can go full *Titanic*." She put her arms out like Kate Winslet on a prow.

"Cool," I said. I looked out at the ocean to mask the abject terror in my eyes. Then I asked, "And when you say Hutch will *deploy*, do you mean *jump*?"

"More or less," Vanessa said, coming over to me now, helping me unbuckle the five-point seat harness and tightening the gunner's belt—which attached to a cable—around my waist. Then she positioned me in a spot where I wouldn't be in anyone's way, but where I could get the shot of Hutch dropping into the water.

I hadn't been thinking about today as particularly windy, but when we got to the scene, I was shocked to see how big the wave swells were. The sky suddenly seemed grayer and stormier, too. As I got my camera ready, I felt a shadow of worry.

Was dropping Hutch into the ocean right now a good idea?

Deploying is more dangerous than it sounds. The helicopter can only—safely—get so low to the water. Fifteen feet above the highest crest is the limit. That's the ideal span for jumping, but of course, there's a reason they call waves *rollers*. They move and undulate and can shift in seconds. A swimmer can deploy for what should be a fifteen-foot drop to the top of the swell, and the water can shift so fast that before he hits the surface, it's forty feet—or more.

"That'll knock the wind out of ya," Hutch had explained during one of our interviews.

"Can forty feet kill you?"

"I mean," Hutch had said, "it's gonna hurt. That's for sure. And you'll probably get a garage sale."

"A what?"

"It's when the water smacks you so hard you lose all your equipment—your snorkel and your goggles and your fins."

"I'm guessing it's not good to lose your fins."

"Correct. It's bad."

"How bad?"

Hutch thought about it. "Your fins are your power and your control. So you don't want to lose that. Especially in a stormy ocean."

Was the ocean below us stormy?

It definitely seemed a little worked up about something.

It was astonishing how calm everybody was. I could hear the crew talking through the headsets. The pilots were serenely discussing procedures and positioning. The flight mechanic was adjusting equipment in the back. And Hutch was waiting in position for the moment when he would drop himself into the ocean.

For me, this was utterly surreal.

For these guys, it was just another day at the office.

Below us, there was a small fishing boat on its side. It had been knocked over by one of these enormous waves. A survivor bobbed in the water close by with an orange life jacket on.

The pilots positioned us over him, and the wind from our rotor rippled the water, making it spray. Hutch had switched his flight helmet out for his yellow swim helmet and put his fins on over his swim shoes. As we hovered in position, Vanessa opened the door and slid it back, and Hutch moved toward the opening, dropping his feet over the side.

"Is it scary?" I had asked him, back in that same interview. "Jumping out of helicopters?"

"Nah," Hutch had said—a light in his eyes confirming his words. "It's fun."

"But there are so many ways you could die," I said.

"If you're a person who thinks about it that way," Hutch said, "you wouldn't be here. You'd never have made it through swim school."

It was pretty clear before, and possibly *extra* clear now, that I never would have made it through swim school. Even just watching Hutch sit there gave me a dropped-stomach feeling.

And then he did exactly the thing my stomach was afraid of.

He shoved off and went over.

I got a very cool shot. Splash and all.

As soon as Hutch was in the water, he was swimming in the direction of the survivor—pumping his arms and shoulders hard in a type of swimming he called *sprinting*. I zoomed in close and watched him work through the spray. He reached the soul, as they called him, and within a few minutes, Hutch was giving the signal for a basket. Vanessa lowered it down and I filmed that, too. As the basket descended, Hutch clamped the survivor into a cross-chest carry to maneuver closer to meet it.

The basket reached the surface and disappeared under the water. Hutch grabbed its wire and helped the survivor get positioned inside.

When Hutch gave the signal, Vanessa raised the basket with the survivor inside. The winch for the hoisting cable was on a hinged metal arm, and when the survivor reached the right height, Vanessa rotated the arm to bring the basket inside the cabin. Hutch was next. She lowered a clip to him, he attached it to his harness, and she raised him up, too.

The survivor was a fifty-something guy in a Hawaiian shirt—looking very much like he hadn't anticipated that his day might end up this way. He didn't have any visible injuries that I could see, but he was definitely wide-eyed, like his brain was still trying to catch up to what was happening. Hutch got him settled, and the pilots got us moving to return to base, and I put my camera away.

For something so extraordinary, they really made it look easy.

Just another life-saving sortie, I guess.

But maybe not for everyone. I snuck a glance at the survivor just before we landed, and saw that he was crying.

BACK AT THE hangar, before Hutch headed off to the locker room to clean up, I stopped him and said, "Do they always cry like that?"

Hutch turned and met my eyes for the first time all day—that sad frown of his back in full force. "People do a lot of strange things."

I felt like that was supposed to mean something.

Enough was enough.

"Did I do something wrong?" I asked.

Hutch considered how to answer before he sighed and said, "No. I'm the one who was wrong."

"Wrong about what?" I said, a tinge of frustration in my voice.

Hutch looked down, then back up. "I talked to Cole on the phone last night. For the first time in a year."

"Okay," I said.

"I've wanted to talk to him for so long. But it wasn't exactly what I was hoping for. A full year of no contact, and now his only topic was you."

"Me?" I asked.

Hutch nodded. "He told me all about you."

From the way he said it, that didn't sound good.

But what would Cole have even said? He barely knew me.

Hutch went on. "He asked me to do your 'Day in the Life' project—and he told me why."

Had Cole told him about Sullivan? Was this why Hutch had been so angry all day? Because Cole was using Hutch's good-heartedness against him—and now he was helping me against his will? Had Cole said Hutch was the only person who could save my job? Did Hutch think I was in on it, too?

"No, no," I protested. "You don't have to—"

"I said yes," Hutch said, with a shrug. "Of course I said yes."

"But you really have a good reason for not—"

"It's fine. It doesn't matter."

"It *does* matter," I countered.

"That phone call," Hutch said then, "shifted my perspective."

"I don't need you to do this for me," I said.

"But Cole does," Hutch said.

I let out a slow breath.

"And if he needs this, then I'm doing it. That's all there is to it."

"But—"

"Let's get it done, though," Hutch said. "I have tomorrow off."

"*Tomorrow?*"

"Why not, right? The sooner the better."

Was I ready to do this tomorrow? Did I even want to? "I really don't think—"

But Hutch cut me off. "It's not up to you."

I shook my head. "Everything about this feels wrong."

Hutch let out a bitter half laugh. "No argument here."

"You realize what the project is, right?" Was I trying to talk him out of it? "I stay at your house for twenty-four hours and I film everything you do."

Hutch gave me a look. "Everything?"

"Everything that's filmable. I'm not, like, following you into the bathroom."

Hutch shrugged. "It's not that different from what you're already doing here."

"But *here*, it's professional—and *there*, it's personal. It's you brushing your teeth and eating Cheerios. Putting on your pajamas. Doing dishes. Answering the phone. It's intimate."

At those words, Hutch looked slightly miserable. "Even more reason to get it over with."

"I don't want to make you do this," I said. "What if I just . . . refuse?"

"You can't."

"Why not?"

"Because then I'm in more trouble with Cole," Hutch said. "And I'm already in enough trouble with Cole."

I felt so indignant. Nothing happening here was any of Cole's business, and he was butting in where he absolutely did not belong. But, of course, it was also *all* Cole's business. It was *his* brother, *his* aunt, *his* transferred assignment. I was only here—had only even met Hutch— because of Cole and all of his complicated motivations. Whatever they were.

"Is there no way out of it?" I asked.

Hutch just frowned into my eyes for what felt like an eternity. Then, as if our fates had already been sealed, he said, "I'll text you my address."

Fifteen

I WASN'T GOING to make a "Day in the Life" documentary about Hutch, of course.

Not to put up on YouTube for all the world to see.

I couldn't do that. I wouldn't. Not knowing everything I knew now.

Here was my plan: I'd make the video—and make it *amazing*—and show it to Sullivan and her executive team to prove my worth and save my job. I'd do my normal thing—but then I'd just never upload it.

That could work, right?

If Hutch didn't want to be famous, then I wouldn't make him any more famous.

I'd just use Hutch's infinite charms to make a video so kick-ass that Sullivan had no choice but to let me keep my job. What was that Steve Martin quote? "Be so good they can't ignore you"? I would be so *amazing* they couldn't *downsize* me.

Not as catchy, but still.

And if I had to objectify Hutch a little bit to delight my she-wolf boss and get that done?

There were worse penances to pay.

This was a way for everybody to win, right?

I typically started the "Day in the Life" sessions around ten in the morning. This gave me plenty of time to get good footage before the sun went down, a night to sleep on it, and then a little time the next morning to capture anything I'd missed.

The next morning at ten sharp, I showed up at Hutch's house. Except it wasn't a house.

It was a houseboat.

Of all things.

In case this needs to be said, it's a very strange feeling to pack up all your favorite camera equipment and borrow your landlord's Mini Cooper and drive to a sleepover with a man who does not want you there.

Twenty-four hours can be a very long time.

And then when your map app leads you to a place called the Sunshine Marina? And the house turns out to be a houseboat? Even stranger.

At first, I thought I must have the address wrong.

Until I saw the hand lettering on the hull that read *Rue the Day.* Perhaps in honor of the only person I'd ever met named Rue. And then, above it, on the rooftop deck, wagging his tail at the sight of me, I saw George Bailey.

Guess this must be it.

But didn't military people live in . . . I don't know—*barracks,* or something?

All the time I'd spent with Hutch, and it had never once occurred to me that he went home every night and *slept on the water.*

It made him even more appealing, if that was possible.

I hesitated a minute before walking down the dock to get things started. I wasn't sure what to make of his hot-cold thing. No doubt he was angry about having to do this. But was he really so angry that it completely nullified all the things he'd said—and done—just two nights before?

It seemed extreme. But he wasn't explaining—and I didn't know how to make him explain.

I didn't see a way out. So I guessed I'd just have to go through.

The good news is, the first load of stuff I carried with me, as I went to go knock on Hutch's door, was just my overnight bag—not the bag with all my camera equipment.

As soon as I stepped off the dock onto the back deck of the boat, two things happened: one, Hutch opened the back door, and two, George Bailey scrambled down the spiral stairs from the rooftop and bounded right at me to catapult himself into my arms.

Thinking, again, contrary to all laws of physics, that I was going to catch him.

Which, of course, I didn't.

But, this time, George Bailey didn't just knock me down.

He knocked me *overboard*.

Me, and himself, and my overnight bag. We all flew backward and plunged into the very cold, very wet, very watery water of the marina.

Yes, I'd been taking swim lessons with Hutch. And yes, I'd passed my SWET training. But those had been controlled conditions. Now I was in a much deeper, much realer *natural* body of water. And now I had all my clothes—and sneakers—on. And now I was tangled in the cross-body strap of my duffel bag. With a Great Dane plunging in after me and then using my body as a climbing structure to scramble back up toward the surface.

Given the shock of it all, I did a pretty good job of pulling myself together. I followed Hutch's advice and said to myself, *You've been underwater before.* And that was enough to help me not panic. I wriggled out of the shoulder strap and reminded myself that my body fat wanted to float. Whatever air was in my lungs would also want to float—though I wasn't sure if George Bailey's impact had knocked all of that out. *Make your hands into fins*, I commanded myself. *Kick your feet.*

Amazingly, I listened.

Even more amazingly, it worked.

I could see sunlight filtering down from above—and I reached for it. And kicked like hell. And before I knew it, I surfaced.

I was halfway through a triumphant breath when Hutch surfaced right next to me.

Without even saying anything, he manhandled me, flipped me around, and maneuvered me toward the boat—exactly like he'd done to the soul he rescued yesterday.

Despite the fact that I'd just handled the moment competently myself, I confess that it did feel surprisingly comforting to be taken in Hutch's arms. It was a physical and undeniable feeling of safety that just doesn't come along too often in day-to-day life.

Still, on principle, I argued.

"What are you doing?" I demanded, as he swam us toward the boat ladder.

"I'm rescuing you."

"But I already rescued myself!"

As he grabbed the ladder, he let go of me.

I turned around, grabbed the ladder, too, and faced Hutch in the water.

He looked at me, realizing that was true. "I guess you did."

"Isn't that what you've been teaching me to do?"

"These are just very different conditions."

At those words, George Bailey paddled up and between us toward the ladder, and, in unison, we both pushed on his butt as he scrambled back up onto the deck and then shook the water out of his fur.

Hutch looked from the dog to me. "Why does he keep trying to jump into your arms?"

"He's your dog, pal."

"I'm sincerely sorry," Hutch said.

"It's okay," I said—and then I noticed my suitcase floating away behind him.

Hutch turned to see it, too, and then he was off like a dolphin to retrieve it for me. "Let's get you inside," he said, when he got back.

"You don't have to push me on the butt like George Bailey," I said, pointing at him before I started up the ladder.

Hutch held up both hands and said, "I wouldn't dare."

I wound up showering and changing into some sweats of Hutch's, while he loaded batches of my marina-water-soaked things into the tiniest washing machine in the world. Even over the noise of the shower water, I could hear him humming "Heart and Soul."

In the shower, the soap stung my breastbone, and I found scratches there as thick as yarn from George Bailey's claws. Later, I showed them to Hutch by pulling the collar of the T-shirt down and tilting my neck back.

Hutch frowned at the sight and then made me sit on a kitchen stool while he dabbed ointment on with a Q-tip—apologizing over and over.

Yes, I probably could have managed that procedure by myself in private in the bathroom. But Hutch was a professional. Plus, it was really—surprisingly—nice to be taken care of.

What can I say? I just went ahead and let it happen.

"I keep thinking about it and thinking about it," Hutch said, standing close and dabbing along the scratch line. "What is it about you?"

No lie: that's a heck of a thing to hear from a man as dreamy as Hutch when he's standing six inches away and giving medical attention to your chest. "You keep thinking and thinking," I echoed, watching his hand as he worked, "what it is about me?"

"You and this dog," Hutch said.

Ah. Yes. The dog. I regrouped. "Maybe I remind him of someone?" I offered. "Or maybe he can sense that I'm very good at hugs?"

"Are you?" Hutch asked, not looking up.

"Of course," I said. "I'm out of practice, but I'm good."

WAS GETTING KNOCKED ass-over-teakettle off the side of a boat the ideal way to start a filming session?

Ordinarily, no.

But starting like this had a huge upside this time: Hutch felt so guilty and responsible, he was much nicer to me afterward.

I'd been anticipating put-upon silence, and maybe that's what I would've gotten—if his dog hadn't almost drowned me. But in the wake of that impromptu water rescue, I got apologies, and hot tea, and a soft T-shirt with the big letters USCG across it. I got eye contact, and chitchat, and kindness. I'd been braced for a solid day of misery, and instead, it was . . . quietly fun. Which sparked a conspiracy theory in my head that I did not share with Hutch. Maybe George Bailey was helping me. Maybe that was the deal with this dog. Maybe he was some kind of canine yenta.

Impossible, of course. But the facts didn't lie.

Everything we had to do in the next twenty-four hours got a lot more fun if Hutch wasn't actively mad at me. And *everything we had to do* included me following him around, filming whatever it was that he did on his day off. Everyday things: folding laundry, making sandwiches, going for a run, cleaning the boat. I got all kinds of beautiful close-ups of the sandwich, the laundry tumbling in the dryer, his sneakers, the bucket of soap bubbles.

I asked if he really did two hundred push-ups every day, and he said yes, but only in the morning. I asked him if he could do some jump-roping tricks, and he obliged. I also happened to show up on a deck-washing day, so I was forced to film shirtless Hutch in his swim trunks scrubbing the deck—soap, hoses, and all.

The things we do for art.

I would apologize for objectifying him, but I didn't have a choice. I had, at this point, an audience of one—Sullivan. Of the six minutes I had to work with, shirtless jump-roping could have as many as it wanted.

The craziest part of the day was taking George Bailey on a walk. I went with them and got wide shots of the two of them playing in the grass at a nearby park, the dog hip-height to the man beside him. Also: close-ups of George Bailey's velvety ears, his sad eyes, and his big paws padding along the weathered wood of the docks. Oh—and a fantastic wide shot of the moment when Hutch patted his own shoulders, and George Bailey lifted up on his hind paws to rest his front ones there— and he was *taller than Hutch*.

The moment just happened to happen in front of a purple-and-orange sunset.

So many great visuals.

On the way back, once I had all my shots, I fell into step beside them.

"I can't believe you live on a houseboat," I said. "Who lives on a houseboat?"

"It's not mine," Hutch said. "It's Rue's. Or, actually—it was her husband, Robert's. He built it himself. He was an engineer. Anyway, she couldn't bring herself to sell it. She kept it in storage all these years. When I moved here, she offered it to me, and one weekend we docked it at the marina."

"It's Rue's? I can't believe she hasn't decorated it for you."

"She wants to. Badly. But I'm holding firm. Just keeping it clean is enough for me."

"It does seem quite clean. Almost brand-new."

Hutch's voice got a little quieter. "Well, Robert had just finished it when . . . the accident happened. They were going to retire and spend summers on it, but they never got the chance."

Just then, George Bailey stopped and dropped his head.

"Shit," Hutch said, dropping to his knee beside him. And in seconds, Hutch had pulled a yellow dishwashing glove out of his pocket and shoved his hand into it, and then took ahold of George Bailey's snout. "Nope, nope, nope. That's a nope."

"What's going on?" I asked.

Hutch put his fingers into George Bailey's mouth, trying to pry his jaws open. "Toad," he said.

"Toad?"

Hutch nodded, still working. "He likes to scoop them up in his mouth."

I stared in horror. "He eats live toads?"

"He doesn't eat them. He just holds them. In his mouth."

"He just—?"

"Which is fine. To each his own, you know? And native toads are fine. No harm, no foul. But there's an invasive species called the cane toad that squirts poison—like lethal in fifteen minutes if you don't do anything. So he just can't be messing around with toads. I keep explaining this to him," Hutch said, still working on George Bailey's jaw, "but he never listens."

Right then, Hutch's fingers must have tripped a gag reflex, because George Bailey made a little hacking noise, lowered his head, and opened his jaw.

Out flopped a medium-sized toad.

Hutch pulled out his flashlight and peered at it while the toad took a second to gather its wits, and then it hopped off into the grass, unharmed.

"Was that a poisonous one?" I asked.

Hutch shook his head. "There's no ridge on the head. We're good."

"Wow," I said, in a tone like *That was close.*

"Yeah," Hutch said. "Normally, I walk him earlier. And watch him closer. But today I'm—" He glanced my way. "Distracted."

By the time we got back, the sun was down. The plan was to film Hutch making dinner, and then eat together, and then sit down for an official interview, where I'd ask him about the Puppy Love rescue. I always filmed the interviews—but since I only used the audio, the visuals didn't matter, and so I generally did those at night.

We had time. No rush.

Hutch made pasta with fresh tomato sauce and basil, and we ate it on the rooftop deck, with the vast starry sky above and the sparkling water below.

And then, after a careful sound check of all the locations on the boat, I determined that Hutch's bedroom, of all places, was the quietest spot for recording sound. I got set up in there while Hutch was off in the kitchen, making George Bailey's dinner.

And then a funny thing happened.

I realized I'd forgotten my extension cord.

"Do you have an extension cord?" I called to Hutch in the other room.

"In the closet! At the bottom! In a plastic tub!" he called back.

And so then I was opening Hutch's closet, having some kind of visceral pheromone reaction to the sensation of all his clothes hanging there together, then pulling out the plastic tub, only to find something else behind it.

Back in the corner of the closet, dropped and forgotten by the look of things, was my little hot-pink hibiscus hair clip. The one Rue had given me. The one I'd lost during the Great Splinter Removal.

I stared at it for a second.

What in the world was my hair clip doing in Hutch's closet?

Was it there on purpose? By accident? Was it a keepsake? A memento? Had he found it and saved it for me—but then forgotten to return it?

I wondered if I should just take it back. Or ask him about it. But I had a feeling like it being there might mean something—which might be embarrassing for Hutch. Or it might mean nothing—which would be embarrassing for me. So when I put the tub back, I set the flower back in place where I'd found it.

Better to let things unfold on their own.

THE INTERVIEW WENT really well. Maybe all Hutch had needed was practice. Or maybe it was the comfort of being in his own bedroom, instead of at work. Or maybe it had been a long day and he was ready to let his guard down. But he told the story of rescuing Jennifer Aniston's dog simply and clearly—in a way that was nothing short of page-turning. I sat beside him on the bed with my headphones on, holding the mic and letting that sandpapery voice of his just flood every nook and cranny of my ears and then wash on down through the rest of me.

And this was before I'd added visuals.

This "Day in the Life" was going to be epic, and gorgeous, and unforgettable.

Too bad nobody would ever see it but me. And Sullivan.

AFTERWARD, WHEN IT was time for bed, Hutch tried to insist on giving me his bedroom.

"I changed the sheets and everything," he said.

"I'm fine on the sofa," I said.

"That doesn't feel polite—to make a guest sleep on the sofa."

"I'm not a guest. I'm a filmmaker."

"Still—"

"Look," I said, "this isn't some corporate thing I normally make in my normal job. This isn't some stiff executive reading cue cards. This is journalism. This is cinema verité. I'm trying to do something important here. I'm trying to capture something true—something that matters about the human spirit. I have to film what's real. I'm trying to capture your actual life. Would I be in your bed in your actual life?"

Hutch blinked.

"That didn't come out right," I said. "You know what I mean."

He nodded. "Okay, then. But don't be surprised if you get licked."

Now it was my turn to blink.

But then I followed Hutch's gaze to George Bailey, dozing on a rug nearby.

Ah.

"This room is kind of his territory."

"Fine. That's fine."

Hutch gave a little headshake, like he was pretty sure it wouldn't be fine.

As he walked away, I called after him, "There is one favor I need to ask of you, though."

He turned. "Shoot."

But this was a terrible question to have to ask. I squeezed my eyes closed. "Can I film you putting on your pajamas?"

Another new Hutch frown for the collection: *Are you insane?* "What?"

How to explain? Cole had definitely told him my job was on the line. But how much had he told him?

"Did Cole tell you about Sullivan?" I asked.

Hutch shook his head.

I took a breath. "Our boss is a lady named Karen Sullivan. She's the main person who gets to decide if I keep my job or not. She will see this video. And I think she will really . . . appreciate your visuals."

"Appreciate my visuals?"

I nodded. "So much so that she might not fire me."

Hutch tilted his head inquisitively. "Are you trying to titillate your boss?"

"Just a little bit," I said. "For a good cause."

At that, Hutch smiled and shook his head. And I suddenly noticed that I'd seen him smile more times today than in all the weeks I'd been following him around.

I hated to belabor it, but I felt the need to justify myself. "I'm just saying," I said, gesturing at his torso, "that thing could save my job."

Now Hutch looked almost embarrassed. "Only one problem," he said. "I don't sleep in pajamas."

Oh, god. "Please tell me you don't sleep naked."

"That would be a tall order for your cinema verité, wouldn't it?"

I flared my nostrils, like *Just tell me.*

"I do not sleep naked," Hutch said.

I let out a relief-drenched sigh—

"I sleep in boxer briefs."

—then I tried to suck it back in.

The sight of this made Hutch laugh. "I can put on pajamas, if you want," Hutch offered.

With most men, I would've jumped at that offer. Of course. *Of course* he shouldn't be sleeping in his underwear.

But there was just something about Hutch.

I thought about a story Rue had told me the other night about a time she and Hutch were traveling together and their flight got delayed. They had to deboard and wait to change planes in the terminal. The hours ticked by, and people were missing connections right and left, and everybody waiting just got angrier and angrier, and people started going up to the reservation desk and yelling at the gate agents—who, of course, had no control over anything.

After watching this for a little while, Hutch got up and walked off.

When he came back, he had a whole tray of coffees. He walked up to the reservation desk, and he set the coffees down, and said to the ticket agent, "I know it's been a tough day, and I know you're all working so hard. Thank you for everything you're doing."

Then he left the coffees there for them.

Rue said the whole area went dead quiet. Everybody witnessed that one act of kindness—and had to confront the humanity of those ticket agents in a whole new way. The man who was mid-rant lowered his arms, closed his mouth, and walked quietly back to his seat. Rue herself, who had been frustrated, too, totally recalibrated. That one action, she told me, shaking her head, just neutralized everybody, and reminded them what human decency was—and let the agents get back to work.

I guess what I'm saying is . . . if a guy like that wanted to sleep in his underwear, he could sleep in his underwear.

It's such a vital skill—learning to recognize who's a good guy and who isn't. Sometimes it's hard to tell, and sometimes it's impossible. But I had to admit right then that I was as sure as a person could be that Hutch was, absolutely, a good guy. From watching him take a sticker burr out of George Bailey's paw on our walk tonight, to the way he'd grabbed my pasta bowl back so he could add a sprig of basil . . . I knew. I just knew.

He was a person it was okay to feel safe with.

"Just sleep how you'd normally sleep," I said. "I'm not uncomfortable." And I meant it. "But," I added then, getting back to Sullivan, "if you're not putting things *on* for bed, could I film you taking a few things *off*?"

Sixteen

I *DID WIND* up getting licked in the middle of the night.

And not just licked. *Sat on.*

Because that night, there was a thunderstorm. And Hutch wasn't kidding when he said that George Bailey had thunder-phobia. Or whatever it was called.

I woke to George Bailey, who had fallen asleep on the rug beside the sofa, clawing his way on top of me, panting, drooling, and trembling all over.

I looked up, and George Bailey looked down.

And then I realized that I couldn't exactly breathe. So I grabbed the frame of the sofa and hauled myself up and out from underneath him. Which should have been fine. But George Bailey, teetering above me, lost his balance as I shifted and then went thrashing off the sofa and collided with the coffee table . . . which flipped on its side.

It was two A.M.

The sound was so loud, it rattled the whole boat.

As George Bailey and I recovered and stared at each other, Hutch came bursting out of the bedroom.

Were you wondering if Hutch had just been teasing about the boxer briefs? That when it came down to it, he would don some modest, gentlemanlike cotton pajamas?

Yeah, no.

At the sound of the crash, Hutch showed up—ready for action—with, honestly, next to nothing on.

Deep breaths: those boxer briefs were not that shocking. If we'd been on the Tour de France, I argued to myself forcefully, they could almost be bike shorts.

Fine: bike shorts that shrank in the wash—but bike shorts, all the same.

"What happened?" Hutch demanded, looking around, arms out like he might have to pummel an intruder barefoot.

I got up off the sofa and started working to right the table, and he helped me. We picked up all his newly fallen books and his backgammon set.

"Um," I said, not even sure how to explain, "I guess it was thundering? And George Bailey climbed on top of me? But I couldn't breathe, so I tried to wriggle out from under him—and then he kind of flopped over and crashed onto the coffee table."

It was such an odd story when you put all the pieces together.

But Hutch just said, "It's thundering?"

Right then, as if the universe wanted to confirm, it thundered.

George Bailey, in response, tried to dive between Hutch's legs—until Hutch was basically riding him like a cowboy. A cowboy in his Tour de France underpants.

I blinked hard. *Pull it together, Katie!*

Hutch scrambled off George Bailey's back, and then he started trying to lead him by the collar back into the bedroom. "This is what we do," Hutch explained, as he tugged. "We go in the bedroom and close all the curtains, and I turn on a white-noise machine, and then I hold him tight until the storm passes like he's a cow in a squeeze chute."

George Bailey braced against the pull.

"Does it work?" I asked.

"Not at all," Hutch said, still tugging. "But it's the best I've got."

Hutch went to the bedroom door and tried to call him. "Come on, buddy," he said. "Let's go!"

But George Bailey wasn't budging.

Hutch got a squeaky squirrel, and threw it into the bedroom for George Bailey to fetch—but nothing. Then he got a rawhide bone and held it out as a lure—also a no-go. Then he went back around to the far side and tried to shove George Bailey from behind.

All to no avail.

"Fine," Hutch said, "I'll play possum," and he walked off to the bedroom.

"Where are you going?" I called after him.

"I'm pretending to give up. Maybe he'll follow of his own accord."

George Bailey did seem interested in why Hutch was leaving the room. After a few seconds, he walked halfway to the bedroom and tilted his head. Then he looked back at me. Then he U-turned and strode toward me like some kind of big cat in a zoo and stopped when he got close.

"Go on," I said. "Hutch is waiting for you."

But in response, almost as if he'd understood my words, George Bailey stepped closer to me and gathered the loose fabric of one of my yoga pant legs in his teeth.

"Hey," I said, trying to tug the fabric back out.

But, as the nonpoisonous toads of the neighborhood could attest, those jaws made their own rules.

When George Bailey started tugging me toward the bedroom—what could I do?

I followed.

Those were my favorite yoga pants.

When we reached the room, there was Hutch—I swear to god—reclining on a double bed in his boxer briefs, arms behind his head, humming "Heart and Soul."

He saw me and sat up, like he'd never expected George Bailey to bring me with him.

Meanwhile, George Bailey had let go of my pant leg and was nudging me toward the bed with his snout.

I stopped when I reached it and looked back at him.

He blocked the door and looked at me.

"I think he wants me to stay in here," I said.

"Maybe he's gathering the pack together?"

"Does he usually do that?"

"I don't usually have"—Hutch glanced at me—"a pack."

Why did it give me a little buzz of joy to hear that?

"What should I do?" I asked.

"Why don't you sit down on the bed and see if he comes over?"

I sat. And then I patted the bed. And then George Bailey walked right over, climbed up, and lay down in the middle between us.

"Good boy," I said, standing up to leave.

But when I stood, George Bailey stood, too—right there on the mattress. His body language said, *Don't you dare.*

"Am I—not allowed to leave?" I asked Hutch.

"I'm not sure," Hutch said. Then he said, "Maybe give him a few minutes to settle?"

"Okay," I said, resting back against the headboard.

At the next clap of thunder, George Bailey raised his head and looked back and forth between the two of us, like *How could you be letting this happen?*

"He's really shaking," I said. The bed was trembling.

"I know," Hutch said, reaching around to clamp an arm against him.

"It must have been really hard for him before"—I couldn't bring myself to say *at the puppy mill*—"when it thundered."

"It must have been loud. They were in a metal structure with no windows."

I stroked George Bailey's soft head. "Monsters," I said.

Hutch nodded and then said, "You might have to wait here until he falls asleep."

I was getting that vibe, too. "The trouble is, I'm wide awake now."

"Me, too."

"Can I ask you about something, then? Since we have nothing else to do?"

"What?" Hutch asked.

"What happened between you and Cole? What's the fight about?"

Hutch shifted to meet my eyes. "He hasn't told you?"

"No."

Hutch frowned. "Huh."

"It might help me to know," I said, trying to make it sound like I wasn't just curious.

Hutch nodded, his worried frown back. Then, when he'd made a decision: "Okay, but you didn't hear it from me. If Cole finds out that you know this story, you've gotta throw Rue—not me—under the bus."

I could tell from the tilt of his eyebrow that he was mostly kidding. "Deal," I said.

"So, this was . . . a year ago. Cole was getting married."

Cole was getting married? I tried not to register surprise on my face.

Hutch went on, "His fiancée—not sure how much he's told you about Scarlett—was really aggressively flirty, you know?"

Why would Cole have told me about Scarlett?

Hutch went on. "She was that way with everybody. She posted bikini pictures online all the time—just had that vibe of someone who wanted the whole world to notice her. It creeped Rue and me out a little, but Cole loved that about her."

I wondered what it would be like to *want* to be on display.

"Anyway," Hutch said, "that's why I didn't see it coming, I guess."

"See what coming?"

"They'd been dating a few years, so I'd met her a few times—mostly just in passing. I'd been stationed in Kodiak for four years, so I didn't get down to the lower forty-eight that much."

"Okay," I said, feeling like this was a slow start.

"On the night of their rehearsal dinner, she got really drunk and grabbed the karaoke mic and made an announcement to everybody there that she . . . wanted me, instead."

"I'm sorry—*what?*"

Hutch sighed. "She said she'd fallen in love at first sight. With me. The first time we met. Seeing me again at the wedding party, she didn't think she could go through with marrying Cole. She said she couldn't spend her whole life with *the next best thing* and then she called Cole *a poor man's Hutch.*"

"Oof," I said.

"I know."

"That is harsh."

"I agree."

"Did Cole hear her say all that?"

"He was right there. Next to her. On the stage."

Another crack of thunder. George Bailey started panting.

Hutch went on. "Then she said she wanted to switch."

"Switch what? Switch *men?*"

Hutch nodded. "And then she proposed to me. Right there. From the stage. In front of everybody."

"So what you're saying is that Cole's fiancée dumped him at their rehearsal dinner and proposed to you—all in the same sentence?"

"Effectively—yeah. But she never dumped him. She just wanted to trade up."

"Then what happened?"

"Then she took a run at me. But a bunch of groomsmen tackled her and hauled her out of the room, writhing like a caught tuna and shouting, 'Hutch! Come find me later!' Then adding that she wasn't wearing panties."

"I'm guessing you did not go find her later."

Hutch nodded in confirmation. "I did not."

"I take it they didn't wind up getting married?"

"No, actually—they *did.*"

I looked over. "They *did* get married?"

Hutch nodded. "They talked that night after she sobered up—and decided to go ahead with everything."

"Must have been a heck of a talk."

"She told him that I'd *entrapped* her. That was the word she used. And somehow, after that, her no-panties karaoke became all my fault."

"But it *wasn't* your fault!"

"My brother disagrees."

"But that's bananas!"

"Yeah. He fired me as best man and went on with the wedding as planned."

Huh. I didn't know Cole was married. He didn't give off married vibes.

But then Hutch said, "It didn't last, of course. They broke up within the month. But Cole hasn't talked to me since."

"Wow."

Hutch looked over at me. "I didn't *entrap* her, by the way."

I snorted a laugh.

"What does that mean?"

I frowned. "I guess it means *of course* you didn't entrap her. I bet you've never entrapped a woman in your life."

Hutch's frown got deeper. "What does *that* mean?"

I waved my hand in his general direction. "Just the idea of you having to do that much work. It's laughable. I mean, *look* at you. I can't imagine you have to do anything at all. I bet women just leap into your arms like flying fish."

But Hutch's frown deepened. "You seem to have an outsized opinion of my appeal to women."

"I think I'm qualified to judge."

But Hutch shook his head. "Women don't *leap* into my arms."

"If you say so." I wasn't going to fight about it. "I'm just saying I agree with you. You'd never entrap a woman in the first place. But also—you'd never have to."

Hutch looked genuinely puzzled.

"I'm not saying it's your fault. *She* got drunk and grabbed that karaoke mic. I'm just saying, I get it."

Hutch looked away.

"I'm not blaming you. You can't help it. But—you do know how handsome you are, right? That can't be news."

Hutch didn't say anything. Just looked back over with those big, dark eyes.

"Hutch?" I asked. I needed a response. "Do you know you're handsome?"

"I guess I'm okay."

"*Okay?*" I demanded, like now he was just being insulting. "You're *heartbreaking.*"

Hutch shook his head like I must be joking.

I needed to make my case. "It's the eyes, I think. Those big, serious, sad eyes—so earnest. The way you look at people when you're listening. The way you pay attention. Or the nose, maybe? You have a thing called a Roman nose, did you know that? It's, like, what all the people who get nose jobs ask for. And then"—I counted off on my fingers—"there's the tallness, and the washboard stomach, and that Adam's apple for the Guinness Book. Plus, is there a pheromone for good-heartedness?" I wafted the air with my hands like I was taking in the aroma of something simmering on the stove. "Because there's something going on there. It's a lot, Hutch, is all I'm saying. It's a lot for the women of the world. Gah. We're only human."

Hutch looked down at George Bailey, who had conked out. Then, like he couldn't stop himself from asking, he said, "Is it a lot for you?"

"Of course!" I had meant it to sound declarative—just stating a scientific fact. But it came out a little softer. Wistful, even.

Hutch sat with that for a while, but I didn't take it back.

Then he looked over at me with an expression a lot like *longing.* The more he looked, the more I got this feeling that he might kiss me.

He *could* kiss me. We weren't that far apart. One upward shove with one of his powerful shoulders and one quick lean in my direction—and we'd be face-to-face. It could happen. It really might.

I hoped it would.

For a moment there, I thought I should be the captain of my own life and just make it happen, myself.

But then I chickened out.

Mostly because I still wasn't sure where, exactly, we stood. He'd been so weird yesterday—hadn't he? Or had I just been reading him wrong? Either way, I was still looking for clues to his feelings. And if he kissed me of his own volition, that would be a big one.

And then it started to look like he would do it. I started to feel like he was ever-so-slowly leaning toward me.

I held my breath.

But then, instead, he looked away. Then he said, all curt, "I think you better go back to the sofa."

Was he mad? "You do?"

"You can't say things like that to me, Katie."

"I can't?"

He brought those dark eyes back to meet mine, and he shook his head.

"You're the one who asked the question. I just answered it."

He nodded, agreeing. "I shouldn't have asked. That's why I need you to get out."

I won't pretend it didn't sting. I had just basically—in the most joking way possible—told him that I, personally, found him irresistible. I'd disguised it as some kind of anthropological statement, but I guess we both saw through that.

How could I even hope to hide something like that? It had to be obvious, right?

I mean, we were in his bed—and he was in his underwear. If you ignored the Great Dane in between us, I'm not sure how much more suggestive I could possibly have been.

But the answer to that suggestion was, apparently, a very unambiguous *Get out*.

"Of course," I said then, trying to gather my dignity back up. "I get it. No problem."

I felt a prickle in my throat like I might actually cry.

That's normal, Beanie would've said. *That's normal for a rejection.*

But it didn't feel normal.

I slid sideways, working not to tug the bedspread or do anything else that might jog George Bailey awake. I made it off the bed and then rotated to tiptoe out.

But before I made it to the door, George Bailey was already there, blocking my way.

Defeated, I walked with him back to the bed.

"Guess I'm staying," I said.

"Guess you are," Hutch said to the ceiling.

This time, as I lay back against the pillow, Hutch clicked the lights off.

And we fell asleep there, in the darkness—as alone as two people in the same bed can be.

BY MORNING, GEORGE Bailey was on top of me again.

I *felt* him before I saw him—draped over my belly as if we slept that way every night. I strategized for a minute before trying to extract myself, since my first attempt last night had gone the opposite of well.

That's when I opened my eyes—and it wasn't George Bailey.

It was Hutch.

George Bailey, for his part, wasn't even in the room anymore.

My stirring awake roused Hutch—and the second he saw me, he jerked back to the other side of the bed like a stuntman on a wire.

"What the hell?" Hutch said.

As if *I'd* been the person on top of *him*.

Maybe I was still a little irritated by his attempt to kick me out of bed last night, but I resented the implication that I was the problem here.

So I did the only dignified thing I could think of.

I got up and walked out of the room.

George Bailey was out in the living room, napping amiably, belly-up on the sofa, as though the concept of thunder didn't even exist.

I started shoving gear and equipment into my bag, breaking down my tripod and zipping lens cases. I didn't change or even brush my teeth. I just grabbed my stuff to make my getaway.

I was closing my last case when I noticed Hutch watching me from the bedroom doorway—now in jeans and a T-shirt—with his sad frown back in place.

"I'm sorry I was so . . . *all over you* just now," he said then. "I must have thought you were the dog."

Insult to injury. "I guess you must have."

"I hope you don't feel . . . upset about it."

"What—you mean, am I worried you were trying to make a move or something?"

Hutch gave a little shrug.

"No, pal. You were clearly fast asleep. And you made your total noninterest pretty clear yesterday."

"That's a good thing, though—right?"

Why the hell would that be a good thing? "If you say so," I said.

"I'm just trying to do the right thing here."

"You think mistaking me for a dog was doing the right thing?"

Hutch's jaw tightened. "Look. I didn't ask you to come over here—"

"Technically, you did."

"Only because Cole told me to."

"Do you have to do everything that Cole says?"

Hutch blinked. "Yeah. Yes, I do."

Was he truly not letting himself date anyone because Cole wasn't dating anyone? Had he just accepted all that incorrect guilt without question? "Well," I said. "I think you're doing penance for something that's not your fault."

"That's not what this is."

I shrugged, like *That's between you and Cole, I guess.* "Okay. But you told me to get out. So I'm getting out."

I hated how hurt my voice sounded. Could Hutch hear it, too?

Hutch checked the time. "I thought you stayed until ten."

It was 9:27. Close enough. "I've got everything I need."

Except for the two hundred push-ups. But even that wasn't worth staying for.

Now that I was leaving, Hutch seemed oddly dismayed about it. "Let me help you with your stuff."

"I got it," I said.

But there was no stopping him. He grabbed my remaining bags and followed me down the dock back to Rue's car. Even after everything was loaded, he was still standing there—lingering. "Thank you," he said then, squinting into the sun. And then, as if we would never see each other again, he said, "I had a weirdly great time yesterday."

I wasn't ready to get nostalgic about *our time together before he rejected me.* "Yeah, well," I said.

"See you at work, then," he said next, stepping back.

But I didn't want to go to work. And it suddenly occurred to me that I didn't have to. I could take a mental health day, right? *I* wasn't in the military, after all. Nobody would know—or care—if I spent a day in bed, eating bad food and watching bad TV.

"I'm pretty sure," I said, "that I'll be skipping work today."

Seventeen

"I'M TAKING A personal day," I told Beanie when I video-called her later.

"Brilliant," Beanie said, when I told her why. "Reclaim your power."

I wasn't sure eating Lindor chocolates for breakfast and binge-watching HGTV was reclaiming my power, exactly. But it would do for now.

Beanie, for the record, was appalled by Hutch kicking me out of bed. "He's given you *yes* after *yes* after *yes*—and now suddenly it's a *no?*"

"Exactly," I said.

"So much for heroes," Beanie said.

"I mean," I said, now feeling an urge to defend him, "he did do the twenty-four hours. Even though he didn't want to."

"But he did it for his brother, not you."

"And he did dive in and save me when his dog knocked me overboard."

"Big whoop. That's his literal job."

"And he sneaked me snacks on the helicopter so I wouldn't barf."

At that, Beanie brought the phone close to her face to stare me down. "Katie," she said, "raise your bar."

Before we hung up, she made me add to the beauty list.

"I don't want to today," I said.

"That's exactly why you have to."

"Can't I take a day off?"

"No," Beanie said. "It's more important than ever."

I frowned, looking for another excuse.

But then Beanie said, "This dude rejected you. So you have to un-reject yourself."

"Fine," I said.

"And don't do anything weird this time. No armpits, or *molars*, or whatever. Pick something normal."

Something normal.

I studied myself in the phone. Finally, I declared: "Mouth."

"Mouth!" Beanie said, throwing up her arms in victory. "Yes! I've been *waiting* for *mouth*!"

I knew the drill. Now I had to tell her why. "It's plump and kind of a nice heart shape. It's a great color—a good shade of pink, even without lipstick." Then, in defiance of whatever Hutch might think, I added: "It's kissable."

"It's a million percent kissable!" Beanie shrieked. "Holy cow—this is personal growth for the hall of fame!"

"*Is* there a personal growth hall of fame?" I asked, as I walked over to the bathroom mirror to double-check all the assessments I'd just made about my mouth.

Yes. Correct. Those were objectively kissable lips.

Infinitely kissable, dammit.

It really was the most incredible realization—and I felt it all the way from my brain down to my heart. I didn't need *a rescue swimmer* to think I was beautiful.

I could do that for myself.

It was such a life-changing thought.

That longing to be *looked at lovingly*? That longing to be lovable . . .

that's really also so much about wanting to be valued, and seen, and connected, and safe, and just deeply, fundamentally *okay*?

Maybe we didn't have to outsource that.

Maybe we could fill that longing for ourselves.

And I'm not saying we don't need other people, or that we should spend our lives alone.

I just suddenly understood in a whole new, sun-breaking-through-the-clouds way that even if we do eternally need and long and want to be seen . . . maybe the most important eyes doing the looking are our own.

"Beanie," I said. "I think my whole understanding of how human life works just shifted."

"About time," Beanie said.

I explained my epiphany while Beanie nodded at me like she was epically impressed. "This is so much better than elbows—or whatever dumbass thing I thought you were going to say."

"I guess I needed a breakthrough today."

"You sure as hell did," Beanie said.

This culture-of-appreciation thing was working. "I feel like the Gottmans would be proud," I said.

"Wouldn't they?"

Now my mind was racing. "Is this why I stayed with Lucas for so long? Because I thought I needed him to do this for me? Because I didn't know I could do it for myself?"

"One hundred percent."

"Beanie, you're a genius," I said.

"I totally am," Beanie said. "And you're a lot less of a dummy than you used to be."

I WAS STILL glowing from all the revelations when Rue knocked at my door not long before dinner.

"Hi, sweetheart," she said, when I opened it. "Did Hutch just tell me you're sick?"

"I'm not sick," I said. "I'm just taking a personal day."

"Wonderful," Rue said. Then she held out another shopping bag from Vitamin Sea. "I've brought you something."

I took the bag.

"It's a sundress," she said, "but there's a choice. Romance red, or funeral black."

I pulled them out, and held them both up, and let the fabric tumble down.

"Pick one, and wear it to dinner," Rue said. "It's Ginger's birthday."

And then, in honor of my new epiphany, I said, "Red." As if there had never been a question. I might not be having a romance with Hutch. But nobody could stop me from having one with myself.

"I'm so glad you said that," Rue said, kissing her fingers and then touching my cheek.

I hadn't planned on going to dinner tonight, to be honest. I had planned on giving myself the gift of not having to see Hutch.

But now I'd discovered a hidden well of inner strength.

"Hutch will be there," Rue added, thinking that would be an inducement.

I let that sit.

Then Rue said, "Or I assume he will be, at least. He only used to come to dinner once a week before you showed up, but now it's pretty much every night."

"He only used to come to dinner once a week?"

"It seemed frequent at the time," Rue said.

"But why so often now?"

Rue looked at me through her red glasses. "I think things became more fun for him recently. For reasons no one on earth could start to guess."

She gave me a wink.

Had I been fun for Hutch?

I wasn't sure.

But it didn't matter.

Hutch or no Hutch . . . Rue was throwing a birthday party for her friend. And my new red dress, my recalibrated worldview, and my kiss-able mouth would all be in attendance.

HUTCH DID SHOW up, in the end.

And the red sundress looked even better on.

If I held my arms out to the sides and lifted the hem, it made a full semicircle from the waist. Combine clothing that voluminous with a hearty island breeze, and add some string lights, an outdoor party, and some yacht rock on the speaker system . . . and you've got some fluttery magic. I walked out of my cottage and toward the party doing some-thing I'd never done in my life: admiring myself.

Was every aspect of me Photoshop perfect?

Irrelevant.

The addition of my kissable lips to my growing collection of lovable visuals had tipped the scales.

I'm no scientist. I don't know why it worked.

But I knew this much: it was enough.

I looked up and saw Hutch stepping in through the picket-fence gate, dressed up in a collared shirt in Ginger's honor and carrying a birthday bouquet for her.

I don't know what he saw in that moment—or what he felt.

But I can tell you that we both held still as we locked eyes—his bou-quet forgotten in his hand and my red dress billowing in the wind—for much longer than people who don't notice each other ever would.

Before we'd broken the stare, the drums for "Copacabana" started up on the speaker system, and Rue raised her arms to The Gals in a round-'em-up gesture and said, "Okay, ladies! You know what to do."

Apparently, they did know what to do. The whole group started as-sembling itself into a conga line, and Nadine and Benita came to pull us in.

"What is happening?" I asked Hutch, as he lined up behind me.

"It's a rule around here," he said. "Whenever 'Copacabana' plays, you have to stop what you're doing and conga."

"I don't know how to conga," I protested, even as I placed my hands on Benita's waist in front of me.

"It's easy," Hutch said, as he settled his hands onto my hips.

"You all just—*do* this?" I asked.

"Resistance is futile," Hutch answered.

I guess it really was.

Were Hutch and I still fighting at this point?

I mean, can you really fight when Barry Manilow is playing?

I felt the warmth of Hutch's hands through the sundress fabric, and I moved in time with the group, and the bulb lights shone overhead, and the breeze caressed us all . . . and I felt myself just giving in to it all—letting go.

What did that headline say about Lucas Banks's ex-fiancée?

She has really let herself go.

Maybe that was right.

And maybe that was a good thing.

The four minutes of that song flew by in a blur of fabric and touch and the warm pressure of Hutch's palms, and as the song wound down and the line broke apart, Hutch slid his hand over to grab mine and then spun me around for a minute. The swells of the wind, the waving fabric, the steadiness of his grip . . . it all felt surreal, and alive, and like I was part of something larger than myself.

Even after I stopped spinning, I was still spinning—you know?

And then The Gals started heckling Hutch to dip me, and never one to disappoint them, he did it . . . and just when I was thinking that this night could not possibly be more surprising, at the lowest point of the dip, with Hutch above me as I leaned back to stretch my neck, just in the seconds of silence between when that song ended and the next one started, a voice called out from across the yard, "Hey! Get your hands off my girlfriend!"

Hutch and I turned at the sound to look over, mid-dip.

And it was Cole.

Eighteen

HUTCH DID *NOT* drop me, right then, at the sound of Cole's voice.

I'm glad to report.

But he did snap me up into a standing position and then push himself back—hot-potato style. And then he stared at his brother like he'd never seen him before, as Rue walked over to give Cole a hug.

"What a fantastic surprise!" Rue sang out, not surprised at all. Cole hugged her tight enough to lift her feet off the ground.

The Gals also came in for hugs, but Hutch and I both just stood there, catching our breath. I tried to classify the frown that now overtook Hutch's face, but this one was new.

Next, the ladies parted, and Cole came through toward Hutch, holding out his hand.

"Hutch," he said, making his voice lower than normal.

"Cole," Hutch said back, taking his hand like they were colleagues at the UN.

"I see you've met my girlfriend," Cole said then.

I looked around. Did Cole have a girlfriend?

"You made sure of that, didn't you?" Hutch said, seeming to know who he meant.

It took me far longer than it should have to realize that Cole—along with everyone else—was looking at me.

I held very still to contain my rising panic as Cole walked around to me and placed his arm—*unfathomably*—around my waist.

What in the ever-loving hell was going on?

"Is Katie your girlfriend?" Ginger asked Cole, seeming delighted. "We've all been trying to set her up with Hutch!"

I stayed frozen in disbelief as Cole nodded, patted me on the hip, shifted into distorted slow motion, and said, "She sure is."

Okay. Time to shut this down. "Cole—" I started, trying to take reality back.

But he interrupted by pointing at Hutch, and saying, in a pretend-scolding tone, "So, hands off the lady, bro."

The whole group gave Cole a generous courtesy laugh.

The whole group, that is, except for Hutch.

Then Cole turned to me. "Hey, babe," he said, pulling me into a tight, full-body, overly long hug.

I let it happen so that I could keep a tense smile on my face, hover near his ear, and whisper through my teeth, "What the hell are you doing?"

I assume his smile was similar as he whispered back, "We've got an emergency right now, so just go with it."

"I don't have an emergency. And I'm not going with anything."

"Just trust me, okay?" Cole said. "Seriously."

"I don't trust you. And I am *not* your girlfriend."

"I know that. I'll explain everything later."

"Explain it right now," I demanded.

But next, before I could reply, I heard a woman's voice behind me. "Is this her?" Then the voice said, "You're adorable together."

I stepped away from Cole and turned to see . . . Sullivan.

Our boss, Sullivan. The she-wolf.

Not back in Texas, in the office, in businesswear. But here, in the keys, wearing a sarong so bright and floral, she could've shoplifted it right out of Vitamin Sea.

All I could do was look back and forth between Cole and . . . Sullivan.

Sullivan, who wanted to fire me.

Sullivan. Standing here at the Starlite.

Cole seized my moment of confusion to take back the narrative.

He grabbed a random sangria glass off a nearby table and held it up. "It's so great to be back," Cole announced—his voice weirdly loud, like he was playing a part on a stage.

At the announcement, the party guests quieted and gave him their attention.

"I'm so happy," Cole said next, "to see my beautiful aunt Rue and my heroic big brother, Hutch."

Okay—that *heroic* sounded sarcastic, but the group lifted their drinks in support.

He was hijacking Ginger's birthday party, by the way! Not cool! But Ginger didn't seem to mind.

She clapped and cheered with the crowd.

Cole kept grandstanding. "And happy birthday to Ginger—and anyone else who's had a birthday lately."

The group kept clapping, like the world hadn't just gone sideways.

I took the chance to step away from Cole and back into the crowd.

Safety in numbers, right?

I glanced over at Hutch, the only other person watching Cole like I was.

Next, Cole just turned toward Sullivan and raised his glass. "You all may know that the company I work for has been doing a promo video for the US Coast Guard starring the one and only Hutch Hutcheson, and I'm so excited to introduce you to the lady who made it all possible, our boss, Karen Sullivan."

Sullivan stepped up next to Cole, and the group went ahead and clapped for her, too.

I looked around. What was going on?

"So before our time together goes any further . . ." Cole went on, turning toward the place next to him where I'd been standing—only to realize I wasn't there. Then he searched the faces until he spotted me. "Katie, could you come up here?"

Oh, shit. Whatever this was, it was bad.

I shook my head, stepping farther back.

"Come on," Cole said, making a *get on over here* gesture with his arm.

I shook again. "I'm fine right here."

Now Cole went overly playful to disguise what he must've thought was a commanding order. "Katie," he said, all cutesy, "get up here."

I wasn't sure what he was planning to do. But I *was* sure I didn't want to find out.

I was done following his lead.

Whatever game this was, I wasn't playing.

The whole crowd was waiting for me to give in, aw-shucks style, and walk up to join them.

But instead, I gave one last headshake. And then I peeled away from the crowd and marched back toward my cottage.

I heard Cole's voice behind me—"Katie? Katie!"—as the crowd shifted into a perplexed murmur. Then I heard him ad-libbing, "Don't be mad, honey!," as if we were having some kind of lovers' quarrel.

Next, feet that could only be Cole's thumped up behind me, and then there he was, falling into step, and trying to put his arm over my shoulder.

"Get off me," I said, sidestepping away.

We were far enough away that they couldn't hear us over the music, but Cole dropped his voice anyway. "What are you doing? I told you to trust me!"

"Yeah—that's not happening," I said, still moving toward my cottage.

Cole tugged at my shirt. "Just talk to me. Just let me explain."

So I stopped and turned. "Okay," I said. "Explain."

But then, instead of explaining, Cole looked back toward the party. "Do you think he can read lips?"

I turned to look. *He* was clearly Hutch. Cole was staring at him, and Hutch was staring at Cole right back.

Next to Hutch, by the way, was Sullivan. Chatting with him the way you might heckle a stony-faced guard in front of a palace.

"Cole!" I said, like *Focus!* "What's going on?"

"Fine," Cole said, turning back. "The other day on the phone, I told Hutch we were dating."

"What?!"

"I had to."

"You told him we were— *Why?!*"

"It worked, didn't it?"

I was so lost. "What worked?" I asked.

"It got him to do the 'Day in the Life' with you."

"But I'd already told you that wasn't happening. I texted you!"

"He said no to you," Cole said, "but I knew I could get him to say yes to me."

"But it was already settled!"

"He owes me," Cole said. "He knows that."

"He knows that *you think that*," I corrected.

Cole shrugged. "I had a nuclear option, and I took it. You should be thanking me."

"You mean—because of what happened at your wedding?"

"He told you about that?"

"So you thought if you told Hutch I was special to you, he'd do anything for me because he'll do anything for you?"

Cole shrugged. "Pretty much. And I was right."

"But . . ." Now it all started clicking into place. Hutch's change of heart about the video—and about me. How he went from kissing me like mad one night to barely tolerating me the next day. How strangely standoffish he became. His kicking me out of bed. "But—you *lied to him*. That's a big lie, Cole!"

"Look, you told him about Sullivan, and he still said no. We *needed* a big lie."

"I never told him about Sullivan."

"You never told him about Sullivan?"

I shook my head.

"Why not?"

"Because he told me why he doesn't want to be famous."

Cole wasn't expecting that. "He did?"

"Yes. And I was respecting his wishes."

"Why doesn't he want to be famous?"

"You don't know?"

He clearly didn't. "I just want to see if your answer and my answer are the same."

I sighed. How much to tell Cole? "Well," I finally said, "he has his reasons."

"You're not going to tell me?"

"Go ask him yourself."

"I'm not asking that guy *shit*."

"Look," I said. "Hutch is . . ." Then I tried, "Hutch isn't . . ."

"What?" Cole demanded.

"He's not someone you can just go around lying to for no reason."

"Oh, I had a reason."

"What—revenge?"

"Why not?"

"He's a person, Cole! He's your brother—and he loves you."

"You've been here three weeks. Don't act like you know everything."

But I was shaking my head. "I'm not doing this. You need to tell him the truth."

"What are you talking about? You barely know this guy!" But then Cole's face shifted. "Wait—do you have a thing for my brother? Did you come down here and fall for him?"

I mean . . . I did. I had.

But I wasn't telling Cole that.

I covered with: "What kind of question is that?"

But I guess I didn't cover very well. "Oh, my god," Cole said, tilting his head back toward the heavens. "You did. Now he's stolen two girls from me."

"I am not yours to steal."

"He doesn't know that."

The whole thing was just so astonishing. How had we gotten here? "This is a mess, Cole," I said. "What on earth were you thinking?"

"I was trying to help you!"

"You were trying to help yourself."

"Okay, that's true. It started that way. I didn't want to have to spend months making a video about what a hero my brother is. But I have also genuinely been trying to help you not get fired."

"Why?"

"Hutch isn't the only person in this family who can rescue people."

"Oh, *god.* You're competing with him?"

"Who cares? You benefit no matter what."

"I'm not sure this is *benefitting.*"

"Are you saying you want to get fired?"

"No! I just want to do whatever non-liars do when things don't go their way."

"Then you'll have to kiss that 'Day in the Life' goodbye."

"I wasn't going to make it, anyway."

That got Cole's attention. "You don't want to keep your job?"

"Not by selling out Hutch."

Cole thought about that. "Well, it's too late now, anyway."

"What does that mean—*it's too late*?"

"I can't tell the truth now, anyway. Even if I wanted to."

"Why not?"

Cole glanced back toward the party. "Because I also told Sullivan we were dating."

I couldn't have heard that right. "You told—?! Sullivan?!"

"That's why she's here."

I put my hand to my forehead.

"It was an accident. I panicked. I saw your name on the termination list in her office, and, you know—I'd already said it to Hutch, so it was just right there in my head."

"You're out of control."

"I don't normally lie. It all just—snowballed."

"You told *Sullivan* we were dating? Sullivan?" It made no sense. "Why?"

"It was the only thing I could think of."

"How would that even help?"

Cole shook his head, like he knew he'd already lost, then ventured, "Because I wouldn't be dating you if you were bad at your job?"

I sighed.

"But then it got worse," Cole said. "Because she didn't believe me. So I had to amp it up."

"No," I said, trying to rewrite history, "you didn't have to amp it up."

"And so I told her I was coming to Key West this weekend to propose to you."

I squeezed my eyes closed. "No, no, no."

"Which was true, by the way. I really was coming here this weekend. Not to propose—but still."

Now I was just shaking my head, like *This can't be happening.*

"But guess what?" Cole said. "Sullivan said, 'Great. I'll come with you.' She said she could call it a business trip and write it off. She knows a guy with a private jet. She flew me here for free. That's why I'm a little tipsy," he added, shrugging. "Open bar."

My mind searched for a question that could make things make sense. But it was starting to look like no question like that existed.

Cole went on. "Sullivan had a few drinks on the flight, too, and told me she wants to meet Hutch."

I shook my head, refusing to take his meaning.

"You know. *Meet* him?"

I looked over again. Sullivan was trying to show Hutch her necklace. Holding it toward him and leaning forward. But Hutch's eyes were still on Cole and me.

I closed my eyes. "You brought Sullivan here for a booty call?"

But Cole lifted his hands like he was innocent. "She brought herself."

I squeezed my eyes closed.

"Where's your feminist solidarity?" Cole said next, taking a stab at a positive spin. "She's had a rough year. Maybe she deserves a little Marvin Gaye–style healing. This could be the answer to everything. *This* could be what saves your job. No video necessary!"

But I just met his eyes and shook my head. "How is it possible that you've made *every single thing* worse?"

Cole shrugged, like he didn't know, either. "Once I started lying, I didn't know how to stop."

"Just—stop!"

"But then everything falls apart."

"So it falls apart. That's got to be better than whatever this is."

"You want me to just come clean? About everything?"

"Yeah," I said, like *Duh*.

"I can't."

"Why not?"

"For lots of reasons. For reasons stacked on top of other reasons."

"Tell me the reasons," I demanded.

"If I tell the truth now, one: you will get fired. And I don't want you to get fired. And, two: I will get fired. And I don't want to get fired, either."

"Maybe she won't fire you. Maybe she'll—"

"What? Let it go? Some douchey manager at her company lied to her face multiple times in cahoots with an underling, and she just doesn't care?"

"We were *never* in cahoots."

"She won't just fire me, by the way. She'll fire me *with extreme prejudice*. And then she'll blackball me with every future employer. I won't just have to change jobs. I'll have to change *industries*."

"This seems extreme."

"And she'll do the exact same thing to you."

"To *me*? I didn't do anything!"

"But that's not the worst of it."

"How is that not the worst of it?"

"The worst of it has nothing to do with Sullivan. And it's got nothing to do with our jobs. The worst of it is the real reason I'm here."

I sighed, like *Seriously?* Then I demanded: "Which is?"

"It's not because I want to be, that's for damn sure. It's because *Rue told me to be.*"

Rue told him to be? "What's going on, Cole?"

But here Cole's tone shifted. He looked away for a second. "So . . ." he said, his voice quieting. "Nobody really knows about this yet, except for me, and now you . . . so don't talk about it with anyone else, okay?"

This was a lot of buildup. "Okay," I said.

"Rue . . ." Cole said then, looking down at the grass and then rubbing the back of his neck as he hesitated to say the words, "is sick."

My first reaction was to demand that he *take that back*. How dare he say that about Rue?

"Of all the lies you've told—" I started.

"You think I'm *lying*? About Rue?"

"You've been lying all night, so it's definitely on-brand."

"I would never lie about this."

Okay, that felt true enough.

I looked over at the party across the way. Rue was relaxing in a chair near the pool, fruity drink in hand, smiling in that purposeful way she had—determined to enjoy every minute. She didn't seem sick. But Rue was also the kind of person who wouldn't seem sick.

I turned back to ask, "What's she sick with?," and saw that Cole was watching her, too.

"Something that has no cure."

"Just say it, Cole," I said.

Cole said, "It's what they call a long-term terminal illness."

"What does that mean?"

Cole looked down, and then he said, "It means she has heart failure."

I wanted to argue with him. But something about his expression stopped me.

"She was having chest pains and shortness of breath," Cole went on.

"She was worried it was lung cancer because she used to smoke back in the seventies, so she insists that run-of-the-mill heart failure is an improvement. Rue said it will be *the thing that gets her*—but not right away. She's convinced that she can make it another ten years."

"What do the doctors say?"

"They love her optimism."

I sat with this idea for a moment, giving it the benefit of the doubt. Then I said, "Okay, so, if you're not lying—*if*—why would Rue being sick mean that I have to go along with all this?"

Cole nodded as he answered. "Because Friday is the anniversary."

"The anniversary of what?"

"The anniversary," Cole explained, "of the accident."

OF THE CAR accident.

Cole studied me to see if I got it. Then he nodded. "It's a big day in our family. And every year, no matter where we are or what we're doing, the three of us find a way to spend it together. We hand out flowers to strangers in honor of our mom, and then we eat an Italian dinner in honor of Rue's husband, and then at the end, we give our waiter a hundred-dollar tip, in honor of our dad. And all through dinner, we tell stories about them, and remember them, and let ourselves miss them."

"That's actually lovely."

Cole nodded. "Except after Hutch stole my fiancée—"

"He did *not* steal your fiancée—"

"—I stayed away. Last year, I didn't go. And I wasn't planning to come this year, either—until Rue called and told me about her diagnosis. She declared she wasn't putting up with any nonsense this year. *It's time to stop wasting time*, she said." Cole shrugged. "So here I am."

"You're here because Rue wanted you to come."

Cole nodded. "She just wants to spend some good time together. And she wants to be together on the anniversary like we should be. And she wants me to, and I'm quoting here, *quit being an ass and get over it* about my fiancée. She wants Hutch and me to make up. She called it her dying wish."

That did sound like Rue.

I said, "Sounds like a good plan."

"I don't disagree," Cole said. "But if we come clean about us now—"

"There is no *us*!" I protested.

"If we tell the truth—"

"If *you* tell the truth," I corrected. "I am *not* a part of this."

"The point is," Cole said, "if I tell Hutch that I lied to him about you, he's going to beat the hell out of me. I mean it. He might really put me in the hospital."

I studied Cole's face.

"All Rue wants," Cole said, "is for us to get along for one night. To have a good time together on a very bad day. But I guarantee: if Hutch finds out I messed with him, she will not get that wish."

"Hutch isn't going to put you in the hospital," I said, like *Come on*.

"You think you know him better than I do?"

"All I know is, you're the biggest liar I've ever seen. Even just now, when you were lying to the whole group about a dating situation"— I gestured between the two of us—"that does not *in any way* exist, you seemed to be enjoying yourself. A lot."

Cole nodded solemnly. "This situation does have a few personal upsides for me."

"Like?"

"Like not having to show up tonight divorced and sad with nothing good in my life. You get that, right? You've been jilted. I got jilted *for my brother*."

I wasn't sure what to say to that.

"You want the truth? Here's the truth: I did enjoy that moment earlier. I did enjoy taking you away from Hutch like that. I did enjoy a little taste of revenge. I did want to win, for once. Even if it's fake. Even if it's temporary. And even if he will—definitely—eventually pummel me for it. For a moment there, it felt good. That's not a lie."

I looked back toward the party.

The music was still playing, and Hutch was still watching us like a sniper. Sullivan was pulling at his arms like she was trying to get him to dance. And Rue and The Gals were watching Sullivan strike out.

There was no way any of this was going to end well.

Cole, glancing that way, too, sighed. "You have no idea how hard it is to be related to Hutch."

"How is it hard?" I said. "He's perfect."

"Exactly. He's perfect."

I thought about Rue, and how fond of her I'd become in such a short time—how full of life and casual wisdom she was. The way she'd taken me on as a project. This sweet little cottagey beachside community she'd made. Her warm and colorful presence in the world.

"She wants me to make up with Hutch," Cole said, "and I will absolutely do that. But it's *not* going to happen if you tell him the truth right now. Do you want to take the one thing a sick old lady wants away from her?"

I sighed. Then I said, "So you're telling me for the sake of Rue— *who I love*—I have to go along with this ridiculous, absurd, insulting lie—*that I hate*?"

"Just until Friday," Cole said, like that wasn't *forever.* "Three days. Then I'll fly home and tell Sullivan we broke up. And then you can tell Hutch all the truths you want. Hang on until Friday, and we all might escape unscathed."

I sighed, and I gave my brain a minute to search for some—any— other idea.

Me getting fired—and blackballed—for something I had nothing to do with? I'd take that to tell Hutch the truth right now. Cole getting fired and blackballed—and then pummeled by his brother? Fine. Hell, he deserved it, anyway.

Where it all broke down was Rue. Lovely Rue, and all she'd lost, and all she'd done for everybody, and all she was facing now. I'd never had to make a decision like this. I didn't know how to begin to think it through. Only one thing in this churning, relentless family mess seemed clear: protect Rue at all costs.

Could I delay the truth for three days to keep from breaking Rue's heart?

For Rue, I could.

I let out a long, uncertain sigh.

"Just until Friday," I said, pointing at Cole. "I will not contradict you *until Friday*. But that's the full extent of what I'm willing to do. I'm not participating in this, or endorsing it, or amplifying it. I'm just letting it stand—temporarily. We're not partners, and we're not playing house. Do not touch me, ogle me, or—god forbid—*propose to me*. If I see you bend either of your knees for any reason, I will murder you in your sleep."

Nineteen

SO. TO SUM up: in an effort to both save my job for me and get revenge on his objectively cooler older brother, my coworker had lied to everyone and forced me into a make-believe relationship with him without my knowledge or consent.

And then he showed up here—and brought our boss with him.

Our lonely, abandoned boss with lots to work through—and some pretty clear-as-day designs on Hutch.

I'm going to be honest and say that I had been thinking—at least up until his brother messed everything up—that Hutch liked me. The kissing, obviously, seemed like a clear giveaway, if nothing else. Not to mention how mad he'd gotten when the internet was mean to me. And the fact that he was the first person in history, including me, to notice the real color of my eyes.

I don't suffer from overconfidence, but my best read on the situation had been that we liked each other. Mutually. In a normal situation, if Cole hadn't intervened like an absolute lunatic, we might have gone on some dates.

Instead, I was somehow in a situation where I had to watch Hutch genuinely detesting me while my boss—my boss!—tried to put the moves on him.

And I'll tell you something else. Sullivan might have been a full ten years older than both of us, but she was a highly put-together, very well-dressed woman with great style.

She was hot.

Point being: *Sullivan* wasn't afraid of bathing suits.

Rue, of course, had rented her a room at the Starlite, and Sullivan set out to enjoy her work trip/vacation with a vengeance, lounging by the pool in a string bikini and straw hat like a Bain de Soleil model and drinking nonstop tropical cocktails.

She wanted to fire me and seduce Hutch, so we were technically enemies, for sure.

But I had to admit: she looked fabulous.

And as weird as the situation had suddenly become, I did not really think that a guy like Hutch was going to—out of nowhere—switch types from someone like me to someone like Sullivan.

But the truth is, there was no question that Hutch was absolutely seething. About everything. And a little revenge sex might not be totally out of the question for him, either.

I guess The Gals felt the same way. I'm not sure any of them fully bought Cole's story. And so—bless them, bless them—over the next three days, rather than letting Sullivan have free rein to stalk Hutch however she liked, The Gals befriended her.

Aggressively.

And it worked. Strength in numbers. The four of them surrounded her and pummeled her with gifts from Vitamin Sea, and signed her up for snorkeling lessons with their *sexy friend Mario*, and drove her to Big Pine Key for shopping and lunch, and plied her with fruity drinks—and basically did everything they could to keep Sullivan far away from whatever nonsense was going down with Cole and Hutch and me.

None of them has ever admitted it to this day, but I'm convinced they were running interference for me. And it worked almost too well. Sullivan got so sunburned while snorkeling that she didn't leave her cottage for a full twenty-four hours. The Gals brought her sandwiches and ice cream, and then hung around in her cottage, keeping her company.

God bless The Gals, Sullivan even missed dinner by the pool the first two of the three nights she was in town.

Not that *my boss not being there* made my situation better.

It just—maybe—kept it from being worse.

COLE DID NOT remember to *never touch me*, by the way.

He went the other direction, in fact, finding all kinds of ways to break my rules, from touching my arm, to squeezing my shoulders, to patting my knee.

When I glared at him, he'd shrug like he was in character.

Which made for a special agony when Hutch came back the next night for dinner. And—after Rue implored him to come back again—the night after that, too.

At those dinners, Hutch sat stiff and tense, averting his eyes from everything, even while The Gals buzzed around in their caftans and teased me and Cole for being what Ginger kept calling *an unlikely couple*.

Meaning, of course, that we had absolutely no chemistry with each other whatsoever.

Props to Ginger. Spot-on.

"But sometimes unlikely couples are the best ones," Benita said.

Nadine agreed: "And sometimes the couples that seem the happiest are secretly miserable."

Hutch looked like he knew a little something about being secretly miserable.

"What do you think, Hutch?" Ginger asked.

Hutch was jaw-grinding his food with an expression like he was eating grass. "What do I think about what?" he asked.

"About Cole and Katie—as a couple?"

For the first time all night, Hutch lifted his eyes and looked at me.

Then he shifted his gaze to Cole. "I hope he's good to her," Hutch said, at last.

I wanted to correct him so badly. But what would I even say? Of course he couldn't stand the sight of me right now. He thought—and now this really hit me—that all this time I'd been both dating his brother and also throwing myself at him.

And I just had to let him think that.

Until Friday. Just until Friday. One more day.

"We don't have to talk about this," I said.

But the ladies *wanted* to talk about it. In fact, this was pretty much all they wanted to talk about. We were like their own personal reality show—right here at the Starlite. A lifetime of life and love and struggle had tuned their antennas so fine that they sensed all was not as it seemed. They were mystery readers, turning pages late into the night, desperate to figure out the answer. This was the topic for all of dinner—and well after.

"In the past, for example," Ginger said then, "Cole has always dated Kewpie doll types of girls."

I frowned at Cole, like *Seriously?*

Cole shrugged.

"But I'm not quite sure what Hutch's type is," Ginger went on. "What's your type, Hutch?" she asked, turning his way and resting her chin on her hand.

Hutch looked around the table. "I don't know," he said then. "Just . . . anybody."

"*Anybody?*" Benita said. "That's your type?"

Hutch looked down at his empty plate. "I'll know her when I see her, I guess."

Cole volunteered: "Pretty sure his type is the Barbarella on the pinball machine at the Rum Shack."

Hutch looked unamused. "She's your type, too."

"I can't believe that place hasn't been shut down," Cole said, clearly glad to have remembered it. "We should go play pinball. Like old times."

"Wonderful idea," Rue said, her eyes bright, clearly loving the notion of the brothers hanging out.

Hutch shook his head.

"Let's go," Cole said. He stood, and then he reached out his hand toward me. "Come on."

I hesitated. My interest in going to a seedy bar to play a Barbarella pinball game—or doing anything unrequired with Cole—was *zero*.

But what would a girlfriend do?

She'd go. She'd *want* to go.

I stood up.

"That place is pretty squalid," Hutch said, giving me an almost-imperceptible headshake.

But Rue wanted this to happen. "She'll be fine! Cole will look after her."

From Hutch's face, I could see that he was suppressing a response. Probably something like, *But Cole can barely look after himself.*

Instead, Hutch stood up.

"You're coming, too?" Cole said.

Hutch rested his dark, miserable eyes on me for less than a second before looking away. Then he said, "I guess I am."

AT THE BAR, which was indeed squalid, it was pretty clear that Cole and Rue had baited Hutch into going. And it was also clear that I was the bait.

Cole tried to steer us toward Barbarella—but she'd been replaced with Dolly Parton in her cowgirl outfit from *9 to 5*.

"Okay, Hutch," Cole said. "Let's have a pinball contest."

"No, thanks," Hutch said back.

"It's *Dolly Parton*," Cole cajoled.

"I'm good."

"Come on, man. Loser buys all the drinks."

"I don't drink," Hutch said.

Cole already knew that. But he said, "Still?"

Hutch glanced at me. "Still," he said.

"I think you need to take a break from that," Cole said.

Hutch looked away.

"You're not an alcoholic," Cole went on. "It's not that you *can't* drink. You just don't drink."

"That's right," Hutch said.

"But you're so serious. All the time," Cole protested. "Don't you want to loosen up now and then?"

Hutch looked back and forth between the two of us, and then sat down at a table. "Not tonight, I don't."

I sat, too, trying to express solidarity.

But then Cole pulled his chair right next to mine and leaned up against me, draping an arm over my shoulder.

As soon as it happened, Hutch stood back up. "Let's play pinball," he said.

"Great," Cole said. "Dolly Parton for the win."

After that, Cole lost pinball game after pinball game—every single one—progressively playing worse and worse as he drank more and more beer. Also getting louder and ruder.

"What are you doing?" I said to Cole, after a while. "Nobody's drinking but you."

"I just want to have some fun tonight." Cole looked over at Hutch. "You remember *fun*?"

Nothing about this seemed fun to me. Or to Hutch, from the look of things.

"Leave him alone, Cole," I said.

"Afraid you might say things you'll regret?" Cole challenged Hutch.

Hutch met my eyes. "Always."

When we finally sat back down at our table, Cole, already half a sheet to the wind, said, "Let's have a drinking contest."

Hutch just shook his head at him.

"I just lost six straight games of pinball," Cole said. "I need a win."

"Why do you want to have a drinking contest with a guy who doesn't drink?" I asked.

"Because that way I can beat him," Cole said—and then burped.

"I'm not doing a drinking contest with you, Cole," Hutch said.

"Afraid I'll win?"

"You'll definitely win," Hutch said. "Let's just pretend that already happened."

But Cole shook his head. "Come on," he said.

Hutch, clearly trying to shut this down, said, "Why don't you drink for both of us?"

But that didn't shut anything down. Instead, Cole stood up. He turned toward the other tables in the bar. "Who wants to have a drinking contest with me?"

The other customers—all of them men—turned toward Cole. He had their attention.

"My brother doesn't want to drink with me," Cole went on. "Can I get a taker?"

Nobody volunteered.

That's when Cole decided to up the ante. "The winner," he declared then, gesturing at me like *Behold!*, "gets a kiss from my girlfriend."

What?!

I stood up—as did Hutch.

"Cole!" I hissed.

But now he was getting some interest.

I waved my hand at the handful of dudes rising off their chairs. "He's kidding!" I called. I wanted to add, *I'm not even his girlfriend*—but, of course, I couldn't.

"I'm not kidding," Cole said. "Who wants her?"

The dudes started closing in on us with notable zombie apocalypse energy.

In response, Hutch stepped between them and me, and—I think—flexed all his shoulder muscles.

"Cole!" I said. "This isn't funny!"

"It's a little funny," Cole said.

"Shut this down," I said. "You can't offer me to a bar full of drunk men!"

"I'm not offering you. They're going to try to win you, fair and square. Every contest needs a prize."

"I'm not a prize," I said, glaring at him.

"I think, actually, you are," Cole said, looking over at Hutch.

And then I got it. This was all to get Hutch motivated. He was using Hutch's good-heartedness against him. Again.

"You don't get to decide who kisses me and who doesn't," I said, on principle, even as, if I'm totally honest, I felt a little flicker in my chest at the idea of Hutch stepping in. Hutch was protecting me. That kind of thing didn't exactly happen every day.

"So?" Cole said to the room then—watching Hutch. "Who's it going to be?"

Hutch turned to Cole, like he knew exactly what he was up to.

It was so weird to now be on Cole's side. But can you blame me? *Come on, Hutch.*

Hutch turned back to the room. "Please take your seats, gentlemen. Nobody's drinking against my brother but me."

I held my breath. Hutch was doing this? *What if he won?* What if he crushed the contest, and, *darn it*, I was forced to kiss him—because those were just the rules? Would that be the worst tragedy in the world?

Cole seemed a little surprised that his ploy worked. "Really?"

Hutch sighed. "You really seem to want this."

"I do," Cole said. "I absolutely do."

Hutch spun his chair around and sat down decisively on it—backward. He leaned forward and said, "Then your wish is my command."

I'd never seen a drinking contest before. I didn't even think they happened in real life. Drinking *games*? Sure. But contests? What was the point? How did anybody even win?

"How does this work?" I asked. "Does somebody have to pass out? Or throw up?"

"No, no," Cole said. "It's just whoever gets impaired first."

"And how do you measure that?"

Cole shrugged at me, like *How does anybody measure that?* "Field sobriety tests."

"Like the police do?"

"Yeah."

Cole explained the rules, like maybe he'd done this a time or two before. They each had to take a shot and then walk a straight grout line in the tile floor for ten steps—heel to toe—from our table to the pinball machine and back. "First one to step off or fall off the line, or stop walking, or put your arms out for balance . . ." Cole said, "is the loser."

"Who's *administering* this test?" I said—trying to show him how dumb it was for two drunk people to test each other.

"You are."

Oh.

"So pay attention. Because you'll be smooching whoever wins."

I glared at Cole. "That won't be happening."

"Never say never."

At that, the bartender showed up with a tray of whiskey shots.

And so it began. A shot for Cole, a shot for Hutch—and then they both had to walk the line.

It went on longer than I would've expected, to be honest. It was a lot of up and down, back and forth. They drank seated, facing each other, and then they got back up, over and over, to walk the line.

Had Cole been wanting to have *fun*? Because neither of them seemed to be having any. Hutch was dead serious times ten, and Cole was prematurely triumphant—so certain that Hutch couldn't possibly have enough of a tolerance to beat him.

It was psychologically transparent—how bad Cole wanted to beat his perfect older brother at literally anything. I was rooting for Hutch for many reasons, but Cole thinking he'd already won was definitely one of them.

Here's what Cole didn't take into consideration: he'd already had several beers back at the pinball machine. He was already half plastered before he even had this idea. So it wasn't that surprising when Cole failed the test: starting along the line, then putting his arms out for balance, then stopping for a second, and then tripping, falling off the line, and hitting the floor.

He didn't just lose. He lost big.

I couldn't help but feel relief when it happened. Hutch, for his part, still seemed completely sober.

"Contest's over," I declared to Cole. "You lost."

"Did I?" Cole asked, squinting up at me from the floor, like I might be trying to pull a fast one.

"You did," I confirmed, letting myself savor it, as Hutch reached out a hand to help him up.

Cole rose to his feet as Hutch pulled, but then, instead of letting go, Cole started pumping Hutch's hand in a hearty handshake.

"Thanks a lot, man," Cole said. "I know you didn't want to do that. I really appreciate it. It was fun for me. You're such a good sport."

Hutch and I looked at each other. That was unexpected.

"Go ahead," Cole said then, letting go and stepping back. "You won, fair and square."

"Go ahead?" Hutch asked.

"Go ahead and take your prize," Cole said, gesturing at me.

Hutch frowned, and eyed me like Cole couldn't possibly mean what it sounded like he meant.

But Cole went on. "For real, man. Make it happen. No questions asked. She's yours."

What was he—a feudal lord? "Cole," I said, shaking my head. "That's not your permission to give."

"No? Why not? He won, fair and square."

"What is this?" I said. "The Middle Ages?"

But now Cole was turning to Hutch. "Just do it," he said. "You know you want to."

"I don't want to," Hutch said.

"You one thousand percent do," Cole said.

But Hutch shook his head. "I really don't. You have no idea how much."

Okay, that was a little emphatic. But of course—right? Hutch's understanding of who I was in this situation was completely wrong. I wouldn't want to kiss me, either.

"You can't fool me," Cole said.

"I wasn't interested in your last girlfriend, and I'm not interested in this one, either."

"Keep telling yourself that, buddy."

"We should go home," Hutch said.

"Absolutely," Cole said. "Just as soon as you kiss my woman."

"Shut up. Let's go."

"I'm serious. I'm giving you this—and you should take it."

"I don't want it."

"Yeah, you do."

"You could beg me all night, and I wouldn't kiss her. You could punch me in the face, and I wouldn't kiss her. You could pay me a thousand dollars, and I still wouldn't kiss her."

Ouch.

It was meant to settle things, I guess.

But wow, did it make things worse. Because at that, one of the gross old men in a booth nearby said, "I'll kiss her for a thousand dollars."

We all turned in his direction. He climbed out of the booth, a fair bit knackered himself. He was a lot bigger standing up.

Silently, Hutch shifted into position to shield me.

"Not *you*," Cole said, walking closer to the old guy. He gestured back at Hutch. "Just *him*."

"I said I'll do it," the gross old man said. "You want to pay somebody to kiss that girl? I'll do it." Then he looked me over. "Heck, I'll do it for free."

"Absolutely not," Cole said. "No way in hell."

"Why not?"

"Look at her!" Cole said. "She's young and pretty! And you are an old, sad, drunk dude at a bar!"

At that, without even hesitating, the old, sad, drunk dude launched a fist forward and punched Cole in the face.

Cole dropped to the floor. And as soon as he did, the old man started kicking him.

That's when Hutch turned to me. "Stay back," he said.

Uh—no argument there.

Hutch moved toward them, Cole now doubled over on the bar floor and coughing. Everything I'd ever seen in any movie primed me to expect that Hutch was about to beat the crap out of this old man. But, instead, to my astonishment, Hutch moved in and grabbed him from behind, clamping him into a position that looked remarkably like the cross-chest carry he used in the water.

So versatile.

I guess the only difference was that he used his swimming arm to subdue the old man's punching arm by bending it behind him.

Then, into the old man's ear, Hutch said, matter-of-factly, "We're not going to do this, sir."

The man seemed baffled to be so immobilized so suddenly. "We're not?"

"Everybody's been drinking, and everybody's looking for a fight. But that's not who we're going to be tonight." The bartender had come over to investigate the commotion, and Hutch met his eyes as if giving instructions, as he went on. "We're going to *call a taxi*"—at that, the bartender gave a nod—"and we're going to go home peacefully."

"But who's kissing the girl?" the old guy protested.

"*No one* is kissing the girl," Hutch said, with surprising force.

"Someone should get to kiss her."

At that, Hutch jacked the man's arm up a little tighter. "That's her decision, and her decision only," Hutch said. Then, like a pain-based PSA, he threw in: "Just the way it is for all the women in our lives." Hutch gave it a second and then said, "And that's the end of that."

BY THE TIME Hutch had loaded the man into his taxi, the bartender and I had dragged a very drunk, and now injured, Cole out front.

Hutch and I roped Cole's arms over our shoulders to walk him back toward the Starlite. Hutch took a minute, once we had Cole in position, to close his eyes and steady himself, and I wondered if he might *seem* more sober than he really was.

"What were you thinking, doing a drinking contest?" I asked Hutch as we walked.

"I was rescuing you," Hutch said. "Did you *want* to kiss a random old man in a sleazy bar?"

"That was never going to happen."

"Also, Cole really wanted me to."

That was a better reason. "You're a good brother."

Hutch shook his head. "I'm trying."

"He doesn't make it easy."

A wry headshake from Hutch. "He does not."

"How did you *win*?" I asked.

Hutch didn't seem sure himself. "Sheer force of will?"

"You didn't have to do this. I was fine."

"You were less fine than you think. Those dudes were ogling you the whole time."

"I'm not the kind of woman who gets ogled."

"Beg to differ."

"I think I'd know."

"Not so sure you would."

"Women can tell."

"Not all women, apparently."

"Why are we arguing about this?"

"Because you're wrong about yourself, and it bothers me."

"Maybe you're the one who's wrong," I said, just to be contrary.

"You think you're this unnoticed, forgettable thing. But you're not."

"Fine," I said. "I'm not forgettable."

"You're not *not forgettable*," Hutch said then, like I was being obtuse. "You're *un*forgettable."

I held my breath at that.

Hutch went on. "You're a TV jingle you never wanted to learn, but can't erase. You're a puzzle that can't be solved—or a question that can't be answered—or a dream you wake up from that feels like it really happened. But it didn't happen. And it can't happen. Because that's not how dreams work."

At that, Cole roused enough to say, "I knew you liked her."

"I *don't* like her," Hutch said.

"You've still got that hall pass, man," Cole said.

"Stop saying that," Hutch said, "or I will make us all regret it."

WHEN WE MADE it back to the Starlite, Rue and The Gals were still out around the tables chatting. They stood up at the sight of Cole.

"What happened?" Rue asked, rushing to us.

"Drinking contest," Hutch said.

Rue took in Cole's darkening, swelling jaw and his drunk-and-beat-up energy. "That wasn't you, was it?" she asked Hutch.

"When has it ever—even once—been me?" he answered.

Rue nodded.

"Can you see to him?" Hutch asked her. Then he tilted his head toward me. "I'm going to need a designated driver."

"The drinking contest was with *you*?" Rue said.

Hutch nodded.

"Who won?" she asked.

Hutch squinted at her. "Who do you think?"

Rue looked back and forth between the two boys. Then she nodded. "Take my car," she said.

Twenty

WE HAD TO fold Hutch up like origami to get him into Rue's Mini Cooper.

Then, when he struggled to get his seat belt fastened, I leaned across to help and found myself face-to-face with him, watching me.

"What are you doing?" Hutch asked.

I paused to meet his eyes. My face was two inches from his. "I'm helping you with your seat belt."

"I don't need help," Hutch said, holding still.

He seemed to be taking in the sight of me more than he was listening—right there, so close—his eyes looking all around my face at close range, lingering on my mouth.

"Yeah, you do," I said. "I've watched you fumble with this thing for two full minutes." I snapped the buckle and said, "You're welcome."

At that, Hutch closed his eyes, and I felt his arm come up behind my shoulders and clamp me down against him into a hug.

I let it happen. And then I lay there for a second, my head pressed to his breathing, thumping chest, until I heard him say, "You're safe now."

I lifted up. "Safe? Safe from what?"

"From me, dummy," he said, turning toward the window. "I just saved us both from that hall pass."

ON THE DRIVE, he tilted his head back against the headrest, displaying that Adam's apple so luxuriously that I almost hit the curb a couple of times, just trying not to look.

Hutch kept his eyes closed.

"I think the alcohol is hitting me," he said then.

"Only now?" I asked.

"Maybe adrenaline delayed the effects?" he suggested, adding an extra *f* to *effects*.

Maybe so.

Whatever it was, back at the marina, I had to pull him out of the car like a tug-of-war.

Then I had to put my arm around his waist to steer him.

"I'm fine," he said. "I think it's wearing off."

"It's not wearing off—it just barely started."

We got halfway to the *Rue the Day* before Hutch tried to get out of my hold.

"I can take it from here," he said.

"No, you can't."

"You should let me go."

"And let you veer off the dock?"

"I'm saying it's better if you go back to the car."

"Once we get you inside, I'll go back to the car."

"You are *not* coming inside."

"Fine. To the door, then. I'm not going to spend all night worrying that you fell into the water and drowned."

"You know what I do for a living, right?"

"But are you drunk when you do it?"

Hutch nodded, like that was a good point. "Never."

At the door, Hutch had some trouble with his keys. The door was locked with a simple hasp and a padlock, and Hutch fiddled with it for a while without getting the lock undone. Finally, I said, "How about I do it?"

"I've got it," Hutch said.

"Not sure you do."

"This isn't rocket science," Hutch said.

"You're not used to being hammered."

"That's true."

I stepped closer to take over, but Hutch didn't move out of the way. Instead, I had to nudge him, and he resisted a minute before finally stepping aside and flipping around to lean back against the doorframe. I could feel him watching me then.

"Cole, huh?" he asked.

"What?" I said, like I hadn't heard the question.

"I would never, in ten thousand years, have put you together with Cole."

I wanted—so, so, so badly—to say, *I'm not.* But if tonight had made anything clear, it was that I couldn't make their animosity worse. *Friday*, I told myself. Just one more day. Finally, I said, "Me neither."

At that, I turned the key, and the padlock released.

"There," I said.

But Hutch's eyes were closed now, and he'd leaned his head back.

"Hutch?" I asked. "Are you okay?"

"I'm fine," Hutch said, without opening his eyes.

"The door's unlocked," I said.

He nodded. "Okay. Got it. You can go."

"I should see you inside," I said, putting my hand on his shoulder.

But Hutch pushed my hand away. "I'm good," he said.

"Go inside, then," I said, stepping back.

He opened his eyes and looked right at me. "I will. After you go," Hutch said.

"I don't want to just leave you here," I said.

"I don't want to open that door with you so close to it."

"What? Why not?"

"Because," Hutch said, looking away.

"Hey," I said then, grabbing for his shoulder again. "Let's not mess around."

But Hutch stopped me again. "I'm not messing around."

"I don't understand what's happening right now," I said. We were here. The door was unlocked. All Hutch had to do was go safely inside. And yet, he wouldn't. "Why are you being difficult?" I asked.

That's when Hutch took a deep breath and let it out. "I'm trying," he said then, "really, really hard . . . not to kiss you."

A funny little joy bloomed through my body. I stepped closer. "You are?"

Hutch put out a hand, like *Stop.* "I am."

Then I said, "But you *can* kiss me. You won the drinking contest."

"That doesn't mean I get the prize."

"But you have Cole's permission," I said.

"Not really."

"You have a hall pass. You can totally kiss me—guilt-free. Cole won't ever know or care."

"That's not real."

"Sure it is," I said. "Cole was insisting."

At last, Hutch opened his eyes. "Cole wasn't insisting. He was *daring.*"

It was beyond frustrating to me in this moment that Hutch was refusing to get anywhere near me for a reason that wasn't even real. Of course, *yes*, it was reasonable for him to refuse—under all circumstances—to kiss his brother's girlfriend.

I just *wasn't his brother's girlfriend.*

"You have *my* permission," I said then.

"Don't say that."

"You've kissed me before."

"That was before I knew about you and Cole. And you should never have let that happen, by the way. Are you a bad person?"

"No."

Hutch closed his eyes again. "Then why the hell were you kissing your boyfriend's brother?"

"You kissed me first."

"But you kissed me back."

"It's weirdly complicated."

Hutch opened his eyes. "What were you thinking?" he asked.

"Look, I had a reason that it was okay, but I just can't tell you about it right now."

He closed his eyes again. "I take it back. I don't want to know."

And then I couldn't resist saying, "It's still okay, actually."

"How? How could it possibly be okay?"

"I can't tell you."

Here was the problem: we were two single, consenting adults. But Hutch didn't know that. And I wasn't honestly sure if he'd still feel the same way about me after he knew the truth. I'd participated in Cole's lie. As much as I thought I could justify my choices logically . . . logic and feelings were hardly the same thing. Who knows what kind of magic goes into one person liking another person? There were no guarantees that this bad situation wouldn't just get worse.

I might never get another kiss, is what I'm saying.

Hutch would never kiss me *before* he knew the truth. But after he knew the truth—he might not want to anymore.

Hutch watched me wrestle with myself. Then he shook his head. "I think you better go now."

I nodded. But I was frozen with indecision. I might never get another chance.

Hutch met my eyes. "I'm serious," he said.

"I know," I said. But I didn't move.

"Katie—do I have to physically move you?"

I shook my head, but I still didn't go.

There was that classic, concerned frown of his—though who he was concerned for wasn't clear. He was breathing deeply, and I was, too. Time seemed to slow down.

He wanted to kiss me. He'd said as much.

He wanted to, but he wouldn't. Even drunk, he wouldn't. It was against everything he stood for. It was against his honor. Good guys didn't kiss their brother's girlfriends. Even with permission.

And Hutch was nothing if not a good guy.

My mind searched desperately for a loophole.

Then it occurred to me that *I* could kiss *him*.

If I kissed him right now—just reached up and pulled him in— I could take him by surprise. Could that work? If Hutch was just a hapless victim of a kiss he never saw coming? He couldn't be held responsible for that, right?

The past was gone, and the future was uncertain, but right now was absolutely clear: I might never get another chance.

You never really know what other people are thinking, but from the way our gazes were locked, I couldn't imagine Hutch felt any way other than the same.

No one would blame him . . .

I took a deep breath. Maybe this was the perfect answer.

. . . But he would blame himself.

I let the breath out.

Somewhere in the multiverse there was a version of this story where I pulled Hutch in with both hands and kissed him senseless until we stumbled backward into his place, and into the bedroom, and into his bed—and everything we did all night made everything else better, not worse.

But this was not that universe.

There was no loophole.

If Drunk Hutch kissed me thinking I was his brother's girlfriend, even if I wasn't, then he was a bad person. And if I kissed him knowing everything I knew, then I was a bad person.

He was holding himself back for a reason.

And for something that wasn't real, that reason was real enough.

I was overthinking it. Maybe *I* should've volunteered for that drinking contest.

But it was what it was. There would be no kissing, no stumbling, no *anything at all* tonight.

I guess George Bailey must have agreed with my line of thinking. Because just as I broke eye contact with Hutch, George Bailey started barking at us through the window.

We both turned, and Hutch let out a long sigh.

"I should go in," he said.

And all I could do was agree.

Twenty-One

THE NEXT DAY was Friday. At last.

My last day of pretending.

Also known as the anniversary of the accident.

Sullivan's sunburn was better by Friday, and she ventured out that afternoon to sit in the shade and enjoy the breeze. The Gals surrounded her and asked her all about how she was feeling. When she heard that Hutch and Cole and Rue were headed out to dinner that night, she tried to invite herself along, but The Gals dissuaded her—saying it was family only.

Which was why she made a not-pleased face when Rue, right in front of her, invited *me* to join.

Rue had sent Cole to pick up flowers, and after he got back, she sat at a poolside table, dividing up the bouquets.

"Who's the fourth one for?" I asked.

Rue looked at me over her glasses. "*You*, sweetheart."

"Oh, no," I said, glancing toward Sullivan. "This is a family day."

Rue turned back to the flowers. "You're close enough."

I looked over at Cole just as Hutch walked up. He had dressed for the occasion, wearing gunmetal-gray dress pants that fit like he'd just stepped out of the pages of *GQ*. If he was hungover from the drinking contest, he was hiding it like a warrior. A freshly shaved warrior in a slim-fit button-down.

Though, to be fair, he was also wearing his standard-issue concerned frown.

"She's close enough to what?" Hutch asked, in response to Rue.

"Family," Rue and Cole said, in unison.

Hutch looked down to count Rue's bouquets. "She's not coming with us, is she?"

"Of course she is," Rue said, like he was nuts to ask.

"But it's our first time back together," Hutch said.

"He's right," I said, trying to join Team Hutch.

But Rue wasn't brooking any nonsense. "She's important to Cole, so she's important to us. If you ever get a girlfriend, she can come, too."

Hutch gave Rue a look, like *Thanks a lot.*

He wasn't wrong. I was a total interloper.

But I couldn't think of a way out. If I feigned an illness, Rue might worry about me. If I suddenly had an "important meeting," she might feel like my impending new family didn't matter. If I "forgot something" back at the Starlite, she'd be waiting for me to return. All I could do was go—and make the best of things.

The Starlite was right off Duval Street, which is one of the main drags in Key West, so we left Sullivan and The Gals behind, gathered up our bouquets, and walked along the bustling sidewalk, handing out flower after flower to tourists, and shoppers, and passersby.

Despite everything, it was fun.

Rue and I paired off, leaving the guys to do the same. They looked companionable—from a distance, at least. Rue and I cradled our bouquets like we were prima ballerinas about to take our bows. Before we began in earnest, Rue snapped two of the flowers' stems short and tucked one behind her ear, and one behind mine.

"Whatever happened to the flower hair clip I gave you?" she asked.

"Lost." I shrugged. At the back of Hutch's closet.

She nodded and said, "We'll snag you another one."

But I shook my head. "Maybe it was for the best. I'm not sure flowers are for me."

But Rue just looked appalled. "Flowers," she declared, "are for everyone."

We'd barely gotten started when we saw Cole, across the street, raise his arms in victory after handing out his last flower.

"It's not a race, Cole," Rue called.

"What do I do now?" Cole answered. "I'm all out!"

"Go get some more!" Rue called back. "We're not done until we're done!"

If it had been a race, Rue and I would've come in dead last.

The flowers were so unexpected—and so lovely. Person after person reacted with blinks of surprise, then bewildered acceptance, then shy smiles. Highly recommend if you ever want to spend an afternoon lifting people up.

While Hutch and Cole were trying to maximize efficiency, Rue and I wanted to maximize joy. "This is a dahlia," Rue would say to a mom with a baby. "They were originally classified as vegetables." Or, "This is a lilac. They're from the same family as olive trees." Or, "This is a peony. The plants can live for a hundred years—and outlive the gardeners who planted them."

"This is my best day of the year now," Rue said to me as we strolled along. "Isn't that something? It started out as my worst day of the year. I'd walk along handing out flowers, wiping away tears before the boys saw. People must have thought I was crazy. But now, after all this time . . . it's become a joy."

Rue held out a lilac to a girl going by on a skateboard, who took it without slowing, calling "Thank you!" behind her.

"I used to dread it," Rue continued, "but now I look forward to it. The flowers, the food, the big, astonishing tip for the waiter at the end. I always drink a glass or two of Robert's favorite cabernet. I wait for it all year in some compartment in my heart, thinking about how nice it will be to do all these things again. It's good before, and it's good during, and it's good after."

"Rue," I said then. "Cole told me something about you when he first showed up." I met her eyes to see if she could intuit what I meant. "And I'm not sure if I believe it. But maybe that's only because I don't want to believe it."

I let that sit.

"It's not a big deal," she said. "It's just a touch of heart failure."

"Can you have *a touch* of heart failure?"

"It's just stage one," Rue said. "If I take good care of myself, I could last a long time—years! But it's not technically *curable*. It will be the thing that gets me, that's pretty clear." Rue gave me a wry smile. "Unless a runaway bus comes along."

"You told Cole," I asked then, "but you didn't tell Hutch?"

Rue nodded. "Well, Cole needed a kick in the pants. He's always been a little too self-focused for his own good."

"And Hutch?" I prompted.

"Hutch doesn't have that problem. The opposite, in fact. He's not nearly as invincible as he seems." Rue sighed. "He had such a hard time after he lost his mom. He really struggled a lot." She looked at me. "That's why he hums all the time."

"It is?"

"Have you noticed he does that?"

"Of course. It's a whole thing."

"I had a therapist friend who told me that humming was soothing to the vagus nerve."

I shook my head, like *Not sure what that means.*

"That's a nerve," Rue explained, "that calms and regulates your system. The vibrations of humming stimulate it. So does laughing. So do deep breaths. And gargling, of all things. So when Hutch was having a hard time when he was little, I taught him about all those things—but humming was the one that stuck."

"That's why he hums? To feel better?"

"It's such a habit now, I'm not sure he notices he's doing it. But that's where it started." Rue patted my hand.

"And 'Heart and Soul'?" I asked.

Rue shrugged. "It was my husband's favorite."

We gave that a moment.

"Anyway," Rue went on at last, "I will tell Hutch about me, of course—but this is always a hard time of year for him. I might wait a little while."

We'd run out of flowers, so we sat on a park bench to wait for the boys.

Next, Rue said, "I was just reading that old people are happier than young people. Do you want to know why?"

I nodded.

"Because old people," Rue said, "don't have as much time left. And they know it. It's called a time horizon—a sense of how much time we have remaining. For teenagers, it's vast. It's *infinite*. But as we get older, it shortens and shortens—and we can't help but feel it. As it shrinks, it makes everything more precious. We appreciate the days more because there are fewer of them to come. And it's really true. I felt it so much today. How fast it all goes. How much we have to be thankful for. What a miracle each breath is."

Without meaning to, I leaned my head against Rue's shoulder.

"We don't last forever, sweetheart. We're not supposed to. It's okay. It's part of it all. I'm good for now, and that's enough."

Across the street, the boys were headed our way, waiting for the light at the crosswalk to change.

As we watched them start toward us, Rue said, "Do you know what my favorite flower is?"

I shook my head against her shoulder.

"Daisies," she said. "The cheapest daisies you can find. So you can hand out lots and lots and lots of them. Anytime you feel like it."

Twenty-Two

DINNER WENT FINE. Dinner went great.

It wasn't until *after* dinner that all hell broke loose.

We went to an old-timey Italian restaurant with white tablecloths a few blocks from the Starlite. We ate bread and most of us drank buttery red wine, and Hutch, Cole, and Rue did what they always did on anniversary day: they told stories.

Everybody at the table took turns. The time in college when Robert stole a street sign and got chased by a Doberman. Cole and Hutch's dad teaching them how to spin a basketball on their fingers—and their mom making pancakes in the shape of the boys' initials. There were beach stories, and camping stories; stories about birthdays and loose teeth; stories about pets lost and found. Stories about ripped pants and forgotten keys. Some of the stories seemed well-worn and well-told, but others got unearthed in the churn of conversation. Either way, I came away feeling like I knew everyone—the whole family, past and present—a little better.

This was what Rue had been missing. This lovely way of remembering together, and holding on, and bringing the past into the present, even if only for a little while.

And at the end, they really did tip the waiter a hundred dollars. And he whooped with joy and hugged everyone.

But then dinner ended.

On the short walk back to the Starlite, the boys started arguing.

It was one hundred percent Cole's fault. It was like he was *trying* to make Hutch mad. Just complaining and provoking and baiting him. He kept listing, for example, all the ways life kept being unfair to him but not to Hutch.

After a while, Hutch started pushing back. "Why are you keeping score? It's like you *want* to be angry," Hutch said then. "Like you're looking for reasons."

"I'm not looking for reasons," Cole said. "You just keep offering them up."

"Like what? I'm just living my life."

"Like everything," Cole answered. "You've got twice as much money in your savings account. You have the coolest job. You're taller."

"You're mad at me for being *taller*?" Hutch demanded.

"You got the best nickname, too," Cole went on, undeterred. "You got Hutch—and I got nothing."

"I didn't take that nickname from you. It just happened!"

"That's exactly my point. *I* don't get a cool nickname because *you* got the cool nickname."

"There's more than one cool nickname to go around!"

"Apparently not!"

"Take it," Hutch said.

"What?"

"Take the nickname. I don't care. You be Hutch."

"I can't be Hutch," Cole said. "It's too late. *You're* Hutch."

"So pick something else! The world is lousy with nicknames."

"What am I supposed to pick?" Cole demanded.

"I don't know!" Hutch said, throwing things out. "Catfish! Lightning! Boots and Saddles!"

"Don't *ever* call me Boots and Saddles."

"I don't know, man! Do an internet search! Pick something. I'll call you whatever you want."

"You can't pick a nickname for yourself off the internet. That's not how that works."

Rue and I looked at each other. This conversation couldn't really be about nicknames, could it?

Hutch was looking Cole up and down now, like *Fine*. "Ace," Hutch declared then.

"What?"

"Ace. That's your new nickname."

"No."

"Yes."

"I'm not an Ace at anything!"

"Better get on that, Ace."

"Now you're trying to piss me off."

"No, Ace. That's *your* thing."

We'd made it back to the Starlite, and The Gals and Sullivan were out by the pool, holding little drinks with parasols. They started to greet us, but then they sensed the argument brewing and got quiet instead. Rue and I took chairs close enough to The Gals to look like we had joined them, but close enough to the boys to eavesdrop.

"Yeah. Fine," Cole was saying. "Maybe I should've forgiven you sooner. But you never should've tried to make me come here and film a whole video about what a hero you are."

"I was trying to *see* you," Hutch said.

"There are lots of ways to see me."

"Not really. But you know what? You could've just said no. Instead, you made me think you were coming. And Rue, too, by the way. And then you sent an underling instead."

For the record, I resented being called an underling.

"Katie's not an underling," Cole said. "She's a colleague."

I was Team Hutch, but . . . *point, Cole.*

"A colleague," Hutch countered, "is the *last* thing she is."

"Our boss, Sullivan, is laying off half the staff. I was trying to do something good for someone. Isn't that your whole thing?"

But Hutch shook his head. "You just didn't want me to get what I wanted."

"What did you want?"

"To see you!"

"But I sent Katie instead."

Hutch glanced over my way. "Yes, you did."

Cole was nodding now. "And then you fell for her."

I waited for the denial, but it didn't come.

Instead, Hutch said, "You never told me she was your girlfriend. I didn't know anything about that. You can't just send a woman like that down here, and make her spend every single second following me around, and tell me to let her *sleep over at my house*—during a thunderstorm— and think I'm not going to react to that. That's on you. You should've said she was yours from the start! But you didn't. And before I knew it . . ." Hutch rubbed the back of his neck. "Before I knew it, it was too late."

The Gals all turned to check each other's wide-eyed reactions.

No one, of course, was more wide-eyed than me.

But that's when Cole said, "It's not too late."

Hutch shook his head. "What does that mean?"

Hutch looked around. He saw us all by the pool. The Gals raised their glasses as if to say *Cheers.*

Cole looked at me. "Should I tell him what it means?"

But I wasn't prepared. "What—right here?"

"Three days ago you wanted to tell him right here."

"It's been a long three days," I said.

"I think it's been long enough," Cole said.

"But"—I glanced over—"what about Rue?"

"Don't worry about Rue!" Rue called.

Then, without any further discussion, Cole just turned to Hutch and said, "Katie isn't actually my girlfriend."

Oh, god.

Hutch held very still. "She's not—what?"

"Or even my friend, to be honest. We barely know each other. I just needed somebody to come down here and take this job."

Hutch stared at Cole, trying to read his face. "You're not together?"

Cole shrugged.

"You lied to me?" Hutch said. "About Katie?"

Cole was maybe trying to shift gears a little too fast. "But that's good news, right?" He gestured my way, like I was a brand-new car. "She's available!"

If Hutch thought it was good news, he didn't care. "You asshole!" he shouted, tackling Cole, and before the words were even spoken, the boys were on the ground.

I was on my feet in an instant, thinking I should stop them.

But Rue put her hand out to hold me back.

"Shouldn't we do something?" I asked Rue.

"Let's give them a minute."

"I'm sorry," I said. "We tried so hard to give you a good anniversary day."

"This is more important than that," Rue said.

We watched them on the grass. It wasn't a choreographed fight like you'd see in a movie. It was messy, and sideways. And full of grunts and elbows and kicks. No satisfying *SMACK!* sound effects, either. Just breathing, and cursing paired with thuds, and cuffs, and gasps, over and over in that order.

"Should we call the cops?" I asked Rue.

She shook her head. "They'll tire themselves out soon enough."

"I do think Hutch could really kill Cole."

"He could, but he won't."

I don't think I'd ever seen grown men fight in real life. How did anyone even win? Did they just thrash in the grass until they got tired?

Whatever winning might be, it seemed like a foregone conclusion— just based on body mass alone. I mean, Cole wasn't a weakling. But working out was *part of Hutch's job description.*

They really were fighting. My money was on Hutch, of course, but we all watched as Cole landed punch after punch to his torso that didn't seem to have any impact.

"This is good for them," Rue said. "They've been ignoring each other for too long. They need to yell and wrestle and clear the air."

"You're not going to stop them?"

"Not unless someone bursts an artery."

"But . . ." It felt so weird not to intervene. "Aren't we all supposed to use our words?"

Rue nodded, watching the boys. "Sometimes words aren't quite enough."

THEY DID, EVENTUALLY, tire themselves out.

By the time they were done fighting—breathless and bleeding, ripped and grass-stained—Cole and Hutch were so exhausted, they wound up lying on their backs with their limbs splayed out, staring up at the starry sky.

And we all—Rue, The Gals, Sullivan, and I—got quiet to eavesdrop.

"What the hell, Cole?" Hutch said. "Why would you lie to me about Katie?"

"I regretted it as soon as I did it," Cole said, "if that helps."

"It doesn't."

"You'd said no over and over for the 'Day in the Life' thing. I wanted to get you to say yes. And I knew you felt so guilty about what happened at the wedding, you'd do anything I asked."

"Two things," Hutch said then. "I never felt guilty about what happened at the wedding—because I *didn't do anything wrong*. And I have always been willing to do anything you asked, anyway."

Cole nodded. "Maybe there was an element of revenge, too."

"Because you knew I liked her? But how did you know? We weren't even talking!"

"Rue knew," Cole said. "Rue could tell."

Hutch ran his palm over his burr cut and turned back to Cole.

"So . . . Rue told you that she thought I liked the coworker you sent down here to do your job—and you decided to lie to me that you were dating her?"

Cole nodded. "When you put it that way, I sound like a dick."

"You have got to stop competing with me, man," Hutch said.

"That's easy to say when you're the reigning champion."

"I'm not the champion of anything."

"Spoken like a champion."

"You must think I'm totally untouchable," Hutch said. "Is that how you see me?"

But Cole was ready to own it. "Of course. Yes. That's who you are. You're Hutch. You're perfect. And you get everything you want. If you want to make straight A's, you just make them. If you decide to run a marathon, you just run one. If you want to be a rescue swimmer, you're one of five guys total who make it through AST school. You're a machine. You're unstoppable. I'll spend my whole life competing with you, and I'll never win."

Wow. That was a lot of self-disclosure.

"But none of that stuff about me," Hutch said, "has anything to do with you."

"It has everything to do with me," Cole said then. "Because you just had to be a hero and save me."

For a second, everything went quiet.

Then Hutch sat up in the grass. "Do you mean," he asked, not looking over at Cole, "the night of the accident?"

Cole sat up, too. Then, after a long pause, in a barely audible voice, he said, "You should've saved Mom instead."

Hutch looked over at Cole like he was seeing him for the first time. "Is that—what this is?"

Cole kept his eyes on the grass.

Hutch was shaking his head at the revelation. "Is that why you're so angry? Is that why you always want to prove yourself?"

Cole didn't answer.

Hutch shook his head, still putting the pieces together. "No wonder. How could you ever measure up to that?"

"To what?" Cole asked.

"To what we lost."

Cole looked away.

Hutch was studying him now. "Was that it? Was that what it's been all this time? You thought you were the reason she wasn't here? You thought I saved you instead of her? That if I had chosen differently, Mom would still be alive?"

Cole was blinking now, like he'd never expected that question.

"Because, Cole . . ." Hutch went on. "I didn't make that choice."

"What?"

Hutch swallowed. "Mom told me to get you."

"She . . ."

"Even as I was climbing out, she was calling to me. 'Get Cole! Hutch, go get Cole!' I was so dazed right then, but Mom made her voice so loud and certain that it cut through everything. When I hesitated, she said, 'Take Cole first, and then come back for me.' And so I just . . . did it. I climbed back into the car, and I unbuckled you. You were dazed, too. And I said, 'Let's go! Let's go!' You took my hand, and followed me, and I led you off to where the crowd was standing. To safety."

"You took me away because Mom told you to?"

Hutch nodded. "Cole, I remember her face. I think about it all the time. She knew there wasn't time for me to come back."

Now Hutch wiped his eyes with the heels of his hands. When he spoke again, his voice was rough. "I didn't save you, Cole. Mom did."

There were tears on Cole's face now, too.

But Hutch went on. "You weren't the *reason she died*. You were her last wish."

Twenty-Three

I NEVER GOT a chance to talk to Hutch that night.

Instead, just at the height of everything, Sullivan, who had been both sulking all night about not getting included in the family dinner and self-medicating with prosecco, started throwing up.

She threw up on the lawn right next to me, but as The Gals swooped in to help take her back to her cottage, she stopped them.

"No," she said, drunkenly. "I want Tracy."

We all looked around, trying to figure out who Tracy might be, until Sullivan pointed at me.

I put my hand on my chest. "I'm *Katie*," I said.

"Whatever," Sullivan said.

Every single one of The Gals offered to take charge of that moment, but Sullivan wasn't having it. "Tracy only," she declared.

What could I do? She was my boss.

As I helped her across the lawn toward her cabin, I said, "Should you be drinking like this? You've barely recovered from sun poisoning."

"My plan was to drink every single night," Sullivan said. "So I'm behind schedule."

Too little, too late anyway.

I hoped to drop her off, set her up with a glass of water and some Tylenol, and get back to the far more interesting spectacle of the brothers duking out their long-held resentments at last. But as soon as we got inside, Sullivan started crying—those big, earth-shaking, all-is-lost tears that you only have when way too much prosecco has removed all your inhibitions.

"I hate my life," Sullivan sobbed as I helped her wash her face and brush her teeth. "How did it wind up like this?"

"Things will get better," I said, finding her baby-doll PJs in her suitcase and helping her into them. "Life isn't a straight line. It's always ups and downs. That's just how it goes."

"I don't want the downs!" Sullivan protested, sounding much more sober. "I only want the ups!"

"Nobody wants the downs," I told her. "But they're good for you."

Sullivan squinted at me, all skeptical, as I hitched up under her shoulder and walked her toward the bed. "Easy for you to say—over there, doing fine."

"Are you kidding?" I said, handing her a glass of water and two Tylenol. "I'm doing the *opposite* of fine."

She looked at me like she was expecting proof.

So I said, "My fiancé cheated on me with a pop star, I might be about to lose my job, I got ridiculed online for being frumpy, I'm a terrible swimmer, I'm in love with someone who hates me, and I've gotten trapped in a web of lies—none of which I told. Not lately, anyway. But all of which I'll be punished for!"

"Wow," she said, starting to look tired. "Your life *is* worse than mine."

"Probably."

"Let's be best friends, then," she said, as I helped tilt her down to her pillow and then pulled up the covers.

"I'll be your best friend," I said, "if you won't fire me."

"Deal," she said.

And then she lifted her hand from under the covers and held it out for me to shake.

Which—what the heck—I went ahead and did.

She'd never remember, anyway.

BY THE TIME I got back outside, Hutch was gone.

Only Cole remained—alone. In a pool chair. Surrounded by The Gals as they tended to his swollen eye and busted lip.

"Where's Hutch?" I asked.

"He left," Cole said, as Ginger opened up the first-aid kit.

"He left? For where?"

But Cole shrugged. "Didn't say. He just took off."

Hutch left?

I mean, granted, it had been a couple of hours, but Hutch had, just tonight, learned that I was single. I got that his first order of business— mid-fight and all—might be addressing that long-standing beef with his brother. But I really had been assuming the whole time that his second order of business would be . . .

Throwing me over his shoulder and carrying me off to bed.

Or something.

Now that I was officially . . . available.

Out of a million possibilities, I would never have predicted *Hutch going home without even saying goodbye.*

I would have expected a moment of closure, at least.

But then I wondered if maybe Hutch had pretended to go home but was actually waiting for me at my cottage. There was more than one way to get a moment of closure.

I pointed at Cole, who had been sleeping on the floor of my place for the last two nights. "You," I said, "find somewhere else to sleep tonight."

Right? Just in case.

"What?" Cole protested. "Where?"

"I'm sure Aunt Rue will take you in," I said. "Or one of The Gals."

"But all my stuff is there!"

"I'll put it out on the porch."

BACK AT MY cottage, alas—no Hutch.

No texts or missed calls, either.

I put Cole's stuff out, anyway.

I tried to call Hutch, but no answer. I sent a text, and then several more. I left a ton of voicemails. Finally, I borrowed Rue's car to drive to the marina, where there was no sign of him. And when I ran out of ideas . . .

I called Beanie.

"Stop trying to make contact," Beanie said. "It's getting embarrassing. I'm embarrassed just hearing about it, and I'm not even you."

"But he didn't say goodbye!"

"I get that it's anticlimactic—"

"I need closure!" I wailed, in a tone that reminded me of Sullivan.

"—but you're just going to have to wait."

"But everything got revealed—and then he just *left*!"

"Maybe he's having a work emergency," Beanie said, like the calm voice of reason. "Maybe he's injured from the fight. Maybe he needs some time to take it all in."

Okay. I hadn't thought of a work emergency. That had potential.

"Whatever it is," Beanie said, "ten more voicemails won't change it."

"Beanieeeee," I whined. "Where's your fighting spirit?"

"It went to bed two hours ago. And then you woke it up."

"Sorry."

"I get it. There's a lot to process. Give the poor man a minute—and take one for yourself, too. Wash your face, put on your softest PJs, and go to bed. Everything's always better in the morning."

BUT THINGS WEREN'T better in the morning.

Hutch was still hardcore unavailable.

And everybody else was suddenly unavailable, too.

Cole and Sullivan were nowhere to be found, and even when I knocked on Sullivan's door to check on her hangover, I got no answer. Rue and The Gals left early to go antiquing on Sugarloaf Key, and Beanie had an eight A.M. client meeting. Not to mention, in the wake of the internet being mean to me, I had decided to take a technology break and deleted all my social media.

So it was just me, and the breeze, and the Starlite swimming pool alone together all day.

I hoped against hope that Hutch might show up for our standard swim lesson that day, but he didn't. I waited thirty minutes, and sent a hopeful text that just said: Still on for swimming?

And then I got into the pool alone.

Alone, and uninformed.

Apparently, there was some kind of storm that had been brewing in the Atlantic for the past few days that I'd been totally unaware of.

The Starlite felt like a ghost town that day—and that was another reason why. Even though the storm was supposed to make landfall much farther north, closer to Orlando, most of Rue's Vrbo guests had canceled their trips.

So things were extra quiet.

For posterity, here are the thoughts I was having that day, as Hurricane Rafael was gathering strength in the Atlantic without my knowledge:

Hutch had every right to feel however he felt. I had gotten myself embroiled in a nasty sibling rivalry. I had pretended—under duress, but still—for three straight days that I was dating his brother . . . who I barely even liked. You could say that I just hadn't volunteered the truth, but there was no question I'd deceived him—and helped his brother mess with his head.

I'd had my reasons, of course, but still.

He had every right to not say goodbye. And to not call. And he might detest me now, fair and square.

But that didn't change the fact that I was in love with him.

The way I was missing him. The way I couldn't stop longing for him. The way my thoughts, and my heart, and my entire body were completely capsized by everything that had just happened . . . there was no other explanation. Based on misery alone, it just had to be love.

❖ ❖ ❖

I KNEW I didn't have much time. But I had much less time than I thought.

When I showed up at the air station the next day, blithely unaware of the looming weather crisis, the place was all business.

At some point overnight, Hurricane Rafael had apparently whipped himself into a Category Four hurricane and shifted course—now headed for Miami, not Orlando—sooner, faster, and angrier than expected. Landfall was now expected in twenty-four hours, not thirty-six, and the air station crews were doing all preparations possible so they'd be ready to render aid after the worst had passed.

So much for my technology break.

Points to Beanie for calling it. Hutch *was* having a work emergency.

I'd been bobbing around in an empty pool, lovelorn and full of regret—while Hutch was preparing to rescue a massive American city from a major hurricane.

Category Four hurricanes, as defined on the Saffir-Simpson Scale, have sustained winds up to 157 miles per hour, in case you're wondering.

I googled it, obviously.

So, yeah: I was maybe not quite as top-of-mind for Hutch as he was for me.

Once I got to the air station, he was there—but I barely saw him. And when I did catch a glimpse, he didn't see me, or talk to me—or even seem to register that I was present.

As if I was already long forgotten.

I got it.

Of course I was forgotten. Hutch had genuine, death-defying heroics to prepare for. I'd done enough research to know how hard the Coast Guard worked in the wake of hurricanes. They were the first responders as soon as the storm had passed.

Depending on the damage, Hutch could be saving lives, transporting people off rooftops, taking patients across the city, rescuing boaters, helping with evacuations, bringing in water and food, saving families and their pets—and anything else that needed doing—for *weeks*, taking the required hours between shifts to sleep and then heading out again, day in and day out.

Which begged the question: Did he hate me? Or was he just . . . *busy?*

I might never know.

This was a real emergency.

One I truly couldn't help with. At all. For many reasons. Not the least of which—I found out at the station in our first morning meeting—was that they were evacuating the Florida Keys.

"Why the keys?" I whispered to Omar, in the back. "This thing's headed for Miami."

"It shifted course again," Omar whispered back.

Sure enough, it had. Now it was headed for Key Largo. Which, if you need a little help with geography, stood directly between us and the mainland.

I quietly panicked while the meeting continued—as the higher-ups laid out all the procedures and everyone got their orders. They were moving all their helicopters to Miami to wait out the storm, which seemed odd at first. But it made sense as I thought about it: if their equipment got damaged, they couldn't help in the aftermath.

AS SOON AS the meeting was over, I walked to the hangar, looking for Hutch.

When I didn't see him, I stood by the open doors and called Rue.

"We're evacuating," I told her, feeling like I had the inside scoop.

"Oh, we're already on the road, sweetheart," she said. "The Gals and I decided to take a road trip to Phoenix in Benita's Suburban. No hurricanes there."

"Brilliant," I said.

"You should probably change your flight home. Everything out of Miami is getting canceled."

"Good point," I said.

"Try Tampa. Or Orlando. Take my car. Heck, if everything's crazy, just drive it home to Texas."

"Take your car?" I said.

"Bring it back eventually," Rue said. Then, with affection, "I trust you."

"So—is this it? I'm just—leaving? This feels very sudden."

"Well, that's how natural disasters can be."

"I didn't even get to say goodbye to you."

"We'll see each other again," Rue said. Then she added, "But you should get going. The Overseas Highway is already filling up."

"Okay," I said. Then, "Rue?"

"Yes?"

"Thank you for everything." And then I could hear a waver in my voice. "I loved living at the Starlite."

"Come back anytime, sweetheart."

I hung up, turned, and caught sight of Hutch, just as he caught sight of me.

He was in his flight suit, with a backpack over his shoulder and his aviators on, about to stride out to the airfield.

"What are you still doing here?" Hutch asked. "You should be on the road by now."

"Are you leaving?" I asked.

Hutch looked over at the waiting helicopter out on the tarmac. "Yes."

"What about George Bailey?" I asked.

"Lieutenant Alonso is driving all the animals up. They'll stay with us."

"It's OK to bring pets?" I asked. He sure was all business.

"Not technically. But the XO there is pet-positive."

"The XO?"

"Executive officer."

"Ah."

Was this the best we could do, conversationally? Didn't we have some other topics to cover? Why were we defining military abbreviations right now?

Hutch assumed I was worried about the storm. "Don't panic," he said, "but you should leave now. Go back to the Starlite and load up your stuff, and then drive to the mainland. Get gas first. Head up as far from the coast as you can get before stopping for the night."

"But . . ." I said, like a dummy. "I wasn't supposed to leave for a week."

"Well," Hutch said, "everybody's leaving now."

"Yeah."

Across the tarmac, the helicopter crew was waiting, watching Hutch like, *Hurry up.* Hutch glanced back at them.

"I want to say I'm sorry," I blurted out then. "About how everything happened."

Hutch just nodded. "Me, too." Were we both sorry in the same way? I really couldn't read his face in those glasses. I thought about reaching up to take them off.

Everyone was still waiting for him. He took another look at the helicopter, and then he said, "I'm sorry about this, too—but I've really gotta go."

He held my gaze for one more second. Then, in slow motion, he turned and strode away.

I watched him go.

That was it? That was all? No goodbye? No closure of any kind? He was just going to tell me to evacuate and then fly off to Miami?

I never made a conscious choice to run after him. By the time I realized it was happening, I'd dropped all my stuff, and I'd launched into a full George Bailey–style gallop.

"Hutch!" I called, but he didn't hear me over the noise of the bird.

I sprinted faster to catch up. "Hutch!" I called again, and this time I caught his wrist.

He turned back and looked at me.

The sight of him there—windblown and suited up for duty—kind of stopped my heart.

"Hutch!" I shouted over the whirring of the blades. "Do me a favor, okay?"

He was listening.

Even recounting it now, I can't believe what I was about to do. All I can figure is that circumstances had raced out ahead of me, and my rational thinking hadn't caught up. That's the only way I could possibly have said what I said:

"Before you go—can you kiss me goodbye?"

"What?"

One more time, louder. "Kiss me goodbye!" I shouted.

Omar was waving his arms now for Hutch to hurry up.

Hutch glanced that way and then back to me. He still had his back-pack over one shoulder and his helmet under his arm. Everybody was waiting. A hurricane was coming. What the hell was I thinking, chasing Hutch down the tarmac?

It was foolish. We hadn't talked about anything or cleared anything up. We were surrounded by the chaos of half-truths and random expla-nations. I had no idea how he felt about me. But it did seem likely that I might evacuate, go home to Texas, and never see Hutch again. And if that's how things were going to go . . . I wanted one last kiss.

The one I hadn't been able to ask for before he knew the truth.

I braced for Hutch to shake his head.

Of course he would.

But then, instead, he took a step closer—and pulled me to him by the waist with his free arm, clamping me to him so tightly that I tilted backward. And then he gave me the only kind of kiss there was time for—or room for, or reason for. A no-time-for-chitchat kind of kiss. A you-asked-for-it-you-got-it kiss. A kiss churning with things unsaid. In-tense. Melting. Just his arm clutching me tight, his mouth eclipsing all my racing thoughts, and the storm, and the future . . . all our time al-ready borrowed. How long did it last? Three seconds, tops? But it was like emotional lightning—as if we'd stepped into a current of something bigger than both of us. Something vast, and awe-inspiring, and some-thing I knew, even as it happened, that I would never—not ever—forget.

And then it was over.

He let go and took a step back.

I blinked at him for a second—breathless, my knees feeble, my heart slumped and panting against my ribs.

"There's your kiss," Hutch said with a nod, taking another step back. "Now get the hell out of here."

Twenty-Four

SO I DID.

I packed up, took Rue's car, and hit the Overseas Highway. But I hadn't even made it to the mainland—or stopped thinking about that kiss for one second—when Rue called.

"Have you left yet?" Rue asked.

I was on Islamorada. "I'm on the road," I said. "What's going on?"

Rue hesitated, like she wasn't sure if she should tell me.

"Rue?" I asked. "What is it?"

Rue let out a sigh. "I just got a call from Lieutenant Alonso."

My first thought was Hutch. "Is everything okay?"

"Looks like he had some trouble with George Bailey."

George Bailey. Not Hutch. Okay. "What does that mean— *trouble*?"

"When he went to Hutch's place, he couldn't get George Bailey to come with him."

"You mean—"

"Apparently the rain had started already, and the thunder . . ."

Oh, god.

"And Lieutenant Alonso had six other pets in his minivan—plus his wife and kids."

"And so he just *left him*?"

"I'm not sure they had much choice. That dog weighs a hundred and sixty pounds. You can't force him to go anywhere he doesn't want to."

"So what you're saying is . . . George Bailey is alone on the *Rue the Day* right now?"

"Do you know anyone who's still in town?"

I didn't. My mind was churning. "Does Hutch have a hidden key somewhere?"

"The lieutenant left the door unlocked."

Then she seemed to intuit what I was thinking. "But not you," Rue said. "You're not going yourself. There's no time to turn back. The traffic's only going to get worse—and the last place you want to be when a hurricane hits is on a seven-mile bridge out over the ocean. Just get to the mainland. I'll find somebody."

"Okay," I said. "I hear you. I'm sure we'll find someone."

But we wouldn't. Right? We wouldn't find anyone. Everybody was either gone or going. And if Lieutenant Alonso—tough as nails with a tattoo of Poseidon on his shoulder—couldn't get George Bailey off the boat, what chance did a mere mortal have?

That dog couldn't be forced.

He could only be *cajoled*.

And the only person I knew of besides Hutch who could cajole George Bailey . . . was me.

I thought of George Bailey on a boat, during a hurricane, endlessly trembling and all alone . . . and then I did what was doubtless, without question, hands-down, one million percent the dumbest thing I've ever done in my life. I U-turned without braking from the packed northbound side of the highway to the utterly deserted southbound side. With a screech.

And then I hauled ass back to Key West.

Would a Great Dane even fit in a Mini Cooper?

We were about to find out.

I MADE IT back to Key West in an hour and fifteen minutes, which is thirty minutes faster than Google thought possible. That's the upside of going against a mass evacuation, I guess. My side of the highway was totally empty, and the cops had other things to do.

I sped, and I ran red lights, and, to be honest, I called Cole.

"Ace Hutcheson," he said when he answered.

"You're kidding, right?"

"I knew it was you. But I'm trying it out."

"I think you should go with Boots and Saddles."

"You were eavesdropping!"

"Of course I was. We all were."

"I *told* you Hutch was going to beat me up."

"You *wanted* him to beat you up."

Cole thought about it. "Maybe that's true."

"I hope you got it out of your system."

"I think, actually, maybe I did."

I was getting close to the marina. I needed to get to the point. "Listen," I said. "Did you say something weird to Hutch that night?"

"Define *weird*."

"Did you talk to him about me?"

"I thought you said you were eavesdropping."

"I missed the end because I was helping Sullivan throw up."

Cole paused. "Yes. At the end, he asked me about you. He wanted to know what you could possibly have been thinking to go along with all my lies."

I felt my core clench up. "What did you tell him?"

"Well, I couldn't tell him it was for Rue's sake—because he still doesn't know about Rue."

"I repeat: What did you tell him?"

"I told him it was all to save your job."

"My *job*?"

"Yeah. So you could do the 'Day in the Life,' and impress Sullivan, and not get fired."

"But we'd already done the filming by then!"

"I told him you were afraid he'd revoke his permission."

"You—what?"

"It was the best I could do. I was thinking fast, okay?"

"But I wasn't even going to upload it anyway."

"He doesn't know that."

"So Hutch thinks that you and I—evilly, *deceitfully*—planned this whole thing from the beginning for nothing more important than not getting fired?"

I could sense Cole shrugging on the other end. "Maybe?"

All that wondering I'd done over why he wasn't taking my calls?

Guess we'd cleared that up.

"Cole! You lied to him! He *detests* me now. He won't even look at me. You can't just leave him thinking that!"

"I can't expose Rue. She hasn't even told him she's sick."

"Rue should tell him the truth now! You both should! About everything!"

"I agree. There's only one problem: he's not answering his phone. And he's probably a little busy right now. But I'll keep trying, okay? I'll find him, and so will Rue, and we'll set all the records straight—okay?"

What else was there to say? "Okay."

"By the way," Cole said. "We're all good with Sullivan now."

"What do you mean, *all good*?"

"I mean, she knows you and I aren't dating, and she's fine with it."

"Why would she be fine with it? I thought she was going to blackball you and destroy your career."

"That was before we spent the night together."

"What!"

"Remember when you kicked me out?"

"Yeah?"

"She took me in. Enthusiastically."

"Please tell me you didn't take advantage of our boss that night! She was so drunk! She vomited up two bottles of prosecco!"

"I did not take advantage of Sullivan that night," Cole said.

"Thank you."

"It was the next morning."

"Oh, my god, Cole. Why do you always have to make everything worse?"

"Pretty sure I made things a whole lot better."

"You *slept* with *Sullivan*?"

"Yep. Except now I call her Sully."

"Now she's really going to fire you."

"Nope."

"Nope?"

"Nope. Because we fell in love."

"Well, that was fast."

"When it's right, it's right."

"You're dating Sullivan now? That's happening?"

"Yes," Cole said. "And guess who she likes me better than?"

"Hutch?" I asked, just as Cole answered at the exact same time: "Hutch."

"This must be very healing for you," I said.

"It's very healing for both of us."

"Congratulations," I said. "Now go call your brother and confess."

IT WAS SHEETING down rain by the time I parked at the marina. The sky was dark and brooding—even though it was four in the afternoon. All the parking lot lamps were off, and so were all the lights on all the marina boats, and I wondered if the power had gone out.

I left everything in Rue's car except my phone, thinking I might need it for a flashlight—and then I ran down the wooden dock toward the boat, my sneakers smacking the drenched wood. But when I stumbled in through the boat door, expecting, I guess, for George Bailey to knock me down as usual . . . he was nowhere to be found.

"George Bailey?" I called.

Nothing. The boat was dark and quiet.

Had Carlos come back for him? Or had Rue enlisted someone else, after all?

"George Bailey!" I called again, shining my phone light around.

When I reached a bank of light switches, I flipped them all—but nothing.

The boat felt quiet as a tomb, rising and falling on the water and bumping against the dock. *He's definitely not here*, I thought, as I looked around, anyway. Where could he have gone?

Then, just as I got close to the closet by Hutch's bed, I heard a whimper.

"George Bailey?" I asked, peering into the closet.

There, below the hanging shirts and pants, I saw two shining eyes.

"Hey, buddy!" I said, squatting down and trying to convince us both with my voice that we were just having a pleasant get-together. "I found you!"

I could hear George Bailey panting. I put my hand on the closet floor near him, not sure how freaked out he would be. Would he be like one of those panicked animals that bites anything that comes near it?

No. I didn't get bitten. He was a gentle giant to the core.

As soon as I put my hand near him, though, I got *licked*—wrist to elbow.

That felt like a good sign. "Hello, friend," I said, reaching in farther to pet his back and feeling his whole body trembling in a way that made me so glad I'd come back for him.

I made pleasant, newscaster-like chitchat. "I know you're not a big fan of thunder," I said. "You don't enjoy thunder, and I don't enjoy power outages, or darkened boats, or hurricanes. So . . . what do you say to the idea of getting out of here?"

Then, like the most trustworthy person who ever lived, I opened the closet door wide, patted the thighs of my jeans, and said, "Come on. Come on, pal. Let's go jump into Rue's Mini Cooper and blow this popsicle stand."

At the sound of Rue's name, George Bailey ooched forward.

That's when I remembered that he did speak a little English.

"Hey, George Bailey," I said. "*Hutch* told me you might want to go on a *walk*."

At the word *walk* his ears shifted forward and his tail started thumping the inside of the closet.

"Do you want to go on a *walk*?" I asked again, standing up.

When I stood, George Bailey stood.

"A *walk*!" I said. "Where is your *leash*?"

At *leash*, he stepped out and followed me. We walked around, flashing the phone light and looking. "Where does Hutch keep your *leash*?" I asked over and over, just to keep the conversation going.

Then I spotted it hanging from a hook near the door.

Is this going to be easy? I wondered.

But I should have known better than to have thoughts like that. George Bailey was totally with me as I got him leashed up . . . until I opened the door to the rain. That's when I noticed how much darker the sky had become, and how much the water in the marina was churning.

And that's when the thunder decided to do its thing.

At the sound, George Bailey planted all four of his feet and sat down.

He did have a point.

"Come on, buddy," I said, walking confidently toward the door.

But as I reached the threshold, I hit the end of the leash line.

George Bailey wasn't budging.

I gestured out at the pouring rain like it was fun. "Don't you want to go for a *walk*?"

Not that much, apparently.

"Hey, friend," I said, hoping maybe I could explain it to him logically. "There's a hurricane coming. A big one. We need to get out of here."

George Bailey was, quite literally, unmoved.

Next, I tried a bunch of other tactics—from luring him with snacks, to tossing his armadillo squeaky toy out the door, to explaining that Hutch was waiting for him at a big dog party in Miami, to attempting *actual brute force*—and none of it budged him even one inch.

I only succeeded in slipping—twice—on the wet entryway floor . . . and landing on my tailbone both times.

As time wore on, I resorted more and more to trying to *explain things.*

Breathless and wet, I kept up a running monologue that George Bailey fully ignored, as I moved around him—pushing from behind, then pulling from the front, desperately trying to set him in motion: "Look, I know you have concerns about all that weather out there, and I get it. I know it seems scarier outside than it does inside right now . . . but we've got a life-threatening storm on our hands. I don't know if anyone's ever told you this, but a houseboat is literally the last place on earth you want to be during a hurricane. A *Category Four* hurricane, by the way, according to the Saffir-Simpson scale! This guy Saffir-Simpson is not kidding around. We could really die. Every single person—*and dog!*—in the keys is evacuating right now. The entire Overseas Highway is one long string of taillights. Come on, buddy! Let's get the hell out of here."

Through it all, George Bailey watched me like some kind of jaded law school professor who was pretty sure I was going to fail his class— just waiting for me to say something, anything, persuasive.

The whole thing was pretty much the definition of a bad idea.

As the thunder got louder, and the rain got harsher, and the houseboat bobbed more and more urgently on the waves, knocking against the rickety dock, I googled *how to move a large dog* on my phone and scanned search results like: *how to motivate a stubborn stallion, coaxing rituals for camels,* and *how to move a grand piano.*

Turns out, this particular situation is a tough one to crowdsource.

I tried calling Hutch for tips, but as it rang, I heard a faint sound coming from the bedroom.

A phone ringing.

I followed the sound, George Bailey trailing equally curious behind me, until I found Hutch's phone, which had fallen behind his mattress and through the bed slats.

Oh, shit. Was *this* why he hadn't texted me back?

I tried to retrieve it, but the bed was on a frame attached to the floor, and the slats were too narrow to get my arm through.

Oh, well. That would be something to solve later.

Back at the door, I was explaining how courage worked to George Bailey—insisting that facing his demons now would ultimately help him reach his personal best—when I felt an eerie pulse of electricity waver through the air.

Then I heard a hissing sound behind me, and then a crack louder than anything I'd ever heard in my life, just as the room lit up in a flash and then went dark again. The sound was beyond full volume: so loud, it seemed to rip the air like fabric. So loud, my unbudgeable friend George Bailey disappeared in a flash and scrambled back into Hutch's closet, leash and all. The light was so bright, it left a green afterimage in my eyes. One of the windows shattered. Then the searing sound retreated, followed by pops and cracks and the whole sky lighting up, and then rolling thunder.

A lightning strike.

Not on the boat itself, but not far away.

Like, *feet* away.

Had it hit a sailboat mast? A cell tower? An antenna?

Whatever it was, in the wake of it, I watched in horror through the hole where the shattered window had just been as the wooden dock *we were moored to* responded to the lightning strike by collapsing in slow motion into the water.

It was almost as if the whole dock just . . . *fainted.*

And then it was gone.

And we weren't moored to anything anymore.

"Oh, shit," I said out loud—feeling an urgency like now we *really* had to get out of here.

But, of course, now there was nowhere to go.

Next, I felt an urge to call Hutch again. But there was no way to do that, either.

We were, apparently, completely screwed.

I stared through the window, trying to make it make sense.

The dock that I'd just been trying to cajole George Bailey out onto . . . was gone.

"George Bailey," I said out loud, in case this wasn't already abundantly clear. "We have a problem."

LOOK, I'M NOT a boat person. I didn't grow up sailing. I'm from *Dallas, Texas*! We're as landlocked as it gets. I was the last person on earth you'd pick to *captain an unmoored houseboat during a hurricane*. I didn't know how to work a maritime radio, and I didn't know anything about boat safety, and up until three weeks ago, I couldn't even swim.

There was probably some way to radio for help in that situation.

But I couldn't work a boat radio even on a normal day in full sunshine.

I commanded myself to *think*. But then I just thought about how *thinking about thinking* didn't help.

I'm not really a fast processor. For any big decision, I prefer forty-eight hours or so to hem and haw, and make lists of pros and cons, and call Beanie and discuss. Like I'd done, in fact, just hours beforehand, in a different lifetime.

I'd driven along on dry land in a Mini Cooper with heated seats— taking all my safety and comfort for granted as I endlessly yammered to Beanie about how simultaneously passionate and dismissive that good-bye kiss with Hutch had been. How manly yet vulnerable, how angry yet tender, how lost yet found. The astonishing way it felt exactly like a beginning and an ending at the same time.

I mean, that was my whole evacuation journey from earlier today: me summoning pairs of opposite words to try to capture the vibes of that life-ruining kiss while fleeing a hurricane on the Overseas Highway—as Beanie, folding laundry a thousand miles away, validated all my interpretations with ever-more-emphatic *Mmmm-hmmms*.

Maybe I should have been listening to the radio.

A little weather information might have come in handy.

And now here I was. Alone with George Bailey, on a handmade pontoon houseboat tethered to absolutely nothing, adrift in the ocean, during a hurricane.

Fuuuuuuuuck.

Should I call Beanie?

But she was worse in emergencies than I was. She'd panic, and then she'd cry, and then I'd end up consoling her. All that would do was waste time.

Instead, I pulled out my cell phone and called 911.

A dispatcher picked up right away. "911. What's your emergency?"

"Hi there!" I said. "I'm so sorry, but I'm on a houseboat called *Rue the Day* at the Sunshine Marina on Key West, and the dock we were moored to just got struck by lightning—and it collapsed into the water."

Yes, the name of the boat had a sudden new irony.

"Your location is the Sunshine Marina?"

"Yes—but not for long. We are adrift."

"I'm making a note of your distress call and your location," the dispatcher said then.

Wait—what? Why wasn't she dispatching someone to come help?

"Um," I said then. "Can you guys come and get me?" I asked next. Then I added, as if it might help my case, "I have a large dog with me who's afraid of thunder."

A pause that might have been sarcastic. Then: "I'm sorry, ma'am. We're in the middle of an active hurricane."

"Yeah! I know! I'm drifting loose in it!"

"No rescues are happening at this time. All personnel are sheltering in place."

Did her voice sound a little irritated? "Are you saying," I asked then, "that you're just going to leave me here? In the ocean? During a Category Four hurricane?"

"The hurricane has been downgraded to a Category Two."

"What's the difference?"

"Wind speeds for Cat Twos top out at ninety-five miles per hour."

"Why is that not comforting?"

"I apologize, ma'am. But anyone who ignored the evac order will just have to ride this one out."

Hold on. Did she think I had just *flouted* the evac order?

Of course she did. She probably dealt with people like that all the time.

"I didn't ignore it!" I said. "My dog did! And he's not even my dog! I was just trying to help him because he's a rescue dog from a puppy mill, and he has thunder-phobia, or whatever it's called, and his life has been hard enough." Then, to stress that I was a nice person who deserved to *not die in the ocean*, I added: "I *was* evacuating! I had already made it to Islamorada! But then I turned around! To save a very frightened dog! But then I couldn't get him off the boat! He literally weighs more than I do!"

Silence on the other end. Was she checking her Instagram?

"Hello?" I went on. "I'm not a—a—*non-evacuator*! The *dog* is!" I said, my voice shifting into a different octave.

Her voice was unmoved. "I'm sorry, ma'am. All personnel are unavailable."

"Look," I said, hoping maybe I could access some general sense of first-responder camaraderie. "This houseboat belongs to a US Coast Guard rescue swimmer—and so does the dog! He got dispatched to Miami to wait out the storm."

"Then I'm sure he'll be the first one back on scene to rescue you once it's safe to fly," the dispatcher said.

"But—" I protested, my voice lifting higher with panic as I pushed *We could be long dead by then* out of my mind and said instead: "Tell me what to do! How do I survive the night?"

The dispatcher sighed. "If that boat you're on really belongs to a rescue swimmer, it'll be well-equipped with safety gear. Find a life jacket and put it on. Turn off your phone to save power, put it in a plastic bag, and keep it with you. Find someplace secure and hunker down. And if it's a choice between you and the dog? This time, save yourself first."

✧   ✧   ✧

WAS THE *RUE the Day* well-equipped with safety gear?

I'll let the full storage tub of flashlights answer that question.

Hutch, it turned out, had several first-aid kits, fresh drinking water, multiple fire extinguishers, and a battery-powered radio that was older than he was. Not to mention a snorkel, flippers, and mask. And a flare gun.

Wait! *Don't call them flippers.*

A snorkel, *fins*, and a mask.

Add to that, a whole closet with life jackets stashed away inside— including, God bless Hutch, a dog-shaped one for George Bailey.

Docile and perhaps slightly catatonic with fear now, he let me zip him into it. Then I did the same for myself.

Next, I found a freezer bag in the kitchenette to waterproof my phone.

Then I turned on a battery-powered lantern.

Then I started to holster the flare gun in the waistband of my jeans before deciding I was more likely to shoot myself with it than do any good—and I put it back in its case.

What next?

Try to figure out the radio? Try to turn on the boat and steer it somehow? Call 911 again? Cry?

Yes. Yes to all those things. At once.

I'm embarrassed to admit how panicked I was. But I wasn't a crisis person. I wasn't a woman of action. I wasn't the dashing hero of the story. I was a mid-level employee at a commercial video-production company!

I didn't want to have adventures: I wanted to be the person in the background *filming the person having adventures*—or, better yet, a person asking a subject to *reminisce about long-past adventures.*

Who could I appeal to for a do-over?

Adrift in a houseboat with a thunder-phobic dog during a hurricane might be a bad fit for anyone—but it was the full-on worst for me.

Meanwhile, George Bailey was staring at me like I was in charge.

I flipped some switches on the radio until I could hear broadcasts and interchanges, but, honestly, it was mostly jargon. People talking about *knots* and *lat and long* and saying random numbers. Suitable mostly for background noise. I tried to leave it on for the voices—but then, as the frantic Maydays started coming in, I turned it off.

The shore was receding, and I could only tell because part of the marina was now on fire. Was it a boat? The boathouse? I couldn't see well enough to know. But the flames were a point of reference, even as they receded into the distance—or we did.

I suddenly felt colder.

And the waves seemed bigger and sharper.

I felt my first rise of nausea, though if it was seasickness or fear, I wasn't sure.

It's possible at this point that George Bailey was starting to regret his choices. As I moved around the cabin, frantically trying to *do something*, he stayed with me like Velcro.

The end of the boat with the shattered window now had a wet floor—in addition to glass shards—one inch of water sliding side to side with the waves.

We stayed at the other end.

Maybe I shouldn't have, but I scolded George Bailey a little.

"I hate to say this is all your fault," I said, "but it totally is. If you'd just gone with Lieutenant Alonso, you'd be in Miami by now, all dry and warm and bedded down for the night. And so would I! But now we'll both die in a watery grave. So thanks for that."

Then, as if George Bailey had responded with, *You're the one who decided to come back for me,* I went on: "What choice did I have? Honestly. I wasn't leaving you here alone. Not after all you've been through. I just wish you had trusted me a little more, you know? Never choose fear, okay? Choose love. Choose trust! When a good person shows up to rescue you, choose that person!"

What was I even saying now?

I wasn't even listening to myself at this point.

Meanwhile, my brain kindly, frantically, tried to generate some hope.

Maybe we'd be okay. Maybe the winds would push us away from the worst of the storm. Or maybe there was a soft, sandy shore just out of sight that we could wash up on. Or maybe Robert's vintage, handmade pontoon houseboat would astonish us all by bobbing pleasantly over the waves all night, rubber-ducky style.

It was possible, anyway.

The world was full of bad luck—but it was full of good luck, too.

Maybe we'd used up all our bad luck for the day.

Or the year.

What would Hutch have done in this situation? Would he have jumped overboard with George Bailey right after the strike and tried to swim to land? Should I have done that? Never mind that if a solid dock had been a tough sell for this dog—a cold black ocean would've been impossible. Or maybe it was better that we'd stayed on the boat. Maybe that post-lightning water was full of electricity? How did physics even work?

Dammit.

All those years of school, and I didn't know anything that could save my life.

No one was coming for us. At least I knew that much.

Hutch wasn't going to *steal a helicopter* and come get us in a hurricane.

We were on our own. With nothing else to do but ride out the storm.

Twenty-Five

RIDE OUT THE *storm* doesn't capture it, though.

What is it they say about seasickness? First you fear you'll die, then you *hope* you'll die, then, after you survive, it feels like you're dead?

That pretty much captures it.

I assume, as the storm got worse, we floated farther from shore, though I really don't know for sure. Between the rain and the darkness, I had zero bearings. All I got was bright flashes when lightning cracked across the sky. Then the sea would appear, all around us, the waves like canyons—so scary, I didn't even want to look. Soon the windows were so covered with sea-foam spray that it was hard to see out of them, anyway—except for the shattered one. Which let in more water with each crashing wave.

The floors were wet. Everything was wet.

And cold.

At first, I was alert—paying attention in every direction to sights and sounds and cracks of thunder. I even found a sheet of paper, thinking I might try to record information, somehow. The number of lightning flashes? Thunder claps at intervals? Vomiting sessions?

Or maybe I could write something—a will, maybe? Some final deep thoughts? A farewell letter that no one would ever see?

So many choices.

But I never did decide. Soon, I was too seasick to write anything at all.

The constant motion was so exhausting. The churn of the water, the shifting of the angles. We'd switch from tilting one direction to fully tilting the other in seconds—over and over. We tipped up on waves that felt almost vertical, and then we crashed back down into the channel between them. The living room chairs and sofa slid back and forth, hitting the walls and piling on top of each other. The refrigerator came unbolted, and all the food fell out.

It was up and down and side to side—randomly and in no order or rhythm. The weirdest part was going weightless for a minute as the waves tossed the boat up—before feeling gravity double as it slammed back down. Sometimes there was a lull in the waves, but other times, a bunch would hit at once. The boat shuddered and clanked and creaked. We got overtaken again and again with seawater. And every hit from the water wanted to break the boat apart—slamming us with a force like sudden car brakes.

I, at least, had a framework for what was happening—but George Bailey couldn't brace himself and kept skittering across the floor, clawing madly with his paws for traction. During one sharp tilt, he slid all the way into the far corner, shattering a ceramic lamp and cutting his paw in the process.

He yelped, and whimpered, and as he limped back over toward me, refusing to even touch that paw to the floor, he left a trail of blood.

Something about the blood made me feel hopeless.

Or maybe it was the whimpering.

"I'm so sorry, buddy," I said to George Bailey, pulling a pillow out of its case and tying the fabric around his paw as a very ill-fitting bandage.

During another lull, I tried to figure out a better place for George Bailey to shelter. Hutch's closet seemed like a good spot. I could fill it up with pillows and blankets for padding. And of course watch for water under the door.

I took all of Hutch's hanging clothes out, gathering them in my arms and getting a big whiff of Hutch's scent that I was too nauseated to enjoy, and I dumped them in the bathroom in a pile and closed the door. Then, as I did the same to the storage boxes at the bottom, I remembered my hibiscus hair clip. Was it still there, I wondered—shoved back in the corner behind Hutch's neat stack of storage tubs? For a second before I looked, I felt this superstitious flash: *If the flower is there, we're going to be okay.*

But it wasn't there.

The back corner was empty.

For a second, I felt so irrationally disappointed in Hutch. Would it have killed him to just send me *one tiny spark of hope*? I really wasn't asking for that much.

And yet, here we were.

That moment gave way to the next, and I found myself seriously wondering where the flower had gone. Had Hutch thrown it away in a fit of disappointed rage after I'd turned out to be a terrible person? Or maybe tossed it overboard? Or lit it on fire and watched the ashes float off on the wind over the water?

Or maybe it was worse than that. Maybe he had just swept it into a dustpan with all his other unremarkable trash—and thrown it away without even noticing.

In the face of the larger questions dominating my life . . . questions like, *Can you die from seasickness dehydration?* And *Do whales eat people?* And *How deadly are jellyfish stings, exactly?* In the midst of all those, you could argue that *What became of my hibiscus hair clip?* was, perhaps, the least pressing.

But I loved that question the best.

It gave me something Hutch-adjacent to turn over in my mind as I padded the closet floor with pillows and gestured to George Bailey to step inside.

George Bailey, like a perfect angel who had never stranded us on a houseboat during a hurricane, stepped easily in. Then he settled into a lion position on the pillows and gingerly lowered his bandaged paw to wait for what was next.

What would be next?

Drowning? Dismemberment? Ripped apart by sharks?

I thought about Hutch saying sharks were always everywhere.

Then I put a fervent request out to the universe. Of all the ways I might be about to die . . . could *sharks* please not be one of them?

Of course, the universe didn't care about my requests.

I'd just have to care about them myself.

I closed the closet door with George Bailey inside, leaned back against it to keep it that way, and braced myself against Hutch's built-in bed frame. If the boat started sinking, of course, I'd let George Bailey out. But he seemed safer in there for now.

Though what did *safer* even mean?

My senses were all haywire. The motion was the worst—but the screeching and howling of the wind, and the angry creaking of the boat, and the rolling of the thunder . . . it was incessant aural chaos. Clanking, wailing, crashing, howling—all of it so loud I couldn't hear my own thoughts. And, from inside the closet, George Bailey still whimpering, like I was being mean.

It wasn't long before I'd thrown up everything I'd ever eaten in my life, and then, in the wake of it, continued dry-heaving on principle. I lost all sense of equilibrium. The room in my head was spinning worse than the churning sea. During lulls, I would lie on the floor, panting, longing to die.

But I didn't die.

And neither did George Bailey.

We survived.

I don't know how many hours the storm raged. I lost all sense of time—and everything else. But at some point when it was still dark out, almost without my realizing it was happening, the churning waters slowed down. And then it got quiet. And the water itself—if not the motion in my head—became calmer.

George Bailey was still whimpering.

I opened the door, and George Bailey stepped out gingerly, his paw still wrapped in the pillowcase, now stained and bloody where the cut had reopened.

"How are you?" I asked. "Are you okay?"

In response, he limped over on three paws, settled next to me, and licked my face for a while. It was surprisingly comforting—and it made us both feel better.

And that's how we fell asleep, right there on the floor.

WHEN WE WOKE again, it was day. The sun was out, the sky was cloudless, and the ocean surface was as calm as a pond.

Almost as if the sea was exhausted, too.

Or maybe ashamed of its tantrum.

George Bailey woke up when I did. I checked his paw, and then he watched my attempts to clean myself up a little—partly in hopes of feeling more normal, and partly to be presentable for any rescue that might happen to come along. I washed my face and brushed my teeth with bottled water. I combed my hair. My jeans were wet, and so were my shoes, but I didn't have better options there. Though I did change into a safety-orange T-shirt of Hutch's for visibility.

I looked out the shattered window. Except for the debris floating all around us—a beer cooler, a sideways mini fridge, a half-full three-liter soda bottle—everything was weirdly normal.

I walked out toward the living room to investigate, feeling like I had the worst hangover of my life. I'd thrown up so many times in the past twenty-four hours, I lost count. The whole place looked about how I felt—food everywhere, broken furniture, glass from the shattered window. I felt a strange urge to clean up.

I needed to sweep up the glass for George Bailey's paws' sake. I opened a kitchen closet to look for a broom—and guess what I found? Hutch's penny jar. Unbroken, with the lid on, and all of his mom's pennies. It was half-full. Maybe forty or fifty pennies? I grabbed the jar and took it out with the broom.

George Bailey was watching me from the bedroom doorway.

"What?" I said. "These are coming with us when we get rescued."

As I swept up, despite feeling like I'd been trampled by some panicked herd of animals, I also couldn't deny one very joyful fact.

We'd survived.

Also: everything was over!

Except . . . maybe not everything.

The floor did seem to be at a funny angle, now that I'd swept it up.

I looked around. One side of the boat was definitely lower than the other.

I made my way to the back deck—where I was confronted with two facts in rapid succession. One: we were definitely far, far out at sea. And two: one of the pontoons was partly detached from underneath. With a gash along it that had to be letting in water.

Were we . . . sinking?

I checked the horizon for some land.

Not much land out there.

I don't know why my first thought was *flare gun*. I've never shot a flare gun in my life. But I went to the first-aid closet, got it out, and had it pointed toward the sky before it occurred to me to try my cell phone.

It was still dry, inside its little plastic bag. Chalk one up for the dispatcher.

But would it get reception? We could be halfway to Antarctica by now.

I turned it on . . . and YES.

I called 911 again.

A woman dispatcher answered. "911. What's your emergency?"

I was, honestly, so moved and overjoyed and discombobulated to hear a human voice that I burst into tears. And then I apologized.

"I'm so sorry," I said, not even sure myself what exactly I was sorry for. For having a problem? For interrupting the dispatcher's day? For having failed to get George Bailey off the boat? For throwing etiquette to the wind and calling twice in a row?

Anything was possible.

"I called yesterday," I said, wincing at how ridiculous I sounded as I finished with, "while being swept out to sea in a houseboat near Key West?"

My voice sounded weirdly hopeful. As if she might remember me.

She did not. She wasn't even the same person.

"What is your location?" she asked.

"That's the thing," I said. "I really did get swept out to sea. That wasn't, like, a metaphor or anything. *Literally* swept out to sea. I was out here all night in the hurricane in a homemade houseboat . . . but I lived. My friend's dog and I both lived, in fact—though he cut his paw on a broken lamp. And now we are . . . adrift? And I'm not seeing much land nearby? And the other wrinkle here," I went on, never a fan of giving bad news, "is that the boat we're on now seems to be sinking?"

My voice kept going up at the end, as if my entire life was nothing but questions.

A solid pause from the dispatcher.

That couldn't be good.

I rushed in with some more info, lest she decide I was hopeless. "This houseboat belongs to Tom Hutcheson, who's a rescue swimmer for the US Coast Guard. Except he goes by Hutch. Isn't that the sexiest name you've ever heard in your life?" This wasn't helping. My brain was jumbled. *Focus!* "He's not with us—on the boat. It was docked at the Sunshine Marina on the west side, but lightning destroyed the dock it was moored to, and the boat drifted off. With us on it. Me and the dog—not me and Hutch." I looked around. "But I really don't know how long it's been. Or how far we've drifted." I looked around one more time. "And I'm really not seeing much around us other than—you know—floating trash and the ocean."

Another pause. Was it hopeless?

Come on! We could put a man on the moon, but we couldn't find one bedraggled lady and one very stubborn Great Dane off the Florida coast?

"Hello?" I asked.

"I'm initiating a search and rescue."

"Oh, my god, I love you," I said.

"What is your weight?" she asked next.

Seriously?

I made up a number and took off ten pounds as a gesture of self-care. Then I added back two for all the pennies I'd be bringing with me.

"And you have an animal with you?"

"Yes," I confirmed. "A Great Dane. With an injured paw."

"What is the animal's weight?"

"One hundred and seventy," I said, assigning George Bailey my ten missing pounds.

"Can you describe your craft?"

My craft? "You mean the boat?"

"Yes, ma'am."

"It's a houseboat named *Rue the Day*. Smallish, but cozy? It used to have hanging bulbs and Adirondack chairs on the back deck—but they're long gone now."

She interrupted. "Ma'am. I meant something identifying. For the search. Color?"

"Oh. Got it. Kind of a Cape Cod gray?"

"And you said the craft is sinking?"

Ah. "Yes. I think so. It's a pontoon boat, and I think one of the pontoons was damaged in the storm. It seems to be taking on water. We're definitely . . . tilting."

I'll tell you something. This lady wasn't going to win any personality prizes.

But I *loved* her.

I have never felt so grateful for a phone conversation. Yes, she was all business, and kind of the opposite of chatty, and at no point had she offered even a courtesy laugh. But she existed! And she knew that *I* existed! She might not have any idea where I was, and she might have a whole board of other emergencies she needed to go deal with, but she could hear me. I was still totally alone in the ocean on a sinking boat—but at least I had a friend. Of sorts.

Until she had to go.

In the strange lull that followed, I drank all the bottled water I could fit into my stomach, and George Bailey did, too. I scavenged some bread for me and some beef-flavored kibble for him. I also slathered on sunscreen, which seemed de rigueur for being shipwrecked.

Then George Bailey and I climbed up onto the roof deck. I brought the jar of pennies with me, the flare gun, and my cell phone.

And we waited to be rescued.

Except guess what? Waiting to be rescued is hard.

It's an agonizing mixture of boredom and terror.

After about three minutes, I was fighting the itch to call Beanie—even though I knew I should save my cell phone battery. It wasn't like she could save me.

But she could keep me company. That wasn't nothing.

I mean, if they never found me . . . this could be *it*. The grand finale of my life.

Did I really want to spend it *not calling Beanie*?

She was the person I processed everything with—from nail polish colors down to bad dreams. For once I had something interesting! *Shipwrecked?* Come on! How could I *not* call her?

I was just about to give in to temptation when I saw something astonishing on the roof with us.

A toad.

Somehow, a toad had blown onto the roof of our houseboat during the storm, held on for dear life, defied every single one of the odds, and survived.

I watched it hop toward us and then stop between me and George Bailey, like it wanted to be friends—a kind of interspecies bonding-through-adversity scenario.

But—wait! What kind of a toad? If this was the poisonous kind, I'd have to kick it overboard. I remembered Hutch checking the last one with his flashlight, and I leaned in closer: no knobs or ridges on the head. So this one was the nonpoisonous kind, right?

I was 99 percent sure—but still deciding—when George Bailey scooped the toad up into his mouth.

"Really?" I said. "Is this how it's going to be?"

George Bailey gave me the side-eye, like *Mind your business*.

"Fine," I said. "We'll give him the benefit of the doubt. But if either one of you dies, I'm gonna be pissed."

George Bailey looked off at the horizon.

"And we're naming him Lucky," I went on, "and I'm putting you in charge of making sure he stays that way."

On the heels of that, of all things, my phone rang.

Beanie.

I checked my battery life: 60 percent. But I would've answered if it had been six.

It was *Beanie*.

"Hey," she said, as I answered.

"Hey," I said.

"What's up?"

I deflected. "What's up with *you*?"

"Not much," Beanie said—and she wasn't kidding. As she elaborated, and told me all about the avocado toast she'd just made for breakfast, the marinara stain she could not get out of her favorite shirt, and the crazy dream she'd just had about her high school boyfriend, I listened with an almost painful glow of gratitude in my chest.

"You have got to stop dreaming about that dude," I said.

"I know, right?"

What an amazing friend/cousin/almost-sister I had. Life hadn't exactly gifted me with the greatest mom on the planet, and I wouldn't say I'd won the stepmother lottery, either . . . but it was all redeemed, I realized right then, because I had Beanie.

Beanie who always picked up. Beanie who always made time to chat. Beanie who knew all my secrets.

And then I remembered I didn't know one big one of hers.

"I want you to tell me your beauty list," I said next.

"What? Why?"

Um, because I was curious? Because I hated not knowing things about Beanie? Because I might be about to die?

"I think I've waited long enough," I said.

"That's probably right."

"So?" I demanded.

"Well," Beanie said then. "Okay. It's just . . . *everything.*"

"Everything?" I challenged.

"You know," Beanie said. "Just . . . all of it."

Now this was distracting. "You like everything about your body? *Everything?* You think you're just—what? Perfect?"

"I don't think I'm *perfect,*" Beanie said, like that idea was preposterous. "I just don't look at myself the way you do."

"How do I look at myself?"

"Like you have a template in your head for how things should look—down to the most *minute* minutia—and how you feel about every part of yourself gets graded on the scale of how far it varies from the template."

Was there any other way to think about it? "Isn't that what everybody does?"

"I guess I don't."

"How do you think about it?"

"It's just, you know, that . . . everything gets a pass because it's mine."

"Everything gets a pass?"

"Yeah. It's like, I know what a supermodel is . . . and I know that I don't look like that. But I just love all of my . . . everything . . . because it's mine."

She loved all of her everything because it was hers.

It was such an astonishing idea, I didn't know what to say.

"Hello?" Beanie said.

"This is why you wouldn't tell me about your beauty list? Because you're so insultingly nice to yourself? Do I have to spend the rest of my life resenting you about this?"

"I mean, you could, I guess," Beanie said. "Or you could just do the same thing."

Would I do the same thing? Unlikely.

But she could have been talking about ceiling paint right then, and I wouldn't have cared. It felt so gloriously good for a minute for things to just feel normal. I knew I should tell her I was shipwrecked. I knew I should level with her about my dire situation. But, second by second, I just kept putting it off.   .

And that's exactly what I was still doing when the *Rue the Day* made a funny groaning sound—and then tilted further, from *a little bit* to a full 45-degree angle.

One side of the roof shifted up. The other side shifted down. And my cell phone, which had been resting on the roof deck beside me, went skittering off, past the railing, and plunked into the ocean.

George Bailey and I also slid, but we caught ourselves on the railing.

For a second, in the aftermath, I wondered if Beanie would intuit what had just happened. But of course she'd just assume my battery had died. The most hollow, gaping loneliness came over me then, as I lost my last connection to civilization. And panic, too.

George Bailey and I both panted at each other.

But that's when I looked down to see, tucked between George Bailey's paws, Hutch's jar of pennies. Still standing.

"Nice catch," I said.

I reached over, took the jar, unscrewed it, and transferred all the pennies to my jeans pockets. Every last one.

IN THE WAKE of my cell phone's untimely demise, I entered, shall we say, a dark period in my life.

It seemed pretty undeniable that I was going to die.

Sooner rather than later.

Braced against a roof railing at a 45-degree angle on a sinking house-boat with no remaining connection to civilization, and only a bandaged, bleeding dog and his pet toad for company, I felt—maybe for the first time in my life—true despair.

It was the silence, I think.

Or possibly the empty sky.

Or the way it kept getting harder and harder to imagine a version of this moment where the dog, the toad, and I wound up surviving.

Time compressed down and stretched out at the same time.

What happens when you drown? What does it feel like? Is it peaceful—or full of thrashing? Does it hurt when the water fills your lungs? I remembered, years ago, when I was a kid, not wanting my grandmother to be cremated because I just couldn't accept that it wouldn't hurt. But now, being cremated seemed like Swedish massage compared to whatever awaited me in the deep ocean. A school of piranhas, maybe—feasting on me like a charcuterie board?

A visual that I couldn't push away took over the movie screen of my mind: of tiny fish nibbling away every single thing about me that made me *me*. The earlobes? Eaten. The eyes? Consumed. The kissable mouth? Devoured.

What does that old song say? "You don't know what you've got till it's gone"?

The very real, very immediate prospect of my body—the one I'd picked on and complained about and disdained so hard for all these years—suddenly just . . . *not being there* . . .

It saturated me with a sadness so deep, so *cellular*, I'd never felt anything like it before.

Grief.

Grief for a body that, it turned out, I'd loved all along.

I'd taken her for granted, this soft, tender, undemanding self—all these years. I'd criticized her, and ignored her, and scorned her, and denied her. And she'd just endured it. She'd stayed with me and taken it all—because she had no choice.

And now it was a love story—but a tragic one. Because now it was too late.

Tears streamed from the corners of my eyes as I watched the sky. I regretted how mean I'd been. I regretted how relentlessly I had refused to show myself any kindness. I felt the most doomed and hopeless protectiveness. I wished beyond anything that I could save her.

But there was nothing I could do.

Nothing except apologize.

The people who hurt us in life almost never apologize. But she deserved it. And if nothing else, before she disappeared, I wanted her to know that.

I should have loved all of my everything. Because it was mine.

As the roof surface tilted another few degrees, I stroked the tummy that I'd always wished had been flatter, and I said, out loud: "You're soft, and welcoming, and lovely. I couldn't see it before. I'm sorry."

I kept going, moving down to my thighs, patting them the way you would a child who needed comfort. "You are velvety and tender," I said, again, out loud, "and I never should have forbidden you to touch each other."

I worked my way around back to my haunch. "You spent a full morning with Hutch," I said, "and I didn't even let you enjoy it."

And on, and on. I apologized to my boobs for all the contraptions I had smushed them into. To my calves for insisting all those years that they were the wrong shape. To my butt for my lifelong, daily assessments that it was *too round*, of all things—when it had been just the perfect amount of round all along. To my pie piece—and just my irises in general—for looking at them so many times without ever really seeing them.

I worked my way around every inch, from arches to collarbones, apologizing, sincerely.

"This is the last chance I have to say it," I said, "and I know it's not enough. But I bullied you. I picked on you like the meanest mean girl in the world. I made you hate yourself. I sucked the joy out of everything—walking down the street, or eating a BLT, or just sitting in the sun. I should have taken you swimming and let you float in the water. I should have let you relax. I should have stood up for you. I should have admired you, and enjoyed you, and kept you company, and celebrated you. I know it's too late," I said. "But I'm so impossibly sorry."

I WAS ALL cried out by the time I finally heard it.

Far and distant and faint, but unmistakable. The sound of air being chopped.

And I suddenly remembered what hope felt like.

My head lifted at the sound, and then I was craning upward, searching the sky. The helicopter looked black at first—backlit by the sun—and I felt this sting of worry that maybe it wasn't the Coast Guard, after all. Maybe it was just some random helicopter flying by. Some irritating billionaire out for a pleasure ride to enjoy the catastrophe.

But then it got closer, and the light shifted: orange.

Orange!

Chromophobia *cured*.

My new favorite color from now until forever. I'd be buying nothing but orange throw pillows for the rest of my life.

"It's them," I told George Bailey, sitting up a bit. "It's definitely them. It's one hundred percent, absolutely, *holy-shit-we're-rescued* them!"

Then, just as I said it, as if to confirm . . . the one waterlogged pontoon with the gash that had been slowly filling with water gave up its struggle to stay afloat. One whole side of the *Rue the Day* went under, and the boat shifted until it was fully on its side.

George Bailey and I slid off the deck and landed in the water.

The flare gun slid off, too—never to be seen again.

I felt a flash of panic before remembering that these guys didn't need a flare. They knew what to look for. And even if most of the boat was submerged, from up there, they could see down into the water. Hutch had told me that. In the clear waters of the keys, they could sometimes see the ocean floor.

They'd find us. They would.

After the houseboat finished shifting, the only thing holding us up was the second—and last—pontoon. Which wasn't really built to do the whole job by itself. It was only a matter of time before the weight of the water pulled the whole boat under, but, for now, one side of it remained sticking straight up out of the water like an iceberg. I found a piece of railing to hold on to, and then I braced one leg against the submerged hull to pin George Bailey next to me.

He sat politely on my thigh, like it was a bench, but the fall had popped his cut open, and now he was bleeding again.

When the helicopter got closer, I started waving and yelling, more like a reflex than for any good reason. Then, as they moved into place to hover above us, I had a bunch of crazy thoughts all at once: What if the rescue swimmer turned out to be Hutch? I mean, it wouldn't be him. It *couldn't* be—of course.

But what if it was?

Even if he still hated me for, ya know, my collusion in a *tragic web of lies*, he'd still have to rescue me, right? The Coast Guard couldn't just selectively rescue only the people they liked. And this was Hutch, after all. No matter how angry he was, he wouldn't just let me drown in the ocean. He wasn't a fair-weather hero.

Plus, I had his dog. We were kind of a package deal at this point.

I realized, even at the time, how bonkers my inner monologue sounded.

Was it dehydration?

It wouldn't be Hutch. Every swimmer from Texas to Maine had probably deployed to help out with this. I was too tired for math at this point, but I think we can all agree that my odds of being rescued by the man who just happened to have given me the *best worst kiss of my life* yesterday—was it only yesterday?—were the *definition* of low.

Impossible, even.

The point was—who cared! It was somebody. Anybody. A person with a helicopter and the skills to get me and my favorite dog and his pet toad up into it.

I didn't need the love of my life, I reminded myself.

Let's not be greedy.

Any rescue swimmer would do.

That's when the helicopter moved closer, and positioned itself lower, and the wind from the blades started kicking up the water in a spray all around the surface. I had to squint against the spray, but I saw some legs—and some fins—hanging from the open side before a swimmer deployed in a free fall into the waiting ocean below.

He wasn't far away, but it doesn't take much to lose sight of someone at water level in the ocean. A swell would lift George Bailey and me up a few inches, and we'd see the swimmer freestyling toward us at a sprint, then the swell would drop, and we'd lose sight of him again.

Note that the swimmer was wearing the standard-issue helmet, and I was only catching glimpses of him between swells. But I swear to god, the minute I saw him drop from the sky, I felt a jolt of ecstasy that firmly thumbed its nose at reality.

That's Hutch, I thought.

It couldn't be. It was impossible.

But based on how much thumping George Bailey's tail was doing against the hull of the boat, he must've thought so, too.

We both had to be hallucinating, I told myself. I, for one, was dehydrated and traumatized and had just come to grips with my own mortality. Anybody could hallucinate her own personal favorite US Coast Guard employee under conditions like that.

As the swimmer got closer and closer, I kept expecting his real face to come into focus, and I was determined not to be disappointed when it did. But the thing was, he just kept on looking like Hutch.

Finally, he reached us—and my anticipation had been so intense for so many minutes that before he could even say his normal spiel about being a Coast Guard swimmer here to rescue me, I jumped the gun and shouted: "I'm sorry, but I'm having a hallucination"—here I smacked the side of my head a couple of times, as if to shake it out—"that you are a different rescue swimmer who I have a tortured crush on. So if I keep calling you Hutch, don't worry. That's all me. That's the dehydration talking. You're just a mirage in my mental desert. I can't seem to clear my head."

"You're not hallucinating," the rescue swimmer said.

"I'm telling you I am."

"You're not."

"Do we have time to argue about this right now?"

"Katie," the swimmer said. "You're not hallucinating. This is Hutch."

Then, as if to confirm, George Bailey whimpered and double-timed the drumbeat of his wagging tail against the hull. And that was the real confirmation: George Bailey's excitement. This was not a hallucination. This had to be the impossible man himself.

And so, it happened.

Of all the shipwrecks in all the waters off all the keys, Hutch swam up to mine.

HUTCH WAS ALL business.

I hadn't exactly been expecting witty banter. But here's all the *hello* I got: "Which one of you is chumming the water?"

I looked around and saw the water was pinkish. "It's George Bailey," I said. "He cut his paw on a broken lamp."

George Bailey was staring intently at Hutch, but not barking. Instead, he just kept thumping his tail.

"Can't let him do that," Hutch said, pulling George Bailey away from the boat and positioning him for me to hold on to farther away.

"Do what?"

"Thump his tail against the hull like that."

I gave Hutch a look, like *How could that possibly matter?*

So he went on: "Repetitive underwater knocking sounds might summon predators."

Oh, shit. I looked around.

Hutch gave a nod, put his arm up to signal for a basket, and then said, "I'll take George Bailey first."

Wait—what? He was taking the dog first?

If I'd been calmer, I'm sure I could've come up with many reasons why it made all the sense in the world to make me wait. George Bailey was injured, and bleeding, and possibly summoning predators. Also, he was a dog. You couldn't exactly give him instructions. You couldn't toss him a raft and expect him to climb into it. I—technically—was a functioning human adult.

In theory, I could hold it together a little longer.

But that's when Hutch's frowny eyes met mine. "We've hit bingo," he said.

"We've hit bingo?" I asked, hoping I was remembering what that meant wrong. *"Hit bingo* hit bingo? Like *run out of fuel* hit bingo?"

"That's right," Hutch said, keeping his eyes on the lowering basket. "We should already be gone. They're gonna want to drop a raft for you and go back."

"Go back?" I choked. "They want to leave me here? Alone?"

"Alone *with a raft.*"

What kind of half-assed rescue was this? "They can't do that!"

"When you're out of fuel, you're out of fuel."

"But I—" I protested. "I can barely swim!"

He was watching the basket meet the water now. "I made that argument."

"Please don't leave me here!" I called after him, as he gripped George Bailey's collar and maneuvered him toward the basket.

"I'll try like hell to come back," Hutch said. "But it's the pilots' call."

He positioned himself in the basket with George Bailey.

"You'll be fine," Hutch called to me, as the basket started to rise. "Just stay with the boat! And hum something!"

"Hum something?!" What terrible advice. "Hum what?!"

"Anything. Just pick a song and hum it!"

This might sound odd, but, in that moment, as I watched Hutch and George Bailey, my only two friends in this entire ocean, lift up and away toward the rescue helicopter . . .

I really kind of felt personally rejected.

I get that the circumstances were extreme. I get that Hutch was on duty doing his professional job in the wake of a natural disaster. I get he'd been on duty many hours, and his dog was bleeding, and his helicopter was out of fuel.

But he just really didn't seem all that excited to see me. You know?

It left me feeling worse than I had before the rescue. And as I watched the hoist from below, I wondered how I would hold it together if they really made the decision to fly away.

Could I even blame them?

Was it reasonable in any way to ask an entire Coast Guard flight crew to endanger their lives for a woman who should never have even come to Florida in the first place?

Seriously. What was I even doing here—clinging to a half-sunk boat in the ocean?

Hum something, Hutch had said.

Fine. But the only song I could think of was the one Hutch always hummed. "Heart and Soul." Good thing he hadn't ordered me to sing— because I didn't know the words.

Remember when I said it was only a matter of time before the water-filled boat sank, dragging its one last working pontoon with it?

Next, the *Rue the Day* hissed like the *Titanic*—and then groaned loud enough to startle me into letting go.

This baby was sinking for real.

On instinct, I started swimming away.

And then, from a few feet away, I turned back to watch in horror as the *Rue the Day* sighed . . . and then sank away under the waves.

Like, *sank* sank.

Like, *disappeared under the surface* sank.

And then I really was alone.

I thought about Lucky—our valiant little nonpoisonous friend, gone down with the ship. I watched bubbles churn the surface for a few minutes, hoping he might pop up, sputtering, and I could swim over to rescue him.

But there was no toad in sight.

Poor little guy. He'd survived all that just to drown in the end.

I said a little prayer for him before what happened next: the undamaged pontoon broke away from the boat's body down below—and shot into the air nearby, like a whale breaching, before slapping back down onto the ocean's surface in the distance.

Then all I could do was wait, treading water in my life jacket.

There are no words for the stark loneliness of being left alone in a vast ocean that way. I might as well have been on Mars. It was bad before, but at least, then, I'd had a boat—and a dog—to hold on to. Now there was no one and nothing.

Nothing but the memory of Hutch's "chumming the water" comment.

Also his comment about thumping sounds *summoning predators.*

Was that really my next worry? *Being eaten by sharks?* Hutch had said that sharks didn't see us as prey—but that was before there was literal blood in the water. Then I remembered hypothermia, and how you could get it even in warm climates. How long would that take, exactly? I spent some time considering which was worse: *eaten by sharks* or *paradoxical undressing.* You'd die either way, of course. But was the agony of being torn limb from limb better than the humiliation of being discovered naked?

Tough call.

I'd always thought there was some upper limit to how many bad things the universe was legally allowed to send your way . . . but maybe not.

I looked up at the helicopter. They hadn't flown away yet—but they hadn't come back, either.

Was George Bailey okay? Was *Hutch* okay?

The Coast Guard wouldn't really leave me here, would they?

Then, like an answer, the helicopter started moving back in—lower and closer.

The ocean spray whipped up again.

I saw the legs dangling again, knowing now for sure they were Hutch's, unless I had truly lost all grasp on reality, and the flippers— dammit, the *fins*—and the free fall.

I started swimming toward Hutch as he sprinted toward me.

When he reached me, he signaled up for a sling.

"No basket?" I asked.

"No time," Hutch said. "We've gotta RTB."

I knew that term: return to base.

The sling lowered but the wind blew it around, and it took Hutch a minute to catch it. "Come on," he said, positioning me inside it and pulling it taut. He had a harness on, too, and he clipped it to the wire so we were face-to-face—and then he gave the thumbs-up for *ready* to the flight mechanic.

With that, we jerked up out of the water—the helicopter above already shifting into forward motion—and we dangled behind it, trailing through the air.

This was not, shall we say, the gentle and loving hoist that George Bailey had received. And I'll tell you something else—those harnesses cinch tight under your arms.

"What the hell?" I asked Hutch.

"Told you," he said, with that half-smile of his. "We've gotta go."

And so the helicopter rose into the sky like that as the hoist cable towed us through the air, behind and below the helicopter, the two of us chest to chest as the wind thrashed all around us.

The closest thing I can compare it to is those chair rides at carnivals, where you spin around loose in the air with only one flimsy lap chain to hold you in.

In another setting, it might've been exhilarating.

But I'd had enough exhilaration for one day.

I didn't look around, or take in the sight of it, or make a memory to marvel at later.

Instead, I leaned forward to press my head against Hutch's chest.

He found my chin to tilt my face up.

"You're okay," he said, over the wind, as I met his eyes. "It's all okay now."

And here's the funny thing: despite everything, I believed him.

"I'm so sorry about the *Rue the Day*," I said.

Hutch looked down at the water.

I went on. "I'm so sorry about *everything*. I never meant to lie to you. But I have to tell you something. I didn't know Cole had lied to you until he showed up here on the night of the conga line. And then I couldn't tell you the truth because I had to protect Rue. I know that doesn't make any sense, and I can't explain why, but—"

"I know," Hutch said.

"You know?"

"Cole called the air station in Miami. And so did Rue. And they both explained everything. Twice."

Okay, this was better. "So, yes, I did lie to you—but I swear I never meant to."

"You didn't lie to me," Hutch said.

"I didn't?"

"You got caught in Cole's lie. That's different."

"But I didn't correct it."

"You were looking out for Rue."

"Does that mean you're not angry at me?"

Now Hutch broke out his iconic frown. "Is that a real question?"

"Of course!"

But now he was unzipping a pocket on his sleeve. And then reaching in with his fingers. And then pulling out . . . my hibiscus hair clip.

I looked at it. Then I looked at him. "That's my flower," I said.

"It's my flower now," Hutch said.

"You took it?"

"I stole it."

"That day? At the pool?"

Hutch nodded.

"But . . . why?"

"Because," Hutch said, looking right into my eyes, "I wanted it."

Whatever he was saying felt like more than he was saying.

"You wanted it—the first day we swam together?"

"Uh-huh."

"But Cole said—"

"Cole says a lot of things."

"Cole said you were a love hater."

Hutch squinted and thought about it. "I guess that's actually true."

Maybe it was the wind, or the ocean below, or the *flying through the air*. But I felt like I couldn't keep up. "It is?"

Hutch nodded. "Love is the worst." But he was smiling at me. "It makes you jealous. And possessive. And desperate. It upsets your orderly life. It haunts you, and worries you, and gets you drunk with your brother. It tempts you. It makes you say yes when you should say no, and it stops you from saying yes when that's the only thing you want to do. It keeps you up all night with worry, and then makes you run out of fuel because you can't stop searching for a woman on a sinking houseboat."

Now I was smiling. "A woman and a dog," I corrected.

"A woman and a dog," Hutch agreed.

"So you really do hate love," I said, smiling bigger.

Hutch nodded. "A lot. So much."

I looked into his dark eyes. "I hate it, too."

"Good choice," Hutch said. "Let's hate it together."

"Thank you for saving me," I said then.

He kept his eyes on mine. "Thank you for saving my dog."

"Guess what else I saved?"

"My cell phone?"

I wrinkled my nose. "No—sorry. That went down with the ship."

Upside: so did all the crazy texts I'd sent him.

"But I did save," I went on, patting my jeans pocket, "your mom's pennies."

Hutch checked the sight of my bulging pocket, and then turned to look down at the spot where the houseboat had gone down, then back at my pocket again. "All of them?"

I shrugged. "I figured, if I really started drowning, I could empty my pockets. But I'd hold on to them for you until then."

"Why would you do that?"

"I wanted to apologize."

"To apologize?"

"And to thank you for kissing me on the tarmac—even if you didn't want to."

"You think I didn't want to?"

"I thought you might hate me—for real."

Now Hutch shook his head. "Did you think that kiss yesterday was a *hate* kiss?"

"I'm not sure?" I said. "I'm not even a hundred percent sure right now that you aren't a hallucination."

"It wasn't a hate kiss," Hutch said.

"No?" I asked.

"No," Hutch said. "Want to know what kind of kiss it was?"

"What kind?"

"This kind," he said. And then, right there, the two of us harnessed all alone together on a cable in the middle of the sky, during a peaceful miracle of an interlude between everything that had just happened and everything that was yet to come, in front of an entire flight crew of Coasties *who would certainly tease him about it for the rest of his life*—he pulled me close and kissed me.

In a way that left no doubt about what he wanted.

Or who we had become to each other.

Or how he really felt about love.

And then Hutch pulled away to say, "It wasn't a hate kiss. It was a *love* kiss. In case you couldn't tell."

And then he dove back in for another one.

Epilogue

HOW DID THE promo turn out?

Better than I ever hoped for, honestly. *Chef's kiss.*

All those things Cole had wanted me to capture? I captured them and more. The excitement. The adrenaline. The beauty. The stakes. The courage and self-sacrifice.

It's all there and then some.

Read between the shots, and you can also tell that the videographer was falling madly in love with the subject. But, as with everything else, all that love just makes it better.

And what about the 'Day in the Life'?

I finished that, too. And if you think you can see the love in the official video, just wait until you're watching shots of Hutch walking by the water with George Bailey at sunset. And doing the jump-rope-boxer-skip shirtless. And swatting at his videographer with a towel when he should be washing the deck.

It's a little time capsule, for sure—of the *Rue the Day* before she was lost, of Hutch and me before we knew who we'd become to each other, of the joys of getting started.

When it was done, I posted it for three days to my YouTube channel set to public. This was so Sullivan could watch it, and show it to whomever she needed to, and make a decision about whether or not to give me the axe.

The plan was to toggle it to "private" as soon as Sullivan had made her decision, but then Hutch asked to see it.

I'd explained to him—clearly—that I barely had any subscribers, and hardly anyone would see it except Sullivan and her cronies. That once she'd made her decision, I'd delete it forever. But Cole had told Hutch all about the details of his original plan—that a viral video could make me too big to fire. At my current job and at future ones. And so guess who Hutch emailed the link to, while it was live?

Jennifer Aniston.

Turns out she sent him occasional updates on how her dog was doing. And they kept up, as Hutch put it, *a friendly, occasional correspondence.*

In a move that must have pained every self-effacing cell in his body, he sent it, and he asked if she'd be willing to share it. And so she posted a clip to her Instagram and encouraged her forty-five million followers to go watch it. Pretty sure her caption read, *Go watch my Puppy Love jump rope shirtless!*

And so they did.

Did it save my job?

Like you wouldn't believe.

EXCEPT IT WASN'T my job for long.

In the wake of Sullivan's trip to Key West, she changed her mind about downsizing me. Maybe it was because I took care of her when she was drunk. Or her sudden romance with Cole—and how falling in love can make you a lot less cranky.

Or maybe it was all Jennifer Aniston.

But not only did she not fire me. She offered me a promotion.

But I didn't take it.

Instead, I went in another direction.

I moved to Key West.

Not *for a man*, of course. God forbid.

For Rue.

Rue—who had decided to semi-retire in the wake of her diagnosis—had a job for me. She needed a manager for the Starlite, which included rent-free residence in the Starlite cottage of my choice, all the poolside dinners I could eat, and unlimited conga line opportunities.

What can I say?

I didn't just take it. I grabbed it with both hands and then clutched it to my chest.

Why would I move back to my sad, gray apartment in Dallas when I could live in one of Rue's fabulous, colorful cottages in the keys? Why would I live alone when I could live with The Gals? And, fine: Why would I live a thousand miles away from Hutch when I could live . . . a whole heck of a lot closer?

I sold all my gray furniture on Craigslist before I left.

But guess what I took with me?

Beanie's Coast-Guard-orange throw pillows.

Maybe they were some kind of foreshadowing, and maybe they weren't. But, either way, Beanie takes full credit.

AS DAY JOBS go, working for Rue is as good as it gets. She thinks I have *a good head for business*, so she's showing me the ropes of her real estate empire. When we're not relaxing by the pool.

But I didn't give up making videos.

I guess there are many industry people among Jennifer Aniston's infinite followers, because I got so many offers to collaborate and do projects in the wake of her post that I had to get a manager. Of all things.

As we speak, I'm working on a documentary about shipwrecks for HBO.

When I'm not doing my scuba lessons, of course.

✿   ✿   ✿

RUE TURNED OUT to be a medical team's dream.

She did everything they suggested—times ten.

They told her not to do any exercises that involved holding her breath, so she started walking laps in the pool instead of swimming. She bought one of those motivational water bottles marked with encouraging phrases like *Time to hydrate!* and *Halfway there!* and *Get quenched!* She cut out all alcohol and switched to virgin sangrias. She started a morning walking group with The Gals, reduced her sodium, bought a cookbook called *One Hundred Salads*, and started going to bed before the double digits.

And it all seems to be working.

Really, to sum up: she's doing great. She made the absolute most of that diagnosis—and she's grateful for the reminder to be grateful.

We all need those once in a while, I guess.

But as far as I can tell, Rue and her lady friends do a better job of appreciating their lives than anyone I've met. Their days might get busy like everybody else's, but they gather at sunset for dinner almost every night—cooking out and then eating and chatting in the breeze until it's time to turn in. They look after each other, they keep each other company, and they crack each other up in waves. They've taken my understanding of friendship to a whole new level.

COLE IS ALSO doing fine, for the record.

He and Sully really did start dating. She's ten years older, and at least twenty years wiser, but for some crazy reason, it's working. And we'll never know if it's just a coincidence, but it certainly seemed like the intensity and pace of her corporate restructuring seemed to ease in the wake of Sullivan's trip to the keys. Maybe that was the plan all along. Or maybe Sully and Cole both found something they'd been looking for with each other.

Did fighting with Hutch solve everything for Cole?

Nah.

He was self-focused and competitive before, and that's still true after.

But something shifted that night—no question. He no longer talks about his brother as *all exterior, no interior.* He no longer picks fights with him, or looks for reasons to be angry. Maybe he goes easier on himself now. We all have parts of our pasts that we keep contending with, over and over.

I don't know what shape time itself is, but I know our minds move through it in spirals—returning over and over to the mysteries that hook us, to the questions we've never been able to answer, to the pieces that don't quite fit. It's the same questions, over and over—and the only thing different is us.

Cole learned something new about his life that night. The old question got a new answer. It didn't change his personality, but it did change his story of his own life.

He's nicer now. That's true.

And being nice has a lot of upsides.

Now, when Cole comes to visit Key West, he brings Sully—and The Gals converge around her like a flock of birds-of-paradise, while the boys go off fishing. Or to play pinball. Sometimes, Cole tries to join Hutch for his morning workout, until he gives up halfway through and collapses, splayed out in the grass, to recover.

Mostly, Cole and Hutch play in the Starlite pool like they're kids. They set up a water polo net and talk The Gals into forming teams. Plus, they're working on a whole compendium of nutty ways to jump into the water. Old standards like cannonballs, jackknifes, and forward-flips made the list, of course—but also made-up moves like the switchblade, the Hammer Time, the corkscrew, the Air Jordan, the flying squirrel, the break-dancer, and the hallelujah.

Cole still complains about Hutch being too perfect—but now it's in a jokey way.

Mostly.

Before, he could only see his brother from the outside, as some two-dimensional antagonist. But one hard conversation—one peek inside Hutch's perspective—was enough to flip on a switch of empathy that never flipped back off.

So, yes, Hutch is still perfect. But in a relatable way. In a human way. In a *just trying to get through life the best we can* way. Cole can't oversimplify him anymore. And something about that just deflated all his anger like air out of a balloon.

I think it put an end to the lying, as well—at least, as far as I can tell.

Before the big talk, Cole really had told a disturbing number of lies for an adult person. It left me wary of him for a long time—like, was this guy *just a liar*? Was that just how he lived his life?

But maybe it was situational.

Maybe when Cole revised the story of his life, he revised his story about Hutch, too. I guess, if you think your big brother resents you, and you always feel like you have to justify your existence, and your brother keeps on being unbeatably perfect, you might feel like he's taunting you.

But once you understand that he's trying to be perfect *for* you . . .

It kind of changes everything.

And you don't have to compete.

Instead, you can both just relax, and—say—sneak up on your respective girlfriends at the same time and toss them both into the pool.

GEORGE BAILEY GOT eight stitches for that paw injury, but they healed up just fine.

And here's something true about the aftermath of our trauma bonding: George Bailey never knocked me down again after that. He'd still gallop toward me—lips flapping and ears undulating—but as soon as he arrived, he'd screech to a halt and just lean against me, instead.

Much better.

After the sinking of the *Rue the Day*, Hutch and George Bailey, of course, needed a new place to live. They came to live at Rue's, too—in the cottage next door to mine. George Bailey amiably split his time between dual residences. He stayed with me while Hutch was out working—making himself right at home, and sleeping diagonally across my bed with such confidence that I wound up sleeping curled into a little ball.

It was nice in theory to be next-door neighbors, but Hutch didn't stay at his place much.

All the fun people, he kept saying, were next door.

HERE'S ONE MORE update from the rescue. Maybe the biggest shocker in this whole shocking story: Lucky the toad lived.

He didn't go down with the ship, after all.

George Bailey was holding him in his mouth *the entire time*, and he hadn't been on board the helicopter five seconds before he opened his mouth, dropped the toad between his crossed paws, and then sat protectively with his new little pal for the rest of the flight.

Proving once again that sometimes it's worth it to take a risk on love.

DOES GETTING KISSED while trailing from a rescue helicopter Tom Cruise–style over the Atlantic Ocean answer every question in your life?

Weirdly, no.

After the rescue, Hutch had to get back to work, and I had to get back to Texas.

There wasn't really time for chitchat.

I had a flight to make. And a cell phone to replace on the way to the airport.

And Beanie to apologize to.

Beanie was, of course, my main guide for everything in life—and so as soon as I'd landed in Texas and been given the go-ahead to switch off airplane mode, I called her while walking to baggage claim.

First, we had to process her rage about *not being told* I was on a sinking boat while she was on the phone with me.

"You didn't think that was an important detail?" she wanted to know. "That wasn't worth mentioning?"

"I was getting to it," I said.

"How?" she demanded. "Backward?"

"I knew that once I told you, you'd panic—"

"Reasonably!"

"—and then it would, you know, change the whole vibe of the conversation."

"Yeah!" Beanie said. "For good reason!"

"But if it was my last conversation with you, I just wanted it to be a good one."

"But it didn't have to be our last conversation! If you would've helped me rescue you!"

"I was about to tell you," I said. "But then my phone fell into the ocean."

"That's why you should have told me sooner!"

"What were you going to do?" I asked. "Call the Coast Guard?"

"Yeah! For starters!"

"I'd already called them. And they were busy, by the way."

"I would've figured something out!"

"I'm sure you would've. But here's the great news. I got rescued anyway."

"Barely."

"It counts."

"The point is, if you have big news in your life, you're supposed to tell me. And being adrift at sea on a sinking houseboat is big news!"

"Fine. Next time I'm on a sinking houseboat, I will tell you before my phone slides into the ocean."

"Fine."

She was a funny mixture of irritated with me and glad I was alive. All of which was fair.

"Next question," I said then. "If I have other big news right now that I'm not sharing because you're mad at me—should I go ahead and share it, or should I wait until you're done being mad?"

"What other big news could you possibly have?" Beanie asked, as if life had a limited supply.

"It's rescue-swimmer related."

Beanie gasped. "Tell me."

"Would you believe me," I asked, "if I told you that of all the rescue swimmers in the entire US Coast Guard, the one who showed up to hoist me out of the ocean from the jaws of death in the nick of time just happened to be Hutch?"

"No," Beanie said.

"Because I'm pretty sure that's what happened."

"*Hutch* was the one who rescued you?"

"There's a slight chance that I hallucinated it, but yes. Hutch rescued me. And then he kissed me midair between the ocean and the helicopter."

"Now you have to marry him," Beanie said, "so you can tell that story at the wedding."

SO NOW I live at the Starlite. I bought a Dutch bicycle for tooling around town. And I hang out with The Gals in the evenings, and help cook dinner, and revel in the freedom of my newly conquered bathing-suit phobia.

More than that, I have fully given in to the Technicolor joy of a Vitamin Sea–based wardrobe. The horror I felt at my first sight of all those colors and prints and undulating fabrics? I barely remember it now. I've got a friends-and-family discount, and I walk around every day in colorful sundresses and skirts that flutter in the breeze.

Chromophobia conquered, too.

I'm like a tropical fish just floating along through my reef.

A tropical fish with all her black jeans and tees folded neatly in her bottom drawer just in case she needs them, but still.

Every now and then, a song about a younger version of me will come on the radio, and I'll take a second to appreciate the contrast between then and now.

All that hard stuff turned out to be good for me, in the end.

It cracked me open. And you know that old saying about cracks: they're how the sea breezes get through.

REMEMBER WHEN BEANIE teased me and said, "You're afraid of a bathing suit?"

She knew what she was doing.

She was trying to remind me that I had a lot more power than I thought I did.

She was trying to get me to see myself differently.

The swimming wasn't just about swimming. Nor was it just about letting myself love color, or reclaiming my right to splash in the water, or learning to be unapologetically alive in the world.

It was about the deep, enduring comfort that comes from looking at your life for exactly what it is, and exactly how it's unfolded—and really seeing it. The past can't hurt you now like it did then. The story of your life is always full of mystery. You can unfold it on a table like a map, and study it, and understand it in new ways.

It's not different, but you are.

I can still hear Beanie saying, *"You have to do the thing you're afraid of."*

Bless her self-help-loving heart. She was right about that, too.

That's what no one ever tells you. You can look around with your own eyes. You can find your own details. Notice for yourself what matters—and decide what it means.

It's as true as it is life-changing.

But the only way to do it is to do it.

And now I have.

We're here to be alive. To keep going. To find all kinds of ways to thrive anyway. We're here to feel it all. To love and cry and love some more.

We're here to rescue ourselves—and everybody else—in every way that we can.

What was it Rue said about courage? That no one's born fearless?

It's true.

EX-FIANCÉE OF LUCAS BANKS HAS REALLY LET HERSELF GO, they said.

They were so infinitely wrong—but so accidentally right.

That's the truth, and I'll take it where I can get it.

She really *has* let herself go.

And as Rue would say: How glorious.

Author's Note

Stories have a unique kind of magic.

They aren't real life—but they're kind of the next best thing.

Especially good stories. If a story is really working, if the writer is really *crushing it*—you don't just step into that story and watch the characters from afar.

In the best stories, you're *in* it. You're a part of it. It's happening all around you—and *to* you. You're not just witnessing the characters—you *are* the characters. You merge with them in this utterly profound way, climbing into their skin and experiencing it like it's real—seeing what they see, and hearing what they hear, but also feeling their emotions with them and as them: hoping for what they hope for, loving what they love, wanting what they want.

Like it's your life. Like it's you.

It's such an astonishing feat of the human imagination.

It's so much magic.

Researchers have done all kinds of studies about what happens to our brains when we get lost in stories. Our mirror neurons flash. Our brains light up like what we're reading is really happening.

We know it's fiction. We know it's not real. But we believe it, anyway.

And so stories have this power to resonate for us like nothing else in human life can. They teach us things we need to learn, and show us new ways of understanding, and answer questions we didn't even know we needed to ask.

Stories go deep. They don't mess around. They don't care about our attitudes, or our prejudices, or what we think we ought to think.

They bypass the head—and go straight to the heart.

I've spent my whole life obsessed with stories. How they work. Why they matter. Where that power comes from.

I've wanted to understand how to harness them for good. How to tell stories that are page-turning and compelling—but also wise and helpful. How to lift us all up—myself included—and help us make the very best of every minute we have.

The characters I write often struggle with the same things I struggle with. Because as I go through those stories with them—and *as* them—they get better at grappling with forgiveness, or vulnerability, or resilience . . . and I get to get better, too.

It's healing to read stories about healing. It's nourishing to read stories about people finding nourishment. It's life-changing to read stories about people changing their lives.

The Love Haters has, I hope, a very delicious, romantic love story going on between Katie and Hutch—in addition to all kinds of extra love stories between friends, and siblings, and parent figures. But it also has another type of love story.

One between Katie and herself.

Specifically: Katie and her body—in a kind of enemies-to-lovers trope.

People say you have to love yourself first before you can love others. But I don't think it's that linear. Learning to love yourself is a process—and a circular one at that.

Not to mention a big project.

We all struggle with what it means to be seen in the world. And while we don't really have much control over how the world chooses to see us, we can—and this may be the smartest thing I've ever figured out in all my years on this earth . . .

We can see ourselves for ourselves.

What I'm saying is, we can train our own eyes to look with kindness, and pay attention to what's beautiful, and focus on what's right instead of what's wrong.

That's how you fall in love—and stay in love—with anyone, including yourself: see the best in that person and enjoy the hell out of it as often as you can.

So welcome to another installment in my infinite series on why love stories can save the world.

Nora Ephron once said something that I think about all the time: "Reading is escape, and the opposite of escape."

She's so right.

Stories take us out of ourselves and deeper into ourselves at the exact same time. They are specific and universal. Big and small. Something and everything.

The best love stories are never just about romantic love. They're always about so much more than that: kindness, and joy, and belonging, and safety—not to mention growing, and changing, and healing from the past. They are always master classes on how we find the best in each other—and, by extension, ourselves.

I once had a friend who told me, with great confidence, that every person in any dream you ever have is *you*. That all the "characters" in your dreams are parts of yourself. That if you die in a dream, that's a part of you dying. If you lose someone in a dream, it's a part of yourself that's lost. *It's all metaphor*, she said.

Who knows if it's true? But it stuck with me.

I'm no scientist, but I've read a lot of love stories. And I feel like that idea applies to them, too. That maybe, as the characters are falling in love with each other, we are falling in love with parts of ourselves.

I wish I could write a PhD dissertation on this—but I don't need a PhD to know there's something profoundly nourishing going on inside your soul when you get overtaken like that.

Along the journey of a romance, we become those characters—and then we do all kinds of healing things. We rethink assumptions, and overcome prejudices, and learn to see more clearly. We soften and empathize and nurture. We go deeply into ourselves—and break up the emotional scar tissue we all carry from our lifetimes of hurts and losses and disappointments.

It's not real life, but we believe it anyway. And it heals us and nourishes us in ways we could never find anywhere else.

That's my theory, and I'm sticking to it.

Reading love stories isn't frivolous. It's profound. It's not escape, it's the opposite.

Trust me, and trust yourself: love stories are the best kind of therapy. They aren't shallow, they're deep. Start looking, and you'll see it, too.

Love stories make us better at love. In all directions. And getting better at love, of course, means getting better at life.

Acknowledgments

Note! There is no real US Coast Guard air station on Stock Island in the Florida Keys! I didn't want to make fictional things happen in a real station!

The Love Haters could never have come into existence without the generous help of the United States Coast Guard.

I did most of my research for this book through the U.S. Coast Guard Motion Picture & Television Liaison Office with the aid of Commander Matthew Kroll, who kindly agreed to an interview and connected me with the good people of Air Station Houston at Ellington Field. I got to spend several days hanging out at the air station and talking with aviation survival technicians, pilots, flight mechanics, and other personnel—and I'm so grateful to everyone I met for their warm welcome and their patience with all my beginner-level questions. Many thanks to Aviation Survival Technician Chief Matthew O'Dell and ASTs Omar Alba, Vincent Neiman, Ashworth Reed-Kraus, Benjamin Sobels, and James Housely and airman Luke Eidem for sharing all kinds of great stories and insights about rescue swimmer life—as well as patiently walking me through the basics, showing me equipment,

demonstrating hand signals, and talking through scenarios. Pilots Jor-
dyn Tolefree, Miranda Fay, Ryan Vandehei, Conner Marek, and Sophia
Quick showed me the ins and outs of the hangar and the helicopters,
gave me tours of the air station, and kindly answered many questions.
Miranda, Conner, and basic aircrew Nacole Nader took me for my first-
ever flight in a helicopter of any kind and it was such an honor to see
them all at work. I was also grateful to talk with yeoman Gabriel Castro
Santiago. Special thanks to Sophia for being so welcoming and helpful
as my main contact person at the air station, and to Omar for helping
me think through the ending of this story—saying "sharks are everywhere," walking me step-by-step through how the rescue would go, and
explaining that Hutch really would hoist the dog first. I can't even begin
to describe how much I loved my days at the air station, how thankful I
am for the time everyone took to help me out, and how awestruck I was
to get to witness such courageous people doing such good work in real
life and up close.

I'd also like to thank our family friend, former US Navy Explosive
Ordnance Disposal diver Chris Seger, for being a resource early on.
Thanks also to his son (and my childhood friend), content producer
Hunter Seger, for talking with me about the art and strategy of making
really amazing videos. Much gratitude also to Emmy Award–winning
documentary filmmaker Anthony Penta for letting me interview him at
length about the details of his vocation. Filmmaker Vicky Wight (who
did the feature adaptations of my novels *The Lost Husband* and *Happiness for Beginners*) also let me ask her all about her documentary work.

Thanks to my big sister, Shelley Stein, for letting me use her pie piece
of heterochromia and her blue-gray iris color (that we've all mistakenly
been calling hazel all this time) in this story. Much gratitude also to my
dear childhood friend Julie Alonso for letting me name a character after
her brother Carlos—the best big brother ever. He is gone too soon, and I
always keep him, and Julie's beautiful mom, Amalia, in my heart.

Much of Hutch's nature trivia comes from Ed Yong's book *An Immense
World: How Animal Senses Reveal the Hidden Realms Around Us*. The
quote from the favorite movie Katie references comes from the Carrie

Fisher classic *Postcards from the Edge*. And the idea of a "culture of appreciation" comes from the real research of psychologists John and Julie Gottman—though I'm not 100 percent sure if they'd recommend applying it in all the renegade ways I have over the years. (Sure does work, though!) I learned about chromophobia from the brilliant Ingrid Fetell Lee, and I learned about time horizons from an interview with psychologist Laura L. Carstensen. Also, much gratitude to Christina Coward at Blue Willow Bookshop for letting me borrow her son's name for Hutch.

In addition to the people who helped me create this particular book, I also need to thank the people who support me writing books in general—and who help those books find as many of the readers who will love them as possible. Heartfelt thanks to my agent of many years, Helen Breitwieser, who has doggedly believed in me this whole time, and to the good people of St. Martin's Press/Macmillan/Macmillan Audio, who have cheered for and supported my books in so many big, beautiful ways. Endless thanks to my brilliant editor, Jen Enderlin, and the whole fantastic SMP team: Katie Bassel, Erica Martirano, Brant Janeway, Kejana Ayala, Lisa Senz, Olga Grlic, Christina Lopez, Anne Marie Tallberg, Ginny Perrin, Lena Shekhter, Lizz Blaise, Erik Platt, Katy Robitzki, Emily Dyer, Matt DeMazza, Devan Norman, Alexis Neuville, and Tom Thompson—and many more. Thanks also to both Patti Murin and Ellie Kemper for their fantastic recent audiobook renditions.

Thanks also to my family, who always cheer so much for my books: My dad. My sisters, Lizzie Fletcher and Shelley Stein. My mostly grown kids, Anna and Thomas. My fantastic mom, Deborah Detering, who I adore in every possible way, and who took a research trip with me to Key West that was pure joy. And my husband, Gordon—possibly the most supportive, enthusiastic team player of a man who ever lived. The absolute best.

And before I go, of course . . . thank *you*. If you're reading this, please know that you, and readers like you, are the reason that I get to keep writing books. Every single person who reads, loves, and recommends my books is ensuring that there will be more of them to come. I appreciate you so much. I truly, truly do.

About the Author

Skylar Reeves Photography

Katherine Center is the *New York Times* bestselling author of twelve novels, including *The Bodyguard, Things You Save in a Fire,* and *The Rom-Commers.* Her 2025 book is *The Love Haters.* Katherine writes "deep rom-coms"—laugh-and-cry books about how life knocks us down, and how we get back up. The movie adaptation of Katherine's novel *Happiness for Beginners* became a Netflix film in 2023 and hit the Global Top 10 in eighty-one countries around the world, and the movie adaptation of her novel *The Lost Husband* hit #1 on Netflix in 2020. Katherine lives in her hometown of Houston, Texas, with her husband, two almost-grown kids, and their fluffy-but-fierce dog.